I0741246

Paul I. Hershon

A Talmudic Miscellany

A thousand and one extracts from the Talmud, the Midrashim and the Kabbalah

Paul I. Hershon

A Talmudic Miscellany
A thousand and one extracts from the Talmud, the Midrashim and the Kabbalah

ISBN/EAN: 9783337234850

Printed in Europe, USA, Canada, Australia, Japan

Cover: Foto ©Andreas Hilbeck / pixelio.de

More available books at **www.hansebooks.com**

A

TALMUDIC MISCELLANY

הַמּוֹנֶה מִסְפָּר :

" He who counts the number."—Psalm cxlvii. 4.

OR

A Thousand and One Extracts

FROM

THE TALMUD

THE MIDRASHIM AND THE KABBALAH

COMPILED AND TRANSLATED BY

PAUL ISAAC HERSHON

AUTHOR OF

" GENESIS ACCORDING TO THE TALMUD," " EXTRACTS FROM THE TALMUD," ETC.

WITH INTRODUCTORY PREFACE BY THE

REV. F. W. FARRAR, D.D., F.R.S.

CHAPLAIN IN ORDINARY TO HER MAJESTY, AND CANON OF WESTMINSTER

With Notes and Copious Indexes

BOSTON

HOUGHTON, MIFFLIN & CO.

1880

PREFACE.

I HAVE been requested by the publishers and translator
of this Talmudic Miscellany to say a few words about it
by way of preface. If I have consented to their request,
it is only because I feel a very deep sense of the importance of making the Talmud more widely known.

Of the constituent parts of the Talmud—of the Mishna
with its six orders (*Sedarim*), its 71 *Massictoth*, its 633
Perakim, and its 4187 *Mishnaioth*—the reader will find a
succinct account in the following introduction. A considerable part of the Mishna has been at different times
translated into English and other modern languages, and
to many theologians it has been known as a whole by the
magnificent work of Surenhusius.

But until very recent times the Gemara, or annotations
upon the Mishna, have been known to very few. The
chief sources of information used by English theologians
have been, until quite recently, the collections of Light-
foot, Schöttgen, and Meuschen, and passages quoted and
referred to in Ugolini's Thesaurus, together with such purely
controversial works like Wagenseil's *Tela Ignea Satanæ*, and
Eisenmenger's *Entdecktes Judenthum*. These works were

little read except by students, since they were written in German and Latin, and never entered into general literature. Had it been otherwise, the mass of English readers would never have been prepared to accept the utterly untenable notions about the Talmud, and the glowing wisdom and exquisite morality by which it was supposed to be pervaded, into which they were betrayed by the learned enthusiasm of the late Dr. Deutsch in his celebrated article on the Talmud in the " Quarterly Review." So simple an English book as the late Dr. M‘Caul's " Old Paths " might have sufficed to undeceive them. Wisdom there is in the Talmud, and eloquence, and high morality; of this the reader may learn something even in the small compass of the following pages. How could it be otherwise when we bear in mind that the Talmud fills twelve large folio volumes, and represents the main literature of a nation during several hundred years? But yet I venture to say that it would be impossible to find less wisdom, less eloquence, and less high morality, imbedded in a vaster bulk of what is utterly valueless to mankind—to say nothing of those parts of it which are indelicate and even obscene—in any other national literature of the same extent. And even of the valuable residuum of true and holy thoughts, I doubt whether there is even one which had not long been anticipated, and which is not found more nobly set forth in the Scriptures of the Old and New Testament.

It is now in the power of any one to verify this statement for himself. Strange to say, the Talmud as a whole has never yet been translated into any other language from the original Hebrew. Every attempt to achieve the task has hitherto failed, and the proposals to publish a complete translation have from time to time been abandoned for want of encouragement. Isolated treatises like the *Avoda Zara* and the *Pirke Avoth* have been translated into English and German; but when the Abbé Chiarini and others have endeavoured to get the whole Mishna and Gemara systematically translated, they have not met with the smallest encouragement. At the present time, however, it seems probable that the immense work will be accomplished. Messrs. Munk, Schwab, and their learned collaborateurs have now published in French the translation of the very important treatise Berachoth, and of five or six other treatises of the Mishna, with both the Jerusalem and the Babylonian Gemara. Thus it seems probable that these strange and venerable tomes, so long buried in the most difficult style of a dead language, will for the first time appear as a whole in a modern dress. It is greatly to be hoped that sufficient purchasers may be found to render possible the heroic effort which these scholars have undertaken.

If the whole Talmud should thus be rendered accessible to modern readers, I cannot but think that two good results will follow. On the one hand, it can hardly fail to happen that multitudes of intelligent and thoughtful Jews, to whom the Talmud is, after all, but a name, will be entirely disenchanted of the extravagant veneration which they now entertain for it, and will see for the first time its absolutely immeasurable inferiority to the living oracles of God. They will see that what they have so long been worshipping is not even a golden idol with feet of clay, but an idol of clay of which it can hardly even be said that so much as the feet are of gold. On the other hand, I am quite sure that all students, in reading the Talmud, will find many sidelights for the interpretation not only of the Old but even of the New Testament. Not only does the Talmud furnish many most interesting illustrations of the thoughts and words of the Apostles, but there are cases in which the key to the true solution of difficulties and the true interpretation of phrases and expressions can only be found in these records of the Rabbinic schools. For the greatest of the Apostles had been trained from childhood in this Hebrew lore; and even those of the Twelve who were despised by the hierarchy as "simple and unlearned" were in some measure familiar with it, because even in the days of Christ the views of those elder Rabbis which are enshrined in the Mishna and Gemara, had passed into the common atmosphere of Jewish thought.

For these reasons I hail the labours of Mr. Hershon. He is, I believe, fitted for the task which he has undertaken by an almost life-long familiarity with Talmudic literature; and the adequacy of his versions no less than the extent of his knowledge have been admitted not only by scholars so eminent as Dr. Delitzsch—whose name should alone be a guarantee to theologians that Mr. Hershon is qualified for his work — but also by the free admission of Jewish critics. And the reader may accept his versions without suspicion, because though they may not always be exempt from those imperfections which must remain in the best human work, yet they are not directly controversial, and are merely intended to represent the Talmud exactly as he finds it. For this reason the notes which he has appended have, for the most part, no other object than to elucidate the text. And here I must caution the reader who is entirely unfamiliar with Rabbinic methods, that he must not at once set down any particular passage as a proof of nothing but the grossest absurdity of uncontrolled imagination. When he reads such a passage as the story of Og king of Bashan on p. 41, and still more that about his *bone* on p. 66—not to allude to others which are here recorded—he may be inclined to turn away with contemptuous disgust, and to wonder that any human beings should waste their time over such absurdities. He will, however, be mistaken. Although this is not the place to furnish the real meaning of such passages, the reader must take it on trust that, sometimes at least, they are elaborate cryptographs— concealed methods of inculcating into the initiated those polemical views which the Rabbis might have found it most perilous to utter in an undisguised form.

Lastly, we may observe that the purely *accidental* bond of connection between the many passages here translated by Mr. Hershon—the very discontinuity which might at first sight be regarded as a weak feature in his book—is really of the greatest value. It absolutely excludes the temptation to all *arbitrary* selection,—to any one-sided representation of. the contents of the Talmud in order to serve a purpose. The passages selected are selected solely because they contain references to certain *numbers*.

There is not a single principle which otherwise unites them together. This very fact will be a security to the reader that he will see specimens of the Talmud exactly as he would do if he possessed a knowledge of Talmudic Hebrew, and dipped at haphazard into its voluminous pages in order to ascertain for himself their character and contents. No competent student can rise without some advantage from the perusal of these pages. They will do something to make the Gemara better known, and that knowledge will, I hope, be still further extended by Mr. Hershon in future labours.

F. W. FARRAR.

AUTHOR'S PREFACE.

In bespeaking the regard of the English public to the following work, the general nature of which is already explicitly enough stated on the titlepage, I feel called upon to explain the object I have had in view in compiling it, the circumstances in which it was suggested to me, and the plan I have seen good to adopt.

The Talmud of the Jews, like the Koran of the Moslem, is a composition so confused and heterogeneous, that, were its twelve folio volumes translated into English, not only would it prove unreadable throughout, but not one in a thousand would have patience to read consecutively the first twelve pages. It is this fact, of which, as will appear,* the Talmud itself is aware, I have had to face; and my object has been, if not to overcome, then to diminish to some extent this drawback. It is with this view the following selections are made, and I have striven to arrange them on a principle which I trust may contribute to awaken a greater interest in and convey a better understanding of its contents.

The special circumstances which suggested the compilation were these. · In the reading-room of the British Museum, many years ago, I happened to light upon a Hebrew book containing no fewer than seventy sermons

* See p. 23, No. 15.

on the short text (Gen. xxxiii. 17) וייעקב נסע סכתה, the English of which is, "And Jacob journeyed to Succoth." This book at once struck me as a typical instance of the treatment to which the Talmud had for long been, and was still, subjected at the hands of its professed expounders. Their mode of procedure was this: First to pick out at random a passage torn from the context, and then, to use an Oriental phrase, pack upon it a camel-load of matter. This passage they so sermonised upon that not only was its sense hidden in a miscellaneous jumble of irrelevant comments, corollaries, and glosses, but the fact of its existence was buried out of sight, like the sunk foundations of an edifice, and the book it was extracted from entombed along with it. The world-old question, "What is the Talmud?" I remarked to myself, could never be resolved in this way, and I determined to try whether I could not disturb the ashes under which it lay concealed, and, if not bring it home, at least bring it near to the general intelligence. The way to do this seemed to me to be to make the Talmud speak for itself; to select and array from its pages a thousand quotations or so, such as to show both the topics of which it treats and its manner of handling and settling them. This, accordingly, is what I have attempted here. Samples of the good, the bad, and the indifferent, especially extracts that throw light on Old and New Testament exegesis, are alike introduced, and references are studiously given to the folios and columns of its sections, so that the learned can check and verify the instances I have quoted. These instances have been all derived word for word, and at first hand, from the Talmud itself, and the original has been consulted again and again to ensure accuracy of reproduction. There is scarcely a treatise, or even chapter in the Talmud, which has not been laid under contribution to my purpose, and reference can be readily made to the quotations in the work by means of the peculiar arrangement adopted, and the two carefully prepared indexes at the end of the volume.

The plan of the work, according to which the quotations are sorted and grouped agreeably to the prominency in them of particular numbers, on which special stress is laid, was suggested to me years ago when I was engaged in a different enterprise. I had published a work on the Talmud in Hebrew, entitled "Genesis according to the Talmud," * and was engaged on a second in continuation, to be entitled "Exodus according to the Talmud," since completed in MS., when, *apropos* to the text (Exod. xxiii. 26), "The *number* of thy days I will fulfil," I was led to remark, which I did in a note, what a prominent part numerical quantities played in Talmudic estimates; and I collected there and then 350 quotations from the Babylonian Talmud all bearing on numbers, which I thereupon proceeded to arrange in proper order. When on the Continent, about four years ago, I took the opportunity of showing the Hebrew MS. referred to to several scholars, and of calling especial attention to the note in question. All were struck with the discovery I had made as a literary curiosity, and Dr. Delitzsch of Leipsig, in particular, was pleased to say he even *admired* it. He asked me how I had managed to collect so many quotations to the point, and I replied by producing a MS. I had prepared by way of key to the Talmud. Encouraged by his approving criticism, I set myself, on my return, in the course of my Talmudic labours, to extend

---

* An English translation of this work is already in print, and will be published in due time.

my researches in the direction indicated, and the result was the expansion of my note into a body of more than 1600 quotations, enough to occupy a volume. Hence the present venture, and the peculiar arrangement adopted. This arrangement I take leave to think is warranted by the obvious emphasis laid on numbers in the selected passages; it becomes thus an arrangement natural in itself, and it supplies a series of threads along which these passages, when once read, easily group themselves in the memory.

In carrying the plan of this work out, it was necessary for me, as a foreigner, to procure the aid of an English scholar, and I had the good fortune to obtain the services of one who wrought along with me with all his heart. Mr. W. R. Brown, the gentleman I refer to, became known to me about the time the idea of the work occurred to me; he caught up my project with enthusiasm, offered gratuitously the assistance I needed, and stood by me, helping me in every way to the last. He aided me in revising and correcting my translation, enriched the text with many of the notes, and crowned the numerous obligations I owe to him by contributing an Introduction to the work, which Introduction, I trust, will be duly and generously appreciated. I, moreover, desire to express my obligations to the Rev. J. Wood, Edin., for the literary service he has rendered to this work in revising and correcting it, and passing it through the press, and for providing it with one of the two indexes appended.

Besides the selections just referred to, I have added a few specimens from the Midrashim and the Kabbalah, which I have thought might prove interesting to the student of Hebrew literature, as, next to the Talmud and the Old Testament Scriptures, these two storehouses of

Rabbinical lore are held in the highest esteem by the orthodox Jews.

In sending this work forth to the public, I desire especially to gain the ear of the pious Jew, the Christian student, and the philosophic thinker. By means of this work the Jew will be able to see his teachers with his own eyes (Isa. xxx. 20), and to judge for himself whether they are or are not able to make him wise unto salvation ; the Christian student will enjoy the advantage of being able to scan as much of the sea of the Talmud as can, so to speak, be seen from the shore, though he may not be able to venture out upon the main, still less essay a voyage through the length and breadth of it; and the philosophic thinker, be he Jew, Turk, infidel, or heretic, will have access in it to forms of morality and humanity which he has not met before in any other religious system. But be that as it may, our enterprise is conceived in the interests of scholarship, morality, and religion, and these interests, whether by our means or not, it is our prayer that the Lord may prosper.

P. I. HERSHON.

Wood Green, *October* 1880.

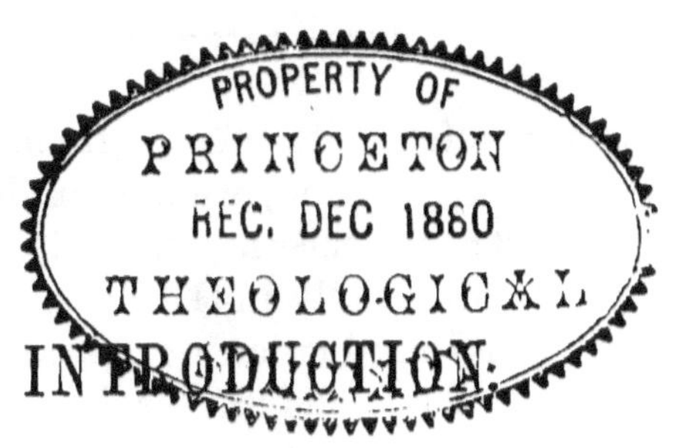

PROPERTY OF
PRINCETON
REC. DEC 1860
THEOLOGICAL

INTRODUCTION.

In Eastern story we read of a dervish who one day presented himself at a palace porch, begging bread. The porter opened the door, beckoned him to enter, and had him conducted, full of expectancy, into the presence of the prince. The prince, who was a grey-haired Barmecide chief, received him compassionately, and made signs as if in preparation for a sumptuous repast. Course after course was ordered, and course after course spread—in imagination — before the hungry visitant. Imaginary soups, fish, flesh, bakemeats, fruits were ceremoniously offered, partaken of with show of relish, and acknowledged with thanks. At length the host called for wine, as unreal as the viands, and offered it to the stranger, who this time politely declined, protesting that he dreaded the consequences should he take too much. Being pressed, however, he yielded, until, affecting elation of spirit under the influence of the fancied liquor, he rose excited, and dealt a blow at his entertainer which had almost fatal results. The host, thus admonished, and pleased with the humour of his guest, thought it time this banter should terminate; so he called his servants to make ready a banquet, and the two sat down together to a substantial and satisfying feast.

Feasts of the Barmecide order are not uncommon in literature, and too often the hungry reader has to satisfy his appetite with the ghost of relief. It is thus the public has been treated with regard to the Talmud; it has again and again been referred to, quoted from, spoken of, and written about, until we fancy we are familiar with it; and yet as regards what it concerns, where it comes from, and what it says, we are wholly in the dark. In the extracts which follow this Introduction we have sought to remove in part this ignorance, and in the Introduction itself it will be our business to give some account of what the Talmud is, how it is divided, and of what it treats.

The Talmud (תַלמוד, from למד, "to learn") is a vast irregular repertory of Rabbinical reflections, discussions, and animadversions on a myriad of topics treated of or touched on in Holy Writ; a treasury, in chaotic arrangement, of Jewish lore, scientific, legal, and legendary; a great storehouse of extra-biblical, yet biblically referable, Jewish speculation, fancy, and faith. Taking the Old Testament Scriptures as a divinely inspired text-book of knowledge and learning, the Talmud claims to be a commentary on these of co-ordinate rank with the texts and the orthodox expositor of their meaning, bearing, and force.

The Talmud proper is throughout of a twofold character, and consists of two divisions, severally called the Mishna and the Gemara. These terms are so closely related to one another as to be of almost synonymous import. Mishna (משנה) being from שנה or תני, "to repeat, to explain, to unfold;" and Gemara (גמרא), from גמר, "to learn" or "to complete." The Mishna, in this connection, may be regarded as the text of the Talmud itself, and the Gemara as a sort of commentary, of which examples will be given as we proceed. The Gemara regularly follows the Mishna, and annotates upon it sentence by sentence, searching out its meaning, arraying the *pros* and *cons* in debatable cases, then summing up results, and deciding, if possible, the point at issue; a בת קול, Bath Kol, or "voice from heaven," at times interposing, and either ratifying the decision or otherwise settling the matter in debate. The Mishna, except where it commences a Perek (or chapter), is invariably introduced by the sign-word כתני׳, while the abbreviation גמ׳ (for גמרא) the sign of a sentence from the Gemara. Besides the Mishna proper as text, a great number of supplementary paragraphs, styled Tosiphtaoth and Boraïthaoth, are scattered up and down the Gemara; but these are not looked upon as authoritative, and, indeed, are of no account if they contradict the Mishna or text. The Tosiphtaoth (תוספתאות, from יסף, "to add") are distinguished by the prefix תנא or תאנא (Tana), "he teaches," or תאני עלה (Tani aleh), "as taught above;" while the Boraïtha is indicated by one or other of the following signs:—ת״ר or תנו רבנן (Tanu Rabbanan), "our Rabbis have taught;" תני חדא (Tani chada), "a certain Rabbi has taught;" תנינא (Tanina), "we have tradition;" תניא אידך (Taniah idach), "elsewhere it is taught," or "another teaches;" or מתניתא (Mathnitha), "it is Mishna." The Tosiphtaoth to the Mishna are distinct from the Tosephoth, or exegetical annotations on the Gemara. Twenty-six of the treatises have no Gemara, and Shekalim has the Gemara of the Talmud Yerushalmi.

There are two Talmuds, the Yerushalmi, or, more correctly, the Palestinian, and the Babli, that is, the Babylonian. The Mishna is pretty nearly the same in both these, but the Gemaras are different. The Talmud Yerushalmi gives the traditional sayings of the Palestinian Rabbis, גמרא דבני מערבא, the "Gemara of the Children of the West," as it is styled; whereas the Talmud Babli gives the traditional sayings of the Rabbis of Babylon. This Talmud is about four times the size of the Jerusalem one; it is by far the more popular, and to it almost exclusively our remarks relate.

What, then, is the Talmud Babli? It is in itself a library of some threescore and ten treatises, so to speak, bound in a dozen volumes. It is a sort of commonplace-book, recording a thousand and one years of Rabbinical thought and wit, with folk-lore and gossip, often quaintly expressed in the allegorical forms of Oriental fancy. There are worthies in it to grace every day in the calendar, and sayings ascribed to some of them enough to invest with a certain halo of immortality their otherwise unnoted names. Here is the mother-stuff of Judaism, the fountain-head of its inspirations, the key to its philosophy and forms of thinking, the fire that burns on its altars, and the vestal flame that lights up and cheers its far-scattered hearths. Nay, the "traditions of the elders," which are here sacredly enshrined, impart to the pile, in the regard of the pious Jew, somewhat of the sanctity of a Temple, and a feeling as if not the high priest only, but the whole race were thereby admitted within the precincts of the Holy of Holies itself. For here, within a veil which no profane person can penetrate, he is privileged, he thinks, to be admitted to a knowledge of the secrets of wisdom, and a familiar acquaintance with the oracles of the Most High; here is the law for the man of thought and the man of action, the law of the household and the law of the state, directions for the health of the body, the attainment of wise knowledge, the conquest of virtue, and the conduct of life.

To the orthodox Jew the Talmud is like the encircling ocean; it inserts itself into and makes itself felt in every nook and corner of the sphere of his existence. Like an atmosphere, it encompasses the whole round of his being, penetrates into all centres of vitality, and presses with its incumbent weight on every class irrespective of age, or sex, or rank; it is all-inspiring, all-including, and all-controlling. It covers, in the regard of the illuminated, the whole field of life, and its principles affect, or ought to affect, every thought and every action of every member in the Jewish state. Such, in the abstract, is the regard in which this book is held in Jewry. Whoso would know it as it is, must, as to know anything else, study it in the detail of its particularity, and this he may in part do through the extracts which succeed, and which are given that he may so far comprehend the substance and bearings of the work.

Meanwhile let us interrogate the Rabbis themselves, and hear what account they have to give. We have just said that the Talmud transmits to us the traditions of the elders. Now the Rabbis and they who take after them assert that Moses received two laws on Sinai—תורה שבכתב, Torah Shebekthab, "the law in writing," and תורה שבעל פה, Torah Shebeâl Peh, "the law upon the lip"—in other words, Scripture and tradition, the written and the oral law. For, as they teach, not only were the חמשה חומשי תורה, "the five-fifths of the law," that is, the Pentateuch, given to Moses, but the Mishna also, which is therefore literally described as the הלכה למשה מסיני (Halachah le Mosheh me Sinai), *i.e.*, the traditional law (given) to Moses on Sinai. It is this law which we have, for convenience' sake, styled the text of the Talmud, and the Hebrew name by which it is designated here might fairly stand as the running title of its every page. If we take the Talmud itself as an authority in this matter, we might go still farther than this (see Berachoth, fol. 5, col. 1); we might assign a Mosaic origin to a great deal more than Scripture and the Mishna; for Rabbi Shimon ben Lakish says, " What is that which is written, ' And I will give thee tables of stone, and the law, and the commandment, which I have written, to teach them ' ? " (Exod. xxiv. 12) " ' Tables,' " he answers, " are the Decalogue, ' law ' is the Scripture, and ' the commandment ' is the Mishna; ' which I have written ' is the Prophets and the Hagiographa; ' to teach them,' that is the Gemara; and this teaches us that all these were given to Moses on Sinai, and ' are the words of the living God.' " (See Gittin, fol. 6, col. 2, &c.)

But be this as it may, what the Rabbis teach respecting the derivation of the Mishna is this :—They say there was a chain of tradition which connected the times of Moses with the times of Rabbi Yehudah the Holy, and that it was put into his heart to compile these oracles into a body, and first impart to them the stamp of the written word.   If some of the links in this chain of tradition seem weak and hardly fit to bear the strain—as, for instance, that between Joshua and Samuel—the orthodox are bound to believe that its sufficiency has been tested, for every part is duly stamped with the re-assuring Rabbinical mark.   The oral law, it is alleged (see Pirke Avoth, chap. 1, &c.), was rehearsed by Moses to Joshua and by him repeated to the elders, and they in turn transmitted it to the prophets, who handed it down from one to another, until Jeremiah dictated it to Baruch the Scribe.   By this last it was communicated to Ezra, who taught it to the men of the Great Synagogue, of whom the last was Simeon the Just.   After this it was handed down from one to another till the time of Hillel the Great, who is said to have arrayed the vast accumulation of traditional explanations of the written law in six Sedarim or Orders, distributed in all into some six or seven hundred sections (see Chaggigah, fol. 14, col. 1, in this Miscellany, chap. xii., No. 86, and Succah, fol. 20, col. 1).   Thus Hillel the Great seems to have arranged the work that Rabbi Yehudah the Holy compiled, as we have represented, and given body to the Mishna pretty much as we now find it.

The Gemara is a voluminous collection of annotations upon the Mishna taken as the text.   That of the Palestinian Talmud, the earlier of the two by at least a century, is said to have been arranged by Rabbi Yochanan ben Eliezer, rector of the College at Tiberias.   That of the Talmud Babli, from which we have given so many excerpts in the pages of this Miscellany, was in the main compiled by Rab Ashi bar Simai, head of the Rabbinical College at Sora, appended to by his successors in the presidential chair, and finally completed by Rabbi Jossi, the last of the Amoraim, somewhere about the year 500 of the present era.

The twelve volumes of the Talmud Babli, whether in folio, quarto, or octavo, are for the most part so printed that not only do the corresponding pages contain the same matter, but line answers to line, word to word, and even letter to letter.* Quotations and references may therefore be readily made when folio and column are specified (as in our Miscellany everywhere), and even the very line can be given where there is any necessity. This arrangement is a great convenience in dealing with such a work as the Talmud, which, with the annotations of Rashi (R. Solomon ben Isaac), the *scholia* called Tosephoth, and the marginal references and footnotes, covers no less than 2947 folio leaves, or, in other words, 5894 pages in Hebrew, Aramaic, and Rabbinic letterpress, crowded with abbreviations, strange grammatical, or rather ungrammatical forms, and mnemonic technicalities, and without one vowel-point from beginning to end.

This vast medley of Rabbinical literature, with its more than cyclopædic range of topic, is roughly classified under half-a-dozen general rubrics, ששה סדרים (Shishah sedarim) six orders or series; the initial letters of which two words give us the technical term ש"ס, Shas, a term by which the Talmud itself is designated, and under which it is known everywhere among Jews.

The names of these six orders are as follows :—

1. Seder Zeraim (זרעים), the order of seeds, containing the laws which concern husbandry, &c.
2. Seder Moed (מועד), the order of festivals, times, and seasons, &c.
3. Seder Nashim (נשים), the order of women, dealing with conjugal laws, marriage duties, &c.
4. Seder Nezikin (נזיקין), the order of injuries, matters of Rabbinic jurisprudence relating thereto, &c.
5. Seder Kodashim (קדשים), the order of consecrations, sacrifices, &c.
6. Seder Taharoth (טהרות), the order of purifications, &c.

---

* Fancy, if all Bibles, of whatever size, had each the same number of pages, each page the same number of lines, and each line the same number of words. You might then be able to prick a pin through several pages and tell the very letters almost of every page the pin had pierced. I have seen this done with the Talmud, and the young Rabbi who performed the feat was, as he might well be, considered as a wonder in his literary world.—H.

The initials of these six names yield the mnemonic term (נ'ק'ט ז'מ'ן), Zeman Nakat, which means "a time accepted or comprehended." These sections are distributed among the twelve volumes thus:—Seder Zeraim occupies volume i.; Seder Moed extends over volumes ii., iii., and iv.; Seder Nashim fills up the next two, *i.e.*, the fifth and the sixth; while the seventh, eighth, and ninth are devoted to Seder Nezikin. These four orders chiefly relate to what is recorded in Exodus, while the other two may, for the most part, be referred to Leviticus. Of these, Seder Kodashim appropriates two of the remaining three volumes, leaving the twelfth to Seder Taharoth. These Sedarim are divided into מסכתות, Massictoth, or treatises, of which there are seventy-one in all, including the מסכתות קטנות, or minor treatises, which usually form an appendix to volume ix. These Massictoth are, in turn, subdivided into פרקים, Perakim, or chapters, of which there are 633 in all, including those of the minor treatises. These chapters again are still further broken up into paragraphs called Mishnaioth, to the number of 4187.

We shall now catalogue the Massictoth and indicate their contents, which we must do briefly; anything like a detailed account would fill a volume.

Seder Zeraim opens with—

1. Berachoth (ברכות, blessings). In this tract there are nine chapters, containing fifty-seven Mishnaioth. Masseketh Beracoth treats of the confession (the Shema) and divine service, thanksgivings for the fruits of the earth, the times and the places where prayer should be offered, &c., &c.—We purpose translating the first Mishna, and so much of its Gemara as is contained on the first page of the Talmud. The entire Gemara to the first Mishna extends to seventeen pages and a half.

2. Peah (פאה, corner) treats of the corner of the field (Lev. xxiii. 22; Deut. xxiv. 19), &c., in eight chapters.

3. Demai (דמאי, doubtful). Here are seven chapters on doubtful matters in regard to tithes, &c., from garden and field produce.

4. Kilaim (כלאים, heterogeneous). The nine chapters of this treatise relate to the mixing of seeds, the arranging of plants, &c., &c.
5. Sheviith (שביעית, the seventh). The Sabbatic year. Here there are ten chapters (Exod. xxiii. 10; Lev. xxv.).
6. Terumoth (תרומות, oblations). This tract contains eleven chapters, all referring to the various offerings, &c., brought for the Temple worship and service.
7. Maaseroth (מעשרות, tithes) deals with the "first tenth" or tithes which belonged to the Levites. Here are five chapters.
8. Maaser Sheni (מעשר שני, second tithe). Here again are five chapters. This tract treats of that which the Levites had to pay out of their tithes to the priests. (Comp. Lev. xxvii. 30; Num. xviii. 28.)
9. Challah (חלה, cake). Here are four chapters about the cake which women were to bring to the priests. (See Num. xv. 20.)
10. Orlah (ערלה, prepuce) Three chapters relating to the fruitage of young trees. (See Lev. xix. 23.)
11. Biccurim (בכורים, first fruits). This tract has four chapters respecting the first fruits which were to be brought to the Temple.

This, the last tract of Seder Zeraim, finishes volume i.

12. Shabbath (שבת, the Sabbath-day). Here are one hundred and thirty-nine Mishnaioth in twenty-four chapters, containing rules relating to the Sabbath.
13. Eiruvin (עירובין, combinations) deals with the various arrangements and limitary combinations, &c., relating to the observance of the Sabbath. Here are ten chapters divided into ninety-six Mishnaioth.

These two Massictoth fill volume ii.

14. P'sachim (פסחים, passovers). This treatise, dealing with the Paschal festival and its accessories, contains ten chapters divided into eighty-nine Mishnaioth.
15. Bitzah (ביצה, the egg), so called from its initial word, also termed Yom Tov, or "the good day." The five chapters of this tract contain restrictions and regulations for the due observance of festivals.
16. Chaggigah (חגיגה, festivity). This tract, in three chapters, deals with the sacrifices for festivals, &c. (Exod. xxiii. 17).

17. Moed Katon (מועד קטון, little feast). The three chapters of this treatise relate to the middle days of Passover and Succoth, &c.

These four tracts are comprised in volume iii.

18. Rosh Hashanah (ראש השנה, the beginning of the year). Here are four chapters in thirty-five Mishnaioth treating of New Year's Day.
19. Yoma (יומא, the day). Here are eight chapters concerning the Day of Atonement.
20. Succah (סוכה, the Feast of Tabernacles). Five chapters relating to the celebration of this festival.
21. Taanith (תענית, fast). Four chapters treating of the public fast days, and how they are to be observed.
22. Shekalim (שקלים, shekels). The eight chapters of this treatise relate to the capitation tax. (See Exod. xiii. 12, &c.)
23. Meggillah (מגילה, roll) contains particulars relating to the Feast of Purim, &c., in four chapters.

Megillah, the last tract of volume iv., finishes Seder Moed. Volume v. contains the three following treatises :—

24. Yevamoth (יבמות, brothers-in-law). Here are sixteen chapters, principally devoted to enforcing the duty of marrying the childless widow of a deceased brother-in-law (see Deut. xxv. 5), and the ceremony of Chalitzah (see ibid., ver. 9).
25. Kethuboth (כתובות. marriage contracts). The thirteen chapters of this treatise relate mainly to marriage documents, dowries, duties and other *et ceteras* concerning married life.
26.. Kiddushin (קדושין, espousals). This tract has four chapters on betrothing, or the "consecration" of a woman, and treats of the various ways this may be done ; by *voie de fait* (ביאה), by money, or by written contract, &c., &c.

The next four tracts occupy volume vi.

27. Gittin (גיטין, divorces). The Get or bill of divorcement and other cognate matters form the subject-matter of the nine chapters of this tract.
28. Nedarim (נדרים, vows) recapitulates and deals with the vows of females and families. Here are eleven chapters.

29. Nazir (נזיר, the Nazarite). The nine chapters of this treatise relate to the vows of Nazarites, &c.

30. Sotah (סוטה, the suspected). This tract in its nine chapters treats principally of conjugal infidelity (Num. v. 11), and with it closes Seder Nashim.

Volume vii., commencing Seder Nezikin, opens with Bava Kama.

31. Bava Kama (בבא קמא, the first gate or place of justice) treats of losses, of damages occasioned by man or beast, fire, &c. Here are ten chapters.

32. Bava Metzia (בבא מציעא, the middle gate). The ten chapters of this treatise deal with things found, with deposits and loans, interest or usury, &c.

33. Bava Bathra (בבא בתרא, the last gate). Here again are ten chapters. These relate chiefly to business matters, buying and selling, inheritances and trusts.

34. Avodah Zarah (עבודה זרה, strange worship). This tract in five chapters treats of idolatry and heresy. It is omitted from some editions because of its objectionable remarks.

Volume ix. commences with—

35. Sanhedrin (סנהדרין, Sanhedrin), which relates to the great ecclesiastical council of the nation, to judges and magistrates, to plaintiffs, defendants, and witnesses, fines, punishments, and forensic matters generally. There are eleven chapters in this treatise.

36. Shevuoth (שבועות, oaths). Eight chapters upon oaths and their administration.

37. Maccoth (מכות, stripes). Here are three chapters upon corporal punishment and other cognate matters. Among other things in reference to the scourging of criminals, the ארבעים חסר אחת, "the forty (stripes) save one" (Deut. xxv. 3; 2 Cor. xi. 24), is commented upon and explained.

38. Horaioth (הוריות, decisions). Another set of three chapters on legal administrations, dealing chiefly with errors of judgment and the offerings which atone for them.

39. Edioth (עדיות, witnesses). Eight chapters upon legal evidence, verdicts, and determinations in lawsuits, &c.

40. Avoth (אבות, fathers), or Pirke Avoth (פרקי אבות, the chapters of the fathers). The six chapters of this treatise which contain the moral apophthegms of the Jewish

sages are among the best known and most popular in the Talmud, and repeated on Sabbath afternoons during the six summer months.

Here follows the treatise entitled the "Avoth de Rabbi Nathan" (אבות דרבי נתן), with its forty-one chapters, and then the rest of the minor treatises styled the "Massictoth Ketanoth" (מסכתות קטנות).

Sophrim (סופרים, scribes). The twenty-one chapters of this treatise relate to the copying of Biblical MSS.

Ebel Rabbathi (אבל רבתי, great mourning), or Semachoth (שמחות, joy), as this tract is euphemistically styled, contains fourteen chapters.

Callah (כלה, the bride). A chapter on marriage ceremonies, &c.

Derech Eretz (דרך ארץ, the way of the world). A compendium of ethics in two divisions; "Rabba," the greater, containing eleven chapters, and "Zuta," the lesser, ten; to which is appended

Perek Hashalom (פרק השלום), as its name implies, "A chapter on peace."

Gerim (גרים, proselytes). Four chapters on the laws concerning proselytes.

Cuthim (כותים, Cuthites). The word Cuthites here, like the Greek βάρβαρος, is used to denote foreigners, especially heathens. This treatise contains two chapters.

Avadim (עבדים, slaves). A small treatise of three chapters.

These minor treatises have no Mishna. They vary in some editions, but occur, as noted above, in the edition of the Talmud Babli used for this Miscellany, that printed at Warsaw. Volume x., commencing Seder Kodashim, begins with—

41. Zevachim (זבחים, sacrifices). A tract of fourteen chapters upon sacrifices, their rules and regulations.

42. Menachoth (מנחות, meat-offerings). Here are thirteen chapters, principally relating to the evening sacrifices.

43. Bechoroth (בכורות, first-born). Primogeniture is the main topic of the nine chapters of this treatise, and with it finishes volume x. Volume xi. opens with—

44. Chulin (חולין, profane). Here we have a dozen chapters upon animals, clean and unclean, for domestic use, &c.

45. Erachin (עֲרכין, valuations). This is a treatise of nine chapters, mostly occupied about estimates, valuing and taxing objects consecrated for divine worship, and with vows.

46. Kerithoth (כריתות, excisions). The half-dozen chapters of this treatise have to do with the sins which are punished by excommunication, or "cutting off" from the people.

47. Temurah (תמורה, commutation). Seven chapters dealing with the substitution of one sacrifice for another.

48. Mehilah (מעילה, trespass). Six chapters upon trespasses with regard to consecrated things being perverted to profane uses.

49. Kinnim (קנים, nests). A treatise of three chapters about birds for sacrifice, nests, &c.

50. Tamid (תמיד, continual offerings). Seven chapters relating to the daily morning and evening sacrifices.

51. Middoth (מדות, measurements). Five chapters upon the dimensions of the Temple. This treatise concludes volume xi.

Seder Taharoth, with its twelve treatises, takes up volume xii. All these treatises except Niddah, the first in the volume, are without Gemara.

52. Niddah (נדה, uncleanness). Ten chapters mostly relating to the matters specified in Lev. xv. 2–12.

53. Kelim (כלים, vessels). Here we have thirty chapters about utensils, furniture, clothes, and other things which contract and communicate uncleanness; with various sanitary rules and regulations, &c.

54. Oholoth (אהלות, tents) treats of houses as well as tents, with special reference to the contaminating presence of a corpse. Here are eighteen chapters.

55. Negaim (נגעים, plagues). Fourteen chapters upon contagious disorders, especially leprosy (Lev. xiii. and xiv.).

56. Parah (פרה, the red heifer). Twelve chapters detailing the laws which relate to Num. xix.

57. Taharoth (טהרות, cleanliness). This treatise takes account of minor impurities which may be got rid of on the same day at sundown. There are ten chapters upon this subject.

58. Mikvaoth (מקואות, baths). Ten chapters upon baths, lavers, &c.

59. Maksheerin (מכשירין, purifiers). Here the rules for purification based upon Lev. xi. 36–38 are expanded into a half-dozen chapters.

60. Zabim (זבים, fluxes). A medical treatise upon Lev. xv. in five chapters.

61. Tevul Yom (טבול יום, ablutions of the day). Four chapters on purifying upon the self-same day on which defilement takes place. (See Lev. xvii. 15, and xxii. 6, 7.)

62. Yadaim (ידים, hands). The washing of the hands is the main topic of the four chapters of this treatise.

63. Okatzin (עקצין, stalks). Three chapters upon fruits and other things which convey impurity by the touch. This treatise finishes volume xii., and with it the Talmud Babli concludes.

We shall now subjoin the first Mishna of Berachoth, and as much of its Gemara as is given upon the first page of the Talmud, the heading to which is :—

מאימתי · פרק ראשון · ברכות

which reads thus: "Meemathai, chapter first, Berachoth." Meemathai = "from what time," is the word with which the chapter commences, and after which, as is usual, this chapter is named.

"From what time is the Shema read in the evening? From the time when the priests enter the sanctuary to eat of their heave-offerings, until the end of the first night-watch. These are the words of Rabbi Eliezer, but the sages say until midnight, and Rabbon Gamliel says until the dawn of morning. It came to pass that the sons of this Rabbi once returned from a banqueting-house after midnight, and said unto him, 'We have not yet read the Shema!' He said unto them, 'If the morning dawn has not yet appeared, ye are bound to read it; and not in this case only, but in every instance where the sages say *until midnight.*' Their precept holds good until the morning daybreak. The precept with regard to the burning of the fat and the joints holds good till the dawn of morning. For all offerings which must be eaten the same day, the precept holds good till the morning dawn rises. If this be the case, why do the sages say, 'until midnight'? In order to keep man far from transgression."

GEMARA.

"The Tanna,* it is asked, to what does he refer when he teaches מאימתי, 'from what time'? And besides, why does he teach about in the evening first, instead of in the morning first? The Tanna rests upon Scripture, where it is written (Deut. vi.), 'When thou liest down and when thou risest up,' and thus he teaches the time of reading the Shema when thou liest down. When does it begin? It begins from the hour when the priests enter to eat their heave-offering. But if thou wishest, I will say that he derives it from the account of the creation of the world, where it is written (Gen. i.), 'And the evening and the morning were day one.' If this be so, why does a later Mishna (fol. 11, col. 1) teach that at dawn two benedictions are to be said before the Shema, and one after it; and at eventide two benedictions are to be repeated before it, and two after it? Ought it not to teach concerning the evening first? The Tanna commences (in the above Mishna) 'in the evening,' then (in the later Mishna) he teaches 'at the dawn.' When he treats of the dawn he explains the particulars relating to the dawn, and then explains the particulars relating to the evening.

"Mar (the master †) says, from the hour when the priests enter to partake of the heave-offering. And from what time do the priests enter to partake of the heave-offering? Reply :—From the time that the stars appear. He should have taught them 'from the time that the stars appear' (which would have been easier to be understood). This he makes us to apprehend by the way. From what point of time do the priests eat the heave-offering? From the appearing of the stars. And then he gives us to understand that the expiatory sacrifice does not hinder (the priests eating of the heave-offering), according to the teaching of tradition (Lev. xxii.), 'And when the sun goes down he shall be clean.' It is the going down of the sun which might hinder him eating of the heave-offering, but the expiatory sacrifice does not hinder him eating it. But whence (do we know), that this 'when the sun is down' means 'when the sun sets,' and 'he shall be clean' is 'the purity of the day'? Perhaps."

So ends the first page of the Talmud.   דילמא (perhaps) is the catchword for the next page; and so the Gemara

---

* This word means a doctor, a learned man, and is applied here to the author of the Mishna.

† Mar refers to the editor and not to the author of the Mishna.

goes on filling page after page with matter of equal interest to that which we have quoted.

As an accompaniment to this we shall here quote two or three of the last Mishnaioth of Ukatzin, and so give the last page of the Talmud as well as the first.

There is no Gemara to any of the twelve treatises of Seder Taharoth except M. Niddah. Mishna 9 of Okatzin commences on the last page but one, and reads thus :—

9. "Tallow or suet of clean cattle (טהורה, clean is the catch-word which finishes one page and commences the next) does not defile like carrion, and requires legal authorisation. Tallow or suet of unclean cattle defiles like carrion, and therefore needs no legal authorisation. Unclean fish and locusts in villages require discrimination.

10 "A beehive, says Rabbi Eleazar, is like landed property, and a title-deed is to be written to give right of possession. In its standing-place it is not liable to become defiled, and he who takes of its honey on the Sabbath is in duty bound to bring a sin-offering. But the sages say it is not like landed property; no title-deed is to be drawn up in regard to it; it is liable to defilement (as it stands) in its place, and he who takes honey from it is not guilty.

11. "From what time does honeycomb become liable to ceremonial defilement as food? The school of Shammai says, from the time the beehive is fumigated; the school of Hillel says, from the time the beehive is emptied.

12. "Rabbi Yehoshua ben Levi says, the Holy One—blessed be He !—will in the future give to every righteous man an inheritance of three hundred and ten worlds, for it is said (Prov. viii.), 'That I may cause those that love me to inherit (יש, by gematria = 310) substance, and I will fill their treasures.' Rabbi Shimon ben Chalapta says, the Holy One—blessed be He !—has found no such vehicle of blessing for Israel as peace, for it is said (Prov. xxix.), 'The Lord will give strength unto His people. The Lord will bless His people with peace.'

END OF MASSICTA OKATZIN."

Such, then, with its opening and closing paragraphs, is an outline of the subject-matter of the Talmud Babli; a work which, in its entirety, has never been translated into any language, and in all probability never will, so incoherent is its structure, so diverse are its oracles, and so barren and questionable often are its results. It is, moreover, so huge in its dimensions that, as the Rabbis allege, it would take one seven years, studying six hours a day, to attain even a moderate acquaintance with its contents.

Enough, we flatter ourselves, has been given in these remarks to supply some real, however meagre, knowledge of its nature, and to mitigate the almost total ignorance which prevails in regard to it. It dates from the time of the Captivity, when the Jewish mind began to open to a sense of the glory of its sacred books, and the wealth of wisdom and knowledge contained within their miraculous pages. To the Jew, in his then mood, these books, conceived and put together by the heroic of the race in direst battle with darkness and disorder, seemed to be fraught with all divine counsel and alone worthy of all regard; until at length not the pious only, but the profane, were smitten with the enthusiasm, or, if not so smitten, made use of it for all sorts of selfish by-ends. It is the fate of all interests, however sacred, when men idly quit the reality for its reflection, and take to merely worshipping the wonderful that has been uttered or done. It would seem to lie in the nature of things that the weak silver age should succeed the rich golden one—the age of pale reflection, the age of glowing action; only in this case, that of silver is ominously all too prolonged. The ages of brass and iron, which among conquering races seem equally fated to follow that of weak admiration, have not yet among the Jews so much as begun to appear. The history they have had is all gone to echo, and the canon of inspiration has been arbitrarily and peremptorily closed.

A TALMUDIC MISCELLANY.

CHAPTER I.

THE 'ONES' OF THE TALMUD.

1. WHERE do we learn that the Shechinah rests even upon *one* who studies the law? In Exodus xx. 24, where it is written, "In all places where I record my name I will come unto *thee*, and I will bless *thee*."

Berachoth, fol. 6, col. 1.

NOTE.—The Chaldee Targums on the Pentateuch strike the same keynote of broad Catholicity, and variously but very beautifully modulate the same sentiment. One example must suffice here. The Targum Yerushalmi says, " In every place in which ye shall memorialize my holy name, my word shall be revealed unto *you*, and bless *you*." The same sentiment has its echo in Matt. xviii. 20.

2. *One* pang of remorse at a man's heart is of more avail than many stripes applied to him. (See Prov. xvii. 10.)

Ibid., fol. 7, col. 1.

3. "Hear, O Israel, the Lord our God is *one* Lord!" (Deut. vi. 4). Whosoever prolongs the utterance of the word (אחד) *one*, shall have his days and years prolonged to him. So also *Zohar*, syn. tit. ii.

Ibid., fol. 13, col. 2.

A

4. Once, as the Rabbis tell us, the Roman Government issued a decree forbidding Israel to study the law. Whereupon Pappus, the son of Yehudah, one day found Rabbi Akiva teaching it openly to multitudes, whom he had gathered round him to hear it. "Akiva," said he, "art thou not afraid of the Government?" "List," was the reply, "and I will tell thee how it is by a parable. It is with me as with the fishes whom a fox, walking once by a river's side, saw darting distractedly to and fro in the stream; and, addressing, inquired, 'From what, pray, are ye fleeing?' 'From the nets,' they replied, 'which the children of men have set to ensnare us.' 'Why, then,' rejoined the fox, 'not try the dry land with me, where you and I can live together, as our fathers managed to do before us?' 'Surely,' exclaimed they, 'thou art not he of whom we have heard so much as the most cunning of animals, for herein thou art not wise, but foolish. For if we have cause to fear where it is natural for us to live, how much more reason have we to do so where we needs must die!' Just so," continued Akiva, "is it with us who study the law, in which (Deut. xxx. 20) it is written, 'He is thy life and the length of thy days;' for if we suffer while we study the law, how much more shall we if we neglect it?" Not many days after, it is related, this Rabbi Akiva was apprehended and thrown into prison. As it happened, they led him out for execution just at the time when "Hear, O Israel!" fell to be repeated, and as they tore his flesh with currycombs, and as he was with long-drawn breath sounding forth the word (אחד) *one*, his soul departed from him. Then came forth a voice from heaven (בת קול), which said, "Blessed art thou, Rabbi Akiva, for thy soul and the word *one* left thy body together."

Berachoth, fol. 61, col. 2.

Note.—בת קול, Bath Kol, *lit.* the echo or daughter of a voice. In this case it is the echo of the voice of God in those who by obeying hear.

5. The badger, as it existed in the days of Moses, was an animal of unique type, and the learned are not agreed whether it was a wild one or a domestic. It had only *one* horn on its forehead; and was assigned for the time to Moses, who made a covering of its skin for the tabernacle; after which it became extinct, having served the purpose of its existence. Rabbi Yehudah says, "The ox, also, which the first man, Adam, sacrificed, had but *one* horn on its forehead." *Shabbath*, fol. 28, col. 2.

6. Once a Gentile came to Shamai, and said, "Proselytise me, but on condition that thou teach me the whole law, even the whole of it, whilst I stand upon *one* leg." Shamai drove him off with the builder's rod which he held in his hand. When he came to Hillel with the same challenge, Hillel converted him by answering him on the spot, "That which is hateful to thyself, do not do to thy neighbour. This is the whole law, and the rest is its commentary" (Tobit, iv. 15; Matt. vii. 12). *Ibid.*, fol. 31, col. 1.

7. When Rabbi Shimon ben Yochai and his son, Rabbi Elazar, came out of their cave on a Friday afternoon, they saw an old man hurrying along with two bunches of myrtle in his hand. "What," said they, accosting him, "dost thou want with these?" "To smell them in honour of the Sabbath," was the reply. "Would not *one* bunch," they remarked, "be enough for that purpose?" "Nay," the old man replied; "*one* is in honour of זכור, 'Remember' (Exod. xxii. 28); and *one* in honour of שמור, 'Keep' (Deut. v. 8)." Thereupon Rabbi Shimon remarked to his son, "Behold how the commandments are regarded by Israel!" *Ibid.*, fol. 33, col. 2.

8. Not *one* single thing has God created in vain. He created the snail as a remedy for a blister; the fly for the sting of a wasp; the gnat for the bite of a serpent; the serpent itself for healing the itch (or the scab); and the lizard (or the spider) for the sting of a scorpion. *Ibid.*, fol. 77, col. 2.

9. When a man is dangerously ill, the law grants dispensation, for it says, " You may break *one* Sabbath on his behalf, that he may be preserved to keep many Sabbaths."

Shabbath, fol. 151, col. 2.

10. Once when Rabbi Ishmael paid a visit to Rabbi Shimon, he was offered a cup of wine, which he at once, without being asked twice, accepted, and drained at *one* draught. " Sir," said his host, " dost thou not know the proverb, that he who drinks off a cup of wine at a draught is a greedy one ? " " Ah ! " was the answer, " that fits not this case ; for thy cup is small, thy wine is sweet, and my stomach is capacious." *P'sachim*, fol. 86, col. 2.

11. At the time when Nimrod the wicked had cast our Father Abraham into the fiery furnace, Gabriel stood forth in the presence of the Holy One—blessed be He !—and said, " Lord of the universe, let me, I pray thee, go down and cool the furnace, and deliver that righteous one from it." Then the Holy One—blessed be He !—said unto him, " I am *One* in my world and he is *one* in his world ; it is more becoming that He who is *one* should deliver him who is *one*." But as God does not withhold His reward from any creature, He said to Gabriel, " For this thy good intention, be thine the honour of rescuing three of his descendants." At the time when Nebuchadnezzar the wicked cast Hananiah, Mishael, and Azariah into the fiery furnace, Yourkami, the prince of hail, arose before God and said, " Lord of the universe, let me, I pray thee, go down and cool the fiery furnace, and rescue these righteous men from its fury." Whereupon Gabriel interposed, and said, " God's power is not to be demonstrated thus, for thou art the prince of hail, and everybody knows that water quenches fire ; but I, the prince of fire, will go down and cool the flame within and intensify it without (so as to consume the executioners), and thus will I perform a miracle within a miracle." Then the Holy One—blessed be He !—said to him,

" Go down." Upon which Gabriel exclaimed, " Verily the truth of the Lord endureth for ever!" (Ps. cxvii. 2).

P'sachim, fol. 118, col. 1.

12. *One* peppercorn to-day is better than a basketful of pumpkins to-morrow. *Chaggigah*, fol. 10, col. 1.

13. *One* day of a year is counted for a whole year.

Rosh Hashanah, fol. 2, col. 2.

Note.—If a king be crowned on the twenty-ninth of Adar (the last month of the sacred year), on the morrow—the first of Nissan—it is reckoned that he commences his second year, that being the new year's day for royal and ecclesiastical affairs.

14. For the sake of *one* righteous man the whole world is preserved in existence, as it is written (Prov. x. 25), " The righteous man is an everlasting foundation."

Yoma, fol. 38, col. 2.

15. Rabbi Meyer saith, " Great is repentance, because for the sake of *one* that truly repenteth the whole world is pardoned; as it is written (Hosea xiv. 4), ' I will heal their backsliding, I will love them freely, for mine anger is turned away from *him*.' " It is not said, "*from them*," but "*from him*." *Ibid.*, fol. 86, col. 2.

16. He who observes *one* precept, in addition to those which, as originally laid upon him, he has discharged, shall receive favour from above, and is equal to him who has fulfilled the whole law. *Kiddushin*, fol. 39, col. 2.

17. If any man vow a vow by only *one* of all the utensils of the altar, he has vowed by the corban, even although he did not mention the word in his oath. Rabbi Yehuda says, " He who swears by the word Jerusalem is as though he had said nothing." *Nedarim*, fol. 10, col. 2.

18. Balaam was lame in *one* foot and blind in *one* eye.

Sotch, fol. 10, col. 1, and *Sanhedrin*, fol. 105, col. 1.

19. One wins eternal life after a struggle of years; another finds it in *one* hour (see Luke xxiii. 43).

Avodah Zarah, fol. 17, col. 1.

> NOTE.—This saying is applied by Rabbi the Holy to Rabbi Eliezer, the son of Durdia, a profligate who recommended himself to the favour of Heaven by one prolonged act of determined penitence, placing his head between his knees and groaning and weeping till his soul departed from him, and his sin and misery along with it; for at the moment of death a voice from heaven came forth and said, "Rabbi Eliezer, the son of Durdia, is appointed to life everlasting." When Rabbi the Holy heard this, he wept, and said, "One wins eternal life after a struggle of years; another finds it in *one* hour." (Compare Luke xv. 11–32.)

20. Whosoever destroyeth *one* soul of Israel, Scripture counts it to him as though he had destroyed the whole world; and whoso preserveth *one* soul of Israel, Scripture counts it as though he had preserved the whole world.

Sanhedrin, fol. 37, col. 1.

21. The greatness of God is infinite; for while with *one* die man impresses many coins and all are exactly alike, the King of kings, the Holy One—blessed be He!—with *one* die impresses the same image (of Adam) on all men, and yet not one of them is like his neighbour. So that every one ought to say, "For myself is the world created."

Ibid., fol. 37, col. 1.

22. "He caused the lame to mount on the back of the blind, and judged them both as *one*." Antoninus said to the Rabbi, "Body and soul might each plead right of acquittal at the day of judgment." "How so?" he asked. "The body might plead that it was the soul that had sinned, and urge, saying, 'See, since the departure of the soul I have lain in the grave as still as a stone.' And the soul might plead, 'It was the body that sinned, for since the day I left it, I have flitted about in the air as innocent as a bird.'" To which the Rabbi replied and said, "Where-

unto this thing is like, I will tell thee in a parable. It is like unto a king who had an orchard with some fine young fig-trees planted in it. He set two gardeners to take care of them, of whom one was lame and the other blind. One day the lame one said to the blind, 'I see some fine figs in the garden; come, take me on thy shoulders, and we will pluck them and eat them.' By and by the lord of the garden came, and missing the fruit from the fig-trees, began to make inquiry after them. The lame one, to excuse himself, pled, 'I have no legs to walk with;' and the blind one, to excuse himself, pled, 'I have no eyes to see with.' What did the lord of the garden do? He caused the lame to mount upon the back of the blind, and judged them both as *one*." So likewise will God re-unite soul and body, and judge them both as *one* together; as it is written (Ps. l. 4), "He shall call to the heavens from above, and to the earth, that He may judge His people." "He shall call to the heavens from above," that alludes to the soul; "and to the earth, that He may judge His people," that refers to the body.   *Sanhedrin*, fol. 91, cols. 1, 2.

> NOTE.—Rabbi Yehudah, surnamed the Holy, the editor of the Mishna, is the personage here and elsewhere spoken of as the *Rabbi* by pre-eminence. He was an intimate friend of the Roman Emperor Antoninus Pius.

23. *One* thing obtained with difficulty is far better than a hundred things procured with ease.
  Avoth d'Rab. Nathan, ch. 3.

24. In the name of Rav, Rabbi Yehoshua bar Abba says, "Whoso buys a scroll of the law in the market seizes possession of another's meritorious act; but if he himself copies out a scroll of the law, Scripture considers him as if he had himself received it direct from Mount Sinai." "Nay," adds Rav Yehudah, in the name of Rav, "even if he has amended *one* letter in it, Scripture considers him as if he had written it out entirely."
  Menachoth, fol. 30, col. 1.

25. He who forgets *one* thing that he has learned breaks a negative commandment; for it is written (Deut. iv. 9), "Take heed to thyself . . . lest thou forget the things."   *Menachoth*, fol. 99, col. 2.

26. A proselyte who has taken it upon himself to observe the law, but is suspected of neglecting *one* point, is to be suspected of being guilty of neglecting the whole law, and therefore regarded as an apostate Israelite, and to be punished accordingly.   *Bechoroth*, fol. 30, col. 2.

Note.—The same sentiment, which is a Jewish one, is more peremptorily and absolutely delivered in James ii. 10.

27. It is written (Gen. xxviii. 11), "And he took from the *stones* of the place;" and again it is written (ver. 18), "And he took the *stone*." Rabbi Isaac says this teaches that all these stones gathered themselves together into one place, as if each were eager that the saint should lay his head upon it. It happened, as the Rabbis tell us, that all the stones were swallowed up by one another, and thus merged into *one* stone.   *Chullin*, fol. 91, col. 2.

Note.—Though the Midrash and two of the Targums, that of Jonathan and the Yerushalmi, tell the same fanciful story about these stones, Aben Ezra and R. Shemuel ben Meir among others adopt the opposite and common-sense interpretation which assigns to the word מאבני, in Gen. xxviii. 11, no such occult meaning.

28. The psalms commencing "Blessed is the man" and "Why do the heathen rage" constitute but *one* psalm.

Berachoth, fol. 9, col. 2.

29. The former Chasidim used to sit still *one* hour, and then pray for *one* hour, and then again sit still for *one* hour.

Ibid., fol. 32, col. 2.

30. All the benedictions in the Temple used to conclude with the words "Blessed be the Lord God of Israel unto eternity;" but when the Sadducees, corrupting the faith, maintained that there was only *one* world, it was enacted

that they should conclude with the words *"from eternity
unto eternity."*   *Berachoth*, fol. 54, col. 1.

> NOTE.—The Sadducees (צדוקים, Zadokim), so called after
> Zadok their master, as is known, stood rigidly by the
> original Mosaic code, and set themselves determinedly
> against all traditional developments. To the Talmudists,
> therefore, they were especially obnoxious, and their bald,
> cold creed is looked upon by them with something like
> horror. It is thus the Talmud warns against them—
> "Believe not in thyself till the day of thy death, for,
> behold, Yochanan, after officiating in the High Priest-
> hood for eighty years, became in the end a Sadducee."
> (*Berachoth*, fol. 29, col. 1.) In Derech Eretz Zuta, chap. i.,
> a caution is given which might well provoke attention—
> "Learn or inquire nothing of the Sadducees, lest thou
> be drawn into hell."

31. Rabbi Yehudah tells us that Rav says a man should
never absent himself from the lecture-hall, not even for *one*
hour; for the above Mishnah had been taught at college for
many years, but the reason of it had never been made
plain till *the hour* when Rabbi Chanina ben Akavia came
and explained it.   *Shabbath*, fol. 83, col. 2.

> NOTE.—The Mishnah alluded to is short and simple, viz.,
> Where is it taught that a ship is clean to the touch?
> From Prov. xxx. 19, "The way of a ship in the midst
> of the sea" (*i.e.*, as the sea is clean to the touch, there-
> fore a ship must also be clean to the touch). The force
> of the maxim is now evident. One hour's absence from
> school may be of serious consequence.

32. It is indiscreet for *one* to sleep in a house as the
sole occupant, for Lilith will seize hold of him.

                    Ibid., fol. 151, col. 2.

> NOTE.—Lilith (לילית, the night-visiting one, from ליל, *night*)
> is the name of a *night spectre*, said to have been Adam's
> first wife, but who, for her refractory conduct, was
> transformed into a demon endowed with power to injure
> and even destroy infants unprotected by the necessary
> amulet or charm.

33. "Thou hast acknowledged the Lord this day to be

thy God; and the Lord hath acknowledged thee this day to be His peculiar people" (Deut. xxvi. 17, 18). The Holy One—blessed be He!—said unto Israel, "Ye have made Me a name in the world, as it is written (Deut. vi. 4), 'Hear, O Israel, the Lord our God is *one* Lord;' and so I will make you a name in the world, as it is said (1 Chron. xvii. 21), 'And what *one* nation in the earth is like Thy people Israel?'"

Chaggigah, fol. 3, col. 1.

34. *One* in the Greek language is Hen (הן = ἔν).

Moed Katon, fol. 28, col. 1.

Note.—This fragment is given to show that the Rabbis did not ignore Greek when it suited their purpose.

35. Why are the words of the Law compared to *fire?* (Jer. xxiii. 29.) Because, as fire does not burn when there is but *one* piece of wood, so do the words of the Law not maintain the fire of life when meditated on by *one* alone (see, in confirmation, Matt. xviii. 20).

Taanith, fol. 7, col. 1.

36. "And Moses went up from the plains of Moab unto the mountain of Nebo" (Deut. xxxiv. 1). Tradition says there were twelve stairs, but that Moses surmounted them all in *one* step.   *Sotah*, fol. 13, col. 2.

37. Pieces of money given in charity should not be counted over by twos, but *one* by *one*.

Bava Bathra, fol. 8, col. 2.

38. "Knowest thou the time when the wild goats of the rock bring forth?" (Job xxxix. 1.) The wild goat is cruel to her offspring. As soon as they are brought forth, she climbs with them to the steep cliffs, that they may fall headlong and die. But, said God to Job, to prevent this I provide an eagle to catch the kid upon its wings, and then carry and lay it before its cruel mother. Now, if that eagle should be too soon or too late by *one* second only, instant death to the kid could not be averted; but

with Me *one* second is never changed for another. Shall
איוב (*Job*) be now changed by Me, therefore, into אויב (*an
enemy*). (Comp. Job. ix. 17, and xxxiv. 35.)

Bava Bathra, fol. 16, cols. 1, 2.

NOTE.—Whatever may be said of the natural history here,
the point of the illustration is beyond question.

39. A generation can have *one* leader only, and not two.

Sanhedrin, fol. 8, col. 1.

40. "Like the hammer that breaketh the rock in pieces"
(Jer. xxiii. 29). As a hammer divideth fire into many
sparks, so *one* verse of Scripture has many meanings and
many explanations. *Ibid.*, fol. 34, col. 1.

NOTE.—In the Machser for Pentecost (p. 69) God is said to
have "explained the law to His people, face to face, and
on every point *ninety-eight explanations* are given."

41. Adam was created *one* without Eve. Why? That
the Sadducees might not assert the plurality of powers in
heaven. *Ibid.*, fol. 37, col. 1.

NOTE.—As the Sadducees did not believe in a plurality of
powers in heaven, but only the Christians, in the regard
of the Jews, did so (by their profession of the doctrine
of the Trinity), it is obvious that here, as well as often
elsewhere, the latter and not the former are intended.

42. "And the frog (צפרדע, *sing. no.*) came up (ותכס,
also *sing.*) and covered the land of Egypt" (Exod.
viii. 1 ; A. V. viii. 6). "There was but *one* frog," said
Rabbi Elazar, "and she so multiplied as to fill the whole
land of Egypt." "Yes, indeed," said Rabbi Akiva, "there
was, as you say, but *one* frog, but she herself was so large
as to fill all the land of Egypt." Whereupon Rabbi
Elazar ben Azariah said unto him, "Akiva, what business
hast thou with Haggadah? Be off with thy legends, and
get thee to the laws thou art familiar with about plagues
and tents. Though thou sayest right in this matter, for

there was only *one* frog, but she croaked so loud that the frogs came from everywhere else to her croaking."

Sanhedrin, fol. 67, col. 2.

NOTE.—(*a.*) Rabba, the grandson of Channa, said that he himself once saw a frog larger than any seen now, though not so large as the frog in Egypt. It was as large as Acra, a village of some sixty houses. (*Bava Bathra*, fol. 73, col. 2.)

(*b.*) Apropos to the part the frog was conceived to play or symbolise in the Jewish conception of the mode and ministry of Divine judgment, we quote the following:—"We are told that Samuel once saw a frog carrying a scorpion on its back across a river, upon the opposite bank of which a man stood waiting ready to be stung. The sting proving fatal, so that the man died; upon which Samuel exclaimed, ' Lord, they wait for Thy judgments this day: for all are Thy servants.' (Ps. cxix. 91)." (*Nedarim*, fol. 41, col. 1.)

43. " According to the days of *one* king " (Isa. xxiii. 15). What king is this that is singled out as *one?* Thou must say this is the King Messiah, and no other.

Sanhedrin, fol. 99, col. 1.

44. Rabbi Levi contends that Manasseh has no portion in the world to come, while Rabbi Yehudah maintains that he has; and each supports his conclusion in contradiction of the other, from *one* and the same Scripture text.   *Ibid.*, fol. 102, col. 2.

45. The words, " *Remember* the Sabbath day," in Exod. xx. 8, and " *Keep* the Sabbath day," in Deut. v. 12, were uttered in *one* breath, as no man's mouth could utter them, and no man's ear could hear.

Shevuoth, fol. 20, col. 2.

46. The officer who inflicts flagellation on a criminal must smite with *one* hand only, but yet with all his force.

Maccoth, fol. 22, col. 2.

NOTE.—More on this topic may be found in " Genesis according to the Talmud," p. 151, n. 12.

47. I would rather be called a fool all my days than sin *one* hour before God. *Edioth*, chap. 5, mish. 6.

48. He who observes but *one* precept secures for himself an advocate, and he who commits *one* single sin procures for himself an accuser. *Avoth*, chap. 4, mish. 15.

> Note.—The word for *advocate* in the above Mishnah is פרקליט, a Hebrew form of the Greek παράκλητος, *advocate*, which occurs in John xiv. 16, &c.

49. He who learns from another *one* chapter, *one* halachah, *one* verse, or *one* word or even a *single letter*, is bound to respect him. *Ibid.*, chap. 6, mish. 3.

> Note.—The above is one evidence, among many, of the high esteem in which learning and the office of a teacher are held among the Jews. Education is one of the virtues— of which the following, extracted from the Talmud, is a list—the interest of which the Jew considers he enjoys in this world, while the capital remains intact against the exigencies of the world to come. These are :— The honouring of father and mother, acts of benevolence, hospitality to strangers, visiting the sick, devotion in prayer, promotion of peace between man and man, and study in general, but the study of the law outweighs them all. (*Shabbath*, fol. 127, col. 1.) The study of the law, it is said, is of greater merit to rescue one from accidental death, than building the Temple, and greater than honouring father or mother. (*Meggillah*, fol. 16, col. 2.)

50. "Repent *one* day before thy death." In relation to which Rabbi Eliezer was asked by his disciples, "How is a man to repent *one* day before his death, since he does not know on what day he shall die?" "So much the more reason is there," he replied, "that he should repent to-day, lest he die to-morrow; and repent to-morrow, lest he die the day after: and thus will all his days be penitential ones." *Avoth d'Rab. Nathan*, chap. 15.

> Note.—This reminds one of Horace's admonition:—"Omnem crede diem tibi diluxisse supremum."

51. He who obliterates *one* letter from the written name of God, breaks a negative command, for it is said, "And

destroy the names of them out of that place. Ye shall *not do so* unto the Lord your God" (Deut. xii. 3, 4).

Sophrim, chap. 5, hal. 6.

52. Rabbi Chanina could put on and off his shoes whilst standing on *one* leg only, though he was eighty years of age. *Chullin*, fol. 24, col. 2.

53. A priest who is blind in *one* eye should not be judge of the plague; for it is said (Lev. xiii. 12), "Wheresoever the priest (with both eyes) looketh."

Negaim, chap. 2, mish. 3.

54. The twig of a bunch without any grapes is clean; but if there remained *one* grape on it, it is unclean.

Okzin, chap. 1, mish. 5.

CHAPTER II.

THE 'TWOS' OF THE TALMUD.

1. Not every man deserves to have *two* tables.

Berachoth, fol. 5, col. 2.

Note.—The meaning of this rather ambiguous sentence may either be, that all men are not able to succeed in more enterprises than *one* at a time ; or that it is not given to every one to make the best both of the present world and of that which is to come.

2. Abba Benjamin used to say " There are *two* things about which I have all my life been much concerned: that my prayer should be offered in front of my bed, and that the position of my bed should be from north to south."

Ibid., fol. 5, col. 2.

Note.—There are several reasons which may be adduced to account for Abba Benjamin's anxiety, and they are all more or less connected with the important consequences which were supposed to depend upon determining his position with reference to the Shechinah, which rested in the east or the west.

(*a*.) Abba Benjamin felt anxious to have children, for " any man not having children is counted as dead," as it is written (Gen. xxx. 1), " Give me children, or else I die." (*Nedarim*, fol. 64, col. 2.)

(*b*.) With the Jew one great consideration of life is to have children, and more especially *male children ;* because when a boy is born all rejoice over him, but over a girl they all mourn. When a boy comes into the world he brings peace with him, and a loaf of bread in his hand, but a girl brings nothing. (*Niddah*, fol. 31, col. 2.)

(*c*.) It is impossible for the world to be without males

and females, but blessed is he whose children are boys, and hapless is he whose children are girls. (*Kiddushin,* fol. 82, col. 2.)

(*d.*) Whosoever does not leave a son to be heir, God will heap wrath upon him. (Scripture is quoted in proof of this, compare Numb. xxvii. 8 with Zeph. i. 15.) (*Bava Bathra,* fol. 116, col. 1.)

3. "There are *two* ways before me, one leading into Paradise, the other into Hell." When Yochanan, the son of Zachai, was sick unto death, his disciples came to visit him; and when he saw them he wept, upon which his disciples exclaimed, "Light of Israel! Pillar of the right! Mighty Hammer! why weepest thou?" He replied, "If I were going to be led into the presence of a king, who is but flesh and blood, to-day here and to-morrow in the grave, whose anger with me could not last for ever, whose sentence against me, were it even unto death, could not endure for ever, and whom perhaps I might pacify with words or bribe with money, yet for all that should I weep; but now that I am about to enter the presence of the King of kings, the Holy One—blessed be He for ever and ever!—whose anger would be everlasting, whose sentence of death or imprisonment admits of no reprieve, and who is not to be pacified with words nor bribed with money, and in whose presence there are *two* roads before me, one leading into Paradise and the other into Hell, and should I not weep?" Then prayed they him, and said, "Rabbi, give us thy farewell blessing;" and he said unto them, "Oh that the fear of God may be as much upon you as the fear of man."   *Berachoth,* fol. 28, col. 2.

NOTE.—See Shakespeare's "Henry VIII.," act iii. sc. 2, and contrast the words of this light of Israel with the words of St. Paul, his contemporary, in 2 Tim. iv. 6–8, uttered in the prospect and near presence of the same dread reality.

4. Rabbi Ami says, "Knowledge is of great price, for it is placed between *two* divine names, as it is written (1 Sam.

ii. 3), "A God of knowledge is the Lord," and therefore mercy is to be denied to him who has no knowledge; for it is written (Isa. xxvii. 11), "It is a people of no understanding, therefore He that hath made them will not have mercy on them." *Berachoth*, fol. 33, col. 1.

Note.—(*a.*) Here we have a clear law, drawn from Scripture, forbidding, or at any rate denying, mercy to the ignorant. The words of Rabbi (the Holy) are a practical commentary on the text worth quoting, " Woe is unto me because I have given my morsel to an ignorant one (עם הארץ)." (*Bava Bathra*, fol. 8, col. 1.)

(*b.*) But who is the ignorant one from whom this mercy is to be withheld? Here the doctors disagree. He, says Rabbi Eliezer, who does not read the שמע, Shema, "Hear, O Israel,"&c., both morning and evening. According to Rabbi Yehudah, he that does not put on phylacteries is an ignorant one. Rabbi Azai affirms that he who wears no fringes to his garment is an ignorant one, &c. Others again say he who even reads the Bible and the Mishna, but does not serve the disciples of the wise, is an ignorant one. Rabbi Huna winds up with the words הלכה כאחרים, "the law is as the others have said," and so leaves the difficulty where he finds it. (*Berachoth*, fol. 47, col. 2.)

(*c.*) Of him " who transgresses the words of the wise, which he is commanded to obey," it is written, " He is guilty of death and has forfeited his life." (*Berachoth*, fol. 4, col. 2, and *Yevamoth*, fol. 20, col. 1.) Whoso, therefore, shows mercy to him contradicts the purpose and incurs the displeasure of God. It was in application of this principle, literally interpreted, that the wise should hold no parley with the ignorant, which led the Jews to condemn the contrary procedure of Jesus Christ.

(*d.*) It was this prohibition to show mercy to the ignorant, together with the solemn threatenings directed against those who neglected the study of the law, that worked such a wonderful revolution in Hezekiah's time ; for it is said that then " they searched from Dan to Beersheba, and did not find an ignorant one." (*Sanhedrin*, fol. 94, col. 2.)

5. When the Holy One—blessed be He !—remembers

that His children are in trouble amongst the nations of the world, He drops *two* tears into the great ocean, the noise of which startles the world from one end to the other, and causes the earth to quake.

Berachoth, fol. 59, col. 1.

6. We read in the Talmud that a Gentile once came to Shamai and said, " How many laws have you ? " Shamai replied, " We have *two*, the written law and the oral law." To which the Gentile made answer, " When you speak of the written law, I believe you, but in your oral law I have no faith. Nevertheless, you may make me a proselyte on condition that you teach me the written law only." Upon this Shamai rated him sharply, and sent him away with indignant abuse. When, however, this Gentile came with the same object, and proposed the same terms to Hillel, the latter proceeded at once to proselytise him, and on the first day taught him Aleph, Beth, Gemel, Daleth. On the morrow Hillel reversed the order of these letters, upon which the proselyte remonstrated and said, " But thou didst not teach me so yesterday." " True," said Hillel, " but thou didst trust me in what I taught thee then ; why, then, dost thou not trust me now in what I tell thee respecting the oral law ? "

Shabbath, fol. 31, col. 1.

7. Every man as he goes on the eve of the Sabbath from the synagogue to his house is escorted by *two* angels, one of which is a good angel and the other an evil. When the man comes home and finds the lamps lit, the table spread, and the bed in order, the good angel says, " May the coming Sabbath be even as the present ; " to which the evil angel (though with reluctance) is obliged to say, " Amen." But if all be in disorder, then the bad angel says, " May the coming Sabbath be even as the present," and the good angel is (with equal reluctance) obliged to say " Amen " to it.   *Ibid.*, fol. 119, col. 2.

8. *Two* are better than three. Alas ! for the one that goes and does not return again.

Shabbath, fol. 152, col. 1.

Note.—As in the riddle of the Sphinx, the " two " here stands for youth with its two sufficient legs, and the " three " for old age, which requires a third support in a staff. The one that goes and does not return is youth after it has faded away.

9. There were *two* things which God first thought of creating on the eve of the Sabbath, which, however, were not created till after the Sabbath had closed. The first was *fire*, which Adam by divine suggestion drew forth by striking together *two* stones ; and the second, was the *mule*, produced by the crossing of *two* different animals.

P'sachim, fol. 54, col. 1.

10. " Every one has *two* portions, one in paradise and another in hell." Acheer asked Rabbi Meyer, " What meaneth this that is written (Eccl. vii. 14), ' God also has set the one over against the other ' ? " Rabbi Meyer replied, " There is nothing which God has created of which He has not also created the opposite. He who created mountains and hills created also seas and rivers." But said Acheer to Rabbi Meyer, " Thy master, Rabbi Akiva, did not say so, but spake in this way : He created the righteous and also the wicked ; He created paradise and hell : every man has *two* portions, one portion in paradise, and the other in hell. The righteous, who has personal merit, carries both his own portion of good and that of his wicked neighbour away with him to paradise ; the wicked, who is guilty and condemned, carries both his own portion of evil and also that of his righteous neighbour away with him to hell." When Rav Mesharshia asked what Scripture guarantee there was for this, this was the reply : " With regard to the righteous, it is written (Isa. lxi. 7), ' They shall rejoice in their portion, therefore in their land (beyond the grave)

they shall possess the *double.*' Respecting the wicked it is written (Jer. xvii. 18), 'And destroy them with *double destruction.*'"   *Chaggigah*, fol. 15, col. 1.

> NOTE.—The question asked above by Acheer has been practically resolved by all wise men from the beginning of the world, but it is the boast of the Hegelians that it has for the first time been resolved philosophically by their master. Others had maintained that you could not *think* a thing but through its opposite; he first maintained it could not *exist* but through its opposite, that, in fact, the thing and its opposite must needs arise together, and that eternally, as complements of one unity : the white is not *there* without the black, nor the black without the white ; the good is not *there* without the evil, nor the evil without the good.

11. Pride is unbecoming in women. There were two proud women, and their names were contemptible; the name of the one, Deborah, meaning *wasp*, and of the other, Huldah, *weasel.* Respecting the wasp it is written (Judges iv. 6), " And she sent and called Barak," whereas she ought to have gone to him. Concerning the weasel it is written (2 Kings xxii. 15), " Tell the man that sent you," whereas she should have said, " Tell the king."

Meggillah, fol. 14, col. 2.

12. If speech is worth one sela (a small coin so called), silence is worth *two.*   *Ibid.*, fol. 18, col. 1.

> NOTE.—The Swiss motto, " Speech is worth silver, silence worth gold," expresses a sentiment which finds great favour with the authors and varied expression in the pages of the Talmud.
>
> (*a.*) If silence be good for wise men, how much better must it be for fools ! (*P'sachim*, fol. 98, col. 2.)
>
> (*b.*) For every evil silence is the best remedy. (*Meggillah*, fol. 18, col. 1.)
>
> (*c.*) Silence is as good as confession. (*Yevamoth*, fol. 87, col. 1.)
>
> (*d.*) Silence in a Babylonian was a mark of his being of good family. (*Kiddushin*, fol. 71, col. 2.)

(*e.*) Simeon, the son of Gamliel, said, "I have been brought up all my life among the wise, and I have never found anything of more material benefit than silence." (*Avoth*, chap. 1.)

(*f.*) Rabbi Akiva said, "Laughter and levity lead a man to lewdness; but tradition is a fence to the law, tithes are a fence to riches, vows are a fence to abstinence, while the fence of wisdom is silence." (*Ibid.*, chap. 3.)

13. When they opened his brain, they found in it a gnat as big as a swallow and weighing *two* selas.

Gittin, fol. 56, col. 2.

NOTE.—The context of the above states a tradition current among the Jews in reference to Titus, the destroyer of Jerusalem. It is said that when, after taking the city, he had shamefully violated and profaned the Temple, he took the sacred vessels of the sanctuary, wrapped them in the veil of the holy place, and sailed with them to Rome. At sea a storm arose and threatened to sink the ship; upon which he was heard reflecting, "It seems the God of these Jews has no power anywhere but at sea. Pharaoh He drowned, and Sisera He drowned (*sic* in original), and now He is about to drown me also. If He be mighty, let Him go ashore and contend with me there." Then came a voice from heaven (בת קול) and said, "O thou wicked one, son of a wicked man and grandson of Esau the wicked, go ashore. I have a creature—an insignificant one in my world—go and fight with it."

This creature was a gnat, and is called insignificant because it must receive and discharge what it eats by one aperture. Immediately, therefore, he landed, when a gnat flew up his nostrils and made its way to his brain, on which it fed for a period of seven years. One day he happened to pass a blacksmith's forge, when the noise of the hammer soothed the gnawing at his brain. "Aha!" said Titus, "I have found a remedy at last;" and he ordered a blacksmith to hammer before him. To a Gentile for this he (for a time) paid four zuzim a day, but to a Jewish blacksmith he paid nothing, remarking to him, "It is payment enough to thee to see thy enemy suffering so painfully." For thirty days he felt relieved, but after, no amount of hammering in the least relieved him. As to what happened after his death, we have this testimony from Rabbi Phineas, the son of Aruba: "I myself was among the Roman magnates when an inquest was held upon the body of Titus, and on opening his brain they found therein a gnat as big as a swallow, weighing two selas." Others say it was as large as a pigeon a year old and weighed two litras. Abaii says, "We found its mouth was of copper and its claws of iron." Titus gave instructions that after his death his body should be burned, and the ashes thereof scattered over the surface of the seven seas, that the God of the Jews might not find him and bring him to judgment. (*Gittin*, fol. 56, col. 2.)

14. "The man with *two* wives, one young and the other old." Rav Ami and Rav Assi were in social converse with Rabbi Isaac Naphcha, when one of them said to him, "Tell us, sir, some pretty legend," and the other said, "Pray explain to us rather some nice point of law." When he began the legend, he displeased the one, and when he proceeded to explain a point of law, he offended the other. Whereupon he took up this parable in illustration of the plight in which their obstinacy placed him. "I am like the man with the two wives, the one young and the other old. The young one plucked out all his grey hairs, (that he might look young), and the old wife pulled out all his black hairs (that he might look old); and so between the one and the other he became bald. So is it with me between you. However, I've something nice for both of you. It is written (Exod. xxii. 6), 'If a fire break out and catch in thorns, so that the stacks of corn, or the standing corn, or the field be consumed therewith, he that kindled the fire shall surely make restoration.' The Holy One—blessed be He!—hath said, 'I must both judge myself and take upon myself to indemnify the evil of the conflagration I have caused, for I have kindled a fire in Zion,' as it is written (Lament. iv. 11), 'He hath kindled a fire in Zion, and hath devoured the foundations thereof.' I must therefore rebuild her with fire, as it is written,

(Zech. ii. 5), ' I will be unto her a wall of fire round about, and will be the glory in the midst of her.' "

Bava Kama, fol. 60, col. 2.

15. Rabbi Oshaia asked, "What is this that is written, (Zech. xi. 7), ' I took unto me *two* staves; the one I called Amiable and the other Destroyer ' ? " The staff called Amiable represents the disciples of the wise in the land of Israel, who were friendly one towards another in their debates about the law. The staff called Destroyer represents the disciples of the wise of Babylon, who in the like debates were fierce tempered and not friendly towards one another. What is the meaning of Babel or Babylon? Rabbi Yochanan says it means בלולה במקרא בלולה במשנה בלולה בהש"ס, that is, "confused in the Bible, confused in the Mishna, and confused in the Talmud." " He hath set me in dark places, as they that be dead of old " (Lam. iii. 6). Rabbi Jeremiah said by this we are to understand the Babylonian Talmud.

Sanhedrin, fol. 24, col. 1.

Note.—(*a*.) הש"ס stands for הששה סדרים, the six sedarim or orders of the Talmud. The Rabbis say these three hate their fellows — dogs, cocks, and conjurors; to which some add, among others, the disciples of the wise of Babylon. (*P'sachim*, fol. 113, col. 2.)

(*b*.) On his return from Babylon to the land of Israel, Rabbi Zira fasted a hundred fasts, during which he prayed that he might be enabled to forget the Babylonian Talmud. (*Bava Metzia*, fol. 85, col. 1, and *Rashi in loco*.)

16. Rabbi Yochanan and Rabbi Yonathan travelled one day together; they came to *two* roads, one of which led by the door of a place devoted to the worship of idols, and the other by a place of ill fame. Upon which one said to the other, "Let us go by the former, because our inclination to the evil that waylays us there is already extinguished." "Nay, rather," said the other, "let us go by the latter, and curb our desires; so shall we receive a

reward in recompense." In this resolution they went on, and as they passed the place the women humbled themselves before them and withdrew ashamed into their chambers. Then Yochanan asked the other, "How didst thou know that this would occur to us?" He made answer, "From what is written (in Prov. ii. 2), 'Discretion (in the law) shall preserve thee.'"

Avodah Zarah, fol. 17, cols. 1, 2.

17. Given *two* dry firebrands and one piece of green wood, the dry will set fire to the green.

Sanhedrin, fol. 93, col. 1.

18. With *two* dogs they caught the lion.

Ibid., fol. 95, col. 1.

Note.—Both these proverbs express the same idea, that a minority, be it ever so strong, must give way to a majority.

19. "And the elders of Moab and the elders of Midian departed together" (Numb. xxii. 7). Midian and Moab, were never friendly towards each other; they were like *two* dogs tending a flock, always at variance. When the wolf came upon the one, however, the other thought, "If I do not help my neighbour to-day, the wolf may come upon myself to-morrow;" therefore the *two* dogs leagued together and killed the wolf. Hence, says Rabbi Pappa, the popular saying, "The mouse and the cat are combined to make a feast on the fat of the unfortunate."

Ibid., fol. 105, col. 1.

Note.—The moral of this is obvious. Herodotus expresses it tersely in Greek, "Τύραννος τυράννῳ συγκατεργάζεται" (One tyrant aids another).

20. Rabbi Yochanan, in the name of Yossi, the son of Zimra, asks, "What is this that is written (Ps. cxx. 3), 'What shall be given unto thee, or what shall be added unto thee, O thou false tongue'?" The Holy One—blessed

be He !—said to the tongue, " All the members of the body
are erect, thou only art recumbent; all other members are
without, thou art within, and not only so, for I have sur-
rounded thee with *two* walls, one of bone and the other of
flesh. What shall be given to thee, or what shall be added
unto thee, O thou false tongue ? " Rabbi Yochanan, in the
name of Yossi, says, " He who slanders is an atheist, for it
is written (Ps. xii. 4), ' Who have said, With our tongues
will we prevail; our lips are with us; who is lord
over us ? ' "   *Erchin*, fol. 15, col. 2.

NOTE.—This may seem the place to append a few sayings
from the Talmud on the abuse of the tongue.

(*a.*) He who slanders, he who receives slander, and he
who bears false witness against his neighbour, deserve to
be cast to the dogs. (*P'sachim*, fol. 118, col. 1.)

(*b.*) All animals will one day remonstrate with the
serpent and say, " The lion treads upon his prey and
devours it, the wolf tears and eats it, but thou, what
profit hast thou in biting?" The serpent will reply
(Eccl. viii. 11), " I am no worse than a slanderer."
(*Taanith*, fol. 8, col. 1.)

(*c.*) Adonijah was deprived of life for no other reason
than that he was given to quarrelling. It is lawful to
slander one so evil-disposed as he was. (*Perek Hashalom.*)

(*d.*) God will say to the prince of hell, " I from
above and thou from below shall judge and condemn the
slanderer." (*Erchin*, fol. 15, col. 2.)

(*e.*) The *third tongue* (*i.e.*, slander) hurts three parties :
the slanderer himself, the receiver of slander, and the
person slandered. (*Ibid.*)

(*f.*) *Four* classes do not receive the presence of the
Shechinah : scorners, liars, flatterers, and slanderers.
(*Sanhedrin*, fol. 103, col. 1.)

21. Where are we told that when *two* sit together and
study the law the Shechinah is with them ? In Mal.
iii. 16, where it is written, " They that feared the Lord
spake often *one to another*, and the Lord hearkened and
heard it."   *Berachoth*, fol. 6, col. 1.

22. Why did Elijah employ *two* invocations, saying

twice over, "Hear me! hear me!" (1 Kings xviii. 37). Elijah first prayed before God, "O Lord, King of the universe, hear me!" that He might send fire down from heaven and consume all that was upon the altar; and again he prayed, "Hear me!" that they might not imagine that the result was a matter of sorcery; for it is said, ' Thou hast turned their heart back again.' "

Berachoth, fol. 9, col. 2.

NOTE.—The twofold invocation of Elijah, which betokens his intense earnestness, anagrammatically expressed, is echoed in the words of the bystanders, יהוה הוא האלהים, " The Lord He is the God, the Lord He is the God."

23. "I dreamed," said Bar Kappara one day to Rabbi (the Holy), "that I beheld *two* pigeons, and they flew away from me." " Thy dream is this," replied Rabbi, " thou hast had *two* wives, and art separated from them both without a bill of divorcement." *Ibid.*, fol. 56, col. 2.

24. The Rabbis teach concerning the *two* kidneys in man, that one counsels him to do good and the other to do evil; and it appears that the former is situated on the right side and the latter on the left. Hence it is written, (Eccl. x. 2), " A wise man's heart is at his right hand, but a fool's heart is at his left." *Ibid.*, fol. 61, col. 1.

25. For *two* sins the common people perish : they speak of the holy ark as a box and the synagogue as a resort for the ignorant vulgar. *Shabbath*, fol. 32, col. 1.

26. On the self-same day when Jeroboam introduced the *two* golden calves, the one into Bethel and the other into Dan, a hut was erected in a part of Italy which was then subject to the Greeks. *Ibid.*, col. 56, fol. 2.

NOTE.—In the context where the above tradition occurs, which, as is obvious, relates to the founding of Rome, we meet with another on the same subject as follows :— When Solomon married the daughter of Pharaoh, the

Angel Gabriel thrust a reed into the sea, stirring up therewith the sand and mud from the bottom. This, gradually collecting, first shaped itself into an island and then expanded so as to unite itself with the continent. And thus was the land created for the erection of the hut which should one day swell into the proportion of a proud imperial city.

27. If Israel kept only *two* Sabbaths, according to the strict requirement of the law, they would be freed at once from their compelled dispersion; for it is written (Isa. lvi. 4, 7), "Thus saith the Lord unto the eunuchs that keep my Sabbaths (שבתותי, dual form), Even them will I bring to my holy mountain."   *Shabbath*, fol. 118, col. 2.

28. Adam had *two* faces; for it is said (Ps. cxxxix. 5), "Thou hast made me behind and before."

Eiruvin, fol. 18, col. 1.

Note.—There is a notion among the Rabbis that Adam was possessed originally of a bisexual organisation, and this conclusion they draw from Gen. i. 27, where it is said, "God created man in His own image; male-female created He them." These two natures, it was thought, lay side by side; according to some, the male on the right and the female on the left; according to others, back to back; while there were those who maintained that Adam was created with a tail, and that it was from this appendage Eve was fashioned. Other Jewish traditions tell us that Eve was made from "the thirteenth rib of the right side" (Targ. Jonath.), and that "she was not drawn out by the head, lest she should be vain; nor by the eyes, lest she should be wanton; nor from the mouth, lest she should be given to garrulity; nor by the ears, lest she should be an eavesdropper; nor by the hands, lest she should be intermeddling; nor by the feet, lest she be a gadder; nor by the heart, for fear she should be jealous; but she was taken out from the side. Yet, in spite of all these precautions, she had all the faults so carefully provided against."

29. If in time of national calamity a man withdraw himself from his kindred and refuse to share in their

sorrow, his *two* guardian angels come and lay their hands upon his head and say, "This man has isolated himself from his country in the day of its need, let him not live to see and enjoy the day when God shall restore its prosperity." When the community is in trouble, let no man say, "I will go home and eat and drink, and say, Peace be unto thee, oh my soul!" (Luke xii. 19); for to him Scripture hath solemnly said (Isa. xxii. 13, 14), "Surely this iniquity shall not be purged from you till you die."

Taanith, fol. 11, col. 1.

30. An infant that has died under a month old is (to be) carried to the grave in the arms (not in a coffin), and buried by one woman and *two* men, but not by one man and two women.   *Moed Katan*, fol. 24, col. 1.

> Note.—Both Rashi and the Tosephoth allude to a case which justifies the rule given here, where a woman actually carried a living child in a coffin, in order to avoid the suspicion of an assignation she had made with a man, who set out to join her. But the Tosephoth, after noticing this version of Rashi, gives another more to the point. The story in the Tosephoth is to this effect:—A woman was once weeping and groaning over the grave of her husband, and not very far away was a man who was guarding the corpse of a person who had been crucified. In the moment of mourning an affection sprung up between the two, and in the engrossment of it the corpse which the man guarded was stolen. He was in great trepidation for fear of the king's command. The woman said, "Don't be afraid; exhume my husband, and hang him up instead." This was accordingly done. (See *Kiddushin*, fol. 80, col. 2.)

31. There were *two* date-trees in the Valley of Hinnom from between which smoke ascended, and this is the gate of hell.   *Succah*, fol. 32, col. 2.

> Note.—According to Jewish tradition, there are *three* gates to Gehinnom, *one* in the desert, *one* in the sea, and *one* in Jerusalem: *In the desert*, as it is written (Numb. xvi. 33), "They went down, and all that belonged to

them, alive into hell." *In the sea*, as it is written (Jonah ii. 2), "Out of the belly of hell have I called," &c. *In Jerusalem*, as it is written (Isa. xxxi. 9), "Thus saith the Lord, whose fire is in Zion, and His furnace in Jerusalem." The gates to Gehinnom (פתחים לניהנם) must not be confounded with the שערי שאול of the Sacred Scriptures, or the Πύλαι ᾅδου of the Greek. "The Gates of Hades" are simply the gates of death.

32. When *two* women are seen sitting on opposite sides of a cross road facing each other, it is to be presumed that they are up to witchcraft and contemplate mischief. What in that case must you do? Go by another road, if there is one, and if not, with a companion, should such turn up, passing the crones arm-in-arm with him; but should there be no other road and no other man, then walk straight on repeating the counter-charm, as you pass them—

> "Agrath is to Asia gone,
> And Blussia's killed in battle."

P'sachim, fol. 111, col. 2.

NOTE.—Agrath and Blussia are two Amazons well known to those familiar with Rabbinic demonology.

33. "If Mordecai, before whom thou hast began to fall, be of the seed of the Jews, expect not to prevail against him, but נפול תפול falling, thou shalt fall" (Esth. vi. 13). Wherefore these *two* fallings? They told Haman, saying, "This nation is likened to the dust, and is also likened to the stars; when they are down, they are down even to the dust, but when they begin to rise, they rise to the stars."

Meggillah, fol. 16, col. 1.

34. If any *two* disciples of the wise, dwelling in the same city, have a difference respecting the Halachah, let them remember what Scripture denounces against them, "And also I gave them statutes that are not good, and judgments by which they shall not live" (Ezek. xx. 25).

Ibid., fol. 32, col. 1.

35. If a man espouse one of *two* sisters, and does not know which he has espoused, he must give both a bill of divorce. If *two* men espouse *two* sisters, and neither of them know which he has espoused, then each man must give *two* bills of divorce, one to each woman.

Yevamoth, fol. 23, col. 2.

36. There is a time coming (*i.e.*, in the days of the Messiah), when a grain of wheat will be as large as the *two* kidneys of the great ox.   *Kethuboth*, fol. 111, col. 1.

> NOTE.—According to a recent discovery, which has been confirmed by subsequent observation and experiment, wheat is a development by cultivation of the tiny grain of the *Ægilops ovata*, a sort of grass ; but we are indebted to Rabbinic lore for the curious information that before the Fall of man wheat grew upon a tree whose trunk looked like gold, its branches like silver, and its leaves like so many emeralds. The wheat ears themselves were as red as rubies, and each bore five sparkling grains as white as snow, as sweet as honey, and as fragrant as musk. At first the grains were as big as an ostrich's egg, but in the time of Enoch they diminished to the size of a goose's egg, and in Elijah's to that of a hen, while at the commencement of the common era, they shrank so small as not to be larger than grapes, according to a law the inverse of the order of nature. Rabbi Yehudah (Sanhedrin, fol. 70, col. 1) says that *wheat* was the *forbidden fruit.* Hence probably the degeneracy.

37. Of *two* that quarrel, the one that first gives in shows the nobler nature.   *Ibid.*, fol. 71, col. 2.

> NOTE.—So also Prov. xx. 3, " It is an honour for a man to cease from strife."

38. He who sets aside a portion of his wealth for the relief of the poor will be delivered from the judgment of hell. Of this the parable of the *two* sheep that attempted to ford a river is an illustration ; one was shorn of its wool

and the other not; the former, therefore, managed to get over, but the latter, being heavy-laden, sank.

Gittin, fol. 7, col. 1.

39. Zoreah and Eshtaol (Josh. xv. 33) were *two* large mountains, but Samson tore them up and grated the one against the other. *Soteh*, fol. 9, col. 2.

> NOTE.—The above tradition is founded on Judges xiii. 25, in which it is said of Samson, "And the spirit of God began to move him at times in the camp of Dan, between Zoreah and Eshtaol," in which the word פעם, translated to "move," signifies also to "strike a stroke" "step a step," and "once." Founding on which last two meanings, Rabbi Yehudah says, "Samson strode in one strides from Zoreah to Eshtaol," *a giant stride of two miles or more.* Taking פעם in the sense of "strike," or "producing a ringing sound," another Rabbi tells us that the hairs of Samson's head stood upright, tinkling one against another like bells, the jingle of which might be heard from Zoreah to Eshtaol. The version in the text takes the same word in the sense of to "strike together."

40. On the day when Isaac was weaned, Abraham made a great feast, to which he invited all the people of the land. Not all of those who came to enjoy the feast believed in the alleged occasion of its celebration, for some said contemptuously, "This old couple have adopted a foundling, and provided a feast to persuade us to believe that the child is their own offspring." What did Abraham do? He invited all the great men of the day, and Sarah invited their wives, who brought their infants, but not their nurses, along with them. On this occasion Sarah's breasts became like *two* fountains, for she supplied, of her own body, nourishment to all the children. Still some were unconvinced, and said, "Shall a child be born to one that is a hundred years old, and shall Sarah, who is ninety years old, bear?" (Gen. xvii. 17). Whereupon, to silence this objection, Isaac's face was changed, so that it became

the very picture of Abraham's; then one and all exclaimed, "Abraham begat Isaac."

Bara Metzia, fol. 87, col. 1.

NOTE.—The Midrash (p. 27) tells the same story almost
  verbatim.

41. Rava relates the following in the name of Rabbi
Yochanan :—" *Two* Jewish slaves were one day walking
along, when their master, who was following, overheard
the one saying to the other, 'There is a camel ahead of us,
as I judge—for I have not seen—that is blind of one eye
and laden with *two* skin-bottles, one of which contains
wine and the other oil, while two drivers attend it, one
of them an Israelite, and the other a Gentile.' 'You
perverse men,' said their master, 'how can you fabricate
such a story as that ?' The slave answered, and gave
this as his reason, 'The grass is cropped only on one
side of the track, the wine, that must have dripped, has
soaked into the earth on the right, and the oil has trickled
down, and may be seen on the left; while one of the
drivers turned aside from the track to ease himself, but
the other has not even left the road for the purpose.'
Upon this the master stepped on before them in order to
verify the correctness of their inferences, and found the
conclusion true in every particular. He then turned back,
and . . . after complimenting the *two* slaves for their
shrewdness, he at once gave them their liberty."

Sanhedrin, fol. 104, col. 2.

NOTE.—A story similar to the above, with additional details,
  is familiar to most readers. This we have given is one
  of many with which the Talmud abounds, and the collection of which would fill a goodly volume.

42. When the disciples of Shamai and Hillel increased
in Israel, contention increased along with them, so much
so, that the one law became as *two* laws (and these contradictory). *Soteh*, fol. 47, col. 2.

43. If *two* parties deposit money with a third, one a single manah and the other two hundred, and both afterwards appear and claim the larger sum, the depositary should give each depositor one manah only, and leave the rest undivided till the coming of Elijah.

Bava Metzia, fol. 37, col. 2.

Note.—"Till Elijah comes" is a phrase which is in use among the Jews to express postponement for ever, like *ad Kalendas Græcas*. It is applied to questions that would take Elijah to settle, which, it is believed, he will not appear to do till doomsday.

44. "And I will make thy windows of agates" (Isa. liv. 12). *Two* of the angels in heaven, Gabriel and Michael, once disputed about this: one maintained that the stone should be an onyx, and the other asserted it should be a jasper; but the Holy One—blessed be He!— said unto them, "Let it be as both say, כדין וכדין," which, abbreviated, is כדכד (*i.e.*, an agate).

Bava Bathra, fol. 75, col. 1.

45. "The horseleech has *two* daughters, crying, Give! give!" (Prov. xxx. 15). Mar Ukva says, "This has reference to the voice of *two* daughters crying out from torture in hell, because their voice is heard in this world crying, ' Give! give!'—namely—*heresy* and *officialism*."

Avodah Zarah, fol. 17, col. 1.

Note.—Rashi says *heresy* here refers to the "heresy of James," or, in other words, Christianity.

46. *Two* cemeteries were provided by the judicial authorities, one for beheaded and strangled criminals, and the other for those that were stoned or burned. When the flesh of these was consumed, they collected the bones and buried them in their own place, after which the relations came and saluted the judge and the witnesses, and said, "We owe you no grudge, for you passed a just judgment.'

Sanhedrin, fol. 46, col. 1.

47. Alas! for the loss which the world has sustained in the degradation of the helpful serpent. If the serpent had not been degraded, every Israelite would have been attended by *two* of kindly disposition, one of which might have been sent to the north, and the other to the south, to bring for its owner precious corals and costly stones and pearls.   *Sanhedrin*, fol. 59, col. 2.

> NOTE.—We here append two or three other sayings from the Talmud relative to the serpent.
>
> (*a.*) Benjamin the son of Jacob, Amram the father of Moses, and Jesse the father of David all died, not because of their own sin (for they had none, says Rashi), but because of the (original) sin committed under the serpent's temptation. (*Shabbath*, fol. 55, col. 2.)
>
> (*b.*) No man was ever injured by a serpent or scorpion in Jerusalem. (*Yoma*, fol. 21, col. 1.)
>
> (*c.*) "And dust is the serpent's food" (Isa. lxv. 25). Rav Ammi says, "To the serpent no delicacy in the world has any other flavour than that of dust;" and Rav Assi says, "No delicacy in the world satisfies him like dust." (*Ibid.*, fol. 75, col. 1.)

48. *Two* negatives or *two* affirmatives are as good as an oath.   *Shevuoth*, fol. 36, col. 1.

49. Like *two* pearls were the *two* drops of holy oil that were suspended from the two corners of the beard of Aaron.   *Horayoth*, fol. 12, col. 1.

50. For *two* to sit together and have no discourse about the law, is to sit in the seat of the scornful; as it is said (Ps. i. 1), "And sitteth not in the seat of the scornful."

Avoth, chap. iii.

51. When *two* are seated together at table, the younger shall not partake before the elder, otherwise the younger shall be justly accounted a glutton.

Derech Eretz, chap. vii.

52. Philemo once asked Rabbi (the Holy), "If a man has *two* heads, on which is he to put the phylactery?"

To which Rabbi replied, "Either get up and be off, or take
an anathema; for thou art making fun of me."

Menachoth, fol. 37, col. 1.

53. It is thus Rav Yoseph taught what is meant when
it is written in Isaiah xii. 1, " I will praise Thee, O Lord,
because Thou wast angry with me: Thine anger will depart and Thou wilt comfort me."   "The text applies," he
says, "to *two* men who were going abroad on a mercantile
enterprise, one of whom, having had a thorn run into his
foot, had to forego his intended journey, and began in
consequence to utter reproaches and blaspheme.   Having
afterwards learned that the ship in which his companion
had sailed had sunk to the bottom of the sea, he confessed
his short-sightedness and praised God for His mercy."

Niddah, fol. 31, col. 1.

CHAPTER III.

THE 'THREES' OF THE TALMUD.

1. THE night is divided into *three* watches, and at each watch the Holy One—blessed be He!—sits and roars like a lion; as it is written (Jer. xxv. 30), " The Lord will *roar* from on high, . . . *roaring*, He will *roar* over His habitation." The marks by which this division of the night is recognised are these:—In the *first* watch the ass brays; in the *second* the dog barks; and in the *third* the babe is at the breast and the wife converses with her husband.

Berachoth, fol. 3, col. 1.

2. The Rabbis have taught that there are *three* reasons why a person should not enter a ruin:—1. Because he may be suspected of evil intent; 2. Because the walls might tumble upon him; 3. And because of evil spirits that frequent such places. Ibid., fol. 3, col. 1.

3. He who *three* times a-day repeats David's psalm of praise (Ps. cxlv.) may be sure of an inheritance in the world to come. Ibid., fol. 4, col. 2.

4. *Three* precious gifts were given to Israel, but none of them without a special affliction: these *three* gifts were the *law*, the *land of Israel*, and the *world to come*.

Ibid., fol. 5, col. 1.

NOTE.—We subjoin a few passages from the Talmud anent Israel and the Israelites.

(*a.*) All Israelites are princes. (*Shabbath*, fol. 57, col. 1.)

(*b.*) All Israelites are holy. (*Ibid.*, fol. 86, col. 1.)

(*c.*) Happy are ye, O Israel! for every one of you,

from the least to the greatest, is a great philosopher. (*Eiruvin*, fol. 53, col. 1.) The Machzor for Pentecost says, Israelites are as "full of meritorious works as a pomegranate is full of pips." (See also *Chaggigah*, fol. 27, col. 1.)

(*d.*) As it is impossible for the world to be without air, so also is it impossible for the world to be without Israel. (*Taanith*, fol. 3, col. 2.)

(*e.*) If the ox of an Israelite bruise the ox of a Gentile, the Israelite is exempt from paying damages; but should the ox of a Gentile bruise the ox of an Israelite, the Gentile is bound to recompense him in full. (*Bava Kama*, fol. 38, col. 1.)

(*f.*) When an Israelite and a Gentile have a lawsuit before thee, if thou canst, acquit the former according to the laws of Israel, and tell the latter such is *our* law; if thou canst get him off in accordance with Gentile law, do so, and say to the plaintiff such is *your* law; but if he cannot be acquitted according to either law, then באין עליו בעקיפין, bring forward adroit pretexts and secure his acquittal. These are the words of the Rabbi Ishmael. Rabbi Akiva says, "No false pretext should be brought forward, because, if found out, the name of God would be blasphemed; but if there be no fear of that, then it may be adduced." (*Ibid.*, fol. 113, col. 1.)

Note.—Contrast this counsel with that of a heathen poet:—

> " If ever called
> To give thy witness in a dubious case,
> Though Phalaris himself should bid thee *lie*
> On pain of torture in his flaming bull,
> Disdain to barter *innocence* for *life*,
> To *which* life owes its lustre and its *worth*."
> *Juvenal, Sat.* 8, 1, 80.

How true are the words of Shakespeare (Henry VIII., act v., sc. 1):—

> "At what ease
> Might corrupt minds procure knaves as corrupt
> To swear against you?"

(*g.*) If one find lost property in a locality where the majority are Israelites, he is bound to proclaim it; but he is not bound to do so if the majority be Gentiles. (*Bava Metzia*, fol. 24, col. 1.)

(*h.*) (Prov. xiv. 34), " Almsgiving exalteth a nation, but benevolence is a sin to nations."   " Almsgiving, צדקה, exalteth a *nation*," that is to say, *the nation* of Israel ; as it is written (2 Sam. vii. 23), " And what one nation in the earth is like thy people, even like Israel ? " but " *benevolence* " is a sin to *nations*, that is to say, for the Gentiles to exercise charity and benevolence is sin. (*Bava Bathra*, fol. 10, col. 2.)

(*i.*) If a Gentile smite an Israelite, he is guilty of death ; as it is written (Exod. ii. 12), " And he looked this way and that way, and when he saw there was no man, he slew the Egyptian."   (*Sanhedrin*, fol. 58, col. 2.)

(*j.*) All Israelites have a portion in the world to come ; as it is written (Isa. lx. 21), " And thy people are all righteous : they shall inherit the land."   (*Ibid.*, fol. 90, col. 1.)

(*k.*) " And they shall fall *one* on account of another " (Lev. xxvi. 37),—one on account of the sins of another. This teaches us that all Israel are surety for one another. (*Shevuoth*, fol. 39, col. 1.)

(*l.*) If one find a foundling in a locality where the majority are Gentiles, then the child is (to be reckoned) a Gentile ; if the majority be Israelites, it is to be considered as an Israelite ; and so also it is to be, providing the numbers are equal. (*Machsheerin*, chap. 2, Mish. 7.)

(*m.*) " One generation passeth away, and another generation cometh, but the earth abideth forever " (Eccl. i. 4).   One empire cometh and another passeth away, but Israel abideth forever.   (*Perek Hashalom.*)

(*n.*) The world was created only for Israel : none are called the children of God but Israel ; none are beloved before God but Israel.   (*Gerim*, chap. 1.)

(*o.*) The Jew that has no wife abideth without joy, without a blessing, and without any good.   Without joy, as it is written (Deut. xiv. 26), " And thou shalt rejoice, thou and thy household ; " without blessing, as it is written (Ezek. xliv. 30), " That He may cause a blessing to rest on thy household ; " without any good, for it is written (Gen. ii. 8), " It is not good that man should be alone."   (*Yevamoth*, fol. 62, col. 2.)

(*p.*) The Jew that has no wife is *not a man ;* for it is written (Gen. v. 2), " Male and female created He them and called their name *man* " (אדם in the singular). To which Rabbi Eleazar adds, " So every one who has no landed property is *no man ;* for it is written (Ps. cxv.

16), ' The heaven, even the heavens, are the Lord's, but the earth (the land, that is), hath He given to the children of man.' " (*Yevamoth*, fol. 63, col. 1.)

5. *Three* things did Moses ask of God:—1. He asked that the Shechinah might rest upon Israel; 2. That the Shechinah might rest upon none but Israel; and 3. That God's ways might be made known unto him; and all these requests were granted. *Berachoth*, fol. 7, col. 1.

NOTE.—What was the Shechinah? Was it the presence of a Divine person or only of a Divine power? The following quotations will show what is the teaching of the Talmud on the matter, and will be read with interest by the theologian, whether Jew or Christian.

(*a.*) Where do we learn that when *ten* persons *pray* together the Shechinah is with them? In Ps. lxxxii. 1, where it is written, "God standeth in the congregation of the mighty." And where do we learn that when two sit together and study the law the Shechinah is with them? In Mal. iii. 16, where it is written, " Then they that feared the Lord spake often one to another, and the Lord hearkened and heard it." (*Berachoth*, fol. 6, col. 1.)

(*b.*) Where do we learn that the Shechinah does strengthen the sick? In Ps. xli. 3, where it is written, " The Lord will strengthen him upon the bed of languishing." (*Shabbath*, fol. 12, col. 2.)

(*c.*) He who goes from the Synagogue to the lecture-room, and from the lecture-room back to the Synagogue, will become worthy to receive the presence of the Shechinah ; as it is written (Ps. lxxxiv. 1), "They go from strength to strength ; every one of them in Zion appeareth before God." (*Moed Katan*, fol. 29, col. 1.)

(*d.*) Rabbi Yossi says, " The Shechinah never came down here below, nor did Moses and Elijah ever ascend on high, because it is written (Ps. cxv. 16), ' The heaven, even the heavens, are the Lord's, but the earth hath he given to the children of men.' " (*Succah*, fol. 5, col. 1.)

(*e.*) Esther " stood in the inner court of the King's house " (Esth. v. 1). Rabbi Levi says, " When she reached the house of the images the Shechinah departed from her. Then she exclaimed, " My God ! my God ! why hast thou forsaken me ?" (*Meggillah*, fol. 15, col. 2.)

(*f.*) "But ye that did cleave unto the Lord your God are alive every one of you this day" (Deut. iv. 4). Is it possible to cleave to the Shechinah? Is it not written (ibid., verse 24), "For the Lord thy God is a consuming fire"? The reply is:—He that bestows his daughter in marriage on a disciple of the wise (that is, a Rabbi), or does business on behalf of the disciples of the wise, or maintains them from his property, Scripture accounts it as if he did cleave to the Shechinah. (*Kethuboth*, fol. 111, col. 25.)

(*g.*) He who is angry has no regard even for the Shechinah; as it is written (Ps. x. 4), "The wicked, when his anger rises, does not inquire after God; God is not in all his thoughts." (*Nedarim*, fol. 22, col. 2.)

(*h.*) He who visits the sick should not sit upon the bed, nor even upon a stool or a chair beside it, but he should wrap his mantle round him and sit upon the floor, because of the Shechinah which rests at the head of the bed of the invalid; as it is written (Ps. xli. 3), "The Lord will strengthen him upon the bed of languishing." (*Ibid.*, fol. 40, col. 1.)

(*i.*) When Israel went up out of the Red Sea, both the babe on its mother's lap and the suckling at the breast saw the Shechinah, and said, "This is my God, and I will prepare Him a habitation;" as it is written (Ps. viii. 2), "Out of the mouths of babes and sucklings thou hast ordained strength." (*Soteh*, fol. 30, col. 2.)

(*j.*) Where do we read that the Shechinah is present everywhere? In Zech. ii. 3, where it is written, "And behold the angel that talked with me went forth, and another angel went out to meet him." It is not said *went out after him*, but "*went out to meet him.*" From this we know that the Shechinah is present everywhere. (*Bava Bathra*, fol. 25, col. 1.)

(*k.*) Many more such-like passages might be adduced, but we will conclude this catena with a phrase which will recall pleasing memories to most of our readers, words "*as familiar as household words*" in Jewry—

לשֵם יחוד קב"ה ושכינתיה ע"י ההוא טמיר ונעלם בריך ה'לעולם !

In the name of the union of the Holy and Blessed One and His Shechinah, the Hidden and the Concealed One! Blessed be the Lord forever!

6. Rabbi Akiva says, "For *three* things I admire the Medes:—1. When they carve meat, they do it on the

table; 2. When they kiss, they only do so upon the hand; 3. And when they consult, they do so only in the field."

Berachoth, fol. 8, col. 2.

7. The stone which Og, king of Bashan, meant to throw upon Israel is the subject of a tradition delivered on Sinai. "The camp of Israel I see," he said, "extends *three* miles; I shall therefore go and root up a mountain *three* miles in extent and throw it upon them." So off he went, and finding such a mountain, raised it on his head, but the Holy One—blessed be He!—sent an army of ants against him, which so bored the mountain over his head that it slipped down upon his shoulders, from which he could not lift it, because his teeth, protruding, had riveted it upon him. This explains that which is written (Ps. iii. 7), "Thou hast *broken* the teeth of the ungodly;" where read not שברת, "*Thou* hast *broken*," but read thus: שרבבת, "*Thou* hast *ramified*," that is, "Thou hast caused to *branch out*." Moses being *ten* ells in height, seized an axe *ten* ells long, and springing up *ten* ells, struck a blow on Og's ankle and killed him. *Ibid.*, fol. 54, col. 2.

> NOTE.—This same story is given with more than Talmudic exaggeration in the Targum of Jonathan ben Uzziel, while the author of the Book of Jasher (chap. lxv., verses 23, 24) makes the camp and the mountain forty miles in extent. The giant here figures in antediluvian tradition. He is said to have been saved at the Flood by laying hold of the ark, and being fed day by day through a hole in the side of the ark by Noah himself. A tradition which says the soles of his feet were forty miles long at once explains all the extraordinary feats ascribed to him.

8. Rav Yehudah used to say, "*Three* things shorten a man's days and years:—1. Neglecting to read the law when it is given to him for that purpose; seeing it is written (Deut. xxx. 20), 'For He (who gave it) is thy life and the length of thy days.' 2. Omitting to repeat the customary benediction over a cup of blessing; for it is

written (Gen. xii. 3), 'And I will bless them that bless thee.' 3. And the assumption of a Rabbinical air; for Rabbi Chama bar Chanena says, 'Joseph died before any of his brethren, because he domineered over them.'"

Berachoth, fol. 55, col. 1.

> Note.—The first of these refers to the reading of the law in public worship, the second to a practice after meals when more than two adult Jews were present, and the third to the dictatorial air often assumed by the Rabbis.

9. *Three* things proceed by pre-eminence from God Himself :—Famine, plenty, and a wise ruler. Famine (2 Kings viii. 2): "The Lord hath *called* for a famine;" plenty (Ezek. xxxvi. 29): "I will *call* for corn and increase it;" a wise ruler; for it is written (Exod. xxxi. 2), "I have *called* by name Bezaleel." Rabbi Yitzchak says, "A ruler is not to be appointed unless the community be first consulted. God first consulted Moses, then Moses consulted the nation concerning the appointment of Bezaleel."

Ibid., fol. 55, col. 1.

10. *Three* dreams come to pass :—That which is dreamed in the morning; that which is also dreamed by one's neighbour; and a dream which is interpreted within a dream; to which some add, one that is dreamed by the same person twice; as it is written (Gen. xli. 32), "And for that the dream was doubled unto Pharaoh twice."

Ibid., fol. 55, col. 2.

11. *Three* things tranquillise the mind of man :—Melody, scenery, and sweet odour. *Three* things develop the mind of man :—A fine house, a handsome wife, and elegant furniture.

Ibid., fol. 57, col. 2.

12. The Rabbis have taught that there are *three* sorts of dropsy :—*Thick*, resulting from sin ; *bloated*, in consequence of insufficient food ; and *thin*, due to sorcery.

Shabbath, fol. 33, col. 1.

13. *Three* things bring a man to poverty:—1. המשתין
כים בפני מטתו ערום; 2. Neglecting the (ceremonial)
washing of the hands; 3. Being cursed to the face by one's
wife.   *Shabbath*, fol. 62, col. 2.

14. These *three* grow stronger as they grow older:—The
fish, the serpent, and the pig.   *Ibid.*, fol. 77, col. 2.

15. It were better to cut the hands off than to touch the
eye, or the nose, or the mouth, or the ear, &c., with them
without having first washed them. Unwashed hands
may cause blindness, deafness, foulness of breath, or a
polypus. It is taught that Rabbi Nathan has said, "The
evil spirit Bath Chorin (בת חורין), which rests upon the
hands at night, is very strict; he will not depart till
water is poured upon the hands *three* times over."

                                         Ibid., fol. 109, col. 1.

Note.—(*a.*) The great importance of this ceremonial washing
    of the hands will appear from the following anecdote,
    which we quote *verbatim* from another part of the Tal-
    mud:—"It happened once, as the Rabbis teach, that
    Rabbi Akiva was immured in a prison, and Yehoshua
    Hagarsi was his attendant. One day the gaoler said to
    the latter as he entered, 'What a lot of water thou hast
    brought to-day! Dost thou need it to sap the walls of
    the prison?' So saying, he seized the vessel and poured
    out half of the water. When Yehoshua brought in
    what was left of the water to Rabbi Akiva, the latter,
    who was weary of waiting, for he was faint and thirsty,
    reproachfully said to him, 'Yehoshua, dost thou forget
    that I am old, and my very life depends upon thee?'
    When the servant related what had happened, the Rabbi
    asked for the water to wash his hands, 'Why, master,'
    said Yehoshua, 'there's not enough for thee to drink,
    much less to cleanse thy hands with.' To which the
    Rabbi replied, 'What am I to do? They who neglect
    to wash their hands are judged worthy of death; 'tis
    better that I should die by my own act from thirst than
    act against the rules of my associates.' And accordingly
    it is related that he abstained from tasting anything till
    they brought him water to wash his hands." (*Eiruvin,*

fol. 21, col. 2. See also *Maimonides, Hilc. Berach.,* vi. 19.)

(*b.*) From the context of the passage just quoted we cull the following, which proves that the Talmud itself bases the precept concerning the washing of hands on oral tradition and not on the written law :—"Rav Yehudah ascribes this saying to Shemuel, that when Solomon gave to the traditional rules that regulated the washing of hands and other ceremonial rites the form and sanction of law, a Bath Kol came forth and said (Prov. xxiii. 15), 'My son, if thy heart be wise, my heart shall rejoice, even mine;' and again it said (Prov. xxvii. 11), 'My son, be wise, and make my heart glad, that I may answer him that reproacheth me.'" (See Prov. xxx. 5, 6.)

(*c.*) There is a great deal in the Talmud about (נטילת ידים), *washing the hands,* in addition to what is said in the treatise Yadaim, which is entirely devoted to the subject. But this topic is subordinate to another, namely, the alleged inferiority of the precepts of the Bible to the prescriptions of the Rabbis, of which the punctilious rules regulative of *hand-washing* form only a small fraction. This is illustrated by an anecdote from the Talmudic leaflet entitled Callah, כלה, respecting Rabbi Akiva, whose fame extends מסוף העולם ועד סופו, from one end of the world to the other. (See *Yevamoth,* fol. 16, col. 2.)

Once upon a time, as the Elders were sitting together, two lads passed by them, one with his head covered and the other bareheaded. Of the latter boy as he passed Rabbi Elazar said, "He is a ממזר," and Rabbi Yehoshua, "He is a בן הנדה," but Rabbi Akiva contended, "He is both a Mamzer and a Ben Haniddah." Upon which the Elders said to Rabbi Akiva, "How darest thou be so bold as dispute the assertion of thy masters?" "Because I can substantiate what I say," was his answer. He then went to the mother of the lad, and found her selling pease in the market-place. "Daughter," said he to her, "if thou wilt answer all that I ask of thee, I will ensure thee a portion in the life to come." She replied, "Let me have thy oath and I will do so." *Then taking the oath with his lips but nullifying it in his heart,* he asked her, "What sort of a son is thy lad?" She replied, "When I entered my bridal chamber I was a Niddah, and consequently my husband kept away

from me," וּבָא עָלַי שׁוֹשְׁבִינִי וְהָיָה לִי בֶּן זֶה. Thus it was
found out that the boy was a Mamzer and a Ben
Haniddah; upon which the sages exclaimed, "Great
is Rabbi Akiva, for he has overcome his masters;"
and as they congratulated him they said, "Blessed be
the Lord God of Israel, who hath revealed His secret
unto Akiva the son of Joseph." Thus did the Rabbi
forswear himself, and thus did his companions compliment him on the success of his perjury; yet the Bible says,
"Thou shalt not take the name of the Lord thy God in
vain" (Exod. xx. 7), and "Keep thou far from a falsehood" (Exod. xxiii. 7).

(*d.*) Here is a companion picture from Yoma, fol. 84,
col. 1 :—"Rabbi Yochanan was suffering from scurvy,
and he applied to a Gentile woman, who prepared a
remedy for the fifth and then the sixth day of the week.
'But what shall I do to-morrow?' said he; 'I must
not walk so far on the Sabbath.' 'Thou wilt not
require any more,' she answered. 'But suppose I do,'
he replied. 'Take an oath,' she answered, 'that thou
wilt not reveal it, and I will tell thee how to compound
the remedy.' This he did in the following words : 'By
the God of Israel (לאלהא הישראל, which also means "To
the God of Israel"), I swear I will not divulge it.'
Nevertheless, when he learned the secret, he went and
revealed it. 'But was not that profaning the name
of God?' asks one. 'No,' pleads another Rabbi, 'for,
as he told her afterwards, that what he meant was that
he would not tell it *to* the God of Israel.' The remedy
was yeast, water, oil, and salt."

(*e.*) The anecdote that follows we take from Sanhedrin,
fol. 97, col. 1 :—"In reference to the remark of Ravina,
who said, 'I used to think that there was no truth in
the world,' one of the Rabbis, Toviah (or Tavyoomah, as
some say), would protest and say, 'If all the riches of
the world were offered me, I would not tell a falsehood.'
And he used to clench his protestation with the following apologue : 'I once went to a place called *Kushta*
(קושטא), where the people never swerve from the truth,
and where (as a reward for their integrity) they do not
die until old age; and there I married and settled down,
and had two sons born unto me. One day as my wife
was sitting and combing her hair, a woman who dwelt
close by came to the door and asked to see her. Thinking that it was a breach of etiquette (that any one should

see her at her toilet), I said she was *not* in. Soon after this my two children died, and the people came to inquire into the cause of their premature decease. When I told them of my evasive reply to the woman, they asked me to leave the town, lest by my misconduct I might involve the whole community in a like calamity, and death might be enticed to their place."

16. Food remains for *three* days in the stomach of the dog, because God knew that his food would be scanty.

Shabbath, fol. 155, col. 1.

17. He who is born on the *third* day of the week will be rich and amorous. *Ibid.*, fol. 156, col. 1.

18. Rabbi Abba, in the name of Shemuel, says, "The schools of Shammai and Hillel were at variance *three* years, the one party contending and saying, 'The Halacha is according to us;' and the other, 'The Halacha is according to us.' Then came a Bath Kol * from the Lord and said, אלו ואלו דברי אלהים חיים, '*Both these and those are the words of the living God*, but yet the Halacha is according to the school of Hillel.' What was the merit of the school of Hillel that the Halacha should be pronounced to be according to it? Its disciples were gentle and for-bearing, for whilst they stood by their own decisions, they also stated those maintained by the school of Shammai, and often even mentioned the tenets of the school of Shammai first and their own afterwards. This teaches us that him who humbles himself, God will exalt; and him who exalts himself, God will abase. Whoso pursueth greatness, greatness will flee from him; and whoso fleeth from greatness, greatness will pursue him."

Eiruvin, fol. 13, col. 2.

19. There are *three* entrances to hell:—One in the desert, one in the sea, and one in Jerusalem.

Ibid., fol. 19, col. 1.

Note.—For more detailed matter on this topic see Chap. II. sect. 31, *supra*.

* Defined at p. 2.

20. These *three* will never see hell:—He who is purified by poverty; he who is purged by a painful flux; and he who is harassed by importunate creditors; and some say, he also who is plagued with a termagant wife.

Eiruvin, fol. 41, col. 2.

NOTE.—In the original, והרשות: *i.e.*, "and government." Rashi renders it "*Creditors;*" Tosephoth renders it, "The yoke of the government of Babylon."

21. *Three* effects are ascribed to Babylonian broth (which was made of mouldy bread, sour milk, and salt):—It retards the action of the heart, it affects the eyesight, and emaciates the body.   *P'sachim*, fol. 42, col. 1.

22. These *three* are not permitted to come between two men, nor is a man allowed to pass between any two of these *three*:—A dog, a palm-tree, or a woman; to which some add the pig, and others the serpent as well.

Ibid., fol. 111, col. 1.

NOTE.—One part of this regulation is rather hard and should surely be abolished; that, viz., which ordains a woman shall not come between two men or a man pass between two women. The compiler of this Miscellany was once witness to a case which illustrates its inconvenience: it occurred at Tiberias. A pious young Jew who had to traverse a narrow road to pass from the lake to the town was kept standing for a very considerable time under a broiling sun, simply because two young women, to tease him, guarded the entrance, and dared him to pass between them. Of course he dared not accept the challenge, otherwise he would have incurred the penalty of death, according to the judgment of the Talmud; for "Whosoever transgresses *any* of the words of the Scribes is guilty of death." (*Eiruvin*, fol. 21, col. 2.)

23. These *three* will inherit the world to come:—He who dwells in the land of Israel; he who brings up his sons to the study of the law; and he who repeats the ritual blessing over the appointed cup of wine at the close of the Sabbath.   *P'sachim*, fol. 113, col. 1.

24. There are *three* whom the Holy One—blessed be He!—Himself proclaims virtuous :—The unmarried man who lives in a city and does not sin; the poor man who restores a lost thing which he has found to its owner; and the rich man who pays the tithes of his increase unostentatiously. Rav Saphra was a bachelor, and he dwelt in a large city. A disciple of the wise once descanted upon the merits of a celibate life in the presence of Rava and this Rav Saphra, and the face of the latter beamed with delight. Remarking which, Rava said to him, " This does not refer to such a bachelor as thou art, but to such as Rabbi Chanena and Rabbi Oshaia." They were single men, who followed the trade of shoemakers, and dwelt in a street mostly occupied by זונות *meretrices*, for whom they made shoes; but when they fitted these on, they never raised their eyes to look at their faces. For this the women conceived such a respect for them, that, when they swore, they swore by the life of the holy Rabbis of the land of Israel. *P'sachim*, fol. 113, cols. 1, 2.

25. There are *three* whom the Holy One—blessed be He! —abhorreth : He who says one thing but thinks another; he who might bear witness in favour of his neighbour but refrains from doing so ; and he who, having seen his neighbour act disgracefully, goes and appears *singly* as a witness against him (thus only condemning, but not convicting, him, as the law requires two witnesses). As, for example, when Toviah transgressed and Zigud appeared against him singly before Rav Pappa, and Rav Pappa ordered this witness to receive forty stripes save one in return. " What ! " said he, " *Toviah has sinned, and should Zigud be flogged ?* " " Yes," replied the Rabbi, " for by testifying singly against him thou bringest him only into bad repute." (See Deut. xix. 15.) *P'sachim*, fol. 113, col. 2.

NOTE.—" *Toviah has sinned and Zigud is flogged,*" has long been a proverb among Jews.

26. There are *three* whose life is no life :—The sympathetic, the irascible, and the melancholy.

P'sachim, fol. 113, col. 2.

27. There are *three* which despise their fellows :—Dogs, cocks, and sorcerers. Some say strange women also, and some the disciples of the Babylonian Rabbis. *Ibid.*

> NOTE.—Cato used to say that he was surprised one soothsayer could keep his countenance when he saw another manipulating, knowing, as he did, the imposture he was practising.

28. These *three* love their fellows :—Proselytes, slaves, and ravens. *Ibid.*

29. These *three* are apt to strut :—Israel among the nations, the dog among animals, the cock among birds. Some say also the goat among small cattle, and some the caper shrub among trees. *Ibid.*, fol. 25, col. 2.

30. There are *three* whose life is no life :—He who lives at another's table; he whose wife domineers over him; and he who suffers bodily affliction. Some say also he who has only a single shirt in his wardrobe.

Ibid., fol. 32, col. 2.

> NOTE.—Χωρὶς ὑγιείας ἄβιος βίος, βίος ἀβίωτος, "Without health life is not life, life is lifeless." (*Ariphon.*)

31. *Three* things are said respecting the finger-nails :—He who trims his nails and buries the parings is a pious man; he who burns these is a righteous man; but he who throws them away is a wicked man, for mischance might follow, should a female (עוברה) step over them.

Moed Katan, fol. 18, col. 1.

> NOTE.—The orthodox Jews in Poland are to this day careful to bury away or burn their nail-parings.

32. *Three* classes appear on the day of judgment :—The perfectly righteous, who are at once written and sealed for

D

eternal life ; the thoroughly bad, who are at once written and sealed for hell; as it is written (Dan. xii. 2), " And many of them that sleep in the dust of the earth shall awake, some to everlasting life, and some to shame and everlasting contempt ;" and those in the intermediate state, who go down into hell, where they cry and howl for a time, whence they ascend again ; as it is written (Zech. xiii. 9), " And I will bring the third part through the fire, and will refine them as silver is refined, and will try them as gold is tried ; they shall call on my name, and I will hear them."   It is of them Hannah said (1 Sam. ii. 6), " The Lord killeth and maketh alive ; He bringeth down to hell and bringeth up."

Rosh Hashanah, fol. 16, col. 2.

33. Our Rabbis have taught that there are *three* voices which can be heard from one end of the world to the other :—The sound emitted from the sphere of the sun ; the hum and din of the city of Rome ; and the voice of anguish uttered by the soul as it quits the body ; . . . but our Rabbis prayed that the soul might be spared this torture, and therefore the voice of its terrors has not since been heard.   *Yoma*, fol. 20, col. 2.

34. In *three* particulars is benevolence superior to almsgiving :—Almsgiving is only the bestowment of money, but benevolence can be exercised by personal service as well.   Alms can be given only to the poor, but benevolence can be shown no less to the rich.   Alms are confined to the living, but benevolence may extend to both the dead and the living.   *Succah*, fol. 49, col. 2.

35. *Three* marks characterise the nation of Israel :— They are compassionate, they are modest, and they are benevolent.   Compassionate, as it is written (Deut. xiii. 18), " And show thee mercy, and have compassion upon thee, and multiply thee."   Modest, as it is written (Exod. xx. 20), " That his fear may be before your faces."   Bene-

volent, as it is written (Gen. xviii. 19), "For I know him,"
&c.   *Yevamoth*, fol. 79, col. 1.

> NOTE.—The Rabbis are not always happy in applying Scrip-
> ture, but No. 35 is the right rendering. Jewish writers
> often quote it as it stands here.

36. Dates are good after meals in the morning and in
the evening, but hurtful in the afternoon; on the other
hand, at noon they are most excellent, and an antidote to
these *three* maladies :—Evil thought, constipation, and
hemorrhoids.   *Kethuboth*, fol. 10, col. 2.

37. Beware of these *three* things :—Do not sit too much,
for it brings on hemorrhoids; do not stand too much, for
it is bad for the heart; do not walk too much, for it is
hurtful to the eyes. But sit a third, stand a third, and
walk a third.   *Ibid.*, fol. 111, col. 1.

38. He who holds his household in terror tempts to
the commission of *three* sins : — Fornication, murder, and
Sabbath-breaking.   *Gittin*, fol. 6, col. 2.

39. *Three* things weaken the strength of man :—Fear,
travel, and sin. Fear, as it is written (Ps. xxxviii. 10),
"My heart palpitates, my strength faileth me." Travel,
as it is written (Ps. cii. 23), "He hath weakened my
strength in the way." . . . Sin, as it is written (Ps. xxxi.
10), "My strength faileth me, because of my iniquity."
                                        Ibid., fol. 70, col. 2.

40. Abraham was *three* years old when he first learned
to know his Creator; as it is said (Gen. xxvi. 5), "Because
(עקב) Abraham obeyed my voice."
                                        Nedarim, fol. 32, col. 1.

> NOTE 1.—The conclusion arrived at here is founded on inter-
> preting the Hebrew letters of the word rendered " be-
> cause " numerically, in which ע = 70 ק = 100 and ב = 2,
> making a total of *one hundred and seventy-two;* so that
> the sense of the text is, " Abraham obeyed my voice "
> one hundred and seventy-two years. Now Abraham died

when he was a hundred and seventy-five, therefore he must have been only three when he began to serve the Lord.

As Abraham plays so important a part both in the history and the imagination of the Jewish race, we may be allowed to quote here a score or so of the Talmudic traditions regarding him. The traditions, as is like, contributed quite as much, if not more, to give character to his descendants as his actual personality and that spirit of faith which was the central fact in his history. Races and nations often draw more inspiration from what they *fancy* about their ancestry and early history than from what they *know ;* their fables therefore are often more illuminative than the facts.

(*a.*) Abraham was Ethan the Ezrahite, who is mentioned Ps. lxxxvii. 1. (*Bava Bathra*, fol. 15, col. 1.)

(*b.*) Abraham's mother was Amathlai, the daughter of Karnebo. (*Ibid.*, fol. 91, col. 1.)

(*c.*) Abraham was the head of a seminary for youth, and kept both laws, *the written and the oral.* (*Yoma*, fol. 28, col. 2.)

(*d.*) Abraham observed the *whole ceremonial law*, even before it was given on Sinai. (*Kiddushin*, fol. 82, col. 1.)

Note.—From the day Abraham was compelled to leave the idolatrous worship and country of his fathers, it is reasonable to suppose that his tent would become a rendezvous for his neighbours who shrunk like himself from the abominations around them. There, from his character, by which he recommended himself as the friend of God, he might very naturally be looked upon as a religious teacher, and men might gather together to learn from his lips or profit by his example. Hence, making due allowance for Eastern hyperbole, the statement of the Book of Jasher (chap. xxvi. verse 36) is not undeserving of credit, where it is said that "Abraham brought all the children of the land to the service of God, and he taught them the ways of the Lord." The same remark applies to what is said in Targ. Yerushalmi (Gen. xxi.), that Abraham's guests went not away until "he had made them proselytes, and had taught them the way everlasting." His son Isaac, says the Targ. of Ben Uzziel, went to school at the "Beth Medrasha de Shem Rabba."

(*e.*) Though Abraham kept all the commandments,

he was not perfect till he was circumcised. (*Nedarim*, fol. 31, col. 2.)

Note.—In whatever sense this may have been written, and whatever the interpretation that may be put upon it, there is one sense in which it is absolutely and eternally true, and that is, that, in order to be perfect, a man's life must be as pronounced on the negative side as the positive, in its denials as in its affirmations, and that it is futile to attempt to obey God unless one at the same time renounce all co-partnery with the devil. Circumcision is the symbol of this renunciation, and it is only as such it has any radical spiritual significance. Till he was circumcised, it is said, God did not speak to Abraham in Hebrew. Not till then is sacredness of speech, any more than sacredness of life, possible. Doubtless among the Jews circumcision was the symbol of their separation from the ethnic religions; and hence the jealousy with which their prophets looked upon any compromise with idolatry. Hatred of that, utter and intense, was the one essential negative pole of genuine Judaism, and circumcision was its sign and seal.

(*f.*) Abraham was the first of the proselytes. (*Succah*, fol. 49, col. 2.)

(*g.*) Abraham it was that ordained the form of prayer for morning worship, which is extant to this very day. (*Berachoth*, fol. 26, col. 2.)

(*h.*) As he himself was pious, so were his very camels, for they would not enter into a place where there were idols; as it is written (Gen. xxiv. 31), "I have prepared," *i.e.*, removed the idols from, "the house and room for the camels." (*Avoth d' Rabbi Nathan*, chap. 8.)

Note.—The Targum of Ben Uzziel suggests the same principle as this tradition: "I have purified the house from strange worship, and have prepared a place for the camels."

(*i.*) Abraham had a daughter, and her name was Bakol. (*Ibid.*, fol. 16, col. 2.)

(*j.*) Abraham was free from evil passion. (*Bava Bathra*, fol. 17, col. 1.)

(*k.*) He was also free from the Angel of Death. (*Ibid.*, fol. 17, col. 1.)

(*l.*) He delivered to the children he had by Keturah a secret name, with which they learned to practise witchcraft and do the works of the devil. (*Sanhedrin*, fol. 91, col. 1.)

(*m.*) Though great, he personally waited on his guests, who had the appearance of Arabs and not of angels. (*Kiddushin*, fol. 32, col. 2.)

(*n.*) Rabbi Yehudah says Abraham planted an ornamental garden with all kinds of choice fruits in it, and Rabbi Nehemiah says he erected an inn for travellers in order to make known the name of God to all who sojourned in it. (*Sotah*, fol. 10, col. 1.)

Note.—Both the Targum of Ben Uzziel and the Yerushalmi say that Abraham planted a paradise at Beersheba for the entertainment and delectation of his guests; and in Jasher (chap. xxvii. verse 37), it is said that "Abraham formed a grove and planted a vineyard there, and had always ready in his tent meat and drink for those that passed through the land, so that they might satisfy themselves in his house."

(*o.*) He ranked as one of the seven shepherds of Israel (Micah v. 5). In this group David was the central figure, with Adam, Seth, and Methusaleh on his right hand, and Abraham, Jacob, and Moses on his left. (*Succah*, fol. 52, col. 2.)

(*p.*) The coin of Jerusalem had the impress of David and Solomon on the one side, and the holy city of Jerusalem on the other. But the impress on the coin of our father Abraham was an old man and an old woman on one side, and a young man and a damsel on the other. (*Bava Kama*, fol. 37, col. 2.)

Note.—This, it is to be presumed, must be taken in some symbolical sense, for coins cannot be traced back to a date so early as this; and when Abraham purchased the cave to bury Sarah in from the sons of Heth, we read that he *weighed* to Ephron the silver.

(*q.*) Abraham pleaded with God on behalf of Israel and said, "While there is a Temple they will get their sins atoned for, but when there shall be no Temple, what will become of them?" God, in answer to his prayer, assured him that He had prepared a prayer for them,

by which, as often as they read it, He would be pro-
pitiated and would pardon all their sins. (*Meggillah*,
fol. 31, col. 2.)

(*r.*) He was punished by his posterity being compelled
to serve the Egyptians two hundred and ten years, because he had *pressed* the Rabbis under his tuition into
military service in the expedition he had undertaken to
recover Lot from those who had carried him off captive;
for it is written (Gen. xiv. 14), "He armed his *instructed.*" Samuel says Abraham was punished because
he perversely distrusted the assurance of God; as it is
written (Gen. xv. 8), "*Whereby shall I know* that I shall
inherit it?" (*Nedarim*, fol. 31, col. 2.)

(*s.*) Abraham was thrown into a fiery furnace by
Nimrod, and God would not permit Gabriel to rescue
him, but did so Himself; because God is *One* and
Abraham was *one*, therefore it behoved the *One* to rescue
the *one.* (*P'sachim*, fol. 118, col. 1.)

Note.—The fire from which Abraham is here said to be
delivered may simply refer to his deliverance by
the hand of God from Ur of the Chaldees; Ur
meaning "fire," and being the name of a place
celebrated for fire-worship. The Midrash (p. 20)
says, "When the wicked Nimrod cast Abraham into
the furnace, Gabriel said, 'Lord of the universe!
permit me to deliver this holy one from the fire!'
But the Lord made answer, 'I am the *One Supreme*
in my world, and he is supreme in his; it is fitting
therefore that *the Supreme* should rescue the
supreme.'"

(*t.*) Abraham was a giant of giants; his height was
as that of *seventy-four* men put together. His food, his
drink, and his strength were in the proportion of seventy-
four men's to one man's. He built an iron city for the
abode of his seventeen children by Keturah, the walls
of which were so lofty that the sun never penetrated
them: he gave them a bowl full of precious stones, the
brilliancy of which supplied them with light in the
absence of the sun. (*Sophrim*, chap. 21.)

(*u.*) Abraham our father had a precious stone suspended
from his neck, and every sick person that gazed upon it
was immediately healed of his disease. But when
Abraham died, God hung up the stone on the sphere of
the sun. (*Bava Bathra*, fol. 16, col. 2.)

(*v.*) Till Abraham's time there was no such thing as a *beard;* but as many mistook Abraham for Isaac, and Isaac for Abraham, they looked so exactly alike, Abraham prayed to God for a beard to enable people to distinguish him from his son, Isaac, and it was granted him; as it is written (Gen. xxiv. 1), " And to Abraham *a beard* came when he was well stricken in age." (*Sanhedrin*, fol. 107, col. 2.)

Note.—Here the word זקן, which the translators of the English version render *was old*, is taken in another of its cognate meanings as *a beard.* The Midrash is a trifle more modest in this legendary assertion. There we read, " Before Abraham there was no special mark of old age," and that for distinction's sake " the beard was made to turn grey."

(*w.*) When he died, all the chiefs of the nations of the world stood in a line and exclaimed, " Alas for the world, that has lost its leader ! Alas for the ship that has lost its helmsman !" (*Bava Bathra*, fol. 91, col. 2.)

(*x.*) As Rabbi Banna went about to measure and to mark off the outward and inward dimensions of the different caves, when he came to the cave of Machpelah he found Eliezar, Abraham's servant, at the entrance, and asked him, " What is Abraham doing?" The answer he received was, " He is asleep in the arms of Sarah." (*Ibid.*, fol. 58, col. 1.)

Note 2.—Abraham being greater than Moses, for whilst the latter is only called by God " My Servant " (Mal. iv. 4), the former is called " My Friend " (Isa. xli. 8), we are fain to devote a little more space for a few more extracts from other Jewish sources than the Talmud, in order to make the picture they supply of our father Abraham's character a little more complete.

(*aa.*) Rabbi Yochanan ben Nuri says:—" The Holy One —blessed be He !—took Shem and separated him to be a priest to Himself, that he might serve before Him. He also caused His Shechinah to rest with him, and called his name Melchizedek, priest of the Most High and king of Salem. His brother Japheth even studied the law in his school, until Abraham came and also learned the law in the school of Shem, where God Himself instructed Abraham, so that all else he had learned from the lips of man was forgotten.   Then came Abraham and prayed to God that His Shechinah might ever rest in the house of Shem, which also was promised to him ; as it is said (Ps. cx. 4), ' Thou art a priest for ever after the order of Melchizedek.' " (*Avodath Hakkodesh*, part 3, chap. 20.)

(*ab.*) Wherever Jacob resided he studied the law as his fathers did.   How is this, seeing the law had not yet been given, it is nevertheless written of Abraham (Gen. xxvi. 5), "And he kept my charge " ?   Whence then did Abraham learn the law ?   Rabbi Shimon says his reins (literally kidneys) were made like two water-jars, from which the law flowed forth.   Where do we learn that it was so ?   From what is said in Ps. xvi. 7, " My reins also instruct me in the night season." (*Bereshith Rabba*, chap. 95.)

(*ac.*) The masters of the Kabbalah, of blessed memory, say that Abraham's Rabbi, *i.e.*, teacher, was the angel Zadkiel. (*Rabbi Menachem's comment on the Pent.*, Exod. iii. 5.)

(*ad.*) Adam's book, which contained celestial mysteries and holy wisdom, came down as an heirloom into the hands of Abraham, and he by means of it was able to see the glory of his Lord. (*Zohar Parashah Bereshith.*)

(*ae.*) Abraham was the author of a (מסכתא) treatise on the subject of different kinds of witchcraft and its unholy workings and fruits, as also of the Book of Creation, ספר יצירה, through holy names, (by means of which, namely, anything could be created.) (*Nishmath Chayim*, chap. 29).

(*af.*) The whole world once believed that the souls of men were perishable, and that man had no pre-eminence above a beast, till Abraham came and preached the doctrine of immortality and transmigration. (More on this subject we give in Part III. of this work.) (*Ibid.*, fol. 171, col. 1.)

(*ag.*) A good son delivers his father from the punishment of hell, for thus we find that Abraham our father delivered Terah, as it is said in Gen. xv. 15, " And thou shalt go to thy *fathers in peace.*"   This implies that God had communicated to him the tidings that his father had a portion in the world to come and was now " *in peace* " there. (*Pesikta Zotarta*, fol. 3, col. 2.)

(*ah.*) Before Abraham was circumcised God spake to him in the Chaldee language, that the angels should not understand it. (This is proved from Gen. xv. i.) (*Yalkut Chadash*, fol. 117.)

(*ai.*) Rabbi Levi said Abraham sits at the gate of hell and does not permit any circumcised Israelite to enter. But if any appear who happen to have sinned unduly, these he (by an indescribable contrivance) causes to become uncircumcised and lets pass without scruple into the region of torment; and this is what is said in Ps. lv. 20, "He hath put forth his hands against such as be at peace with him : he hath broken his covenant." (*Yalkut Shimoni*, fol. 33, col. 2, sec. 18.)

(*ak.*) Abraham was circumcised on the Day of Atonement, and God looks that day annually on the blood of the covenant of our father Abraham's circumcision as atoning for all our iniquities, as it is said in Lev. xvi. 30, "For on that day shall he make an atonement for you, to cleanse you from all your sins." (*Yalkut Chadash*, fol. 121, col. 1, sec. 3.)

(*al.*) "And it came to pass that when *Abram* was come into Egypt" (Gen. xii. 14). And where was Sarah? He confined her in a chest, into which he locked her, lest any one should gaze on her beauty. When he came to the receipt of custom, he was summoned to open the chest, but declined, and offered payment of the duty. The officers said, "Thou carriest garments;" and he offered duty for garments. "Nay, it is gold thou carriest;" and he offered the impost laid on gold. Then they said, "It is costly silks, belike pearls, thou concealest;" and he offered the custom on such articles. At length the Egyptian officers insisted, and he opened the box. And when he did so, all the land of Egypt was illumined by her beauty. (*Bereshith Rabba*, chap. 40.)

(*am.*) The question may naturally be asked why Abraham hid his wife from the gaze of others first then and not before. The reply is to be deduced from the following double rendering of Gen. xii. 11 :—"Behold *now* I know that thou art a fair woman." As if to say, "Usually people lose their good looks on a long journey, but thou art as beautiful as ever." The second explanation is this :—Abraham was so piously modest that in all his life he never once looked a female in the face, his own wife not excepted. As he approached Egypt and was crossing some water, he saw in it the reflection of her face, and it was then that he exclaimed, "Behold *now* I know that thou art a fair woman." As the Egyptians

arc swarthy, Abraham at once perceived the magnitude
of the danger, and hence his precaution to hide her
beauty in a chest. (*Zeenah Ureenah* (1877 in Russia),
fol. 28, col. 1.)

(*an.*) When Abraham came to the cave of Machpelah
to bury Sarah, Adam and Eve rose from their grave and
protested against his committing her to the dust in that
receptacle. "For," said they, "we are ever ashamed in
the presence of the Holy One—blessed be He!—on account
of the sin which we committed, and now comest thou to
add to our shame by the contrast therewith of the good
works which ye two have done." On Abraham's assurance that he would intercede with God on their behalf
that they should not bear the shame any longer, Adam
immediately retired to his sepulchre, but Eve being still unwilling to do so, Abraham took her by the hand and led
her back to the side of Adam ; and then he buried Sarah.
(*Yalkut Chadash*, fol. 14, col. 3, sec. 68.)

(*ao.*) Abraham's father, Terah, was both an idolater,
a manufacturer of idols, and a dealer in them. Once
when Terah had some engagement elsewhere he left his
son Abraham to attend to his business. When a customer came to purchase an idol, Abraham asked him,
"How old art thou?" "Lo! so many years," was the
ready reply. "What," exclaimed Abraham, "is it possible
that a man of so many years should desire to worship
a thing only a day old?" The customer, being ashamed
of himself, went his way ; and so did all other customers,
who underwent a similar inquisition. Once an old woman
brought a measure of fine flour and wished to present
it as an offering to the gods. This so enraged Abraham
that he took a staff and broke all the images, excepting
the largest, into whose hands he fixed the staff. When
his father came and questioned him about the destruction of the gods, he replied, "An old woman placed an
offering of flour before them, which immediately set
them all by the ears, for every one was hungrier than
another, but the biggest god killed all the rest with this
staff which thou now seest he still holds in his hands."
Superstition, especially when combined with mercenary
motives, knows neither reason nor human affection,
therefore the father handed over his son Abraham to the
inquisition of Nimrod, who threw him into the fiery
furnace, as recorded elsewhere in this Miscellany. This
is an historical fact, to the truth of which the whole

orthodox Jewish world will bear testimony, and is solemnly recorded in *Shalsheleth Hakkabalah,* fol. 2, col. 1.

(*N.B.*—Consult Index for more on the subject of Abraham.)

41. There are *three* graces :—The grace of a place in the eyes of its inhabitants; the grace of a woman in the eyes of her husband; the grace of a purchase in the eyes of the buyer.   *Soteh,* fol. 47, col. 1.

42. A man should divide his capital into *three* parts, and invest one-third in land, employ one-third in merchandise, and reserve one-third in ready money.

Bava Metzia, fol. 42, col. 1.

43. All who go down to hell shall come up again, except these *three :*—He who commits adultery; he who shames another in public; and he who gives another a bad name.

Ibid., fol. 58, col. 2.

44. These *three* complain, but no one sympathises with them :—He who lends money without witnesses; he who buys to himself a master; and he who is lorded over by his wife.   *Ibid.,* fol. 75, col. 2.

Note.—The sense in all these cases is the same, viz., that no one pities the man who brings his troubles upon himself. The expression, "buy a master to himself," finds illustration in the Latin proverb, "*Chius dominum emit,*" "The Chian buys himself a master." This proverb originated thus : When Mithridates conquered Chios, he gave over the inhabitants into the hands of the very slaves they themselves had imported.

45. There are *three* things on which the world stands :— The law, the temple service, and benevolence.

Avoth, chap. 1.

46. If *three* eat at one table and do not converse together on the law of the Lord, it is as if they ate from the sacrifices for the dead; but they, on the contrary, are as if they

partook from a table of the Lord's own furnishing who, while they sit down to meat, season their talk with its holy precepts. *Avoth*, chap. 3.

47. There are *three* crowns:—The crown of the law, the crown of the priesthood, and the crown of royalty; but the crown of a good name surpasses them all.

Ibid., chap. 4.

48. He who possesses these *three* virtues is a disciple of Abraham our father, and he who possesses the *three* contrary vices is a son of Balaam the wicked. The disciples of our father Abraham have a kindly eye, a loyal spirit, and a lowly mind. The disciples of Balaam the wicked have an evil eye, a proud spirit, and a grasping soul. *Ibid.*, chap. 5.

49. *Three* things are said respecting the children of men:—He who gives alms brings a blessing on himself; he who lends does better; he who gives away half of what he hath to spare does best of all.

Avoth d'Rab. Nathan, chap. 41.

50. There are *three* classes of disciples, and among them *three* grades of worth:—He ranks first who asks and answers when asked; he who asks but does not answer ranks next; but he who neither asks nor answers ranks lowest of all. *Ibid.*

51. Over these *three* does God weep every day:—Over him who is able to study the law but neglects it; over him who studies it amidst difficulties hard to overcome; and over the ruler who behaves arrogantly towards the community he should protect. *Chaggigah*, fol. 5, col. 2.

52. Rabbi Yochanan says there are *three* keys in the hand of the Holy One—blessed be He!—which He never intrusts to the disposal of a messenger, and they are

these :—(1.) The key of rain, (2.) the key of life (היה), and (3.) the key of reviving the dead. The key of rain, for it is written (Deut. xxviii. 12), "The Lord shall open unto thee His good treasure, the heaven to give the rain unto thy land in season;" the key of life, as it is written (Gen. xxx. 22), "God hearkened unto her, and opened her womb;" the key of reviving the dead, for it is written (Ezek. xxxvii. 13), "When I have opened your graves, and brought you up out of your graves, and shall put my spirit in you, and ye shall live," &c.

Taanith, fol. 2, col. 1, 2.

53. A disciple of the wise who makes light of the washing of hands is contemptible; but more contemptible is he who begins to eat before his guest; more contemptible is that guest who invites another guest; and still more contemptible is he who begins to eat before a disciple of the wise; but contemptible before all these *three* put together is that guest which troubles another guest.

Derech Eretz Zuta, chap. viii.

54. A roll of the law which has two mistakes to a column should be corrected; but if there be *three,* it should be stowed away altogether.   *Menachoth,* fol. 29, col. 2.

55. All creatures משמשין פנים כנגד עורף except *three,* and these do it, פנים כנגד פנים,—fish, man, and the serpent. Why should the action of these three differ from the rest? When Rav Dimi came he said, "They in the west say it is because the Shechinah conversed with them." Of the camel is it recorded אחור כנגד אחור.   *Bechoroth,* fol. 8, col. 1.

56. The wolf, the lion, the bear, the leopard, the panther, the elephant, and the sea-cat, each bear *three* years.   *Ibid.*

57. Rav Yehudah says, in the name of Rav, "The butcher is bound to have *three* knives; one to slaughter

with, one for cutting up the carcase, and one to cut away
the suet.* *Chullin*, fol. 8, col. 2.

58. *Three* classes of ministering angels raise a song of
praise every day. One class says, *Holy!* the second re-
sponds, *Holy!* and the third continues, *Holy is the Lord
of hosts!* But in the presence of the Holy One—blessed
be He!—Israel is more beloved than the ministering
angels; for Israel reiterates the song every hour, while
the ministering angels repeat it only once a day, some
say once a week, others once a month, others once a year,
others once in seven years, others once in a jubilee, and
others only once in eternity. Again, Israel mentions *The
Name* (יהוה) after two words, as it is said (Deut. vi. 4),
שמע ישראל יהוה, "*Hear Israel, Yehovah,*" but the ministering angels do not mention *The Name* (יהוה) till after
three, as it is written (Isa. vi. 3), קדוש קדוש קדוש יהוה
צבאות, "*Holy! holy! holy! Yehovah Zebaoth.*" Moreover,
the ministering angels do not take up the song above till
Israel has started it below; for it is said (Job xxxviii. 7),
" When the morning stars sang together,† then all the sons
of God shouted for joy." *Ibid.*, fol. 91, col. 2.

59. ת"ר The Rabbis have taught, a man should not
sell to his neighbour shoes made from the hide of a beast
that has died of disease, as if of a beast that had been
slaughtered in the shambles, for two reasons : first, because
he imposes on him (for the skin of a beast that dies of
itself is not so durable as the hide of a slaughtered
animal) ; second, because there is danger (for the beast
that died of itself might have been stung by a serpent,
and the poison remaining in the leather might prove fatal
to the wearer of shoes made of that leather). A man
should not send his neighbour a barrel of wine with oil
floating upon its surface ; for it happened once that a

---

* Suet being as unlawful for food as pork.
† " Israel are likened to stars," says Rashi.

man did so, and the recipient went and invited his friends to a feast, in the preparation of which oil was to form a chief ingredient; but when the guests assembled, it was found out that the cask contained wine, and not oil; and because the host had nothing else in preparation for a worthy feast, he went and committed suicide. Neither should guests give anything from what is set before them to the son or daughter of their host, unless the host himself give them leave to do so; for it once happened during a time of scarcity that a man invited *three* of his friends to dine, and he had nothing but *three* eggs to place before them. Meanwhile, as the guests were seated at the board, the son of the host came into the room, and first one of the guests gave him his share, and then the other two followed his example. Shortly afterwards the host himself came in, and seeing the child with his mouth full and both hands, he knocked him down to the ground, so that he died on the instant. The mother, seeing this, went and threw herself headlong from the housetop, and the father followed her example. Thus Rabbi Eliezer ben Yacob said, "There perished in this affair *three* souls of Israel." *Chullin*, fol. 94, col. i.

60. Once the Roman Government issued a decree that the Israelites should neither observe the Sabbath nor circumcise their sons and שיבעלו את הנדות. Thereupon Reuben the son of Istrubli trimmed his hair as a Gentile, and went among the Roman senators and plied them with wise remonstrance. "If one," said he, "has an enemy, does he wish him to be poor or rich?" "To be poor," was the reply. "Then," he argued, "won't he be poorer if you prohibit him from working on the Sabbath?" "It is well said," observed the senators; and they at once abolished their decree respecting the Sabbath. Again he asked, "If one has an enemy, does he wish him to be weak or strong?" "Why, weak, to be sure," was the inevitable answer. "Then," said he, "let the Jews cir-

cumcise their children, then will they be weakened."
"The argument is good," said they, and the decree against
circumcision was rescinded. Again he asked, "If one
has an enemy, does he wish him to increase or decrease?"
"To decrease, of course," said they. "Then," argued he,
"‏לא יבעלו נדות‎." The decree against catamenia was
accordingly abolished. When, however, they found out
that he was a Jew, they at once re-enacted the decrees
they had cancelled. Upon this the question arose who
should go to Rome and appeal against these enactments.
It was resolved that Rabbi Shimon ben Yochai, who was
reputed experienced in miracles, should go, accompanied by
Rabbi Elazar, the son of Rabbi Yossi. . . . As they journeyed
along, the question was proposed to them, "Whence is it
proved that the blood of a reptile is unclean?" Rabbi
Elazar replied with a curl of the lip, and quoted Lev. ii.
29, "And these shall be unclean unto you." Rabbi
Shimon said unto him, "By the curl of thy lip art thou
recognisable as a disciple of the wise! May the son
never return to his father!" for he was annoyed that he
should presume to teach a Halachah in his presence, and
then and there he condemned him to death. (See *Berachoth*,
fol. 31, col. 2.) Thereupon Ben Temalion (an evil sprite
or imp) came, and greeting him, said, "Do ye wish me to
accompany you?" Rabbi Shimon wept and said, "Alas!
a maid-servant of my ancestor (Abraham) was assisted by
three angels,* and I have not one to attend me! However, let a miracle be worked for us anyhow." Then the
evil spirit entered into the Emperor's daughter, and when
the Rabbi was called in to cure the princess, he exorcised
the spirit by saying, "Depart, Ben Temalion! Ben
Temalion, depart!" and the evil spirit left her. By way
of reward the Rabbis were bidden to ask whatsoever they
pleased, and admitted into the imperial treasury that
they might choose what seemed good to them. Espying

---

* The word angel occurs three times in the narrative.

there the edict against Israel, they chose it, and tore it
to pieces.　　　　　　　　　*Megilah*, fol. 17, col. 1, 2.

61. At the time when the high priest enters to worship, *three* acolytes take hold of him, one by the right
hand and another by the left, while the third lifts the
gems attached to the train of his pontifical vestment.

Tamid, chap. 7 ; *Mishna*, 1.

62. "I once, when a grave-digger," says Abba Shaul, as
the Rabbis relate, "chased a roe which had entered the
shin-bone of a dead man ; and though I ran *three* miles
after it, I could not overtake it, nor reach the end of the
bone.　When I returned, I was told that it was a bone of
Og, king of Bashan."　　　*Niddah*, fol. 24, col. 2.

63. The Rabbis have taught that during the first *three*
months (of pregnancy) the child lies in the lower part (of
the uterus) ; during the next *three* it occupies the middle
part ; and during the last *three* it is in the upper part ;
and that when the time of parturition comes, it turns
over first, and this causes the birth-pains.　We are also
taught that the pains caused by a female child are greater
than those caused by a male.　Rabbi Elazar said, "What
Scripture is there for this ?　'When I was made in secret
and curiously wrought, רקמתי, in the lowest parts of the
earth' (Ps. cxxxix. 15).　It is not said, דרתי, '*I abode*,'
but, רקמתי, 'I was curiously wrought.'　Why the difference ?　Why are the pains caused by a girl greater
than those caused by a boy ?" זה בא כדרך תשמישו
וזה בא כדרך תשמישו· זו הופכת פנים וזה אינו הופך פניו·

Niddah, fol. 31, col. 1.

64. The Rabbis teach there are *three* that have a share
in a man ; God, and his father and mother.　The father's
part consists of all that is white in him—the bones, the
veins, the nails, the brain, and the white of the eye.　The
mother's part consists of all that is red in him—the skin,

the flesh, the hair, and the black part of the eye.   God's part consists of the breath, the soul, the physiognomy, sight and hearing, speech, motive power, knowledge, understanding, and wisdom.   And when the time comes that the man should depart from the world, God takes away His part, and leaves those which belong to the father and mother.   Rav Pappa says, "This is the meaning of the proverb, 'Shake off the salt and throw the flesh to the dogs.'"   *Niddah*, fol. 31, col. 1.

> NOTE.—Rashi's explanatory note is this : "Shake off the salt from the flesh and it becomes fit only for dogs.   The soul is the salt which preserves the body ; when it departs, the body putrefies."

CHAPTER IV.

THE 'FOURS' OF THE TALMUD.

1. *Four* things require fortitude in the observance:—
The law, good works, prayer, and social duties. Respecting the law and good works it is written (Josh. i. 7), " Be
thou strong and firm, that thou mayest observe to do all
the law;" in which the word "strong" refers to the law,
and the word "firm" to good works. Of prayer it is
written, " Wait on the Lord; be strong, and He shall make
thine heart firm; wait, I say, upon the Lord" (Ps. xxvii.
14). In respect to social duties it is written (2 Sam. x. 2),
" Be strong, and let us strengthen ourselves for our people,
and for the cities of our God." *Berachoth*, fol. 32, col. 2.

2. There are *four* signs which tell tales:—Dropsy
(הדרוקן, Gr. ὕδρωψ) is a sign of sin; jaundice is a sign
of hatred without a cause; poverty is a sign of pride; and
quinsy is a sign of slander. *Shabbath*, fol. 33, col. 1.

3. "Unto Mamre, unto the city of Arbah," *i.e.*, *four*
(Gen. xxxv. 27). Rabbi Isaac calls it the city of four
couples, *i.e.*, Adam and Eve, Abraham and Sarah, Isaac
and Rebekah, Jacob and Leah. These four couples being
buried in Mamre, it was therefore called "the city of
four." *Eiruvin*, fol. 53, col. 1.

Note.—There is, according to the Rabbis, no anachronism
here, as the name was given by prophetic anticipation.

4. The sun makes *four* quarterly circuits. In April,
May, and June, *i.e.*, Nisan, Iyar, and Sivan, his circuit is

between the mountains, in order to dissolve the snow; in July, August, and September, *i.e.*, Tamuz, Ab, and Ellul, his circuit is over the habitable parts of the earth, in order to ripen the fruits; in October, November, and December, *i.e.*, Tishri, Marcheshvan, and Kislev, his circuit is over the seas, to evaporate the waters; in January, February, and March, *i.e.*, Tebeth, Shebat, and Adar, his circuit is over the deserts, in order to protect the seed sown from being scorched. *P'sachim*, fol. 94, col. 2.

5. *Four* persons are intolerable:—A poor man who is proud, a rich man who is a liar, an old man who is incontinent, and a warden who behaves haughtily to a community for whom he has done nothing. To these some add him who has divorced his wife once or twice and married her again. *Ibid.*, fol. 113, col. 2.

6. *Four* things cancel the decrees of Heaven:—Alms, prayer, change of name, and reformation of conduct. Alms, as it is written (Prov. x. 2), "But alms (צדקה, more correctly, righteousness) delivereth from death." Prayer, as it is written (Ps. cvii. 6), "Then they cried unto the Lord in their trouble, and He delivered them out of their distresses." Change of name, as it is said (Gen. xvii. 15, 16), "As for Sarai thy wife, thou shalt not call her name Sarai, but Sarah shall be her name." And after this change of name it is written, "And I will bless her, and give thee a son of her." Reformation of conduct, as it is written, (Jonah iii. 10), "And God saw their works," and "God repented of the evil," &c. Some say also change of residence has the effect of turning back the decree of Heaven (Gen. xii. 1), "And the Lord said unto Abram, Get thee out of thy country;" and then it is said, "I will make of thee a great nation." *Rosh Hashanah*, fol. 16, col. 2.

7. *Four* things cause an eclipse of the sun:—When a chief magistrate dies and is not mourned over with the due

lamentation; when a betrothed damsel calls for help and no
one comes to the rescue; when the people commit the
sin of Sodom and Gomorrah; and when brother murders
brother.   *Succah*, fol. 29, col. 1.

8. *Four* things cause an eclipse among the luminaries
of heaven: The writing of false documents; the bearing
false witness; the breeding of small cattle, such as sheep
and goats, in the land of Israel; and the cutting down
of fruit-trees.   *Ibid.*, fol. 29, col. 1.

9. There are *four* things God repents of having created:
—The Captivity, the Chaldeans, the Ishmaelites, and the
evil passion in man. The Captivity, as it is written (Isa.
lii. 5), "What have I here, saith the Lord, that my people
are taken away for nought?" &c. The Chaldeans, as it is
written (Isa. xxiii. 13), "Behold the land of the Chaldeans: this people was not." The Ishmaelites, as it is
written (Job xii. 6), "The tents of robbers prosper, and
they that provoke God are secure, into whose hand God
bringeth abundance." The evil passion, as it is written
(Micah iv. 6), ‏ואשר הרעתי‎, "And whom I have caused
.to be evil."   *Ibid.*, fol. 52, col. 2.

10. There have been *four* beautiful women in the world:
—Sarah, Abigail, Rahab, and Esther.
                                  Meggillah, fol. 15, col. 1.

Note.—(a.) Tosephoth, *in loco*, asks, "Why was not Eve
    numbered among these beauties, since even Sarah, in
    comparison with Eve, was as an ape compared to a
    man?" The reply is, "Only those *born* of woman are
    here enumerated."

(b) In fol. 13, col. 1, of the same treatise from which the
    above is quoted, we are informed by Ben Azai that
    Esther was like the myrtle-tree, neither tall nor short
    statured, but middle-sized. Rabbi Yehoshua ben Korcha
    states that Esther's complexion was of a yellow or gold
    colour.

11. One cup of wine is good for a woman, two are disgraceful, three demoralising, and *four* brutalising.

Kethuboth, fol. 65, col. 1.

12. He who traverses so much as *four* ells in the land of Israel is sure of everlasting life.   *Ibid.*, fol. 111, col. 1.

13. To walk even *four* ells without bowing the head is an offence to Heaven; for it is written (Isa. vi. 3), " The whole earth is full of His glory."

Kiddushin, fol. 31, col. 1.

14. There are *four* who are accounted as dead:—The pauper, the leper, the blind man, and he who has no male children.   *Nedarim*, fol. 64, col. 2.

15. *Four* things mark the characters of men:—He who says what is mine is mine, and what is thine is thine, is, according to some, a moderate man, but, according to others, a child of Sodom; he who says what is mine is thine, and what is thine is mine, is an ignorant man (עם הארץ); he who says what is mine is thine and what is thy own is also thine, is a pious man; he who says mine and thine are both my own, is a wicked man.

Avoth, chap. 5, sec. 16.

16. There are four kinds of men, according to their degrees of passionateness:—He who is easily provoked and as readily pacified, and who loses more than he gains; he whom it is difficult to rouse and as difficult to appease, and who gains more than he loses; he who is not readily provoked, but easily pacified, who is a pious man; he who is easily provoked and with difficulty appeased, who is a wicked man.   *Ibid.*, chap. 5, sec. 19.

17. There are *four* classes of men who give alms, and they are thus distinguished:—He who is willing to give, but unwilling that others should do so, he has an evil eye

towards others; he who wishes others to give, but does not do so himself, he has an evil eye towards himself; he who gives, and induces others to give, he is pious; he who gives not, nor wishes others to give, he is wicked.

Avoth, chap. 5, sec. 19.

18. There are *four* marks by which one disciple differs from another:—One learns and does not teach, one teaches and does not learn, one learns and teaches, and one neither learns nor teaches. *Avoth d'Rab. Nathan*, chap. 29.

19. *Four* things, if kept in view and gravely pondered over, deter from sin:—That a man consider whence he cometh, whither he goeth, who the judge will be, and what the future will bring to pass. *Derech Eretz*, chap. 3.

20. What is the meaning of that which is written (Ps. lxxxvii 2), "The Lord loveth the gates of Zion more than all the dwellings of Jacob?" The answer is, The Lord loveth the gates (המצויינים בהלכה) *that are marked with the Halachah* more than the synagogues and the schools; and this agrees with what Rabbi Cheeya bar Ami has said, in the name of Ulla, that since the destruction of the Temple nothing else has remained to God in His world but *four* ells of the Halachah.

Berachoth, fol. 8, col. 1.

NOTE.—המצויינים is an example of what is a very common pastime of the Rabbis of a play upon words. The word ציון in Talmudic Hebrew means *a mark*, and the allusion is to the little cells or rooms, often only about *four* ells square, set apart for the study of the Halachoth. These God is said to prefer to the places where large assemblies gather to study the Mishna, or even the Bible; as, for instance, חברה משנה and the חברה ת"נך.

21. Whoso walks even *four* ells with a proud unbending gait is as though he spurned with his haughty head the feet of the Shechinah; for it is written (Isa. vi. 3), "The whole earth is full of His glory." *Ibid.*, fol. 43, col. 2.

22. *Four* are in duty bound to return thanks to God:—
They that have returned from a voyage at sea (Ps. cvii.
23, 24, 31); those who have travelled in the desert (verses
4–8); they who have recovered from a serious illness
(verses 17–21); and those that are liberated from prison
(verses 10–15). *Berachoth*, fol. 54, col. 2.

23. If one does not walk, say *four* cubits, before falling
asleep after a meal, that which he has eaten, being un-
digestible, causes foulness of breath.

Shabbath, fol. 41, col. 1.

24. *Four* have died in consequence of the seduction of
the serpent:—Benjamin, the son of Jacob; Amram, the
father of Moses; Jesse, the father of David; and Chileab,
the son of David. *Ibid.*, fol. 55, col. 2.

> Note.—These *four* are reckoned to have died on account of
> original sin, and not solely because of actual transgres-
> sion, which, says Rashi, they never committed.

25. The traveller who is overtaken with the approach of
Sabbath-eve before he has completed his journey should
hand over his purse to a Gentile to carry; and if there be
no Gentile at hand, let him stow it away on his ass. As
soon as the nearest halting-place is reached, those burdens
which may be lifted on the Sabbath should then be removed,
and then the cords should be slackened that the rest may
slip off of its own accord. *Ibid.*, fol. 153, col. 1.

> Note.—Here the Gemara very graciously appends a direction
> as to the disposal of the purse, in case the traveller should
> happen to be on foot and have no Gentile attendant. He
> *may* take care of it himself, provided he halt at every
> other step and deposit it on the ground, for at least a dis-
> tance of four cubits.

26. A master is bound to rehearse a lesson to his pupil
four times. *Eiruvin*, fol. 54, col. 2.

27. Alas for the power which prepares a grave for its possessor, for there is not a prophet who hath not in his lifetime witnessed the decadence of *four* kings; as it is said (Isa. i. 1), "The vision of Isaiah . . . in the days of Uzziah, Jotham, Ahaz, and Hezekiah, kings of Judah" (see also Hosea i. 1).   *P"sachim*, fol. 87, col. 2.

28. Once Rav Papa and Rav Hunnah partook together of a common meal, and as the latter ate only one morsel the former ate *four*. After this, when Rav Hunnah and Ravina ate together, the latter devoured eight portions to the other's one, upon which Rav Hunnah jocularly remarked, "A hundred (Rav) Papas to one Ravina."

Ibid., fol. 89, col. 2.

29. No food may be eaten on Passover-eve from the time of the offering of the evening sacrifice (in order, *i.e.*, that abstinence may whet the appetite for the *Matsoth*). Even the poorest in Israel may not break his fast till the hour of reclining; nor is he to partake of less than *four* glasses of wine, even though he has been reduced so low as to subsist on the porridge doled out by public charity.

Ibid., fol. 99, col. 2.

NOTE.—The *four* cups severally commemorate *four* expressions made use of in connection with the deliverance from Egypt (see Exod. vi. 67, and the *Hagadah for Passover*) :—

והוצאתי ' והצלתי ' וגאלתי ' ולקחתי

"I will bring you, I will rid you, I will redeem you, I will take you."

30. There are *four* things the doing of which by man brings judgment upon his own head:—If he turn in between a wall and a date-palm; if he turn in between two date-palms; if he drink borrowed water; and if he step across spilt water, such even as his own wife may have thrown away. (All these doings, says Rashi, are bound to annoy the evil genii.)   *Ibid.*, fol. 111, col. 1.

31. *Four* precepts did our holy Rabbi (Yehudah Hakadosh) urge upon his children :—Not to choose Shechentzia * as a dwelling-place, for scoffers resided there ; not to use the bed of a Syrian odalisque ; not to shirk the payment of fiscal dues, lest the collector should confiscate all their property ; not to face an ox when he came up (ruffled) from the cane-brake, for Satan sported betwixt his horns.

P'sachim, fol. 112, col. 2.

32. Whosoever prieth into the *four* things in the matter of the chariot in Ezekiel's vision—what is above, what is beneath, what is before, or what is behind—it were better for him if he had never been born.

Chaggigah, fol. 11, col. 2.

Note.—The מעשה מרכבה, the *work* or *matter of the chariot,* the Rabbinic term for the Vision of Ezekiel, ranks among the *Arcana Judaica,* which are not to be told save to the initiated.

33. *Four* men entered Paradise—these are their names :—Ben Azai, Ben Zoma, Acher, and Rabbi Akiva. Rabbi Akiva thus warned his companions : " When you come across pavements of pellucid marble, do not cry out ' Water ! water ! ' for it is said (Ps. ci. 7), ' He that uttereth falsehood shall not dwell in my sight.' " Ben Azai looked and died ; concerning him the Scripture says (Ps. cxvi. 15), " Precious in the sight of the Lord is the death of his saints." Ben Zoma looked and went out of his mind ; of him the Scripture says (Prov. xxv. 16), " Hast thou found honey ? eat only so much as is sufficient for thee, lest thou be filled therewith and vomit it." Acher cut the plants. Only Akiva departed in peace. *Ibid.,* fol. 14, col. 2.

Note.—*Rashi* explains this by saying these men *went up to heaven;* but Maimonides much more rationally teaches that *the Paradise* (פרדס) or *garden* here is merely the retreat of profound philosophic meditation. These *five*

* Shechentzia is the name of a place near Nahardaa. See " La Géographie du Talmud," by Dr. A. Neubauer, p. 363.

intuitions were technically styled the הפרדס:—(1.) *To know that there is a God; (2.) to ignore every other beside Him; (3.) to feel His unity; (4.) to love His person; and (5.) to stand in awe of His Majesty* (see Yad Hachaz., chap. 4, sec. 19). Deep thought in these matters was spoken of by the Rabbis as *promenading in the garden.*

34. *Four* times a year is the world subject to an ordeal of judgment:—At Passover, which is decisive of the fruits of the field; at Pentecost, which is decisive of the fruits of the garden; at the feast of Tabernacles, which is decisive in respect of rain; on New Year's Day, when all who come into the world pass before the Lord like sheep, as it is said (Ps. xxxiii. 15), "Who formed their hearts together; who understandeth all their works."

Rosh Hashanah, fol. 16, col. 1.

35. There are *four* varieties of cedar:—Erez, Karthom, Etz-Shemen, and Berosh.   *Ibid.*, fol. 23, col. 1.

36. Ben Kamzar would not teach the art of writing, and yet it is related of him that he could, by taking *four* pens between his fingers, write off a word of four letters at one stroke.   *Yoma*, fol. 38, col. 2.

37. There are *four* kinds of quails:—Sichli, Kibli, Pisyoni, and the common quail. The first was of superior quality, and the last inferior.   *Ibid.*, fol. 75, col. 2.

38. A man may obtain forgiveness after the third transgression, but if he repeat the offence a fourth time, he is not pardoned again; for it is said (Amos ii. 4), "For three transgressions of Judah, and for *four*, I will not turn away the punishment thereof;" and again (Job xxxiii. 29), "Lo! all these things doth God *two* or *three* times" (*and so inferentially not four times*) "with man, to bring back his soul from the pit."   *Ibid.*, fol. 86, col. 2.

39. For *four* reasons does their property pass out of the

hands of the avaricious:—Because they are backward in paying the wages of their hired servants; because they altogether neglect their welfare; because they shift the yoke from themselves and lay the burden upon their neighbours; and because of pride, which is of itself as bad as all the rest put together; whereas of the meek it is written (Ps. xxxvii. 11), "The meek shall inherit the earth." *Succah*, fol. 29, col. 2.

40. "And the Lord showed me *four* carpenters" (Zech. i. 20). Who are these *four* carpenters? Rav Chana bar Bizna says that Rabbi Shimon Chassida said they were Messiah the son of David, Messiah the son of Joseph, Elijah, and the Priest of Righteousness.

Ibid., fol. 52, col. 2.

41. No Synagogue is to be sold except on condition that there be power of re-purchase. These are the words of Rabbi Meir; but the sages say it may be sold unconditionally, except in these *four* particular cases: that it be not turned into a bath-house, a tannery, a wash-house, or a laundry. *Meggillah*, fol. 27, col. 2.

42. Rabbi Yochanan ben Zachai was once asked by his disciples how he had attained such length of days. "Never once," he said, " in my life השתנתי מים within *four* cubits of a place where prayer is offered; never have I called a person by a wicked name; nor have I ever failed to sanctify the Sabbath over a cup of wine. Once my aged mother sold her head-dress to buy the consecration wine for me." *Ibid.*, fol. 27, col. 2.

43. When a sage is approaching, one should rise up before he gets within *four* ells' distance, and remain standing until he has gone as far past. When a chief magistrate is about to pass, one must rise as soon as he comes in sight, and not resume the seat until he has passed *four* ells. When a prince passes, one must stand up whenever

he appears, and not sit down again until the prince himself is seated; for it is said (Exod. xxxiii. 8), "All the people rose up, . . . and looked after Moses *until* he was gone *into* the tabernacle." *Kiddushin*, fol. 33, col. 2.

44. When Nero came to the Holy Land, he tried his fortune by *belemnomancy* thus:—He shot an arrow eastward, and it fell upon Jerusalem; he discharged his shafts towards the *four* points of the compass, and every time they fell upon Jerusalem. After this he met a Jewish boy, and said unto him, "Repeat to me the text thou hast learned to-day." The boy repeated, "I will lay my vengeance upon Edom (*i.e.,* Rome) by the hand of my people Israel" (Ezek. xxv. 14). Then said Nero, "The Holy One—blessed be He!—has determined to destroy His Temple and then avenge Himself on the agent by whom its ruin is wrought." Thereupon Nero fled and became a Jewish proselyte, and Rabbi Meir is of his race.

Gittin, fol. 56, col. 1.

45. They whose banquet is accompanied with *four* kinds of instruments of music bring five calamities on the world; as it is said (Isa. v. 11–15), "Woe unto those that get up early in the morning, that they may run after strong drink; and continue until late at night, till flushed with wine. And the harp and psaltery, tambourine and flute, and wine are at their carousals." *Soteh*, fol. 48, col. 1.

46. Let him carry the purse, and halt every time he accomplishes less than *four* cubits forward.

Shabbath, fol. 153, col. 1, 2.

Note.—Rav Yitzchak here explains how the good Jew, belated on Sabbath-eve, may carry his purse himself, and so save his conscience. The traveller is to halt at about every other step, and so measure off the journey in *four-cubit stages.*

47. Though ever since the destruction of the Temple the Sanhedrin has ceased to exist, the *four* kinds of capital

punishment have not failed to assert themselves. If a man incurs the penalty of death by stoning, he is in the course of Providence either punished by a fatal fall from a roof or slain by some beast of prey; if he has exposed himself to the penalty of death by burning, it happens that he is either burned to death in the end or mortally stung by a serpent; if the penalty of the law is that he should be beheaded for his offence, he meets his death either from the Government officer or by the hand of an assassin; if the penalty be strangulation, he is sure to be drowned or suffocated. *Sanhedrin*, fol. 37, col. 2.

48. When a person is in a state of apprehension and cannot make out the cause of it (the star that presided at his birth and his genii know all about it), what should he do? Let him jump from where he is standing *four* cubits, or else let him repeat, "Hear, O Israel," &c. (Deut. vi. 4); or if the place be unfit for the repetition of Scripture, let him mutter to himself, "The goat at the butcher's is fatter than me." *Ibid.*, fol. 94, col. 1.

49. It is written in 2 Chron. xxxiii. 7, "A carved image;" and again it is written in verse 19, "Graven images." Rabbi Yochanan said, "At first he made the image with one face, but afterwards he made it with *four—four*, so that the Shechinah might see it from every point, and thus be exasperated." *Ibid.*, fol. 103, col. 2.

50. Moses uttered *four* judgments upon Israel, but *four* prophets revoked them:—(1.) First *Moses* said (Deut. xxxiii. 28), "Israel then shall dwell in safety alone;" then came *Amos* and set it aside (Amos vii. 5), "Cease, I beseech thee," &c.; and then it is written (verse 6), "This shall not be, saith the Lord." (2.) First *Moses* said (Deut. xxviii. 65), "Among these nations thou shalt find no ease;" then came *Jeremiah* and set this saying aside (Jer. xxxi. 2), "Even Israel, when I went to cause him to rest." (3.)

First *Moses* said (Exod. xxxiv. 7), " Visiting the iniquities of the fathers upon the children ;" then came *Ezekiel* and set this aside (Ezek. xviii. 4), " The soul that sinneth, it shall die."   (4.) First *Moses* said (Lev. xxvi. 38), " And ye shall perish among the heathen;" then came *Isaiah* and reversed this (Isa. xxvii. 13), " And it shall come to pass in that day that the great trumpet shall be blown, and they shall come which were ready to perish."

Maccoth, fol. 24, col. 1.

51. When Akavyah ben Mahalalel appealed to *four* halachahs contradicting the judgment of the wise on a certain important point of law, " Retract," they said, " and we will promote thee to be president of the tribunal."   To which he replied, " I would rather be called a fool all the days of my life than be judged wicked for one hour before Him who is omnipresent."   *Edioth*, chap. 5, mish. 6.

52. Let thy house be open wide towards the south, the east, the west, and the north, just as Job, who made *four* entrances to his house, in order that the poor might find entrance without trouble from whatever quarter they might come.   *Avoth d'Rav Nathan*, chap. 7.

53. Rabbah once saw a sea-monster on the day it was brought forth, and it was as large as Mount Tabor.   And how large is Mount Tabor ?   *Four miles* ארבע פרסי.   Its neck was three miles long, and where it laid its head a mile and a half.   Its dung choked up the Jordan, till, as Rashi says, its waters washed it away.

Bava Bathra, fol 73, col. 2.

54. Shemuel said, " We know remedies for all maladies except three :—That induced by unripe dates on an empty stomach; that induced by wearing a damp linen rope round one's loins; and that induced by falling a sleep after meals without having first walked a distance of at least *four* cubits " (see 23 supra).

Bava Metzia, fol. 113, col. 2.

CHAPTER V.

THE 'FIVES' OF THE TALMUD.

1. THE *five* times repeated " Bless the Lord, O my soul " (Ps. ciii. civ.), were said by David with reference both to God and the soul. As God fills the whole world, so does the soul fill the whole body ; as God sees and is not seen, so the soul sees and is not seen ; as God nourishes the whole world, so does the soul nourish the whole body ; as God is pure, so also is the soul pure ; as God dwelleth in secret, so does the soul dwell in secret. Therefore let him who possesses these *five* properties praise Him to whom these *five* attributes belong. *Berachoth*, fol. 10, col. 1.

2. *Five* things have in them a sixtieth part of *five* other things :—Fire, honey, the Sabbath, sleep, and dreams. Fire is a sixtieth of hell, honey a sixtieth of manna, the Sabbath a sixtieth of the rest in the world to come, sleep the sixtieth of death, and a dream the sixtieth of prophecy. *Ibid.*, fol. 57, col. 2.

3. There are *five* weak things that are a source of terror to the strong :—The mosquito is a terror to the lion, the gnat is a terror to the elephant, the ichneumon-fly is a terror to the scorpion, the flycatcher is a terror to the eagle, and the stickleback is a terror to the leviathan.*

Shabbath, fol. 77, col. 2.

* Dr. Lewysohn of Worms has published a very able work in German on the Zoology of the Talmud.

F

4. These *five* should be killed even on the Sabbath :—
The fly of Egypt, the wasp of Nineveh, the scorpion of
Hadabia, the serpent of the land of Israel, and the mad
dog anywhere and everywhere.

Shabbath, fol. 121, col. 2.

5. *Five* things did Canaan teach his children :—To love
one another, to perpetrate robbery, to practise wantonness,
to hate their masters, and not to speak the truth.

P'sachim, fol. 113, col. 2.

6. *Five* things were in the first Temple which were not
in the second :—The ark and its cover, with the cherubim ;
the fire ; the Shechinah ; the Holy Spirit ; and the Urim
and Thummim.　　*Yoma*, fol. 21, col. 2.

7. *Five* things are said respecting the mad dog :—Its
mouth gapes wide, it drops its saliva, its ears hang down,
its tail is curled between its legs, and it slinks along
the side of the road.　Rav says that a dog's madness is
caused by witches sporting with it.　Samuel says it is
because an evil spirit rests upon it.　*Ibid.*, fol. 83, col. 2.

8. When a man has betrothed one of *five* women, and
does not remember which of the five it is, while each of
them claims the right of betrothment, then he is in
duty bound to give to each a bill of divorcement, and to
distribute the dowry due to one among them all.　This
decision is according to Rabbi Tarphon, but Rabbi Akiva
holds that he must not only divorce each, but give to each
the legal dowry, otherwise he fails in his duty.

Yevamoth, fol. 118, col. 2.

9. When a person having robbed one of *five* does not
remember which of the five it was he had robbed, and each
claims to have been the victim of the robbery, then he is to
part the stolen property (or the value of it) among them
all, and go his way.　So says Rabbi Tarphon, but Rabbi

Akiva argues that the defaulter does not in this way fully exonerate himself; he must restore to each and all the full value of the plunder. *Yevamoth*, fol. 118, col. 2.

10. *Five* things are said concerning garlic :—It nourishes, it glows inwardly, it brightens the complexion, it increases virility, and kills the כינים שבבני מעיים. Some say that it is a philtre for love, and that it exterminates jealousy (see No. 21 *infra*). *Bava Kama*, fol. 82, col. 1.

> NOTE.—Garlic was in high repute in Egypt, where the Israelites may have learned to appreciate it. Dioscorides (Book i. p. 80) says—
>
> > " The gods were recommended by their taste ;
> > Such savoury deities must needs be good
> > Which served at once for worship and for food."
>
> Juvenal makes this the *point d'appui* of one of his sarcastic pieces (Sat. 15)—
>
> > " How Egypt, mad with superstition grown,
> > Makes gods of monsters, but too well is known.
> > 'Tis mortal sin an onion to devour ;
> > *Each clove of garlic has a sacred power.*
> > Religious nation, sure and blest abodes,
> > Where every garden is o'errun with gods."

11. *Five* things cause forgetfulness :—Partaking of what has been gnawed by a mouse or a cat, eating bullock's heart, habitual use of olives, drinking water that has been washed in, and placing the feet one upon the other while bathing. *Horayoth*, fol. 13, col. 2.

12. *Five* things restore the memory again :—Bread baked upon coals, soft-boiled eggs without salt, habitual use of olive oil, mulled wine, and plenty of salt. *Ibid.*

13. He who does not cheer the bridegroom whose wedding breakfast he has enjoyed transgresses against the *five* voices (mentioned in Jer. xxxiii. 11):—" The voice of joy, the voice of gladness, the voice of the bridegroom, and the voice of the bride, the voice of them that shall say ' Praise ye the Lord of Hosts.' " *Berachoth*, fol. 6, col. 2.

14. Mount Sinai had *five* names :—(1.) Wilderness of *Zin*, because on it the Israelites were *commanded* to observe the law; (2.) Wilderness of *Kadesh*, because on it the Israelites were *consecrated* to receive the law; (3.) Wilderness of *Kedemoth*, because *precedence* was there given to Israel over all other nations; (4.) Wilderness of *Paran*, because there the Israelites were *fruitful* and multiplied; (5.) Wilderness of *Sinai*, because from it *enmity* came to be cherished to the Gentiles. It was denominated *Horeb* according to Rabbi Abhu, because from it came down *destruction* to the Gentiles.

Shabbath, fol. 89, cols. 1, 2.

15. Mar (the master) has said, "From dawn to the appearance of the sun is *five* miles" (מילין, from Lat. *mille* = a thousand, that is, a thousand paces). How is this proved? It is written (Gen. xix. 15), "When the dawn arose the angels hurried Lot;" and it is added (verse 25), "The sun was risen upon the earth when Lot entered into Zoar." And Rabbi Chanena said, "I myself have seen that place, and the distance is *five* miles."

P'sachim, fol. 93, col. 2.

16. He that cooks in milk the ischiadic sinew (גיד הנשה) on an annual festival is to be scourged *five* times forty stripes save one:—For cooking the sinew, for eating the sinew, for cooking flesh in milk, for eating flesh cooked in milk, and for lighting the fire.   *Baitza,* fol. 12, col. 1.

NOTE.—To this very day the גיד הנשה is extracted from the hind quarters of all animals before it is allowable for a Jew to eat them. This operation, in popular parlance, is termed *porging.*

17. The mysteries of the law are not to be communicated except to those who possess the faculties of these *five* in combination :—"The captain of fifty, and the honourable man, and the counsellor, and the cunning artificer, and the eloquent orator" (see Isa. iii. 3).

Chaggigah, fol. 13, col. 1.

18. "Captain of fifty." This should be read, not captain of fifty, but captain of *five*, that is, such as knew how to manage the חמשה חומשי תורה, the *five-fifths of the law* (or Pentateuch).   *Chaggigah*, fol. 14, col. 1.

19. *Five* characteristics were ascribed to the fire upon the altar :—It crouched there like a lion, it shone as the sun, it was perceptible to the touch, it consumed liquids as though they were dry materials, it caused no smoke.

Yoma, fol. 21, col. 2.

20. How is it that the word ואכבד, "And I will be glorified," occurs in Hag. i. 8 without the letter ה, and yet it is read ואכבדה, as if it had the letter ה? It indicates the absence of *five* things from the second Temple which were to be found in the first (ה being the symbol that stands for 5). (1.) The ark, *i.e.*, the mercy-seat of the cherubim ; (2.) the fire from heaven upon the altar ; (3.) the visible presence ; (4.) the Holy Spirit (of *prophecy*, says Rashi) ; and (5.) the Urim and Thummim.   *Ibid.*

> NOTE.—How then, it may be asked, if these five tokens of the Divine presence and favour which rendered the first Temple so glorious were wanting in the second could it be said (Hag. ii. 9), "The glory of this latter house shall be greater than of the former"? It is a question which it is natural to ask, and it should be ingenuously answered. Is it that these were tending to usurp the place of the spiritual, of which they were but the assurance and the symbol, and darken rather than reveal the eternal reality they adumbrated ?

21. The Israelites relished any flavour they fancied in the manna except the flavour of these *five* things (mentioned in Num. xi. 59) :—"Cucumbers, melons, leeks, onions, and garlic" (see No. 10 *supra*).

Ibid., fol. 75, col. 1.

> NOTE.—The reason why exception was made with regard to the five things enumerated above is given by Rashi. "*Quia hæc illis quæ mammis infantes nutrire gravidisque solent, detrimentosa sunt.*"

22. *Five* things happened to our forefathers on the 17th of Tammuz, and *five* on the 9th of Ab. On the 17th of Tammuz (1.) the tables of the covenant were broken; (2.) the daily sacrifice was done away with; (3.) the city walls were cleft asunder; (4.) Apostumes burned the roll of the law, (5.) and set up an idol in the temple. On the 9th of Ab (1.) the decree was uttered that our ancestors should not enter the land of Canaan; both the (2.) first and the (3.) second Temple were destroyed; (4.) Byther was subjugated and (5.) the city was ploughed up.

Taanith, fol. 26, cols. 1, 2.

23. The Rabbis have taught where it is we learn that if one has *five* sons by *five* wives he is bound to redeem each and all of them. It is from what is taught in Exod. xxxiv. 20, where it is said, "*All* the *firstborn* of *thy sons* shalt thou redeem." *Kiddushin*, fol. 29, col. 2.

24. If Israel had not sinned they would have had no other Scriptures than המשה הומשי תורה, *the five-fifths of the law* (that is, the Pentateuch) and the book of Joshua, which last is indispensable, because therein is recorded how the land was distributed among the sons of Israel; but the remainder was added, " Because in much wisdom is much grief" (Eccles. i. 18). *Nedarim*, fol. 22, col. 2.

25. "If a man steal an ox or a sheep and kill it or sell it, *five* oxen shall be given in restitution for one ox, and four sheep for one sheep" (Exod. xxii. 1). From this observe the value put upon work. For the loss of an ox, because it involves the loss of labour, the owner is recompensed with *five* oxen; but for the loss of a sheep, which does no work, he is only recompensed with four.

Bava Kama, fol. 79, col. 2.

26. "And Esau came from the field, and he was faint" (Gen. xxv. 29). Rabbi Yochanan said that wicked man committed on that day *five* transgressions:—He committed

rape, committed murder, denied the being of God, denied the resurrection from the dead, and despised the birthright. *Bava Bathra*, fol. 16, col. 2.

27. There are *five* celebrated idolatrous temples, and these are the names of them:—The Temple of Bel in Babylon, the Temple of Nebo in Chursi, the Temple of Thretha in Maphog, the Temple of Zeripha in Askelon, and the Temple of Nashra in Arabia. When Rabbi Dimmi came from Palestine to Babylon he said there were others, viz., the Temple of Yarid in Ainbechi, and that of Nadbacha in Accho. *Avodah Zarah*, fol. 11, col. 2.

28. "And they *also* transgressed my covenant, which I have commanded them; and they *also* have taken of the accursed thing, and have *also* stolen, and dissembled *also*, and have *also* put it among their own stuff" (Josh. vii. 11). Rav Illaa says, in the name of Rav Yehudah ben Mispartha, the *fivefold* repetition of the particle *also* shows that Achan had trespassed against all the *five* books of Moses. The same Rabbi further adds that Achan had obliterated the sign of the covenant, for it is said in relation to him, "And they have also transgressed my covenant;" and with reference to circumcision, "He hath broken my covenant." *Sanhedrin*, fol. 44, col. 1.

29. He who eats an ant is flogged *five* times with forty stripes save one. *Maccoth*, fol. 16, col. 2.

30. Rabbi Akiva used to say there are *five* judgments on record each of twelve months' duration:—That of the deluge, that of Job, that of the Egyptians, that of Gog and Magog, and that of the wicked in hell. This last is said of those whose demerits outweigh their virtues, or those who have sinned against their bodies. *Edioth*, chap. 2, mish. 10.

31. *Five* possessions hath the Holy One—blessed be He!—purchased for Himself in this world:—(1.) The law is *one* possession (Prov. viii. 22); (2.) Heaven and earth is *one* possession (Isa. lxvi. 1, Ps. civ. 24); (3.) Abraham is *one* possession (Gen. xiv. 9); (4.) Israel is *one* possession (Exod. xv. 16); (5.) the Temple is *one* possession, as it is said (Exod. xv. 17), " The sanctuary, O Lord, Thy hands have established."   And it is also said (Ps. lxxviii. 54), " And He brought them to the border of His sanctuary, even to this mountain, which His right hand had purchased."

Avoth, chap. 6.

32. Rabbi Akiva says he who marries a woman not suited to him violates *five* precepts:—(1.) Thou shalt not avenge; (2.) thou shalt not bear a grudge; (3) thou shalt not hate thy brother in thy heart; (4.) thou shalt love thy neighbour as thyself; (5.) and that thy brother may live with thee.   For if he hates her he wishes she were dead, and thus he diminishes the population.

Avoth d'Rab Nathan, chap. 26.

33. *Five* have no forgiveness of sins:—(1.) He who keeps on sinning and repenting alternately; (2.) he who sins in a sinless age; (3.) he who sins on purpose to repent; (4.) he who causes the name of God to be blasphemed. The fifth is not given in the Talmud.   *Ibid.*, chap. 39.

34. He who has no fringes to his garment transgresses *five* positive commands (see Num. xv. 38, &c.; Deut. xxii. 12).   *Menachoth*, fol. 44, col. 1.

35. A learner who, after *five* years, sees no profit in studying, will never see it.   Rabbi Yossi says, after three years, as it is written (Dan. i. 4, 5), " That they should be taught the literature and the language of the Chaldeans," so educating them in three years.

Chullin, fol. 24, col. 1.

36. Any one who doeth any of these *five* things sinneth against himself, and his blood is upon his own head:—He that (1.) eats garlic, onions, or eggs which were peeled the night before; (2.) or drinks water drawn over night; (3.) or sleeps all night in a burying-place; (4.) or pares his nails and throws the cuttings into the public street; (5.) והמקיז דם ומשמש מטתו׃ *Niddah,* fol. 17, col. 1.

37. Rabbi Yossi said:—"Never once in all my life have the walls of my house seen the hem of my shirt; חמש בעילות בעלתי and I have planted *five* cedars (sons are figuratively so termed, see Ps. xcii. 12) in Israel—namely, Rabbis Ishmael, Eliezar, Chalafta, Artilas, and Menachem. Never once in my life have I spoken of my wife by any other name than *house,* and of my ox by any other name than *field.* In all my life I have never once gazed במילה שלי׃ *Shabbath,* fol. 118, col. 2.

CHAPTER VI.

THE 'SIXES' OF THE TALMUD.

1. *Six* things are a disgrace to a disciple of the wise:—
To walk abroad perfumed, to walk alone by night, to wear
old clouted shoes, to talk with a woman in the street, to
sit at table with illiterate men, and to be late at the synagogue.   Some add to these, walking with a proud step or
a haughty gait.   *Berachoth*, fol. 43, col. 2.

2. A soft-boiled egg is better than *six* ounces of fine
flour.   *Ibid.*, fol. 44, col. 2.

3. *Six* things are a certain cure for sickness:—Cabbage,
beetroot, water distilled from dry moss, honey, the maw
and the matrix of an animal, and the edge of the liver.

Ibid.

4. These *six* things are good symptoms in an invalid:—
Sneezing, perspiration, evacuation, seminal emission, sleep,
and dreaming.   *Ibid.*, fol. 57, col. 2.

5. *Six* things bear interest in this world and the capital
remaineth in the world to come:—Hospitality to strangers,
visiting the sick, meditation in prayer, early attendance
at the school of instruction, the training of sons to the
study of the law, and judging charitably of one's neighbours.   *Shabbath*, fol. 127, col. 1.

6. There are *six* sorts of tears, *three* good and *three* bad:
—Those caused by smoke, or grief, or constipation are

bad; and those caused by fragrant spices, laughter, and aromatic herbs are good.

Shabbath, fol. 151, col. 2; fol. 152, col. 1.

7. *Six* things are said respecting the illiterate (עַם הָאָרֶץ):—No testimony is to be borne to them, none is to be accepted from them; no secret is to be disclosed to them; they are not to be appointed guardians over orphans, nor keepers of the charity-box, and there should be no fellowship with them when on a journey. Some say also no public notice is to be given of their lost property. *P'sachim*, fol. 49, col. 2.

NOTE.—עַמֵּי הָאָרֶץ, here rendered "illiterate," are described in chap. ii. 4 numb. of this Miscellany. The expression means literally "people of the land," and was, there is reason to believe, originally applied to the primitive inhabitants of Canaan, traces of whom may still be found among the fellahin of Syria. They appear, like the aboriginal races in many countries of Christendom in relation to Christianity, to have remained generation after generation obdurately inaccessible to Jewish ideas, and so to have given name to the ignorant and untaught generally. This circumstance may account for the harshness of some of the quotations which are appended in reference to them.

(*a.*) He who aspires to be a fellow (חָבֵר) of the learned must not sell fruit, either green or dry, to an illiterate man, nor may he buy fresh fruit of him. He must not be the guest of an ignorant man, nor receive such an one as his guest. (*Demai*, chap. 2, mish. 2.)

(*b.*) Our Rabbis teach, Let a man sell all that he has and marry the daughter of a תַּלְמִיד חָכָם learned man. If he cannot find the daughter of a learned man, let him marry the daughter of one of the great men of his day. If he does not find such a one, let him marry the daughter of one of the heads of the congregation, or, failing this, the daughter of a charity collector, or even the daughter of a schoolmaster; but let him not marry the daughter of an עַם הָאָרֶץ (*i.e.*, an illiterate man), for the unlearned are an abomination, as also their wives and their daughters. (*P'sachim*. fol. 49, col. 2.)

(*c.*) It is said that Rabbi (the Holy) teaches that it is illegal for an unlearned man to eat animal food, for it is said (Lev. xi. 46), " This is the *law* of the *beast* and the fowl ; " therefore he who studies the law may eat animal food, but he who does not study the law may not. Rabbi Eliezar said, " It is lawful to split open the nostrils of an unlearned man, even on the Day of Atonement which happens to fall on a Sabbath." To which his disciples responded, " Rabbi, say rather *to slaughter him.*" He replied, " Nay, that would require the repetition of the usual benediction ; but in tearing open his nostrils no benedictory formula is needed." Rabbi Eliezar has also said, " It is unlawful to travel with such a one, for it is said (Deut. xxx. 20), ' For it is thy life and the length of thy days.' The unlearned does not ensure his own life (since he has no desire to study the law, which would prolong life), how much less then will he regard the life of his neighbour ? " Rabbi Samuel, son of Nachman, says on behalf of Rabbi Yochanan, that it is lawful to split open an unlearned man like a fish. " Aye," adds Rabbi Samuel, " and that *from his back.*" (*Ibid.,* fol. 49, col. 2.)

(*d.*) Rav Yehudah says it is good to eat the pulp of a pumpkin with beetroot as a remedy, also the essence of hemp seed in Babylonian broth ; but it is not lawful to mention this in the presence of an illiterate man, because he might derive a benefit from the knowledge not meant for him. (*Nedarim,* fol. 49, col. 1.)

(*e.*) No contribution or heave-offering should be given to an ignorant priest. (*Sanhedrin,* fol. 90, col. 2.)

(*f*) No boor (בור) can be pious, nor an ignorant man (עם הארץ) a saint. (*Avoth,* chap. 2, mish. 6.)

(*g*) Sleep in the morning, wine at mid-day, the idle talk of inexperienced youth, and attending the conventicles of the ignorant drive a man out of the world. (*Ibid.,* chap. 3, mish. 16.)

(*h.*) Rabbi Jonathan says, " Where do we learn that no present is to be made to an ignorant priest ? " In 2 Chron. xxxi. 4, for there it is said Hezekiah " commanded that all the people that dwelt in Jerusalem should give a portion *to the priests* and *to the Levites,* that they *might be strong in the law* of the Lord." He who firmly lays hold of the law has a claim to a portion, otherwise he has none. (*Chullin,* fol. 130, col. 2.)

(*i.*) The aged, if ignorant, grow weaker in intellect the older they become in years, for it is written (Job xii. 20), " He removeth away the speech of the trusty, and taketh

away the understanding of the aged" But it is not so
with them that are old in the study of the law, for the
older they grow the more thoughtful they become, and
the wiser, as it is said (Job xii. 12), " With the ancient
is wisdom, and in length of days understanding."
(*Kinnin*, chap. 3.)

(*j.*) The salutation of the ignorant should be responded
to quietly, and with a reluctant nod of the head.
(*Taanith*, fol. 14, col. 2.)

(*k.*) No calamities ever befall the world except such
as are brought on by the ignorant. (*Bava Bathra*, fol. 8,
col. 1.)

(*l.*) Rav Hunna's widow once appeared before Rav
Nachman as plaintiff in a lawsuit. " What shall I do?"
he said. " If I rise before her (to honour her as the
widow of a Rabbi), the defendant, who is an *amhuaretz*,
will feel uneasy; and if I don't rise I shall break the
rule which ordains that the wife of an associate is to be
treated as an associate." So he said to his servant,
" Loose a young goose over my head, then I'll get up."

Rav bar Sheravyah had a lawsuit with an *amhuaretz*
before Rav Pappa, who bade him be seated, and also
asked the other to sit down. When the officer of the
court raised the *amhaaretz* with a kick, בטש ביה ואוקמיה.
the magistrate did not request him to be seated again.
(*Shevuoth*, fol. 30, col. 2.)

8. *Six* things are said respecting demons. In three particulars they are like angels, and in three they resemble
men. They have wings like angels; like angels they fly
from one end of the world to the other, and they know the
future, as angels do, with this difference, that they learn
by listening behind the veil what angels have revealed to
them *within*. In three respects they resemble men. They
eat and drink like men, they beget and increase like men,
and like men they die. *Chaggigah*, fol. 16, col. 1.

Note.—The Talmud is particularly rich in demonology, and
many are the forms which the evil principle assumes in
its pages. We have no wish to drag these shapes to the
light, and interrogate them as to the part they play in
this intricate life. Enough now if we mention the circumstance of their existence, and introduce to the reader
the story of Ashmedai, the king of the demons. The

story is worth relating, both for its own sake and its historical significance.

In Ecclesiastics ii. 8, we read, " I gat me men singers and women singers, the delights of the sons of men, as *musical instruments, and that of all sorts.*" These last *seven* words represent only two in the original Hebrew, שרה ושדות, *Shiddah-veshiddoth.* These two words in the original Hebrew translated by the last *seven* in this verse, have been a source of great perplexity to the critics, and their exact meaning is matter of debate to this hour. They in the West say they mean severally carriages for lords and carriages for ladies, while we, says the Babylonish Talmud, interpret them to signify male demons and female demons. Whereupon, if this last is the correct rendering, the question arises, for what purpose Solomon required them? The answer is to be found in 1 Kings vi. 7, where it is written, " And the house, when it was in building, was built of stone made ready before it was brought thither," &c. For before the operation commenced Solomon asked the Rabbis, " How shall I accomplish this without using tools of iron ? " and they remembering of an insect which had existed since the creation of the world, whose powers were such as the hardest substances could not resist, replied, " There is the *Shameer,* with which Moses cut the precious stones of the Ephod." Solomon asked, " And where, pray, is the Shameer to be found ? " To which they made answer, "אייתי שידה ושידתין, *Let a male demon and a female come,* and do thou coerce them both ; mayhap they know and will reveal it to thee." He then conjured into his presence a male and a female demon, and proceeded to torture them, but in vain, for said they, " We know not its whereabouts and cannot tell ; perhaps Ashmedai, the king of the demons, knows." On being further interrogated as to where he in turn might be found, they made this answer : " In yonder mount is his residence ; there he has dug a pit, and, after filling it with water, covered it over with a stone, and sealed with his own seal. Daily he ascends to heaven and studies in the school of wisdom there, then he comes down and studies in the school of wisdom here ; upon which he goes and examines the seal, then opens the pit, and after quenching his thirst, covers it up again, re-seals it, and takes his departure.'

Solomon thereupon sent Benaiah, the son of Jehoiada,

provided with a magic chain and ring, upon both of which the name of God was engraved. He also provided him with a fleece of wool and sundry skins with wine. Then Benaiah went and sank a pit below that of Ashmedai, into which he drained off the water and plugged the duct between with the fleece. Then he set to and dug another hole higher up with a channel leading into the emptied pit of Ashmedai, by means of which the pit was filled with the wine he had brought. After levelling the ground so as not to rouse suspicion, he withdrew to a tree close by, so as to watch the result and wait his opportunity. After a while Ashmedai came, and examined the seal, when, seeing it all right, he raised the stone, and to his surprise found wine in the pit. For a time he stood muttering and saying, it is written, " Wine is a mocker : strong drink is raging, and whosoever is deceived thereby is not wise." And again, " Whoredom and wine and new wine take away the heart." Therefore at first he was unwilling to drink, but being thirsty, he could not long resist the temptation. He proceeded to drink therefore, when, becoming intoxicated, he lay down to sleep. Then Benaiah came forth from his ambush, and stealthily approaching, fastened the chain round the sleeper's neck. Ashmedai, when he awoke, began to fret and fume, and would have torn off the chain that bound him, had not Benaiah warned him, saying, " The name of thy Lord is upon thee." Having thus secured him, Benaiah proceeded to lead him away to his sovereign master. As they journeyed along they came to a palm-tree, against which Ashmedai rubbed himself, until he uprooted it and threw it down. When they drew near to a hut, the poor widow who inhabited it came out and entreated him not to rub himself against it, upon which, as he suddenly bent himself back, he snapt a bone of his body, and said, " This is that which is written (Prov. xxv. 15), ' And a gentle answer breaketh the bone.' " Descrying a blind man straying out of his way, he hailed him and directed him aright. He even did the same service to a man overcome with wine, who was in a similar predicament. At sight of a wedding party that passed rejoicing along, he wept ; but he burst into uncontrollable laughter when he heard a man order at a shoemaker's stall a pair of shoes that would last seven years ; and when he saw a magician at his work he broke forth into shrieks of scorn.

On arriving at the royal city, three days were allowed to pass before he was introduced to Solomon. On the first day he said, "Why does the king not invite me into his presence?" "He has drunk too much," was the answer, "and the wine has overpowered him." Upon which he lifted a brick and placed it upon the top of another. When this was communicated to Solomon, he replied, "He meant by this, go and make him drunk again." On the day following he asked again, "Why does the king not invite me into his presence?" They replied, "He has eaten too much." On this he removed the brick again from the top of the other. When this was reported to the king, he interpreted it to mean, "Stint him in his food."

After the third day, he was introduced to the king; when measuring off four cubits upon the floor with the stick he held in his hand, he said to Solomon, "When thou diest, thou wilt not possess in this world (he referred to the grave) more than four cubits of earth. Meanwhile thou hast conquered the world, yet thou wert not satisfied until thou hadst overcome me also." To this the king quietly replied, "I want nothing of thee, but I wish to build the Temple and have need of the *Shameer*." To which Ashmedai at once answered, "The Shameer is not committed in charge to me, but to the Prince of the Sea, and he intrusts it to no one except to the great wild cock, and that upon an oath that he return it to him again." Whereupon Solomon asked, "And what does the wild cock do with the Shameer?" To which the demon replied, "He takes it to a barren rocky mountain, and by means of it he cleaves the mountain asunder, into the cleft of which, formed into a valley, he drops the seeds of various plants and trees, and thus the place becomes clothed with verdure and fit for habitation." This is the *Shameer* (Lev. xi. 19), נגר טורא, Nagger Tura, which the Targum renders *Mountain Splitter.*

They therefore searched for the nest of the wild cock, which they found contained a young brood. This they covered with *a glass*, that the bird might see its young, but not be able to get at them. When accordingly the bird came and found his nest impenetrably glazed over, he went and fetched the Shameer. Just as he was about to apply it to the glass in order to cut it, Solomon's messenger gave a startling shout, and this so agitated the bird that he dropped the Shameer, and Solomon's messenger caught it up and made off with it. The cock thereupon went and strangled himself, because he was unable to keep the oath by which he had bound himself to return the Shameer.

Benaiah asked Ashmedai why, when he saw the blind man straying, he so promptly interfered to guide him? "Because," he replied, "it was proclaimed in heaven that that man was perfectly righteous, and that whosoever did him a good turn would earn a title to a place in the world of the future." "And when thou sawest the man overcome with wine wandering out of his way, why didst thou put him right again?" Ashmedai said, "Because it was made known in heaven that that man was thoroughly bad, and I have done him a good service that he might not lose all, but receive some good in the world that now is." "Well, and why didst thou weep when thou sawest the merry wedding-party pass?" "Because," said he, "the bridegroom was fated to die within thirty days and the bride must needs wait thirteen years for her husband's brother, who is now but an infant" (see Deut. xxv. 5–10). "Why didst thou laugh so when the man ordered a pair of shoes that would last him seven years?" Ashmedai replied, "Because the man himself was not sure of living seven days." "And why," asked Benaiah, "didst thou jeer when thou sawest the conjuror at his tricks?" "Because," said Ashmedai, "the man was at that very time sitting on a princely treasure, and he did not, with all his pretension, know that it was under him."

Having once acquired a power over Ashmedai, Solomon detained him till the building of the Temple was completed. One day after this, when they were alone, it is related that Solomon, addressing him, asked him, "What, pray, is your superiority over us, if it be true, as it is written (Num. xxiii. 22), 'He has the strength of a unicorn,' and the word '*strength*,' as tradition alleges, means '*ministering angels*,' and the word '*unicorn*' means '*devils*'?" Ashmedai replied, "Just take this chain from my neck, and give me thy signet-ring, and I'll soon show thee my superiority." No sooner did Solomon comply with this request, than Ashmedai, snatching him up, swallowed him; then stretching forth his wings—one touching the heaven and the other the earth—he vomited him out again to a distance

of four hundred miles.   It is with reference to this time
that Solomon says (Eccl. i. 3 ; ii. 10), " What profit hath
a man of all his labour which he taketh under the sun ?
This is my portion of all my labour."   What does
the word *this* mean ?   Upon this point Rav and Samuel
are at variance, for the one says it means his *staff*, the
other holds that it means his *garment* or *water-jug ;*
and that with one or other Solomon went about from
door to door begging; and wherever he came he said
(Eccl. i. 12), " I, the preacher, was king over Israel in
Jerusalem."   When in his wanderings he came to the
house of the Sanhedrin, the Rabbis reasoned and said,
if he were mad he *would not* keep repeating the same
thing over and over again; therefore what does he
mean ?   They therefore inquired of Benaiah, " Does the
king ask thee into his presence ? "   He replied, " No ! "
They then sent to see whether the king visited the
hareem.   And the answer to this was, " Yes, he comes."
Then the Rabbis sent word back that they should look
at his feet, for the devil's feet are like those of a cock.
The reply was, " He comes to us in stockings."   Upon this
information the Rabbis escorted Solomon back to the
palace, and restored to him the chain and the ring, on
both of which the name of God was engraven.   Arrayed
with these, Solomon advanced straightway into the
presence-chamber.   Ashmedai sat at that moment on
the throne, but as soon as he saw Solomon enter, he
took fright, and raising his wings, flew away, shrieking
back into invisibility.   In spite of this, Solomon continued in great fear of him ; and this explains that which
is written (Song of Songs, iii. 7, 8), " Behold the bed
which is Solomon's ; threescore valiant men are about it,
of the valiant of Israel ; they all hold swords, being
expert in war ; every man has his sword upon his thigh,
because of fear in the night."   (See *Gittin*, fol. 68,
cols. 1, 2.)

Note.—Ashmedai, אשמדאי, is the *Asmodeus* (Ἀσμοδαῖος)
of the Book of Tobit, iii. 8, vi. 14, &c.   The
Shameer, שמיר, is mentioned in Jer. xvii. 1 ; Ezek.
iii. 9 ; Zech. vii. 12.   The Seventy in the former
passage and the Vulgate *passim* take it for the
diamond.   It is possibly allied to our word *emery*
(Greek, σμίρις or σμύρις).

9. *Six* things are said respecting the children of men,

in three of which they are like angels, and in three they are like animals. They have intelligence like angels, they walk erect like angels, and they converse in the holy tongue like angels. They eat and drink like animals, they generate and multiply like animals, and they relieve nature like animals. *Chaggigah,* fol. 16, col. 1.

10. *Six* months did the Shechinah hesitate to depart from the midst of Israel in the wilderness, in hopes that they would repent. At last, when they persisted in impenitence, the Shechinah said, " May their bones be blown ; " as it is written (Job xi. 20), " The eyes of the wicked shall fail, they shall not escape, and their hopes shall be as the blowing out of the spirit."

Rosh Hashanah, fol. 31, col. 1.

11. *Six* names were given to Solomon :—Solomon, Jedidiah, Koheleth, Son of Jakeh, Agur, and Lemuel.

Avoth d'Rab Nathan, chap. 39.

12. *Six* years old was Dinah when she gave birth to Asenath, whom she bore unto Shechem.

Sophrim, chap. 21.

13. " And the Lord blessed Obed-edom and all his household " (2 Sam. vi. 11). In what did the blessing consist ? Rav Yehudah bar Zavidah says it consisted in this, that Hamoth, his wife, and her eight daughters-in-law gave birth each to *six* children at a time, שילדו ששה בכרס אחד. (This is proved from 1 Chron. xxvi. 5, 8.)

Berachoth, fol. 63, col. 2.

14. *Six* things were done by Hezekiah the king, but the sages praised him for three only :—(1.) He dragged the bones of his father Ahaz on a hurdle of ropes, for this they commended him ; (2.) he broke to pieces the *brazen serpent,* for this they commended him ; (3.) he hid the ספר רפואות, *Book of Remedies,* and for this too they praised him. For three they blamed him :—(1.) He stripped the

doors of the Temple and sent the gold thereof to the King of Assyria; (2.) he stopped up the upper aqueduct of Gihon; (3.) he intercalated the month Nisan.

P'sachim, fol. 56, col. 1.

> NOTE.—The hiding of the Book of Remedies, harsh and inhuman as it might seem, was dictated by high moral considerations. It seemed right that the transgressor should feel the weight of his sin in the suffering that followed, and that the edge of judgment should not be dulled by a too easy access to anodyne applications. The reason for stopping the aqueduct of Gihon is given in 2 Chron. xxxii. 3, 4. The inhabitants of Jerusalem did the very same thing when the Crusaders besieged the city, A.D. 1099. Rashi tries to explain why this stratagem was not commended; the reason he gives is that Hezekiah ought to have trusted God, who had said (2 Kings xix. 34), "I will defend the city."

15. *Six* things are said of the horse:—It is wanton, it delights in the strife of war, it is high-spirited, it despises sleep, it eats much and it voids little. There are some that say it would fain kill its own master.

Ibid., fol. 113, col. 2.

16. The Rabbis have taught that there are *six* sorts of fire:—(1.) Fire that eats but drinks not, *i.e.*, common fire; (2.) fire that drinks but does not eat, *i.e.*, a fever; (3.) fire that eats and drinks, *i.e.*, Elijah, as it is written (1 Kings xviii. 38), "And licked up the water that was in the trench;" (4.) fire that burns up moist things as soon as dry, *i.e.*, the fire on the altar; (5.) fire that counteracts other fire, *i.e.*, like that of Gabriel; (6.) fire that consumes fire, for the Master has said (Sanhed., fol. 38, col. 2), "God stretched out His finger among the angels and consumed them," *i.e.*, by His own essential fire.

Yoma, fol. 21, col. 2.

17. For *six* months David was afflicted with leprosy; for it is said (Ps. li. 7), "Purge me with hyssop, and I shall be clean; wash me, and I shall be whiter than snow."*

---

* The use of hyssop is prescribed only in declaring a leper healed.

At that time the Shechinah departed from him; for it is said (Ps. li. 12), "Restore unto me the joy of Thy salvation;" and the Sanhedrin kept aloof from him, for it is said (Ps. cxix. 79), "Let those that fear thee turn unto me." That this ailment lasted six months is proved from 1 Kings ii. 11, where it is said, "And the days that David reigned over Israel were *forty* years; *seven* years he reigned in Hebron, and *thirty-three* years he reigned in Jerusalem;" whereas in 2 Sam. v. 5 it is said, "In Hebron he reigned over Judah *seven years and six months.*" The reason why these six months are omitted in Kings is because during that period he was afflicted with *leprosy.*

Sanhedrin, fol. 107, col. 1.

18. The tables of stone were *six* ells long, *six* broad, and *three* thick. *Nedarim,* fol. 38, col. 8.

> NOTE.—It may perhaps help the reader to some idea of the strength of Moses if we *work out* arithmetically the size and probable weight of these *stone slabs* according to the Talmud. Taking the אמה, cubit or ell, at its lowest estimate, that is eighteen inches, *each* slab, being *nine* feet long, *nine* feet wide, and *four and a half* feet thick, would weigh upwards of *twenty-eight tons,* reckoning *thirteen cubic feet to the ton,*—the right estimate for such stone as is quarried from the Sinaitic cliff. The figures
>
> $$\text{are } 9 \times 9 \times \frac{9}{2} = \frac{729}{2} = 364.5 \times 173.5 = 63240.75 = 28 \text{ tons,}$$
>
> 4 cwt., 2 qrs., 16 lbs. avoirdupois.

19. The Rabbis have taught that these *six* things possess medicinal virtue:—Cabbage, lungwort, beetroot, water, and certain parts of the offal of animals, and some also say little fishes. *Avodah Zarah,* fol. 29, col. 1.

20. Over *six* the Angel of Death had no dominion, and these were:—Abraham, Isaac, and Jacob, Moses, Aaron, and Miriam. Respecting the first *three* it is written, בכל, מכל, כל, "*in all*" (Gen. xxiv. 1), "*of all*" (Gen. xxvii. 33) "*all*" (A. V. "enough," Gen. xxxiii. 11). Re-

specting the last *three* it is written, עַל פִּי יְהוָה, "*by the mouth of Jehovah*" (see Num. xxxiii. 38, and Deut. xxxiv. 5).　　　　　*Bava Bathra*, fol. 17, col. 1.

> NOTE.—According to Jewish tradition, there are 903 kinds of death, as is elicited by a Kabbalistic rule called *gematria*, from the word תוֹצָאוֹת, *outlets* (Ps. lxviii. 20); the numeric value of the letters of which word is 903. Of these 903 kinds of death, the *divine kiss* is the easiest. God puts His favourite children to sleep, the sleep of death, by kissing their souls away. It was thus Abraham, Isaac, and Jacob fell asleep, as may be inferred from the word כֹּל, *all;* that is to say, *they had all the honour* God could confer upon them. Moses and Aaron fell asleep by the *divine kiss*, for it is plainly stated to have been עַל פִּי יְהוָה, "*by the mouth of Jehovah.*" So also Miriam passed away, only the Scripture does not say עַל פִּי יְהוָה, lest the scoffer should find fault. We are also informed that quinsy is the hardest death of all. (See *Berachoth*, fol. 8, col. 1.)

21. "These *six* of barley gave he me." What does this mean? It cannot surely be understood of *six barleycorns*, for it could not be the custom of Boaz to give a present of six grains of barley. It must, therefore, have been *six measures*. But was it usual for a woman to carry such a load as six measures would come to? What he intended by the number six was to give her a hint that in process of time *six* sons would proceed from her, each of which would be blessed with *six* blessings; and these were David, the Messiah, Daniel, Hananiah, Mishael, and Azariah. David, as it is written (1 Sam. xvi. 8), (1.) "Cunning in playing," (2.) "and a mighty and valiant man," (3.) "a man of war," (4.) "prudent in matters," (5.) "a comely person," (6.) and "the Lord is with him." The Messiah, for it is written (Isa. xi. 2), "And the Spirit of the Lord shall rest upon him," viz., (1.) "The spirit of wisdom and (2.) understanding, (3.) the spirit of counsel and (4.) might, (5.) the spirit of knowledge, and (6.) the fear of the Lord." Daniel, Hananiah, Mishael, and Azariah, for regarding them it is written (Dan. i. 4), (1.) "Young men in whom

was *no blemish*," (2.) " handsome in looks," (3.) "intelligent in wisdom," (4.) " acquainted with knowledge," (5.)
" and understanding science, and such as (6.) had ability
to stand in the palace of the king," &c.   But what is the
meaning of *unblemished ?*   Rav Chama ben Chanania says
it means that not even the scar of a lancet was upon
them.   *Sanhedrin*, fol. 93, cols. 1, 2.

Note.—(*a.*) The words "not even the scar of a lancet was
upon them," bespeak the prevalence of blood-letting in
the East, and the absence of the scar of the lancet on
the persons of Daniel and his companions is a testimony
to their health of body and moral temperance and purity.

(*b.*) In Taanith (fol. 21, col. 2) mention is made of
a certain phlebotomist—a noteworthy exception to the
well-known rule (see Kiddushin, fol. 82, col. 2) that
phlebotomists are to be regarded as *morally depraved*,
and in the same class with goldsmiths, perfumers, hair-
dressers, &c., — Abba Umna by name, who had a
special mantle with slits in the sleeves for females, so
that he could surgically operate upon them without seeing their naked arms, while he himself was covered over
head and shoulders in a peculiar cloak, so that his own
face could not by any chance be seen by them.

(*c.*) From Shabbath, fol. 156, col. 1, we learn that
a person born under the influence of מאדים, Maadim,
i.e., Mars, will in one way or another be a shedder of
blood, such as a *phlebotomist*, a butcher, a highwayman,
&c., &c.

22. The lion has *six* names (in Hebrew), viz., ארי, כפיר,
לביא, ליש, שחל, שחץ.   *Ibid.*, fol. 95, col. 1.

Note.—The foregoing are all Biblical terms, of which the
first five occur in Job iv. 10, 11 : " The roaring of the
lion (ארי), the voice of the fierce lion (שחל), and the
teeth of the young lion (כפיר) are broken ; the old lion
(ליש) perisheth for lack of prey, and the whelps of the
lioness (לביא) have to scatter themselves abroad." The
remaining term, שחץ, occurs in Job xxviii. 8.

23. The serpent has *six* names (in Hebrew), viz., נחש,
שרף, תנין, צפעוני, אפעה, עכשוב.
                    Avoth d'Rab. Nathan, chap. 39.

THE 'SEVENS' OF THE TALMUD.

1. HE who passes *seven* nights in succession without dreaming deserves to be called wicked.

Berachoth, fol. 14, col. 1.

2. Gehinnorn has *seven* names:—Sheol (Jonah ii. 2), Avadon (Ps. lxxxviii. 11), Shachath (Ps. xvi. 2), Horrible pit (Ps. xl. 2), Miry clay (Ps. xl. 2), the Shadow of death (Ps. cvii. 14), the Subterranean land. *Eiruvin*, fol. 19, col. 1.

3. A dog in a strange place does not bark for *seven* years. *Ibid.*, fol. 61, col. 1.

4. *Seven* things were formed before the creation of the world:—The Law, Repentance, Paradise, Gehenna, the Throne of Glory, the Temple, and the name of the Messiah.

P'sachim, fol. 54, col. 1.

NOTE.—The Midrash Yalkut (p. 7) enumerates the same list almost word for word, and the Targum of Ben Uzziel develops the tradition still further, while the Targum Yerushalmi fixes the date of the origin of the *seven* prehistoric wonders at "two thousand years before the creation of the world."

5. *Seven* things are hid from the knowledge of a man:— The day of death, the day of the resurrection, the depth of judgment (*i.e.*, the future reward or punishment), what is in the heart of his fellow-man, what his reward will be, when the kingdom of David will be restored, and when the kingdom of Persia will fall. *Ibid.*, fol. 54, col. 2.

6. *Seven* are excommunicated before heaven :—A Jew who has no wife, and even one who is married but has no male children; and he that has sons but does not train them up to study the law; he who does not wear phylacteries on his forehead and upon his arm and fringes upon his garment, and has no mezuzah on his doorpost; and he who goes barefooted.   *P'sachim*, fol. 113, col. 2.

> NOTE.—The first and second of these unhappy ones upon whom the ban of Heaven is said to rest are further commented on in this Miscellany, chap. 1, sec. 9, note; chap. 2, sec. 2, notes. The third case receives illustration from the Book of Zohar (Syn. Tit. 1), " He who takes his son morning and evening to the house of a Rabbi is as if he had twice received the law on Mount Sinai," &c.

7. There are *seven* skies :—Villon, Raakia, Shechakim, Zevul, Maaon, Maachon, and Aravoth.

Chaggigah, fol. 12, col. 2.

8. *Seven* days before the Day of Atonement they removed the high priest from his own residence to the chamber of the President (פרהדרין = πάρεδρον), and appointed another priest as his deputy in case he should meet with such an accident as would incapacitate him from going through the service of the day.   Rabbi Yehudah says they also had to betroth him to another woman lest his own wife should die meanwhile, for it is said, " And he shall make an atonement for himself and for his house,"—his *house*, that is, his *wife*.   In reference to this precautionary rule it was observed, there might then be no end to the matter (Rashi), should this woman die also.   *Yoma*, fol. 2, col. 1.

9. They associated with the high priest the senior elders of the Sanhedrin, who read over to him the *agenda* of the day, and then said to him, " My lord high priest, read thou for thyself; perhaps thou hast forgotten it, or maybe thou hast not learned it at all."   On the day before the Day of Atonement he was taken to the East Gate, when they caused oxen, rams, and lambs to pass before

him, that he might become well-versed and expert in his official duties. During the whole of the *seven* (preparatory) days neither victuals nor drink were withheld from him, but towards dusk on the eve of the Day of Atonement they did not allow him to eat much, for much food induces sleep. Then the elders of the Sanhedrin surrendered him to the elders of the priesthood, and these conducted him to the hall of the house of Abtinas, and there they swore him in; and after bidding him good-bye, they went away. In administering the oath they said, "My lord high priest, we are ambassadors of the Sanhedrin; thou art our ambassador and the ambassador of the Sanhedrin as well. We adjure thee, by Him who causes His name to dwell in this house, that thou alter not anything that we have told thee!" Then they parted, both they and he weeping. He wept because they suspected he was a Sadducee, and they wept because the penalty for wrongly suspecting persons is scourging. If he was a learned man he preached (during the night); if not, learned men preached before him. If he was a ready reader, he read; if not, others read to him. What were the books read over to him? Job, Ezra, and the Chronicles. Zechariah the son of Kevootal says, "I have often read before him the Book of Daniel." If he became drowsy, the juniors of the priestly order fillipped their middle fingers before him, and said, "My lord high priest, stand up and cool thy feet upon the pavement." Thus they kept him engaged till the time of slaughtering (the sacrifices). *Yoma*, fol. 18, cols. 1, 2; fol. 19, col. 2.

Note.—(*a.*) *Sacerdos nascitur, non fit,*—a priest is born, not made, we may truly say (just altering one word of a well-known proverb). His father was a priest, and so were his forefathers as far back as the time of Aaron; his sons and his sons' sons after him will belong to the priestly order, and so the name was far too often only the badge for exclusive and hereditary privilege. This rule, that applies to the כהנים (priests), holds good also with regard to the Levites. (*Berachoth*, fol. 29, col. 1.)

(*b.*) There was a town in the land of Israel called Gophnith,* where there were eighty couples of brother priests who married eighty couples of sister priestesses in one night. (*Berachoth*, fol. 44, col. 1.)

(*c.*) Flay a carcase and take thy fee, but say not it is humiliating because I am a priest, I am a great man. (*P'sachim*, fol. 113, col. 1.)

Note.—Philo Judæus, De Sac. Honor. (p. 833), says, "The hides of the burnt-offerings proved a rich perquisite of the priesthood."

(*d.*) The number of high priests who officiated in succession during the 410 years of the continuance of the first Temple was only *eighteen*, but the number who held office during the 420 years of the second Temple amounted to more than *three hundred*, most of them having died within a year after their entrance upon the office. The reason *naïvely* assigned by the Talmud for the long lives of the former and the short lives of the latter is the text given in Prov. x. 27, "The fear of the Lord prolongeth days, but the years of the wicked shall be shortened." (*Yoma*, fol. 9, col. 1.)

(*e.*) Before a priest could be admitted into active service in the Temple he had to undergo bodily inspection at the hands of the syndicate of the Sanhedrin. If they found the least defect in his body, even a mole with hair upon it, he was ordered to dress in black and be dismissed; but if he was perfectly free from blemish, he was arrayed in white, and at once introduced to his brother priests and official duties. (*Ibid.*, fol. 19, col. 1.)

(*f.*) The daughters of a male proselyte who has married the daughter of a female proselyte are eligible to marry priests. (*Yevamoth*, fol. 57, col. 1.)

(*g.*) If thou seest an impudent priest, think not evil of him; for it is said (Hosea iv. 4), "Thy people are as they that strive with the priest" (see chap. ii. p. 25, Note *c.*). (*Kiddushin*, fol. 70, fol. 2.)

(*h.*) So long as there is a diadem on the head of the priest, there is a crown on the head of every man. Remove the diadem from the head of the high priest and you take away the crown from the head of all the people. (This is a Talmudic comment on Ezek. xxi. 31; A. Ver., 26). (*Gittin*, fol. 7, col. 1.)

---

* Gophnith was a very populous place in Palestine. See "La Géographie du Talmud," by Dr. A. Neubauer.

(*i.*) A king shaved his head every day, a high priest did the same once a week, and an ordinary priest once a month. (*Sanhedrin*, fol. 22, col. 2.)

(*j.*) When a priest performs the service of the Temple in a state of defilement, his brother priests are not required to lead him before the tribunal, but the juniors of the priestly order are to drag him out into the hall and brain him with clubs. (*Ibid.*, fol. 81, col. 2.)

(*k.*) When kings were anointed, the holy oil was laid on the forehead in the form of a coronet (⩛), and when, says Rabbi Mansi bar Gadda, priests were anointed, the operation was performed in the shape of the Greek letter κ (κ). (*Horayoth*, fol. 12, col. 1.)

(*l.*) A learned man who is of illegitimate birth is preferable to an ignorant priest. (*Ibid.*, fol. 13, col. 1.)

(*m.*) A priest who makes no confession during service has no part in the priesthood. (He forfeits his emoluments). (*Menachoth*, fol. 18, col. 2.)

(*n.*) The bald-headed, the dwarfed, and the blear-eyed are ineligible for the priesthood. (*Bechoroth*, fol. 43, col. 2.)

(*o.*) Rav Chasda says, "The portions that fall to the priests are not to be eaten except roasted and that with mustard," because Scripture says (Num. xviii. 8), "by reason of the anointing," *i.e.*, by way of distinction, for only kings (who, of course, are anointed) eat roast meat with mustard. (*Chullin*, fol. 132, col. 2.)

(*p.*) If a case of mistaken identity should occur between the child of a priestess and the child of her female slave, so that the one cannot be distinguished from the other, they both are to eat of the heave-offering and to receive one share from the threshing-floor. When grown up, each is to set the other free. (*Gittin*, fol. 42, col. 2.)

(*q.*) From the old clothes of the priests the wicks were made for the lamps in the Temple. (*Shabbath*, fol. 21, col. 1.)

(*r.*) More on the subjects of priest, priestess, and priesthood may be found in "Exodus, according to the Talmud." One other item only we will add here. Scripture authority is given in proof that the very garments possessed the faculty of making atonement for sin every whit as effectually as animal sacrifices. We are taught that the priest's shirt atones for murder, his drawers atone for whoredom, his mitre for pride, his girdle for evil thoughts, his breastplate for injustice, his ephod for idolatry; his overcoat atones for slander, and the golden plate on his forehead atones for impudence. (*Zevachim*, fol. 88, col. 2.)

Note.—All this and a great deal more on the subject may be found in the Selichoth for Yom Kippur, notably in the prayer beginning אבל אנחנו חטאים.

10. For *seven* years was the land of Israel strewn with brimstone and salt. *Yoma*, fol. 54, col. 1.

11. "Then shall we raise against him *seven* shepherds" (Micah v. 5). Who are these seven shepherds? David in the middle; Adam, Seth, and Methuselah on his right hand; Abraham, Jacob, and Moses on his left.

Succah, fol. 52, col. 2.

12. Who were the *seven* prophetesses? The answer is, Sarah, Miriam, Deborah, Hannah, Abigail, Huldah, and Esther. *Meggillah*, fol. 14, col. 2.

13. It is lawful to look into the face of a bride for *seven* days after her marriage, in order to enhance the affection with which she is regarded by her husband, and there is no Halachah (or law) like this. *Kethuboth*, fol. 17, col. 1.

NOTE.—The Rabbis are especially careful to caution their daughters to guard against such habits as might lower them in the regard of their husbands, lest they should lose aught of that purifying and elevating power which they exercised as maidens. It is thus, for instance, Rav Chisda counsels his daughters: "Be ye modest before your husbands, and do not even eat before them. Eat not vegetables or dates in the evening, and touch not strong drink." מרגניתא אחוי להו וכורא לא אחוי להו עד דמצטערין. (*Shabbath*, fol. 140, col. 2.)

14. Once upon a time a demon in the shape of a *seven*-headed dragon came forth against Rav Acha and threatened to harm him, but the Rabbi threw himself on his knees, and every time he fell down to pray he knocked off one of these heads, and thus eventually killed the dragon.

Kiddushin, fol. 29, col. 2.

15. On the *seventh* of the month Adar, Moses died, and on that day the manna ceased to come down from heaven.

Kiddushin, fol. 38, col. 1.

> Note.—The *seventh* of Adar is still, and has long been, kept *sacred* as the day of the death of Moses our Rabbi—peace be with him!—and that on the authority of T. B. Kiddushin (as quoted above), and Soteh, fol. 10, col. 2; but Josephus (Book iv. chap. 8, sec. 49) most distinctly affirms that Moses died "*on the first day of the month*," and the Midrash on Esther may be quoted in corroboration of his statement. The probability is that the Talmud is right on this matter, but it is altogether wrong in connecting with this event the stoppage of the manna (see Josh. v. 10, 12).

16. *Seven* years did the nations of the world cultivate their vineyards with no other manure than the blood of Israel. Rabbi Chiya, the son of Abin, says that Rabbi Yehoshua, the son of Korcha, said, "An old man, an inhabitant of Jerusalem, related to me that Nebuzaradan, captain of the guard, killed in this valley 211 myriads (about 2,110,000), and in Jerusalem he slaughtered upon one stone 94 myriads (940,000), so that the blood flowed until it reached the blood of Zechariah, in order that that might be fulfilled which is said (Hosea iv. 2), ' And blood toucheth blood.' "

Gittin, fol. 57, col. 1.

> Note.—Historical facts like these speak for themselves and need no comment.

17. The *seventh* of Adar, on which Moses died, was the same day of the same month on which he was born.

Soteh, fol. 10, col. 2.

18. A male hyæna after *seven* years becomes a bat; this after *seven* years, a vampire; this after other *seven* years, a nettle; this after *seven* years more, a thorn; and this again after *seven* years is turned into a demon. If a man does not devoutly bow during the repetition of the daily prayer which commences מודים אנחנו, "we reverently acknowledge," his spine after *seven* years becomes a serpent.

Bava Kama, fol. 16, col. 1.

19. It is related of Benjamin the righteous, who was keeper of the poor-box, that a woman came to him at a period of famine and solicited food. " By the worship of God," he replied, " there is nothing in the box." She then exclaimed, " O Rabbi, if thou dost not feed me I and my *seven* children must needs starve." Upon which he relieved her from his own private purse. In course of time he fell ill and was nigh unto death. Then the ministering angels interceded with the Holy One—blessed be He!—and said, " Lord of the Universe, Thou hast said he that preserveth one single soul of Israel alive is as if he had preserved the life of the whole world ; and shall Benjamin the righteous, who preserved a poor woman and her *seven* children, die so prematurely ? " Instantly the death-warrant which had gone forth was torn up, and twenty-two years were added to his life.

Bava Bathra, fol. 11, col. 1.

20. *Seven* prophets have prophesied to the nations of the world, and these were Balaam and his father, Job, Eliphaz the Temanite, Bildad the Shuhite, Zophar the Naamathite, and Elihu the son of Barachel the Buzite.

Ibid., fol. 15, col. 2.

21. There are *seven* who are not consumed by the worm in the grave, and these are Abraham, Isaac, and Jacob, Moses, Aaron, and Miriam, and Benjamin the son of Jacob. *Ibid.,* fol. 17, col. 1.

22. *Seven* men form an unbroken series from the creation down to our own time. Methuselah saw Adam, Shem saw Methuselah, Jacob saw Shem, Amram saw Jacob, and Ahijah the Shilonite saw Amram, and Ahijah was seen by Elijah, who is alive to this day,

Ibid., fol. 121, col. 2.

23. *Seven* years' famine will not affect the artisan.

Sanhedrin, fol. 29, col. 1.

Note.—The Polish Jews have a saying parallel to this : מלאכה מלוכה, *i.e.,* " A trade is a kingdom."

24. *Seven* years of pestilence will not cause a man to die before his time.   *Sanhedrin*, fol. 29, col. 1.

25 "And it came to pass after *seven* days that the waters of the flood were upon the earth" (Gen. vii. 10). Why this delay of *seven* days? Rav says they were the days of mourning for Methuselah; and this teaches us that mourning for the righteous will defer a coming calamity. Another explanation is, that the Holy One—blessed be He!—altered the course of nature during these *seven* days, so that *the sun arose in the west and set in the east.*

Ibid., fol. 108, col. 2.

26. The first step in transgression is evil thought, the second scoffing, the third pride, the fourth outrage, the fifth idleness, the sixth hatred, and the *seventh* an evil eye.   *Derech Eretz Zuta*, chap. 6.

27. *Seven* things cause affliction :—Slander, shedding of blood, perjury, adultery, pride, robbery, and envy.

Erchin, fol. 17, col. 2.

28. A ram has but one voice while alive but *seven* after he is dead. How so? His horns make two trumpets, his hip-bones two pipes, his skin can be extended into a drum, his larger intestines can yield strings for the lyre and the smaller chords for the harp.

Kinnim, chap. 3, mish. 6.

29. Rav Chisda said, The soul of a man mourns over him the first *seven* days after his decease; for it is said (Job xiv. 22), "And his soul shall mourn over him."

Shabbath, fol. 152, col. 2.

Note.—In the context of this quotation there are several other interesting items of folk-lore on the same topic, of equal credibility with the above.

30. The Rabbis have taught that a man should not drink water on Wednesdays and Saturdays after night-

fall, for if he does, his blood, because of risk, will be upon his own head. What risk? That from an evil spirit who on these evenings prowls abroad. But if the man be thirsty, what is he to do? Let him repeat over the water the *seven* voices ascribed to the Lord by David in Psalm xxix. 3–9, "The voice of the Lord is upon the waters," &c.

P'sachim, fol. 112, col. 1.

31. *Seven* precepts did Rabbi Akiva give to his son Rabbi Yehoshua:—(1.) My son, teach not in the highest place of the city; (2.) Dwell not in a city where the leading men are disciples of the wise; (3.) Enter not suddenly into thine own house, and of course not into thy neighbour's; (4.) Do not go about without shoes; (5.) Rise early and eat in summer time because of the heat, and in winter time because of the cold; (6.) Make thy Sabbath as a week-day rather than depend for support on other people; (7.) Strive to keep on close friendly terms with the man whom fortune favours (lit. on whom the present hour smiles). Rav Pappa adds, "This does not refer to buying or selling, but to partnership." *Ibid.*

32. How is it proved that mourning should be kept up *seven* days? It is written (Amos viii. 10), "I will turn your feasts into mourning," and these in many cases lasted seven days. *Moed Katon*, fol. 20, col. 1.

NOTE.—The first instance of the שבעה, or *week* of mourning, dates much farther back than that of the Scripture authority here quoted for its observance. The mourning for Jacob (Gen. l. 10) and the mourning for Saul (1 Sam. xxxi. 13) may be cited among others. It may interest some of our readers to know that the שבעה is observed to this day.

33. Rav Chisda said there are *seven* kinds of gold:—Gold, good gold, the gold of Ophir, purified gold, beaten gold, shut-up gold, and gold of Parvain.

Yoma, fol. 44, col. 2.

NOTE.—The shut-up gold (זהב סגור, see the original in

1 Kings vi. 12) was of the purest and rarest quality, so that when it appeared in the market for sale, all shops in the locality were "*shut up*," for there could be no sale of any other gold before that. All gold-dealers "*shut up*" their shops in order to be present on so rare an occasion; and hence the name of this kind of gold— "*shut-up gold.*"

34. Each day of the Feast of Tabernacles they walked round the altar once, and said, "O Lord, save us, we beseech Thee! O Lord, prosper us, we beseech Thee!" But on the last day they encompassed it seven times. On their departure they said, "Beauty belongeth to thee, O altar! Beauty belongeth to thee, O altar!"

Succah, fol. 45, col. 1.

Note.—It deserves to be noted here for the information of some of our readers that the words נא הושיעה, translated above, *Save now,* or *Save, we beseech thee,* are the original of our word Hosanna. The 25th and 26th verses of Psalm cxviii., which begin with this expression, were repeated at the Feast of Tabernacles; and hence the bundles of palm and willow branches (carried on this occasion), the prayers, and the festival itself, were so named, *i.e.,* Hosanna.

35. The Tempter is known by *seven* distinctive epithets: —(1.) The Holy One—blessed be He!—calls him *evil;* as it is said, "For the imagination of man's heart is *evil.*" (2.) Moses calls him *uncircumcised;* as it is said (Deut. x. 16), "Circumcise therefore the *uncircumcised* foreskin of your heart." (3.) David calls him *unclean;* as it is said (Ps. li. 10), "Create in me a *clean* heart, O God!" Consequently there must be an *unclean* one. (4.) Solomon calls him *enemy;* as it is said (Prov. xxv. 21, 22), "If thine *enemy* hunger, give him bread to eat; if he be thirsty, give him water to drink; for thus thou shalt heap coals of fire upon his head, and the Lord shall reward thee," (*i.e.,* oppose him with the *law.* לחם, in the sense of bread, is metaphorically taken for the law, Prov. ix. 5, so that *give him water to drink* means also the *law,* Isa.

lv. 1—*Rashi.* *And the Lord reward thee*, read not *reward*, ישלם, but *cause him to make peace with thee*, ישלימנו, not to war against thee). (5.) Isaiah calls him *stumbling-block;* as it is said (Isa. lvii. 14), " Cast ye up, cast ye up, prepare the way, take up the *stumbling-block* out of the way of my people." (6.) Ezekiel calls him *stone;* as it is said (Ezek. xxxvi. 26), " I will take away the heart of *stone* out of your flesh and I will give you a heart of flesh." (7.) Joel calls him the *hidden one;* as it is said (Joel ii. 20), " I will remove far from you *the hidden one*," צפוני, *i.e.,* the tempter who remains hidden in the heart of man: " and I will drive him into a land barren and desolate," *i.e.,* where the children of men do not usually dwell; " with his face towards the former sea," *i.e.,* with his eyes set upon the first Temple, which he destroyed, slaying the disciples of the wise that were in it; " and his hinder part towards the latter sea," *i.e.,* with his eyes set on the second Temple, which he destroyed, also slaying the disciples of the wise that were in it. *Succah, fol. 52, col. 1.*

36. Once a Jewish mother with her seven sons suffered martyrdom at the hands of the Emperor. The sons, when ordered by the latter to do homage to the idols of the Empire, declined, and justified their disobedience by quoting each a simple text from the sacred Scriptures. When the seventh was brought forth, it is related that Cæsar, for appearance' sake, offered to spare him if only he would stoop and pick up a ring from the ground which had been dropped on purpose. " Alas for thee, O Cæsar ! " answered the boy; " if thou art so zealous for thine honour, how much more zealous ought we to be for the honour of the Holy One—blessed be He ! " On his being led away to the place of execution, the mother craved and obtained leave to give him a farewell kiss. " Go, my child," said she, " and say to Abraham, Thou didst build an altar for the sacrifice of one son, but I have erected altars for seven sons." She then turned away and threw herself down

headlong from the roof and expired, when the echo of a
voice was heard exclaiming (Ps. cxiii. 9), " The joyful
mother of children " (or, the mother of the children
rejoiceth). *Gittin,* fol. 57, col. 2.

> NOTE.—The story of this martyrdom is narrated at much
> greater length in the Books of Maccabees (Book iii.
> chap. 7, Book iv. chaps. 8–18).   In a Latin version the
> names are given, that of the mother Solomona, and her
> sons respectively Maccabeus, Aber, Machir, Judas,
> Achaz, Areth, while the hero of our Talmudic reference,
> the seventh and last, is styled Jacob.   Josephus, Ant.,
> Book xii. chap. 6, sec. 4, may also be referred to for
> further and varying details.

37. The land of Israel was not destroyed till the *seven*
courts of judgment (בתי דינין) had fallen into idolatry, and
these are they :—Jeroboam, the son of Nebat ; Baasha, the
son of Ahijah ; Ahab, the son of Omri ; Jehu, the son of
Nimshi ; Pekah, the son of Remaliah ; Menahem, the son
of Gadi ; and Hoshea, the son of Elah ; as it is written
(Jer. xv. 9), " She that hath borne *seven* languisheth : she
hath given up the ghost ; her sun is gone down while it
is yet day ; she hath been ashamed and confounded."

Ibid., fol. 88, col. 1.

38. " *He stood* and measured the earth ; *he beheld* and
freed the Gentiles (A.V., he drove asunder the nations,
Hab. iii. 6) ; *he beheld* that the *seven* precepts which the
children of Noah accepted were not observed ; *he stood
up* and set their property *free* for the service of Israel."

Bava Kama, fol. 38, col. 1.

> NOTE.—This is one of the weightier expositions met with
> from time to time in the Talmud, in which one recog-
> nises a more than ordinarily deep and earnest feeling
> on the part of the commentator.   The interpreter ex-
> presses himself as a man instinct with the exclusive
> Hebrew spirit, and as such claims his title to the whole
> inheritance.   It is a claim abstractly defensible, and the
> just assertion of it is the basis of all rights over others.
> The only question here is whether the Jew alone is

invested with the privilege. There can be little doubt
that the principle on which he claims enfeoffment in the
estate is a sound one, that the earth belongs in no case
to the sons of Belial, only to the sons of God.

39. *Seven* things distinguish an ill-bred man and *seven*
a wise man:—The wise man (1.) does not talk before his
superior in wisdom and years; (2.) he does not interrupt
another when speaking; (3.) he is not hasty to make reply;
(4.) his questions are to the point, and his answers are
according to the Halachah; (5.) his subjects of discourse
are orderly arranged, the first subject first and the last
last; (6.) if he has not heard of a thing, he says, I have
not heard it; and (7.) he confesseth the truth. The characteristics of the ill-bred man are just the contrary of these.

Avoth, chap. 5. mish. 10.

40. If a man does not work during the six days of the
week, he may be obliged to work all the *seven*.

Avoth d'Rab. Nathan, chap. 11.

41. *Seven* have no portion in the world to come:—A
notary, a schoolmaster, the best of physicians, a judge who
dispenses justice in his own native town, a wizard, a congregational reader (or law-officer), and a butcher.

Ibid., chap. 36.

Note.—The reason is these seven are apt to be in some cases
harsh, in others unjust, and in others unscrupulous.

42. *Seven* attributes avail before the Throne of Glory,
and these are:—Wisdom, righteousness, judgment, grace,
mercy, truth, and peace. *Ibid.*, chap. 37.

43. *Seven* epithets are applied to the earth in the Hebrew
language as follows:—ארץ · אדמה · ארקא · חרבה · יבשה ·
תבל · חלד. *Ibid.*

44. There are *seven* points in which a righteous man
excels another:—(1.) The wife of the one is more comely

than the other's; (2.) so are the children of the one as compared with those of the other; (3.) if the two partake of one dish, each enjoys the taste according to his doings; (4.) if the two dye in one vat, by one the article is dyed properly, by the other not; (5, &c.) the one excels the other in wisdom, in understanding, in knowledge, and stature, as it is said (Prov. xii. 26), "The righteous is more excellent than his neighbour."

Avoth d'Rab. Nathan, chap. 37.

45. *Seven* patriarchs were covenant-makers :—Abraham, Isaac, and Jacob, Moses, Aaron, Phinehas, and David.

Derech Eretz Zuta, chap. 1.

46. *Seven* liquids are comprehended under the generic term drink (Lev. xi. 34) :—Dew, water, wine, oil, blood, milk, and honey.   *Machshirin*, chap. 6, mish. 6.

47. For tertian fever take *seven* small grapes from *seven* different vines; *seven* threads from *seven* different pieces of cloth; *seven* nails from *seven* different bridges; *seven* handfuls of ashes from *seven* different fireplaces; *seven* bits of pitch from *seven* ships, one piece from each; *seven* scrapings of dust from as many separate doorways; *seven* cummin seeds; *seven* hairs from the lower jaw of a dog and tie them upon the throat with a papyrus fibre.

Shabbath, fol. 66, col. 2.

CHAPTER VIII.

THE 'EIGHTS' OF THE TALMUD.

1. THE Rabbis teach that the precept relating to the lighting of a candle at the Feast of Dedication applies to a whole household, but that those who are particular light a candle for each individual member, and those that are extremely particular light up *eight* candles on the first day, seven on the second, decreasing the number by one each day. This is according to the school of Shammai; but the school of Hillel say that he should light up *one* on the first day, two on the second, increasing the number by one each of the eight days of the feast. . . . What is the origin of the Feast of Dedication? On the twenty-fifth day of Kislev (about December), the eight days of the Dedication commence, during which term no funeral oration is to be made, nor public fast to be decreed. When the Gentiles (Greeks) entered the second Temple, it was thought they had defiled all the holy oil they found in it; but when the Hasmoneans prevailed and conquered them, they sought and found still one jar of oil stamped with the seal of the High Priest, and therefore undefiled. Though the oil it contained would only have sufficed for one day, a miracle was performed so that the oil lasted to the end of the week (during which time more oil was provided and consecrated for the future service of the Temple). On the anniversary of this occasion the Feast of Dedication was instituted.   *Shabbath*, fol. 21, col. 2.

NOTES.—(*a.*) The Feast of Dedication (חֲנֻכָּה, Chanuca, the ἐγκαίνια of John x. 22), is annually celebrated by all

Jews everywhere, to commemorate the purifying of the Temple and the restoration of its worship after its desecration by Antiochus Epiphanes, of which an account may be found in 1 Maccabees iv. 52–59. It is very probable that some of our Christmas festivities are only adaptations of the observances of this Jewish feast in symbolism of Christian ideas. During the eight days of the festival they light up wax candles or oil lamps, according to the rubric of the school of Hillel. Previous to the lighting, the following benedictions are pronounced :—

"Blessed art Thou, O Lord, our God! King of the universe, who hath sanctified us with Thy commandment, and commanded us to light the light of Dedication."

"Blessed art Thou, O Lord, our God! King of the universe, who wrought miracles for our fathers in those days and in this season."

"Blessed art Thou, O Lord, our God! King of the universe, who hath preserved us alive, sustained us, and brought us to enjoy this season."

(*b.*) After the lighting, the following form is repeated : —"These lights we light to praise Thee for the miracles, wonders, salvation, and victories which Thou didst perform for our fathers in those days and in this season by the hands of Thy holy priests. Wherefore by command these lights are holy all the eight days of the Dedication, neither are we permitted to make any other use of them, but to view them, that we may return thanks to Thy name for Thy miracles, wonderful works, and salvation."

(*c.*) Another commemorative formula is repeated six or seven times a day during this festival ; viz., during morning and evening prayers and after each meal.

2. Rabbi Yoshua ben Levi has said a man should never utter an indecent word, for the Scripture (Gen. vii. 6) uses eight letters more rather than make use of a word which, without them, would be indecent.

P'sachim, fol. 3, col. 1.

NOTE.—In the passage referred to, the words אשר איננה טהרה (*that* are *not clean*) are used instead of טמאה (unclean) ; but see verse 2 ; there another word for *not* (לא) is used, which brings down the excess to *five* letters.

3. When the doors of the Temple were opened the creaking of the hinges was heard at the distance of *eight* sabbath days' journeys. *Yoma*, fol. 39, col. 2.

NOTE—It may be proper to remind our readers that the תחום שבת is about nine furlongs, or one mile and one eighth, so that the distance alluded to is nearly *ten miles.*

4. The *eight* princes alluded to in Micah (v. 5) are Jesse, Saul, Samuel, Amos, Zephaniah, Zedekiah, the Messiah, and Elijah. *Succah*, fol. 52, col. 2.

5. It is related of Rabbi Shimon, the son of Gamaliel, that at the rejoicing during the festival of the drawing of water on the Feast of Tabernacles, he threw *eight* flaming torches, one after the other in quick succession, into the air, and caught them again as they descended without suffering one to touch another. He also (in fulfilment of Ps. cii. 14) stooped and kissed the stone floor, supporting himself upon his two thumbs only,—a feat which no one else could perform. And this is what is termed stooping properly. *Ibid.*, fol. 53, col. 1.

6. Levi once in the presence of Rabbi (the Holy) conjured with *eight* knives. Samuel in the presence of Shavur the king (of Persia, Sapor 1, 240–273) performed the same feat with *eight* cups of wine. Abaii in the presence of Rava did likewise with *eight* eggs; some say with four only. *Ibid.*

7. *Eight* prophets, who were priests as well, were descended from Rahab the harlot, and these are they:— Neraiah, Baruch, Seraiah, Maaseiah, Jeremiah, Hilkiah, Hanameel, and Shallum. Rabbi Yehudah says Huldah the prophetess was one of the grandchildren of Rahab.

Meggillah, fol. 14, col. 2.

8. The last *eight* verses of the Law (Torah) were written by Joshua. *Bava Bathra*, fol. 14, col. 1.

NOTE.—There is a touching story in this very same tract,

fol. 15, col. 1, which is repeated in Menachoth, fol. 30, col. 1, and noticed by Rashi in his commentary, to the effect that Moses himself wrote the verses which record his own death at the dictation of the Almighty. The account literally rendered is, "The Holy One—blessed be He!—spake, and Moses wrote in tears." הק״בה אומר ומשה כותב בדמע.

9. There are *eight* sects of Pharisees, viz., these :—(1.) The *shoulder* Pharisee, *i.e.*, he who, as it were, shoulders his good works to be seen of men. (2.) The *time-gaining* Pharisee, he who says, "Wait a while; let me first perform this or that good work." (3.) The *compounding* Pharisee, *i.e.*, he who says, "May my few sins be deducted from my many virtues, and thus atoned for," (or the *blood-letting* Pharisee, *i.e.*, he who for fear lest he should look by chance on a woman shuts his eyes and wounds his face). (4.) The Pharisee who so bends his back, stooping with his head towards the ground, that he wears the appearance of an inverted mortar. (5.) The Pharisee who proudly says, "Remains there a virtue which I ought to perform and have not?" (6.) The Pharisee who is so out of love for the reward which he hopes to earn by his observances. (7.) The Pharisee who is so from fear lest he should expose himself to punishment. (8.) The Pharisee who is born so.

Avoth d'Rab. Nathan, chap. 37.

Note.—Both Talmuds as a rule enumerate only seven sorts of Pharisees (T. Yerush, Berachoth, fol. 13, Sotah, fol. 20, T. Babli, fol. 22, col. 2, and elsewhere); but Rabbi Nathan, as above, adds a new species to the genus. The freehand sketches of Pharisees given in the Talmud are the reverse of complimentary; but rather than instance any more of them here, we prefer to subjoin the words of the late E. Deutsch, who was a Talmudist of no mean repute;—and who will venture to stigmatise these as *non versiones sed eversiones?* We quote from the "Quarterly Review," vol. cxxiii. p. 439. "The Talmud inveighs even more bitterly and caustically than the New Testament against what it calls 'the plague of Pharisaism,' 'the dyed ones,' 'who do evil deeds like Zimri, and require a goodly reward like

Phinehas,' ' they who preach beautifully, but do not act beautifully.' Parodying their exaggerated logical arrangements, their scrupulous divisions and subdivisions, the Talmud distinguishes seven classes of Pharisees, *one* of whom only is worthy of that name. The real and only Pharisee is he ' who does the will of his Father which is in heaven *because he loves Him.*' "

10. He who neglects to wear phylacteries transgresseth *eight* commandments. *Menachoth*, fol. 44, col. 1.

Note.—The following extract states the occasion when the wearing of phylacteries was prescribed as an equivalent that would be accepted instead of the observance of the law :—" Rabbi Eliezer said the Israelites complained before God one day, ' We are anxious to be occupied day and night in the law, but we have not the necessary leisure.' Then the Holy One—blessed be He !—said to them, ' Perform the commandment of the phylacteries, and I will count it as if you were occupied day and night in the law.' " (*Yalhut Shimeoni.*) Phylacteries, fringes, and Mezuzah, these three preserve one from sin ; as it is said (Eccl. iv. 2), " A threefold cord is not quickly broken ;" as also in Ps. xxxiv. 7, " The angel of the Lord encampeth about them that fear Him, and delivereth them." (*Menachoth*, fol. 43, col. 2.)

11. The harp in the time of the Messiah will have *eight* strings ; as it is written (Ps. xii. 1), " The chief musician upon eight," &c. *Eirchin*, fol. 13, col. 2.

CHAPTER IX.

THE 'NINES' OF THE TALMUD.

1. ON the *ninth* day of the month Ab (about August) both the *first* Temple and the second were destroyed.

Rosh Hashanah, fol. 18, col. 2.

> NOTE.—In 2 Kings xxv. 8, the *seventh* of Ab is the date given for the first of these events, whereas Jeremiah (lii. 12) mentions the *tenth* as the fatal day. *Josephus* (Wars of the Jews, Book vi. chap. 4, sec. 15) coincides with the latter. Query, which is right?

2. On the *ninth* of Ab one must abstain from eating and drinking, and anointing one's self, and wearing shoes, and matrimonial intercourse. He may not read the Bible, the Talmud, the Midrash, the Halachoth, or the Haggadoth, excepting such portions as he is not in the habit of reading, such he may then read. The Lamentations, Job, and the hard words of Jeremiah should engage his study. Children should not go to school on this day, because it is said (Ps. xix. 8), "The statutes of the Lord are right, rejoicing the heart." *Taanith*, fol. 30, col. 1.

> NOTE.—Nowadays, on the date referred to, Jews do not wear their *tallith* and *phylacteries* at morning prayer; by this act laying aside the outward signs of their covenant with God; but, contrary to custom, they put them on in the evening, when the fast is nearly over.

3. He who does any work on the *ninth* of Ab will never see even a sign of blessing. The sages say, whoso does any work on that day and does not lament over Jerusalem

will never see her joy ; for it is said (Isa. lxvi. 10), " Rejoice ye with Jerusalem, and be glad with her; rejoice for joy, all ye that mourn for her."   *Taanith*, fol. 30, col. 2.

4. If there be *nine* shops all selling the meat of animals which have been legally butchered, and *one* selling the meat of animals which have not, and if a person who has bought meat does not know at which of these shops he bought it, he is not entitled to the benefit of the doubt ; the meat he has purchased is prohibited.

Kethuboth, fol. 15, col. 1.

5. A woman prefers one measure of frivolity to *nine* measures of Pharisaic sanctimoniousness (פרישות).

Soteh, fol. 20, col. 1.

Note.—The Talmud has much to say, and does say a great
deal, about women. And although what it says tends
rather to discountenance than to promote their development, it is not insensible to what they might become
under refinement of culture, and occasionally enforces
the duty of attending to their higher education. In
proof of both positions we appeal to the following quotations :—
(*a*.) In the Mishna, from which the above quotation
is taken, we are told that Ben Azai (the son of impudence)
says, a man is bound to instruct his daughter in the law,
although Rabbi Eliezer, who always assumes an oracular
air, and boasts, שהלכה כמותו בכל מקום. *that the Haluchah
is always according to his decision* (*Bava Metzia*, fol. 59,
col. 2), insists, on the other hand, that he who instructs
his daughter in the law must be considered as training
her into habits of frivolity ; and the saying above ascribes
to the sex such a power of frivolity as connects itself
evidently with the foregone conclusion that they are by
nature incapable of being developed into any solidity of
worth or character. The Gemara, Tosephoth, and Rashi
as well all support Rabbi Eliezer in laying a veto on
female education, for fear lest, with the acquisition of
knowledge, women might become cunning, and do things
on the sly which ought not to be done by them. שמתוכה
היא מבינה ערמומית ועושה דברים בהצנע. Literally this
is :—For from it (*i.e.*, the acquisition of knowledge) she

comes to understand cunning, and does things on the quiet.　(*Soteh*, fol. 21, col. 2, Rashi.)

(*b.*) Another good reason for neglecting female education those who take the Talmud as an authority find in these words : נשים דעתן קלות עליהן, *women are light-minded, i.e,,* of shallow natural endowment, on which any serious discipline would be thrown away.　(*Kiddushin*, fol. 80, col. 2.)

(*c.*) Another argument to the same effect is, that there is no distinct command in the law of Moses inculcating the duty ; for in Deut. xi. 19 it is merely said, "And ye shall teach them to your children," a command which, as it passes refracted through the Rabbinic medium, becomes בניכם ולא בנותיכם, *your sons, but not your daughters.* (*Ibid.*, fol. 29, col. 2.)

(*d.*) As the immediately preceding command, so interpreted, cannot be carried out by any one not favoured with male children, the well-known Talmudic dictum acquires force and point, "Blessed is the man whose children are sons, but luckless is he whose children are daughters."　(*Bava Bathra*, fol. 16, col. 2.)

(*e.*) More on this topic may be found in "Genesis according to the Talmud" (chap. 2, ver. 23).

6. A man prefers one measure obtained by his own earning to *nine* measures collected by the exertion of his neighbour.　　　　　　　　*Bava Metzia*, fol. 38, col. 1.

Note.—This is thus explained by Rashi :—"His own *kab* (measure), the remnant of his own labour, is dearer to him than nine *kabs* of others, which he might buy with money were they offered in the market."

7. *Nine* have entered alive into paradise, and these are they :—Enoch, the son of Jared ; Elijah ; the Messiah ; Eliezer, the servant of Abraham ; Hiram, king of Tyre ; Ebed Melech, the Ethiopian ; Jabez, the son of Rabbi Yehuda the prince ; Bathia, the daughter of Pharaoh ; and Sarah, the daughter of Asher.　Some say also Rabbi Yoshua, the son of Levi.　　*Derech Eretz Zuta*, chap. 1.

Note.—As the last-mentioned personage, Rabbi Yoshua, entered paradise "not by the door," but some "other way," it may be interesting to not a few to know how he succeeded, and here accordingly we append the story of the feat. As Rabbi Yoshua's earthly career drew to a close, the angel of death was instructed to wait upon him, and at the same time show all respect for his wishes. The Rabbi, remarking the courteous demeanour of his visitant, requested him, before he despatched him, to favour him with a glimpse of the place he was to occupy in paradise above, and meantime commit to him his sword, as a gage that he would grant his petition and not take advantage of him on the journey. This request being granted and the sword delivered up, the Rabbi and his attendant took the road, pacing along till they halted together just outside the gates of the celestial city. Here the angel assisted the Rabbi to climb the wall, and proceeded to point out the place he would occupy some day in the future, when deftly throwing himself over, he left the angel standing outside and holding him fast by the skirt of his garment. When pressed to return, he swore he would not go back, protesting that, as he had never sought to be relieved of the obligation of his oath on earth, he would not be cajoled or coerced into an act of perjury within the precincts of heaven. He declined at first to give up the sword of the angel, and would have stood to his point but for the echo of a voice which peremptorily ordered its immediate restoration. (See *Kethuboth*, fol. 77, col. 2.)

CHAPTER X.

THE 'TENS' OF THE TALMUD.

1. WHERE is it taught that when *ten* join together in prayer the Shechinah is with them? In Ps. lxxxii. 1, where it is said, "God standeth in the *congregation* of the mighty." *Berachoth*, fol. 6, col. 1.

> NOTE.—According to Rabbinic law, it takes at least *ten* men to constitute a legally convened congregation. Nearly a thousand pounds were expended every year by the synagogues of the metropolis to hire מנין (minyan) men to make up the congregational number, and thus ensure the due observance of this regulation. (See *infra*, Nos. 2 and 12.)

2. When the Holy One—blessed be He!—enters the synagogue, and does not find *ten* men present, His anger is immediately stirred; as it is said (Isa. l. 2), "Wherefore, when I came, was there *no man?* When I called, there was none to answer?" *Ibid.*, fol. 6, col. 2.

> NOTE.—The passion of anger here ascribed to God is by not a few regarded as an attribute wholly alien to the proper nature of the Deity. Such, however, is evidently not the judgment of the Talmudists. Nor is this surprising when we see elsewhere how boldly they conceive and how freely they speak of the Divine Majesty. The Rabbis are not in general a shamefaced generation, and are all too prone to deal familiarly with the most sacred realities. The excerpts which follow amply justify this judgment.
>
> (*a.*) God is represented as *roaring like a lion*, &c., &c. (*Berachoth*, fol. 3, col. 1. See chap. iii. No. 1, *supra*.)
>
> (*b.*) God is said to wear *phylacteries*. (*Berachoth*, fol. 6, col. 1.)

This is referred to in the morning service for Yom Kippur, where it is said He showed "the knot of the phylacteries to the meek one " (*i.e.*, Moses).

(*c.*) He is said *to pray ;* for it is written (Isa. lvi. 7), " Them will I bring to my holy mountain, and make them joyful in the house of תפלתי, *my prayer.*" It is thus He prays : " May it please me that my mercy may overcome my anger, that all my attributes may be invested with compassion, and that I may deal with my children in the attribute of kindness, and that out of regard to them I may pass by judgment." (*Berachoth,* fol. 7, col. 1.)

(*d.*) He is *a respecter of persons ;* as it is written (Num. vi. 26), " The Lord lift up His countenance *upon thee.*" (*Ibid.*, fol. 20, col. 2.)

(*e.*) When accused by Elijah of having turned Israel's heart back again (1 Kings xviii. 37), He confesseth the evil He had done (Micah iv. 6). (*Ibid.*, fol. 31, col. 2.)

(*f.*) God, when charged by Moses as being the cause of Israel's idolatry, *confesseth* the justice of that accusation by saying (Num. xiv. 20), " I have pardoned according to thy word." (*Ibid.*, fol. 32, col. 1.)

(*g.*) He drops *two tears* into the ocean, and this causes the earth to quake. (*Ibid.*, fol. 59, col. 1.)

(*h.*) He is represented as a *hairdresser ;* for it is said He plaited Eve's hair (and some have actually enumerated the braids as 700). (*Eiruvin,* fol. 18, col. 1.)

In a Hagada (see Sanhedrin, fol. 95, col. 2), God is conceived as acting the *barber* to Sennacherib, a sort of parody on Isaiah vii. 20.

(*i.*) He is said to have created the *evil* as well as the *good* passions in man. (*Berachoth,* fol. 61, col. 1.)

(*j.*) God weeps every day. (*Chaggigah,* fol. 3, col. 2. See chap. iii. No. 51 *supra.*)

(*k.*) He dresses Himself in a veil and shows Moses סדר תפלה, *the Jewish Liturgy,* saying unto him, " When the Israelites sin against me, let them copy this example, and I will pardon their sins." (*Rosh Hashanah,* fol. 17, col. 2.)

(*l.*) God is said to have regretted creating certain things. (*Succah,* fol. 52, col. 2. See chap. iv. 9 *supra.*)

(*m.*) God is represented as irrigating the land of Israel, but leaving the rest of the earth to be watered by an angel. (*Taanith,* fol. 10, col. 1.)

(*n.*) It is said that He will make a dance for the righteous, and as He places Himself in the centre, they will point at Him with their fingers, and say (Isa. xxv. 9), " Behold, this is our God ; we have waited for Him ; . . . we will be glad and rejoice in His salvation." (*Taanith*, fol. 31, col. 1.)

Note.—Non-Talmudic readers may find this, and much more on the same topic, in the Machzor for Pentecost (p. 100). But it occurs in a Piyut, and *of course*, as the translator remarks, it is to be understood in a figurative sense.

(*o.*) God is said to have prevaricated in making peace between Abraham and Sarah, which is not so surprising ; for while one Rabbi teaches that prevarication is under certain circumstances allowable, another asserts it absolutely as a duty ; for it is written (1 Sam. xvi. 2), " And Samuel said, How can I go? if Saul hear it, he will kill me. And the Lord said, Take a heifer with thee, and say, I am come to sacrifice unto the Lord." (*Yevamoth*, fol. 65, col. 2.)

Note.—This teaching may be easily matched by parallels from *heathen literature*, but we have room only for two or three examples :—Maximus Tyrius says, " There is nothing (essentially) decorous in truth, yea, truth is sometimes hurtful and lying profitable." Darius is represented by Herodotus (Book iii., p. 191) as saying, "When telling falsehood is profitable, let it be told." Menander says, " A lie is better than an annoying truth." These must suffice.

(*p.*) God utters a curse against those who remain single after they are *twenty* years of age ; and those who marry at *sixteen* please Him, and those who do so at fourteen still more. (*Kiddushin*, fol. 29, col. 2.)

(*q.*) Elijah binds and God flogs the man who marries an unsuitable wife. (*Ibid.*, fol. 70, col. 1.)

(*r.*) God acknowledges His weakness in argument, נצחוני בני ,נצחוני בני, " My children have vanquished me ! my children have vanquished me !" He exclaims. " They have defeated me in argument." (*Bava Metzia*, fol. 59, col. 2.)

(*s.*) God's decision was controverted by the Academy in heaven, and the matter in debate was finally settled by a

Rabbi, who had to be summoned from earth to heaven expressly to adjudicate in the case. (*Bava Metzia*, fol. 86, col. 1.)

Note.—The classical student will recognise in this a parallel to the Greek myth in which the Olympian divinities refer their debate in the matter of the apple of discord to the judgment of Paris. May there not in both fables lie a dim forefeeling of the time when Justice shall transfer her seat from the skies, so that whatever her ministers bind on earth may be bound in heaven?

(*t.*) God will bear testimony before all the nations of the earth that His people Israel have kept the whole of the law. (*Avodah Zarah*, fol. 3, col. 1.)

(*u.*) God is occupied for *twelve hours* every day in study, at work, or at play. (See *ibid.*, fol. 3, col. 2, and chap. 11, No. 16 *infra*.)

(*v.*) God does not act without first consulting the assembly above; as it is said (Dan. iv. 17), "This matter is by the decree of the watchers and the demand of the word of the Holy One," &c. (*Sanhedrin*, fol. 38, col. 2.)

(*w.*) God Himself is described as exacting an atonement for His own miscreations; as, for instance, His diminishing the size of the moon. (*Shevuoth*, fol. 9, col. 1.)

Note.—Though the above are only samples of more, enough has been given to show how the Rabbis deal with the Divine, and how this too often figures in their imagination only as a huge shadow of their own distortions. What if the whole be but a certain imaginative, arbitrary assertion of a reconciliation which some preach and all anticipate between the human and the Divine?

3. The general height of the Levites was *ten* ells.

Shabbath, fol. 92, col. 1.

NOTE.—Moses was a Levite, and he was of that stature. See chap. 3, No. 7 *supra*, for an interesting *morceau* about this.

4. *Ten* things cause hemorrhoids:—Eating cane leaves, the foliage and tendrils of the vine, the palate of cattle, the backbones of fish, half-cooked salt fish, wine lees, &c.

Berachoth, fol. 55, col. 1.

5. *Ten* things provoke a desperate relapse in a convalescent:—Eating beef, fat meat, broiled meat, fowl, or roasted eggs, shaving, eating cress, taking milk or cheese, or indulging in a bath. Some say also eating walnuts, others say eating cucumbers, which are as dangerous to the body as swords. *Berachoth*, fol. 57, col. 2.

6. *Ten* curses were pronounced against Eve:—The words "greatly multiply," "thy sorrow," (alluding to rearing a family), "thy conception," "in sorrow shalt thou bring forth," "thy desire shall be to thy husband," "he shall rule over thee," express six of these. The remainder are:—She should be wrapped up like a mourner (that is, she should not appear in public without having her head covered); she was restricted to one husband, though he might have more wives than one, and was to be kept within doors like a prisoner. *Eiruvin*, fol. 100, col. 2.

7. *Ten* things were created during the twilight of the first Sabbath-eve. These were:—The well that followed Israel in the wilderness, the manna, the rainbow, the letters of the alphabet, the stylus, the tables of the law, the grave of Moses, the cave in which Moses and Elijah stood, the opening of the mouth of Balaam's ass, the opening of the earth to swallow the wicked (Korah and his clique). Rav Nechemiah said, in his father's name, also fire and the mule. Rav Yosheyah, in his father's name, added also the ram which Abraham offered up instead of Isaac, and the Shameer. Rav Yehudah says the tongs also, &c. *P'sachim*, fol. 54, col. 1.

8. To the *ten* things said to have been created on Sabbath-eve some add the rod of Aaron that budded and bloomed, and others malignant demons and the garments of Adam. *Ibid.*

9. Rav Yehuda said, in the name of Rav, *ten* things were created on the first day:—Heaven and earth, chaos

and confusion, light and darkness, wind and water, the measure of day and the measure of night. " Heaven and earth," for it is written, " In the beginning God made the heavens and the earth." " Chaos and confusion," for it is written, " And the earth was chaos and confusion." " Light and darkness," for it is written, " And darkness was upon the face of the abyss." " Wind and water," for it is written, " The wind of God hovered over the face of the waters." " The measure of day and the measure of night," for it is written, " Morning and evening were one day."

Chaggigah, fol. 12, col. 1.

10. *Ten* facts witness to the presence of a supernatural power in the Temple :—No premature birth was ever caused by the odour of the sacrifices ; the carcases never became putrid ; no fly was ever to be seen in the slaughter-houses ; the high-priest was never defiled on the day of atonement ; no defect was ever found in the wave-sheaf, the two wave-loaves, or the shewbread ; however closely crowded the people were, every one had room enough for prostration ; no serpent or scorpion ever stung a person in Jerusalem ; and no one had ever to pass the night without sleeping-accommodation in the city.

Yoma, fol. 21, col. 1.

11. Tradition teaches that Rabbi Yossi said :—The Shechinah has never descended below, nor did Moses and Elijah ever ascend on high ; for it is said (Ps. cxv. 16), " The heavens, even the heavens, are the Lord's ; but the earth hath He given to the children of men." True, it is written, he admitted (Exod. xix. 20), " And the Lord came down *upon* Mount Sinai ; " but that, he remarked, was *ten* handbreadths above the summit. And true, too, is it written (Zech. xiv. 4), " And His feet shall stand in that day upon the Mount of Olives ; " but that, too, he added, is *ten* handbreadths above it. And so, in like manner, Moses and Elijah halted ten handbreadths from heaven.

Succah, fol. 5, col. 1.

12. What entitles a place to rank as a large town ? When there are in it *ten* unemployed men. Should there be fewer than that number, it is to be looked upon as a village.   *Meggillah*, fol. 3, col. 2.

> NOTE.—In places where there are not *ten* Batlanim, *men of leisure*, that is, men always free to be present at every synagogue service, a *minyan* (number) has to be hired for the purpose. The notion that *ten* constitutes a congregation is based on the authority of Num. xiv. 27 " How long shall I bear with this (עֵדָה) *congregation ?* " As the term " congregation " here refers to the *ten spies* who brought the evil report, it is concluded forsooth that *ten* men, and never less, is the orthodox minimum for a congregation. We have already referred to the tax which the synagogues impose upon themselves in this country. In reference to this regulation in the Report of the United and Constituent Synagogues for last year (1878), the treasurers say " that there is an element of absurdity in the system of paying officials to read, and then paying other officials to constitute an audience." The " Jewish World " (January 31, 1879), reviewing the Report, thus remarks :—" The sooner the system is weeded out the better ; it is productive of no possible good ; it is a lasting disgrace to a community, whose most holy charge, and whose principal bond of union and element of homogeneity, is the religion which they profess to hold in such reverence."

13. *Ten* lights, said he, could not extinguish *one ;* how shall *one* extinguish *ten ?*   *Ibid.*, fol. 16, col. 2.

> NOTE.—These words are said to have been spoken by Joseph to his brethren, who, after the death of their father Jacob, feared lest Joseph should revenge himself upon them (Gen. l. 21). The Midrash and the Targums as usual furnish much additional information.

14. Rav Assi said :—Nowadays, if a Gentile should betroth a Jewess, there is reason for regarding the betrothal as not therefore invalid, for he may be a descendant of the *ten* tribes, and so one of the seed of Israel.   *Yevamoth*, fol. 16, col. 2.

15. Rabbi Yochanan said :—If, after the death of her husband, a woman should remain unmarried for *ten* years and then marry again, she will have no children. Rav Nachman added :—Provided she have not thought of marrying all the while; but if she had thought of marrying again, in that case she will have children. Rava once said to Rav Chisda's daughter (who bore children to Rava, though she did not marry him until *ten* years after her first husband's death), " The Rabbis have their doubts about you." She replied, " I had always set my heart upon thee." A woman once said to Rav Yoseph, " I waited *ten* years before I married again, and then I had children." " Daughter," said he, " *do not* bring the words of the wise into discredit. It is thou, not they, that are mistaken." Then the woman confessed that she had been a transgressor. *Yevamoth*, fol. 34, col. 2.

16. The Rabbis teach that if a man live with a wife *ten* years without issue he should divorce her and give her the prescribed marriage portion, as he may not be deemed worthy to be built up by her (that is, to have children by her). *Ibid.*, fol. 64, col. 2.

Note.—As a set-off we append here a romantic story paraphrased from the Midrash Shir Hashirim. A certain Israelite of Sidon, having lived many years with his wife without being blessed with offspring, made up his mind to give her a bill of divorcement. They went accordingly together to Rabbi Shimon ben Yochai, that legal effect might be given to the act of separation. Upon presenting themselves before him, the Rabbi addressed them in these fatherly accents :—" My children," said he, " your divorce must not take place in pettishness or anger, lest people should surmise something guilty or disgraceful as the motive for the action. Let your parting, therefore, be like your meeting, friendly and cheerful. Go home, make a feast, and invite your friends to share it with you ; and then to-morrow return and I will ratify the divorce you seek for." Acting upon this advice, they went home, got ready a feast, invited their friends, and made merry together. " My dear," said the husband at length to his wife, " we have lived for many a long year lovingly together, and now that we are about to be separated, it is not because there is any ill-will between us, but simply because we are not blessed with a family. In proof that my love is unchanged, and that I wish thee all good, I give thee leave to choose whatever thou likest best in the house and carry it away with thee." The wife with true womanly wit promptly replied, "Well and good, my dear!" The evening thereafter glided pleasantly by, the wine-cup went round freely and without stint, and all passed off well, till first the guests one by one, and then the master of the house himself, fell asleep, and lay buried in unconsciousness. The lady, who had planned this result, and only waited its *dénouement*, immediately summoned her confidential handmaids and had her lord and master gently borne away as he was to the house of her father. On the following morning, as the stupor wore off, he awoke, rubbing his eyes with astonishment. "Where am I?" he cried. "Be easy, husband dear," responded the wife in his presence. " I have only done as thou allowedst me. Dost thou remember permitting me last night, in the hearing of our guests, to take away from our house whatever best pleased me? There was nothing there I cared for so much as thyself; thou art all in all to me, so I brought thee with me here. Where I am there shalt thou be; let nothing but death part us." The two thereupon went back to Rabbi Shimon as appointed, and reported their change of purpose, and that they had made up their minds to remain united. So the Rabbi prayed for them to the Lord, who couples and setteth the single in families. He then spoke his blessing over the wife, who became thenceforth as a fruitful vine, and honoured her husband with children and children's children.

A parallel to this, illustrative of wifely devotion, is recorded in the early history of Germany. In the year 1141, during the civil war in Germany between the Guelphs and the Ghibellines, it happened that the Emperor Conrad besieged the Guelph Count of Bavaria in the Castle of Weinsberg. After a long and obstinate defence the garrison was obliged at length to surrender, when the Emperor, annoyed that they had held out so long and defied him, vowed that he would destroy the place with fire and put all to the sword except the women, whom he gallantly promised to let go free and pass out unmolested. The Guelph Countess, when she heard of this, begged as a further favour that the women might be allowed to bear forth as much of their valuables as they could severally manage to carry. The Emperor having pledged his word and honour that he would grant this request, on the morrow at daybreak, as the castle gates opened, he saw to his amazement the women file out one by one, every married woman carrying her husband with her young ones upon her back, and the others each the friend or relation nearest and dearest to her. At sight of this, the Emperor was tenderly moved, and could not help according to the action the homage of his admiration. The result was that not only was life and liberty extended to the Guelphs, but the place itself was spared and restored in perpetuity to its heroic defenders. The Count and his Countess were henceforth treated by the Emperor with honour and affection, and the town itself was for long after popularly known by the name of Weibertreue, *i.e.*, the abode of womanly fidelity.

17. Benedictory condolences are recited by *ten* men, not reckoning the mourners; but nuptial blessings are recited by *ten* men, including the bridegroom.

Kethuboth, fol. 8, col. 2.

18. The Mishnic Rabbis have ordained that *ten* cups of wine be drunk in the house by the funeral party; *three* before supper, to whet the appetite; *three* during supper, to aid digestion; and *four* after the meal, at the recitation of the four benedictions. Afterwards *four* complimentary cups were added, one in honour of the precentors,* one in honour of the municipal authorities, another in remembrance of the Temple, and the fourth in memory of Rabbon Gamliel. Drunkenness so often ensued on these occasions that the number had to be curtailed to the original *ten* cups. The toast to the memory of Rabbon Gamliel was to commemorate his endeavours to reduce the extrava-

---

* The precentors of the synagogue were either readers of public worship or civil officers.

gant expenses at burials, and the consequent abandonment of the dead by poor relations. He left orders that his own remains should be buried in a linen shroud, and since then, says Rav l'appa, corpses are buried in canvas shrouds about a *zouz* in value.   *Kethuboth*, fol. 8, col. 2.

19. At the age of *ten* years a child should begin to study the Mishna.   *Ibid.*, fol. 50, col. 1.

20. Rabbi the Holy, when dying, lifted up his *ten* fingers towards heaven and said:—"Lord of the Universe, it is open and well-known unto Thee that with these *ten* fingers I have laboured without ceasing in the law, and never sought after any worldly profit with even so much as my little finger; may it therefore please Thee that there may be peace in my rest!" A voice from heaven immediately responded (Isa. lvii. 2), "He shall enter peace : they shall rest in their beds."

                    Ibid., fol. 104, col. 2.

21. *Ten* measures of wisdom came down to the world ; the land of Israel received nine and the rest of the world but one only. *Ten* measures of beauty came down to the world; Jerusalem monopolised nine and the rest of the world had only one. *Ten* measures of riches came down to the world ; Rome laid hold of nine and left the rest of the world but one for a portion. *Ten* measures of poverty came down to the world; nine fell to the lot of Babylon and one to the rest of the world. *Ten* measures of pride came down to the world; Elam appropriated nine and to the rest of the world but one remained over. *Ten* measures of bravery came to the world; Persia took nine, leaving but one for the rest of the world. *Ten* measures of vermin came to the world ; nine fell to the Medes and one to the rest of the world. *Ten* measures of sorcery came down to the world; Egypt received nine and one was shared by the rest of the world. *Ten* measures of plagues came

into the world; nine measures were allotted to the swine and the rest of the world had the other. *Ten* measures of fornication came into the world; nine of these belong to the Arabs and to the rest of the world the other. *Ten* measures of impudence found its way into the world; Mishan appropriated nine, leaving one to the rest of the world. *Ten* measures of talk came into the world; women claimed nine, leaving the tenth to the rest of the world. *Ten* measures of early rising came into the world; they of Ethiopia received nine and the rest of the world one only. *Ten* measures of sleep came to the world; the servants took nine of them, leaving one measure to the rest of the world.

Kiddushin, fol. 49, col. 2.

22. *Ten* different sorts of people went up from Babylon :—(1.) Priests, (2.) Levites, (3.) Israelites, (4.) Disqualified Cohanim, (5.) Freedmen, (6.) Illegitimate, (7.) Nethinim, (8.) Unaffiliated ones, and (10.) Foundlings.

Ibid., fol. 63, col. 1.

23. *Ten* characteristics mark the phlebotomist:—He walks sideling along; he is proud; he stoops awhile before seating himself; he has an envious and evil eye; he is a gourmand, but he defecates little at a time; he is suspected of incontinence, robbery, and murder.

Ibid., fol. 82, col. 1.

24. Rabbi Chanena ben Agil asked Rabbi Cheya ben Abba, "Why does the word טוב (*i.e.*, that it may be well with thee) not occur in the first copy of the *ten* commandments (Exod. xx.) as it does in the second ?" (Deut. v.) He replied, "Before thou askest me such a question, first tell me whether the word טוב occurs in Deuteronomy or not? for I don't know if it does." The required answer was given by another Rabbi, "The omission of the word טוב in the first publication of the *ten* commandments is due to the foresight of what was to befall the first tables, for if the word

טוב (or *good*) had been in the tables, and broken withal, then goodness would have ceased to bless the sons of Israel."

Bava Kama, fol. 55, col. 1.

NOTE.—The Tosephoth in Bava Bathra (fol. 113, col. 1) ingenuously admits that the Rabbis were occasionally ignorant of the letter of Scripture. The above quotation may be taken as a sample of several in corroboration. (See also chap. xi. No. 33 *infra*.)

25. The Rabbis have taught that when pestilence is abroad no one should walk along the middle of the road, for there the angel of death would be sure to cross him. Neither when there is pestilence in a town should a person go to the synagogue alone, because there, provided no children are taught there, and *ten* men are not met to pray there, the angel of death hides his weapons. The Rabbis have also taught that (like the Banshee of Ireland), the howling of dogs indicates the approach of the angel of death, whereas when they sport it is a sign that Elijah the prophet is at hand, unless one of them happen to be a female, for it is her presence among them, and not any supernatural instinct, that is to be understood as the cause of the demonstration. *Ibid.*, fol. 60, col. 2.

26. *Ten* constitutions were founded by Ezra :—The reading of a portion of Scripture during the afternoon prayers on the Sabbath-day, and during morning prayers on the second and fifth days of the week (a rule that is to this day observed in orthodox places of worship), and this for the reason that three days should not pass by without such an exercise ;* to hold courts for the due administration of justice on the second and fifth days of the week, when the country people came to hear the public reading of the Scriptures ; to wash their garments, &c., on the fifth day, and to prepare for the coming Sabbath ; *to eat garlic*

* See Exod. xv. 22-24 for the reason of this. The children of Israel had gone three days in the wilderness and had found no water (that is, the Word of God), and they murmured, &c.

on the sixth day of the week, as this vegetable has the property of promoting secretions (see Exod. xxi. 10); that the wife should be up betimes and bake the bread, so as to have some ready in case any one should come begging; that the women should wear a girdle round the waist for decency sake; that they should comb their hair before bathing; that pedlars should hawk perfumes about the streets in order that women should supply themselves with such things as will attract and please their husbands; and that certain unfortunates (see Lev. xv.) should bathe themselves before they came to the public reading of the law.

Bava Kama, fol. 82, col. 1.

27. Ten things are said about Jerusalem:—(1.) No mortgaged house was ever eventually alienated from its original owner (which was the case elsewhere in Jewry). (2.) Jerusalem never had occasion to behead a heifer by way of expiation for an unproved murder (see Deut. xxi. 1–9). (3.) She never could be regarded as a repudiated city (Deut. xiii. 12, &c.). (4.) No appearance of plagues in any house at Jerusalem rendered the house unclean, because the words of Lev. xiv. 34 are "*your* possession," an expression which could not apply to Jerusalem, as it had never been portioned among the ten tribes. (5.) Projecting cornices and balconies were not to be built in the city. (6.) Limekilns were not to be erected there. (7.) No refuse-heaps were allowed in any quarter. (8.) No orchards or gardens were permitted, excepting certain flower-gardens, which had been there from the times of the earlier prophets. (9.) No cocks were reared in Jerusalem. (10.) No corpse ever remained over night within its walls; the funeral had to take place on the day of decease. *Ibid.,* fol. 82, col. 2.

28. In the Book of Psalms David included those which were composed by *ten* elders:—Adam (Ps. cxxxix.); Melchizedek (Ps. cx.); Abraham (Ps. lxxxix.); Moses (Ps.

xc.); the others alluded to were by Heman, Jeduthun, Asaph, and the three sons of Korah.

Bava Bathra, fol. 14, col. 2.

29. A man once overheard his wife telling her daughter that, though she had *ten* sons, only one of them could fairly claim her husband as his father. After the father's death it was found that he had bequeathed all his property to one son, but that the testament did not mention his name. The question therefore arose, which of the *ten* was intended? So they came one and all to Rabbi Benaah and asked him to arbitrate between them. "Go," said he to them, "and beat at your father's grave, until he rises to tell you to which of you it was that he left the property." All except one did so; and he, because by so doing he showed most respect for his father's memory, was presumed to be the one on whom the father had fixed his affections; he accordingly was supposed to be the one intended, and the others were therefore excluded from the patrimony. The disappointed ones went straight to the government and denounced the Rabbi. "Here is a man," said they, "who arbitrarily deprives people of their rights, without proof or witnesses." The consequence was that the Rabbi was sent to prison, but he gave the authorities such evidence of his shrewdness and sense of justice, that he was soon restored to freedom.

Ibid., fol. 58, col. 1.

30. Till *ten* generations have passed speak thou not contemptuously of the Gentiles in the hearing of a proselyte. *Sanhedrin*, fol. 94, col. 1.

31. The ten tribes will never be restored, for it is said (Deut. xxiii. 28), "God cast them into another land, as it is *this* day." As *this* day passes away without return, so also they have passed away never more to return. So says Rabbi Akiva, but Rabbi Eleazar says, "'*As* it is this day' implies that, as the day darkens and lightens up again, so

the ten tribes now in darkness shall in the future be restored
to light." The Rabbis have thus taught that the *ten* tribes
will have no portion in the world to come; for it is said
(Deut. xxix. 28), "And the Lord rooted them out of their
land in anger, and in wrath, and in great indignation."
"And He rooted them out of *their* land," that is, from this
world, "and cast them into another land," that is, the
world to come. So says Rabbi Akiva. Rabbi Shimon
ben Yehuda says, "If their designs continue as they are
at *this* day, they will not return, but if they repent they
will return." Rabbi (the Holy) says, "They will enter
the world to come, for it is said (Isa. xxvii. 13), 'And it
shall come to pass in that day that the great trumpet
shall be blown, and they shall come which were ready to
perish.'" *Sanhedrin*, fol. 110, col. 2.

32. Ten things are detrimental to study :—Going under
the halter of a camel, and still more passing under its
body; walking between two camels or between two women ;* to be one of two men that a woman passes between ;
to go where the atmosphere is tainted by a corpse; to
pass under a bridge beneath which no water has flowed
for forty days; to eat with a ladle that has been used for
culinary purposes; to drink water that runs through a
cemetery. It is also dangerous to look at the face of a
corpse, and some say also to read inscriptions on tomb-
stones. *Horayoth*, fol. 13, col. 2.

33. *Ten* strong things were created in the world (of
which the one that comes after is stronger than that
which preceded). A mountain is strong, but iron can
hew it in pieces; the fire weakens the iron; the water
quenches the fire; the clouds carry off the water; the
wind disperses the clouds; the living body resists the
wind; fear enervates the body; wine abolishes fear; sleep
overcomes wine, and death is stronger than all together;
yet it is written (Prov. x. 2), "And alms delivereth from

* See chap. iii. No. 22 *supra*.

death " (the original word, צדקה, has two meanings, right-eousness and alms). *Bava Bathra, fol. 10, col. 1.*

34. With the utterance of *ten* words was the world created. *Avoth, chap. 5, mish. 1.*

35. There were *ten* generations from Adam to Noah, to show how great is God's long-suffering, for each of these went on provoking Him more and more, till His forbearance relenting, He brought the flood upon them.

Ibid., mish. 2.

36. There were *ten* generations from Noah to Abraham, to show that God is long-suffering, since all those succeeding generations provoked Him, until Abraham came, and he received the reward that belonged to all of them.

Ibid., mish. 3.

NOTE.—The greatest sinner is uniformly presumed throughout the Talmud to have a certain amount of merit, and therefore a corresponding title to reward (see chap. 2, No. 10 = Ps. xxxvii. 35–37). Much of this last is enjoyed by the wicked themselves in the present world, and the surplus is often transferred to the credit of the righteous in the world to come (see " Genesis," page 482, No. 173 = Matt. xiii. 12).

37. Abraham our father was tested *ten* times; in every case he stood firm; which shows how great the love of our father Abraham was. *Ibid., mish. 4.*

38. *Ten* miracles were wrought for our forefathers in Egypt, and *ten* at the Red Sea. *Ten* plagues did the Holy One—blessed be He !—inflict on the Egyptians in Egypt, and *ten* at the sea. *Ten* times did our ancestors tempt God in the wilderness, as it is said (Num. xiv. 22), " And have tempted me now these *ten* times, and have not hearkened to my voice." *Ibid., mish. 5, 6, 7.*

39. *Ten* times did God test our forefathers, and they were not so much as once found to be perfect.

Avoth d'Rab. Nathan, chap. 34.

40. *Ten* times the Shechinah came down unto the world:—At the garden of Eden (Gen. iii. 8); at the time of the Tower (Gen. xi. 5); at Sodom (Gen. xviii. 21); in Egypt (Exod. iii. 8); at the Red Sea (Ps. xviii. 9); on Mount Sinai (Exod. xix. 20); into the Temple (Ezek. xliv. 2); in the pillar of cloud (Num. xi. 25). It will descend in the days of Gog and Magog, for it is said (Zech. xiv. 4), "And His feet shall stand in that day upon the Mount of Olives" (the tenth is omitted in the original.)

Avoth d'Rab. Nathan, chap. 34.

41. The Shechinah made *ten* gradual ascents in passing from place to place:—From the cover of the ark to the cherub (2 Sam. xxii. 11); thence to the threshold of the house (Ezek. ix. 3); thence to the cherubim (Ezek. x. 18); thence to the roof of the Temple (Prov. xxi. 9); thence to the wall of the court (Amos vii. 7); thence to the altar (Amos ix. 1); thence to the city (Micah vi. 9); thence to the mount (Ezek. xi. 23); thence to the wilderness (Prov. xxi. 9); whence the Shechinah went up, as it is said (Hosea v. 15), "I will go and return to my place." *Ibid.*

42. *Ten* different terms are used to designate idols.

שקוצים, גילולים, מסכות, פסולים, אלילים,
אשירים, חמנים, עצבים, און, תרפים,

Ibid.

43. *Ten* different terms are employed to express the title of prophet:—Ambassador, Faithful, Servant, Messenger, Seer, Watchman, Seer of Vision, Dreamer, Prophet, Man of God. *Ibid.*

44. *Ten* distinct designations are applied to the Holy Spirit:—Proverb, Interpretation, Dark Saying, Oracle, Utterance, Decree, Burden, Prophecy, Vision. *Ibid.*

45. Joy is expressed in Hebrew by *ten* different terms,

ששון, שמחה, גילה, רינה, דיצה, צהלה, עליזה חדוה תפארה
עליצה.

Ibid.

46. *Ten* are designated by the term Life or Living:—God, the law, Israel, the righteous, the garden of Eden, the tree of life, the land of Israel, Jerusalem, benevolence, the sages; and water also is described as *life*, as it is said (Zech. xiv. 8), "And it shall be in that day that living water shall go out from Jerusalem."

Avoth d'Rab. Nathan, chap. 34.

47. If there are *ten* beds piled upon one another, and if beneath the lowermost there be any tissue woven of linen and wool (Lev. xix. 19), it is unlawful to lie down upon them.   *Tamid*, fol. 27, col. 2.

48. Alexander of Macedon proposed *ten* queries to the elders of the south:—"Which are more remote from each other, the heavens from the earth or the east from the west?" They answered, "The east is more remote from the west, for when the sun is either in the east or in the west, any one can gaze upon him; but when the sun is in the zenith or heaven, none can gaze at him, he is so much nearer." The Mishnaic Rabbis, on the other hand, say they are equidistant; for it is written (Ps. ciii. 11, 12), "As the heavens are from the earth, . . . so is the east removed from the west." Alexander then asked, "Were the heavens created first or was the earth?" "The heavens," they replied, "for it is said, 'In the beginning God created the heavens and the earth.'" He then asked, "Was light created first or was darkness?" They replied, "This is an unanswerable question." They should have answered darkness was created first, for it is said, "And the earth was without form and void, and darkness was upon the face of the deep," and after this, "And God said, Let there be light, and there was light."

Ibid., fol. 31, col. 2.

49. There are *ten* degrees of holiness, and the land of Israel is holy above all other lands.

Kelim, chap. 1, mish. 6.

50. There are *ten* places which, though Gentile habitations, are not considered unclean :—(1.) Arab tents; (2.) A watchman's hut; (3.) The top of a tower; (4.) A fruitstore; (5.) A summer-house; (6.) A gatekeeper's lodge; (7.) An uncovered courtyard; (8.) A bath-house; (9.) An armoury; (10.) A military camp.

Oholoth, chap. 18, mish. 10.

51. "An Ammonite or Moabite shall not enter the congregation of the Lord, even to the *tenth* generation," &c. (Deut. xxiii. 4). One day Yehuda, an Ammonite prophet, came into the academy and asked, "May I enter the congregation (if I marry a Jewess)?" Rabban Gamliel said unto him, "Thou art not at liberty to do so;" but Rabbi Joshua interposed and maintained, "He is at liberty to do so." Then Rabban Gamliel appealed to Scripture, which saith, "An Ammonite or Moabite shall not enter into the congregation of the Lord, even to the *tenth* generation." To this Rabbi Joshua retorted and asked, "Are then these nations still in their own native places? Did not Sennacherib, the king of Assyria, transplant the nations? as it is said (Isa. x. 13), 'I have removed the bounds of the people, and have robbed their treasures, and have put down the valour of the inhabitants.'" Rabban Gamliel replied, "Scripture saith (Jer. xlix. 6), 'Afterward I will bring again the captivity of the children of Ammon,' and so," he argued, "they must have already returned." Rabbi Joshua then promptly rejoined, "Scripture saith (Jer. xxx. 3), 'I will bring again the captivity of my people Israel and Judah,' and these have not returned yet." And on this reasoning the proselyte was permitted to enter the congregation.

Yadayim, chap. 4, mish. 4.

CHAPTER XI.

TALMUDIC NUMBERS RANGING FROM 'ELEVEN' TO
'NINETY-NINE' INCLUSIVE.

1. Go and learn from the tariff of donkey-drivers, ten miles for one *zouz*, *eleven* for two *zouzim*.

Chaggigah, fol. 9, col. 2.

2. When Israel went up to Jerusalem to attend the festivals, they had to stand in the Temple court closely crowded together, yet when prostrated there was a wide space between each of them (Rashi says about four ells), so that they could not hear each other's confession, which might have caused them to blush. They had, however, when prostrated, to extend *eleven* ells behind the Holy of Holies (בית הכפורת).

Yoma, fol. 21, col. 1.

3. In the days of Joel, the son of Pethuel, there was a great dearth, because (as is said in Joel i. 4) "That which the palmerworm hath left hath the locust eaten," &c. That year the month of Adar (about March) passed away and no rain came. When some rain fell, during the following month, the prophet said unto Israel, "Go ye forth and sow." They replied, "Shall he who has but a measure or two of wheat or barley eat and live or sow it and die?" Still the prophet urged, "Go forth and sow." Then they obeyed the prophet, and in *eleven* days the seed had grown and ripened; and it is with reference to that generation that it is said (Ps. cxxvi. 5), "They that sow in tears shall reap in joy."

Taanith, fol. 5, col. 1.

4. What is a female in her minority? One who is between *eleven* years and one day, and twelve years and one day. When younger or older than these ages she is to be treated in the usual manner. *Yevamoth*, fol. 100, col. 2.

5. Whoever gives a *prutah* to a poor man has six blessings bestowed upon him, and he that speaks a kind word to him realises *eleven* blessings in himself (see Isa. lviii. 7, 8). *Bava Bathra*, fol. 9, col. 2.

Note.—(*a.*) On the next page of the same tract it is said, "For one *prutah* given as alms to a poor man one is made partaker of the beatific vision." (See also Midrash Tillim on Ps. xvii. 15.)

(*b.*) The *prutah* was the smallest coin then current. It is estimated to have been equal to about one-twentieth of an English penny. In some quarters of Poland the Jews have small thin bits of brass, with the Hebrew word פרוטה (*prutah*) impressed upon them, for the uses in charity on the part of those among them that cannot afford to give a kreutzer to a poor man. The poor, when they have collected a number of these, change them into larger coin at the almoner's appointed by the congregation. Thus even the poor are enabled to give alms to the poor. (See my "Genesis," p. 277, No. 31.)

6. Rabbi Yochanan said *eleven* sorts of spices were mentioned to Moses on Sinai. Rav Hunna asked, "What Scripture text proves this?" (Exod. xxx. 34), "Take unto thee sweet spices" (the plural implying two), "stacte, myrrh, and galbanum" (these three thus making up five), "sweet spices" (the repetition doubling the five into ten), "with pure frankincense" (which makes up eleven). *Kerithoth*, fol. 6, col. 2.

7. "Zion said, The Lord hath forsaken and forgotten me" (Isa. xlix. 14). The community of Israel once pleaded thus with the Holy One—blessed be He !—"Even a man who marries a second wife still bears in mind the services of the first, but Thou, Lord, hast forgotten me." The Holy

One—blessed be He !—replied, "Daughter, I have created *twelve* constellations in the firmament, and for each constellation I have created thirty armies, and for each army thirty legions, each legion containing thirty divisions, each division thirty cohorts, each cohort having thirty camps, and in each camp hang suspended 365,000 myriads of stars, as many thousands of myriads as there are days in the year; all these have I created for thy sake, and yet thou sayest, 'Thou hast forsaken and forgotten me !' Can a woman forget her sucking-child, that she should not have compassion on the son of her womb?   Yea, they may forget, yet will I not forget thee."

Berachoth, fol. 32, col. 2.

8. No deceased person is forgotten from the heart (of his relatives that survive him) till after *twelve* months, for it is said (P's. xxxi. 12), " I am forgotten as a dead man out of mind ; I am like a lost vessel" (which, as Rashi explains, is like all lost property, not thought of as lost for twelve months, for not till then is proclamation for it given up).   *Ibid.*, fol. 58, col. 2.

9. Rabbi Yehudah, Rabbi Yossi, and Rabbi Shimon (ben Yochai) were sitting together, and Yehudah ben Gerim (the son, says Rashi, of proselyte parents) beside them. In the course of conversation Rabbi Yehudah remarked, " How beautiful and serviceable are the works of these Romans ! They have established markets, spanned rivers by bridges, and erected baths." To this remark Rabbi Yossi kept silent, but Rabbi Shimon replied, " Yea, indeed ; but all these they have done to benefit themselves. The markets they have opened to feed licentiousness, they have erected baths for their own pleasure, and the bridges they have raised for collecting tolls." Yehudah ben Gerim thereupon went direct and informed against them, and the report having reached the Emperor's ears, an edict was immediately issued that Rabbi Yehudah should be pro-

moted, Rabbi Yossi banished to Sepphoris, and Rabbi Shimon taken and executed. Rabbi Shimon and his son, however, managed to secret themselves in a college, where they were purveyed to by the Rabbi's wife, who brought them daily bread and water. One day mistrust seized the Rabbi, and he said to his son, " Women are light-minded; the Romans may tease her and then she will betray us." So they stole away and hid themselves in a cave. Here the Lord interposed by a miracle, and created a carob-tree bearing fruit all the year round for their support, and opened a perennial spring for their refreshment. To save their clothes they laid them aside except at prayers, and to protect their naked bodies from exposure they would at other times sit up to their necks in sand, absorbed in study. After they had passed *twelve* years thus in the cave, Elijah was sent to inform them that the Emperor was dead, and his decree powerless to touch them. On leaving the cave, they noticed some people ploughing and sowing, when one of them exclaimed, " These folk neglect eternal things and trouble themselves with the things that are temporal." As they fixed their eyes upon the place, fire came and burnt it up. Then a Bath Kol was heard exclaiming, " What! are ye come forth to destroy the world I have made? Get back to your cave and hide you." Thither accordingly they returned, and after they had stopped there *twelve* months longer, they remonstrated, pleading that even the judgment of the wicked in Gehenna lasted no longer than *twelve* months; upon which a Bath Kol was again heard from heaven, which said, " Come ye forth from your cave." Then they arose and obeyed it.   *Shabbath,* fol. 33, col. 2.

10. Rabbi Yehoshua ben Levi said that at every utterance which proceeded from the mouth of the Holy One— blessed be He!—on Mount Sinai, Israel receded *twelve* miles, being conducted gently back by the ministering angels; for it is said (Ps. lxviii. 12), " The angels (reading

מלאכי instead of מלכי, kings) of hosts kept moving." Read not ידודון (intransitive), but ידדון (transitive).

Shabbath, fol. 88, col. 2.

11. A Sadducee once said to Rabbi Abhu, " Ye say that the souls of the righteous are treasured up under the throne of glory; how then had the Witch of Endor power to bring up the prophet Samuel by necromancy ?" The Rabbi replied, " Because that occurred within *twelve* months after his death; for we are taught that during twelve months after death the body is preserved and the soul soars up and down, but that after twelve months the body is destroyed and the soul goes up never to return."

Ibid., fol. 152, col. 2.

Note.—Clever answers to puzzling questions, like the above, are of frequent occurrence in the Talmud; and we can't resist the temptation ;to select here a few out of the many to be met with, as specimens of Rabbinical ready wit and repartee. A reference to others may be found by referring to Index II. appended to this Miscellany.

(*a*.) Turnus Rufus once said to Rabbi Akiva, " If your God is a friend to the poor, why doesn't He feed them ?" To which he promptly replied, " That we by maintaining them may escape the condemnation of Gehenna." " On the contrary," said the Emperor, " the very fact of your maintaining the poor will condemn you to Gehenna. I will tell thee by a parable whereto this is like. It is as if a king of our own flesh and blood should imprison a servant who has offended him, and command that neither food nor drink should be given him, and as if one of his subjects in spite of him should go and supply him with both. When the king hears of it, will he not be angry with that man ? And ye are called *servants*, as it is said (Lev. xxv. 55), ' For unto me the children of Israel are servants.'" To this Rabbi Akiva replied, " And I too will tell thee a parable whereunto the thing is like. It is like a king of our own flesh and blood who, being angry with his son, imprisons him, and orders that neither food nor drink be given him, but one goes and gives him both to eat and drink. When the king hears of it will he not handsomely reward that man ? And we are *sons*, as it is

written (Deut. xiv. 1), ' Ye are the sons of the Lord your God.'" "True," the Emperor replied, "ye are both *sons* and *servants; sons* when ye do the will of God; *servants* when ye do not; and now ye are *not* doing the will of God." (*Bava Bathra*, fol. 10, col. 1.)
Note.—The Emperor possibly alluded to Ps. lxxxi. 13, 14, in proof of his assertion, to which Rabbi Akiva had nothing to say in reply.

(*b.*) Certain philosophers once asked the elders at Rome, "If your God has no pleasure in idolatry, why does He not destroy the objects of it?" "And so He would," was the reply, "if only such objects were worshipped as the world does not stand in need of; but you idolaters will worship the sun and moon, the stars and the constellations. Should He destroy the world because of the fools that are in it? No! The world goes on as it has done all the same, but they who abuse it will have to answer for their conduct. On your philosophy, when one steals a measure of wheat and sows it in his field it should by rights produce no crop; nevertheless the world goes on as if no wrong had been done, and they who abuse it will one day smart for it." (*Avoda Zarah*, fol. 54, col. 2.)

(*c.*) Antoninus Cæsar asked Rabbi (the Holy), "Why does the sun rise in the east and set in the west?" "Thou wouldst have asked," answered the Rabbi, "the same question if the order had been reversed." "What I mean," remarked Antoninus, "is this, is there any special reason why he sets in the west?" "Yes," replied Rabbi, "to salute his Creator (who is in the east), for it is said (Neh. ix. 6), 'And the host of heaven worship Thee.'" (*Sanhedrin*, fol. 91, col. 2.)

(*d.*) Cæsar once said to Rabbi Tanchum, "Come, now, let us be one people." "Very well," said Rabbi Tanchum, "only we, being circumcised, cannot possibly become like you; if, however, ye become circumcised we shall be alike in that regard anyhow, and so be as one people." The Emperor said, "Thou hast reasonably answered, but the Roman law is, that he who nonpluses his ruler and puts him to silence shall be cast to the lions." The word was no sooner uttered than the Rabbi was thrown into the den, but the lions stood aloof and did not even touch him. A Sadducee, who looked on, remarked, "The lions do not devour him because they are not hungry," but, when at the royal command, the Sadducee himself was thrown in, he had scarcely reached the lions before they fell upon him and began to tear his flesh and devour him. (*Sanhedrin*, fol. 39, col. 1.)

(*e.*) A certain Sadducee asked Rabbi Abhu, "Since your God is a priest, as it is written (Exod. xxv. 2), 'That they bring *Me* an offering,' in what did He bathe Himself after He was polluted by the burial (Num. xix. 11, 18) of the dead body of Moses? It could not be in the water, for it is written (Isa. xl. 12), 'Who has measured the waters in the hollow of His hand?' which therefore are insufficient for Him to bathe in." The Rabbi replied, "He bathed in fire, as it is written (Isa. lxvi. 15), 'For behold the Lord will come with fire.'" (*Ibid.*)

(*f.*) Turnus Rufus asked this question also of Rabbi Akiva, "Why is the Sabbath distinguished from other days?" Rabbi Akiva replied, "Why art thou distinguished from other men?" The answer was, "Because it hath pleased my Master thus to honour me." And so retorted Akiva, "It hath pleased God to honour His Sabbath." "But what I mean," replied the other, "was how dost thou know that it is the Sabbath-day?" The reply was, "The river Sambatyon proves it; the necromancer proves it; the grave of thy father proves it, for the smoke thereof rises not on the Sabbath." (*Ibid.*, fol. 65, col. 2.)

> *Note.*—See Bereshith Rabba, fol. 4, with reference to what is here said about Turnus Rufus and his father's grave. The proof from the necromancer lies in the allegation that his art was unsuccessful if practised on the Sabbath-day. The Sambatyon, Rashi says, is a pebbly river which rushes along all the days of the week except the Sabbath, on which it is perfectly still and quiet. In the Machsor for Pentecost (D. Levi's ed. p. 81), it is styled "the incomprehensible river," and a footnote thereto informs us that "This refers to the river סמבטיון, said to rest on the Sabbath from throwing up stones, &c., which it does not cease to do all the rest of the week." (See Sanhedrin, fol. 65, col. 2; Yalkut on Isaiah, fol. 3, 1; Pesikta Tanchuma, sect. כי תשא. See also Shalsheleth Hakabbala and Yuchsin.)

12. Those Israelites and Gentiles who have transgressed

with their bodies (the former by neglecting to wear phylacteries, and the latter by indulging in sensuous pleasures), shall go down into Gehenna, and there be punished for *twelve* months, after which period their bodies will be destroyed and their souls consumed, and a wind shall scatter their ashes under the soles of the feet of the righteous; as it is said (Mal. iv. 3), "And ye shall tread down the wicked; for they shall be as ashes under the soles of your feet." But the Minim, the informers, and the Epicureans, they who deny the law and the resurrection of the dead, they who separate themselves from the manners of the congregation, they who have been a terror in the land of the living, and they who have sinned and have led the multitude astray, as did Jeroboam the son of Nebat and his companions,—these shall go down into Gehenna and there be judged for generations upon generations, as it is said (Isa. lxvi. 24), "And they shall go forth and look upon the carcases of the men that have transgressed against me," &c. Gehenna itself shall be consumed, but they shall not be burned up in the destruction; as it is said (Ps. xlix. 14; Heb. xv.), וצורם לבלות שאול, "And their figures shall consume hell from being a dwelling."

Rosh Hashanah, fol. 17, col. 1.

13. Once when Israel went up by pilgrimages to one of the three annual feasts at Jerusalem (see Exod. xxxiv. 23, 24), it so happened that there was no water to drink. Nicodemon ben Gorion therefore hired of a friendly neighbour *twelve* huge reservoirs of water, promising to have them replenished against a given time, or failing this to forfeit *twelve* talents of silver. The appointed day came and still the drought continued, and therewith the scarcity of water; upon which the creditor appeared and demanded payment of the forfeit. The answer of Nicodemon to the demand was, "There's time yet; the day is not over." The other chuckled to himself, inwardly remarking, "There's no chance now; there's been no rain all the

season," and off he went to enjoy his bath. But Nicodemon, sorrowful at heart, wended his way to the Temple. After putting on his prayer scarf, as he prayed, he pled, " Lord of the Universe! Thou knowest that I have not entered into this obligation for my own sake, but for Thy glory and for the benefit of Thy people." While he yet prayed the clouds gathered overhead, the rain fell in torrents, and the reservoirs were filled to overflowing. On going out of the house of prayer he was met by the exacting creditor, who still urged that the money was due to him, as, he said, the rain came after sunset. But in answer to prayer the clouds immediately dispersed, and the sun shone out as brightly as ever.

Taanith, fol. 19, col. 2.

NOTE.—נקדימון בן גוריון, Nicodemon ben Gorion of the above story is by some considered to be the Nicodemus of St. John's Gospel, iii. 1–10 ; vii. 50 ; xix. 30

14. Would that my husband were here and could listen to me; I should permit him to stay away another *twelve* years.

Kethuboth, fol. 63, col. 1.

NOTE.—Hereto hangs a tale stranger than fiction, yet founded on fact. Rabbi Akiva was once a poor shepherd in the employ of Calba Shevua, one of the richest men in all Jerusalem. While engaged in that lowly occupation his master's only daughter fell in love with him, and the two carried on a clandestine courtship for some time together. Her father, hearing of it, threatened to disinherit her, to turn her out of doors and disown her altogether, if she did not break off her engagement. How could she connect herself with one who was the base-born son of a proselyte, a reputed descendant of Sisera and Jael, an ignorant fellow that could neither read nor write, and a man old enough to be her father? Rachel—for that was her name—determined to be true to her lover, and to brave the consequences by marrying him and exchanging the mansion of her father for the hovel of her husband. After a short spell of married life she prevailed upon her husband to leave her for a while, in order to join a certain college in a distant land, where she felt sure that his talents would be recognised and his genius fostered into development worthy of it. As he sauntered along by himself he began to harbour misgivings in his mind as to the wisdom of the step, and more than once thought of returning. But when musing one day at a resting-place a waterfall arrested his attention, and he remarked how the water, by its continual dropping, was wearing away the solid rock. All at once, with the tact for which he was afterwards so noted, he applied the lesson it yielded to himself. "So may the law," he reasoned, "work its way into my hard and stony heart;" and he felt encouraged and pursued his journey. Under the tuition of Rabbi Eliezer, the son of Hyrcanus, and Rabbi Yehoshua, the son of Chananiah, his native ability soon began to appear, his name became known to fame, and he rose step by step until he ranked as a professor in the very college which he had entered as a poor student. After some *twelve* years of hard study and diligent service in the law he returned to Jerusalem, accompanied by a large number of disciples. On nearing the dwelling of his devoted wife he caught the sound of voices in eager conversation. He paused a while and listened at the door, and overheard a gossiping neighbour blaming Rachel for her *mésalliance*, and twitting her with marrying a man who could run away and leave her as a widow for a dozen of years or more on the crazy pretext of going to college. He listened in eager curiosity, wondering what the reply would be. To his surprise, he heard his self-sacrificing wife exclaim, "Would that my husband were here and could listen to me; I should permit, nay, urge him to stay away other *twelve* years, if it would benefit him." Strange to say Akiva, taking the hint from his wife, turned away and left Jerusalem without ever seeing her. He went abroad again for a time, and then returned for good; this time, so the story says, with twice *twelve* thousand disciples. Well-nigh all Jerusalem turned out to do him honour, every one striving to be foremost to welcome him. Calba Shevua, who for many a long year had repented of his hasty resolution, which cost him at once his daughter and his happiness, went to Akiva to ask his opinion about annulling this vow. Akiva replied by making himself known as his *quondam* servant and rejected son-in-law. As we may suppose, the two were at once reconciled, and Calba Shevua looked upon himself as favoured of Heaven above all the fathers in Israel.

15. The Rabbis say that at first they used to communicate the Divine name of *twelve* letters to every one. But when the Antinomians began to abound, the knowledge of this name was imparted only to the more discreet of the priestly order, and they repeated it hastily while the other priests pronounced the benediction of the people. (What the name was, says Rashi, is not known.) Rabbi Tarphon, the story goes on to say, once listened to the high priest, and overheard him hurriedly pronouncing this name of twelve letters while the other priests were blessing the people.   *Kiddushin*, fol. 71, col. 1.

16. *Twelve* hours there are in the day :—The first three, the Holy One—blessed be He !—employs in studying the law; the next three He sits and judges the *whole* world ; the third three He spends in feeding *all* the world ; during the last three hours He sports with the leviathan ; as it is said (Ps. civ. 26), " This leviathan Thou hast created to play with it."   *Avodah Zarah*, fol. 3, col. 2.

17. Rabbi Yochanan bar Chanena said :—The day consists of *twelve* hours. During the first hour Adam's dust was collected from all parts of the world; during the second it was made into a lump; during the third his limbs were formed ; during the fourth his body was animated; during the fifth he stood upon his legs; during the sixth he gave names to the animals; during the seventh he associated with Eve ; during the eighth Cain and a twin sister were born (Abel and his twin sister were born after the Fall, says the Tosephoth); during the ninth Adam was ordered not to eat of the forbidden tree ; during the tenth he fell; during the eleventh he was judged; and during the twelfth he was rejected from paradise ; as it is said (Ps. xlix. 13, A.V. 12), " Man (Adam) בל ילין, abode not one night in his dignity."
        Sanhedrin, fol. 38, col. 2.

18. Rabbi Akiva used to say :—Of five judgments, some

have lasted *twelve* months, others will do so ;—those of the deluge, of Job, of the Egyptians, of Gog and Magog, and of the wicked in Gehenna.   (See chap. v. 30 *supra*.)

Edioth, chap. 2, mish. 10.

19. Plagues come upon those that are proud, as was the case with Uzziah (2 Chron. xxvi. 16), "But when he was strong (proud), his heart was lifted up to destruction." When the leprosy rose up in his forehead, the Temple was cleft asunder *twelve* miles either way.

Avoth d'Rab. Nathan, chap. 9.

Note.—This hyperbole is evidently a mere fiction joined on to a truth for the purpose of frightening the proud into humility.   The end sanctifieth the means, as we well know from other instances recorded in the Talmud and quoted in this Miscellany, which may easily be found by referring to Index II. appended.

20. Those who mourn for deceased relatives are prohibited from entering a tavern for thirty days, but those who mourn for either father or mother must not do so for *twelve* months.   *Semachoth*, chap. 9.

21. A creature that has no bones in its body does not live more than *twelve* months.   *Chullin*, fol. 58, col. 1.

Note.—The gnat (יתוש) of Titus is an exception, for it lived seven years according to Gittin, fol. 56, col. 2.

22. The Alexandrians asked Rabbi Joshua *twelve* questions ; three related to matters of wisdom, three to matters of legend, three were frivolous, and three were of a worldly nature—viz., how to grow wise, how to become rich, and how to ensure a family of boys.   *Niddah*, fol. 69, col. 2.

23. There was once a man named Joseph, who was renowned for honouring the Sabbath-day.   He had a rich neighbour, a Gentile, whose property a certain fortune-teller had said would eventually revert to Joseph the Sabbatarian.   To frustrate this prediction the Gentile dis-

posed of his property, and with the proceeds of the sale he purchased a rare and costly jewel which he fixed to his turban. On crossing a bridge a gust of wind blew his turban into the river and a fish swallowed it. This fish being caught, was brought on a Friday to market, and, as luck would have it, it was bought by Joseph in honour of the coming Sabbath. When the fish was cut up the jewel was found, and this Joseph sold for *thirteen* purses of gold denarii. When his neighbour met him, he acknowledged that he who despised the Sabbath the Lord of the Sabbath would be sure to punish.

Shabbath, fol. 119, col. 1.

Note.—(*a.*) This story cannot fail to remind those who are conversant with Herodotus or Schiller of the legend of King Polycrates, which dates back five or six centuries before the present era. Polycrates, the king of Samos, was one of the most fortunate of men, and everything he took in hand was fabled to prosper. This unbroken series of successes caused disquietude to his friends, who saw in the circumstance foreboding of some dire disaster; till Amasis, king of Egypt, one of the number, advised him to spurn the favour of fortune by throwing away what he valued dearest. The most valuable thing he possessed was an emerald signet-ring, and this accordingly he resolved to sacrifice. So, manning a galley, he rowed out to the sea, and threw the ring away into the waste of the waters. Some five or six days after this, a fisherman came to the palace and made the king a present of a very fine fish that he had caught. This the servants proceeded to open, when, to their surprise, they came upon a ring, which on examination proved to be the very ring which had been cast away by the king their master. (See Herodotus, book iii.)

(*b.*) Among the many legends that have clustered round the memory of Solomon, there is one which reads very much like an adaptation of this classic story. The version the Talmud gives of this story is quoted in another part of this Miscellany (chap. vi. No. 8, note), but in Emek Hammelech, fol. 14, col. 4, we have the legend in another form, with much amplitude and variety of detail, of which we can give here only an outline.

When the building of the Temple was finished, the king of the demons begged Solomon to set him free from his service, and promised in return to teach him a secret he would be sure to value. Having cajoled Solomon out of possession of his signet-ring, he first flung the ring into the sea, where it was swallowed by a fish, and then taking up Solomon himself, he cast him into a foreign land some four hundred miles away, where for three weary long years he wandered up and down like a vagrant, begging his bread from door to door. In the course of his rambles he came to Mash Kemim, and was so fortunate as to be appointed head cook at the palace of the king of Ammon (Ana Hanun, see 1 Kings xii. 24; LXX.). While employed in this office, Naama, the king's daughter (see 1 Kings xiv. 21, 31, and 2 Chron. xii. 13), fell in love with him, and, determining to marry him, eloped with him for refuge to a distant land. One day as Naama was preparing a fish for dinner, she found in it a ring, and this turned out to be the very ring which the king of the demons had flung into the sea, and the loss of which had bewitched the king out of his power and dominion. In the recovery of the ring the king both recovered himself and the throne of his father David.

(*c.*) The occurrence of a fish and a ring on the arms of the city of Glasgow memorialises a legend in which we find the same singular combination of circumstances. A certain queen of the district one day gave her paramour a golden ring which the king her husband had committed to her charge as a keepsake. By some means or other the king got to know of the whereabouts of the ring, and cleverly contriving to secure possession of it, threw it into the sea. He then went straight to the queen and demanded to know where it was and what she had done with it. The queen in her distress repaired to St. Kentigern, and both made full confession of her guilt and her anxiety about the recovery of the ring, that she might regain the lost favour of her husband. The saint set off at once to the Clyde, and there caught a salmon and the identical ring in the mouth of it. This he handed over to the queen, who returned it to her lord with such expressions of penitence that the restoration of it became the bond and pledge between them of a higher and holier wedlock.

L

24. There were *thirteen* horn-shaped collecting-boxes, and *thirteen* tables, and *thirteen* devotional bowings in the Temple service. Those who belonged to the houses of Rabbi Gamliel and of Rabbi Chananiah, the president of the priests, bowed *fourteen* times. This extra act of bowing was directed to the quarter of the wood store, in consequence of a tradition they inherited from their ancestors that the Ark of the Covenant was hidden in that locality. The origin of the tradition was this :—A priest, being once engaged near the wood store, and observing that part of the plaster differed from the rest, went to tell his companions, but died before he had time to relate his discovery. Thus it became known for certain that the Ark was hidden there.   *Shekalim*, chap. 3, hal. 1.

Note.—It is more than probable that the Chananiah, the סגן הכהנים mentioned above, is the person alluded to in the Acts, chap. xxiii. 2, as " the high priest Ananias." For the tradition about the Ark, see also 2 Macc. ii. 4, 5.

25. There were *thirteen* horn-shaped collecting-boxes in the Temple, and upon them were inscribed new shekels, old shekels, turtle-dove offerings, young-pigeon offerings, firewood, contribution for Galbanus, gold for the mercy-seat; and six boxes were inscribed for voluntary contributions. New shekels were for the current year, old shekels were for the past one.   *Yoma*, fol. 55, col. 2.

26. Once on account of long-continued drought Rabbi Eliezer proclaimed *thirteen* public fasts, but no rain came. At the termination of the last fast, just as the congregation was leaving the synagogue, he cried aloud, " Have you then prepared graves for yourselves ? " Upon this all the people burst into bitter cries, and rain came down directly.   *Taanith*, fol. 25, col. 2.

27. A boy at *thirteen* years of age is bound to observe the usual fasts in full, *i.e.*, throughout the whole day. A girl is bound to do so when only twelve. Rashi gives this as

the reason :—A boy is supposed to be weaker than a girl
on account of the enervating effect of much study.

Kethuboth, fol. 5, col. 1.

28. A poor man once came to Rava and begged for
a meal. "On what dost thou usually dine?" asked Rava.
"On stuffed fowl and old wine," was the reply. "What!"
said Rava, "art thou not concerned about being so burden-
some to the community?" He replied, "I eat nothing be-
longing to them, only what the Lord provides;" as we are
taught (Ps. cxlv. 15), 'The eyes of all wait upon Thee, and
Thou givest them their meat (בעתו) in *his* season.' It is
not said (בעתם) in *their* season, for so we learn that God
provides for each individual in his season of need." While
they were thus talking, in came Rava's sister, who had not
been to see him for *thirteen* years, and she brought him
as a present a stuffed fowl and some old wine also. Rava
marvelled at the coincidence, and turning to his poor
visitor said, "I beg thy pardon, friend; rise, I pray thee,
and eat." *Ibid.*, fol. 67, col. 2.

29. So great is circumcision that *thirteen* covenants
were made concerning it. Tosafoth says that covenant
is written *thirteen* times in the chapter of circumcision.

Nedarim, fol. 31, col. 2.

30. Rabbi (the Holy) says sufferings are to be borne
with resignation. He himself bore them submissively for
thirteen years; for six he suffered from *lithiasis*, and for
seven years from *stomatitis* (or, as some say, six years from
the former and seven from the latter). His groans were
heard three miles off. (See "Gen. acc. to the Talmud,"
p. 286, No. 6.)   *Bava Metzia*, fol. 85, col. 1.

31. The Rabbis have taught *thirteen* things respecting
breakfast (פת שחרית, morning-morsel):—It counteracts
the effects of heat, cold, or draught; it protects from malignant demons; it makes wise the simple by keeping the
mind in a healthy condition; it enables a man to come off

clear from a judicial inquiry; it qualifies him both to learn and to teach the law; it makes him eagerly listened to, to have a retentive memory, &c.

Bava Metzia, fol. 107, col. 2.

32. The land of Israel is in the future to be divided among *thirteen* tribes, and not, as at first, among twelve.

Bava Bathra, fol. 122, col. 1.

33. Rabbi Abhu once complimented Rav Saphra before the Minim by singling him out in their hearing as a man distinguished by his learning, and this led them to exempt him from tribute for *thirteen* years. It so happened that these Minim once posed Saphra about that which is written in Amos iii. 2, "You only have I known of all the families of the earth; therefore I will punish you for all your iniquities." "Ye say you are God's friends, but when one has a friend does he pour out his wrath upon him?" To this Rav Saphra made no reply. They then put a rope round his neck and tormented him. When he was in this sorry plight, Rabbi Abhu came up and inquired why they tormented him thus. To this they made answer, "Didst thou not tell us that he was a very learned man, and he does not even know how to explain a text of Scripture?" "Yes, I did so say," replied Rabbi Abhu; "he is an adept in the Talmud only, but not in the Scriptures." "Thou knowest the Scriptures;" they replied, "and why ought he not to know them as well?" "I have daily intercourse with you," said the Rabbi, "and therefore I am obliged to study the Scriptures, but he, having no intercourse with you, has no need to trouble himself, and does not at all care about them." (See chap. x. No. 24, and note *supra*.) *Avodah Zarah*, fol. 4, col. 1.

Note.—In order to understand aright the grounds on which Rabbi Abhu would fain excuse Rav Saphra for not caring at all about the Scriptures, certain passages from both Talmuds should be read, which, in the usual metaphorical style of the Rabbis, set forth the respective merits of

Scripture and Tradition. The three times three in Sophrim (chap. 15), in which the Scripture is compared to water, the Mishna to wine, and the Gemara to mulled wine, and that in which the Scripture is likened to salt, the Mishna to pepper, and the Gemara to spice, and so on, are too well known to need more than passing mention ; but far less familiar and much more explicit is the exposition of Zech. viii. 10, as given in T. B. Chaggigah, fol. 10, col. 1, where, commenting on the Scripture text, " Neither was there any peace to him that went out or came in," Rav expressly says, " He who leaves a matter of Halachah for a matter of Scripture shall never more have peace ; " to which Shemuel adds, " Aye, and he also who leaves the Talmud for the Mishna ; " Rabbi Yochanan chiming in with אפילו מש"ס לש"ס, " even from Talmud to Talmud ; " as if to say, " And he who turns from the Babli to the Yerushalmi, even he shall have no peace." If we refer to the Mishna (chap. 1, hal. 7) of Berachoth in the last-named Talmud, we read there that Rabbi Tarphon, bent, while on a journey, on reading the Shema according to the school of Shammai, ran the risk of falling into the hands of certain banditti whom he had not noticed near him. " It would have served you right," remarked one, " because you did not follow the rule of Hillel." In the Gemara to this passage Rabbi Yochanan says, " The words of the scribes are more highly valued than the words of the law, for, as Rabbi Yuda remarks, ' If Rabbi Tarphon had not read the Shema at all he would only have broken a positive command, but since he transgressed the rule of Hillel he was guilty of death, for it is written, ' He who breaks down a hedge (the Rabbinic hedge to the law, of course), a serpent shall bite him ' " (Eccles. x. 8). Then Rabbi Chanina, the son of Rabbi Ana, in the name of Rabbi Tanchum, the son of Rabbi Cheyah, says, " The words of the elders are more important than the words of the prophets." A prophet and an elder, whom do they resemble ? They are like two ambassadors sent by a king to a province. About the one he sends word saying, " If he does not present credentials with my signature and seal, trust him not ; " whereas the other is accredited without any such token ; for in regard to the prophet it is written (Deut. xiii. 2), " He giveth thee a sign or token ; " while in reference to the elders it is written (Deut. xvii. 11), " According to the decision which they may say unto thee shalt thou do; thou shalt not depart from the sentence which they may tell thee, to the right or to the left." Rashi's comment on this text is worth notice: "Even when they tell thee that right is left and left is right." In a word, חכם עדיף מנביא, a wise man (*i.e.*, a Rabbi) is better than a prophet. (*Bava Bathra*, fol. 12, col. 1.)

34. Oved, the Galilean, has expounded that there are *thirteen vavs* (*i.e.*, ו occurs thirteen times) in connection with wine. *Vav* in Syriac means woe.

Sanhedrin, fol. 70, col. 1.

NOTE.—The Rabbis have a curious Haggada respecting the origin of the culture of the vine. Once while Noah was hard at work breaking up the fallow ground for a vineyard, Satan drew near and inquired what he was doing. On ascertaining that the patriarch was about to cultivate the grape, which he valued both for its fruit and its juice, he at once volunteered to assist him at his task, and began to manure the soil with the blood of a lamb, a lion, a pig, and a monkey. " Now," said he, when his work was done, " of those who taste the juice of the grape, some will become meek and gentle as the lamb, some bold and fearless as the lion, some foul and beastly as the pig, and others frolicsome and lively as the monkey." This quaint story may be found more fully detailed in the Midrash Tanchuma (see Noah) and the Yalkut on Genesis. The Mohammedan legend is somewhat similar. It relates how Satan on the like occasion used the blood of a peacock, of an ape, of a lion, and of a pig, and it deduces from the abuse of the vine the curse that fell on the children of Ham, and ascribes the colour of the purple grape to the dark hue which thenceforth tinctured all the fruit of their land as well as their own complexions.

35. At *thirteen* years of age, a boy becomes bound to observe the (613) precepts of the law.   *Avoth*, chap. 5.

36. Rabbi Ishmael says the law is to be expounded according to *thirteen* logical rules.

Chullin, fol. 63, col. 1.

NOTE.—The שלש־עשרה מדות, thirteen rules of Rabbi Ishmael above referred to, are not to be found together in any part of the Talmud, but they are collected for repetition in the Liturgy, and are as follows :—

1. Inference is valid from minor to major.

2. From similar phraseology.

3. From the gist or main point of one text to that of other passages.

4. Of general and particular.

5. Of particular and general.

6. From a general, or a particular and a general, the ruling both of the former and the latter is to be according to the middle term, *i.e.*, the one which is particularised.

7. From a general text that requires a particular instance, and *vice versâ*.

8. When a particular rule is laid down for something which has already been included in a general law, the rule is to apply to all.

9. When a general rule has an exception, the exception mitigates and does not aggravate the rule.

10. When a general rule has an exception not according therewith, the exception both mitigates and aggravates.

11. When an exception to a general rule is made to substantiate extraneous matter, that matter cannot be classed under the said general rule, unless the Scripture expressly says so.

12. The ruling is to be according to the context, or to the general drift of the argument.

13. When two texts are contradictory, a third is to be sought that reconciles them.

37. Rabbi Akiva was forty years of age when he began to study, and after *thirteen* years of study he began publicly to teach. *Avoth d'Rab. Nathan.*

38. *Thirteen* treasurers and seven directors were appointed to serve in the Temple. (More there might be, never less.) *Tamid*, fol. 27, col. 1.

39. *Thirteen* points of law regulate the decisions that require to be made relative to the carcase of a clean bird. *Taharoth*, chap. 1, mish. 1.

40. A man must partake of *fourteen* meals in the booth during the Feast of Tabernacles. *Succah*, fol. 27, col. 1.

41. Traditional chronology records that the Israelites killed the Paschal lamb on the *fourteenth* day of Nisan, the month on which they came out of Egypt. They came out on the *fifteenth;* that day was a Friday.

Shabbath, fol. 88, col. 1.

42. The *fifteen* steps were according to the number of the Songs of Degrees in the Psalms. It is related that whosoever has not seen the joy at the annual ceremony of the *water-drawing*, has not seen rejoicing in his life. At the conclusion of the first part of the Feast of Tabernacles, the Priests and Levites descended into the women's ante-court, where they made great preparations (such as erecting temporary double galleries, the uppermost for women, and those under for men). There were golden candelabra there, each having four golden bowls on the top, four ladders reaching to them, and four of the young priests with cruses of oil ready to supply them, each cruse holding one hundred and twenty logs of oil. The lamp-wicks were made of the worn-out drawers and girdles of the priests. There was not a court in all Jerusalem that was not lit up by the illumination of the "water-drawing." Holy men, and men of dignity, with flaming torches in their hands, danced before the people, rehearsing songs and singing praises. The Levites, with harps, lutes, cymbals, trumpets, and innumerable musical instruments, were stationed on the fifteen steps * which led from the ante-court of Israel to the women's court; the Levites stood upon the steps and played and sang. Two priests stood at the upper gate which led from the ante-court for Israel to that for the women, each provided with a trumpet, and as soon as the cock crew (תקעו) they blew one simple blast (והריעו), then a compound or fragmentary one, and then a modulated or shouting blast. This was the preconcerted signal for the drawing of the water. As soon

* These fifteen steps were according to the number of the Songs of Degrees in the Psalter (Ps. cxx.-cxxxiv.).

as they reached the tenth step, they blew again three blasts as before. When they came to the ante-court for women, they blew another three blasts, and after that they continued blowing till they came to the east gate. When they arrived at the east gate, they turned their faces westward (*i.e.*, towards the Temple) and said, " Our fathers, who were in this place, turned their backs towards the Temple of the Lord, and their faces towards the East, for they worshipped the sun in the East; but we turn our eyes to God!" Rabbi Yehudah says, " These words were repeated, echoing, 'We are for God, and unto God are our eyes directed!'" *Succah*, fol. 51, col. 1, 2.

43. Rabbon Shimon ben Gamliel has said there were no such gala-days for Israel as the *fifteenth* of Ab and the Day of Atonement, when the young maidens of Jerusalem used to resort to the vineyard all robed in white garments, that were required to be *borrowed*, lest those should feel humiliated who had none of their own. There they danced gleefully, calling to the lookers-on and saying, " Young men, have a care; the choice you now make may have consequences." *Taanith*, fol. 26, col. 2.

44. Rabbi Elazar the Great said, " From the *fifteenth* of Ab the influence of the sun declines, and from that day they leave off cutting wood for the altar fire, because it could not be properly dried (and green wood might harbour vermin, which would make it unfit for use)." *Ibid.*, fol. 31, col. 1.

45. He who eats turnips to beef, and sleeps out in the open air during the night of the *fourteenth* and *fifteenth* days of the months of summer (that is, when the moon is full), will most likely bring on an ague fever. *Gittin*, fol. 70, col. 1.

46. A lad should, at the age of *fifteen*, begin to apply himself to the Gemara. *Avoth*, chap. 5.

47. "So I bought her to me for *fifteen*" (Hosea iii. 2), that is, on the fifteenth day of Nisan, when Israel was redeemed from the bondage of Egypt. "Silver;" this refers to the righteous. "An homer and a half-homer;" these equal forty-five measures, and are the forty-five righteous men for whose sake the world is preserved. I don't know whether there are thirty here (that is, in Babylon), and *fifteen* in the land of Israel, or *vice versâ*; as it is said (Zech. xi. 13), "I took the thirty pieces of silver and cast them to the potter in the house of the Lord." It stands to reason that there are thirty in the land of Israel, and, therefore, fifteen here. Abaii says that the greater part are to be found under the gable end of the synagogue. Rav Yehudah says the reference is to the thirty righteous men always found among the nations of the world for whose sake they are preserved (but see No. 103 *infra*). Ulla says it refers to the thirty precepts received by the nations of the world, of which, however, they keep three only; *i.e.*, they do not enter into formal marriage-contracts with men; they do not expose for sale the bodies of such animals as have died from natural causes; and they have regard for the law.

Chullin, fol. 92, col. 1.

48. Rabbi Cheyah bar Abba says, "I once visited a householder at Ludkia, and they placed before him a golden table so loaded with silver plate, basins, cups, bottles and glasses, besides all sorts of dishes, delicacies, and spices, that it took *sixteen* men to carry it. When they set the table in its place they said (Ps. xxiv. 1), 'The earth is the Lord's and the fulness thereof,' and upon removing it, they said (Ps. cxv. 16), 'The heaven, even the heavens, are the Lord's, but the earth hath He given to the children of men.' I said, 'Son, how hast thou come to deserve all this?' 'I was,' replied he, 'a butcher by trade, and I always set apart for the Sabbath the best of the cattle.' 'How happy art thou,' I re-

marked (adds Rabbi Cheyah), 'to have merited such a reward, and blessed be God who has thus rewarded thee.'"

Shabbath, fol. 119, col. 1.

49. Rash Lakish said, "I have seen the flow of milk and honey at Tzipori; it was *sixteen* miles by *sixteen* miles."

Megillah, fol. 6, col. 1.

Note.—Rashi explains the above as follows :—The goats fed upon figs from which honey distilled, and this mingled with the milk which dropped from the goats as they walked along. On the spot arose a lake which covered an area of sixteen miles square. (See also Kethuboth, fol. 111, col. 2.)

50. A cedar-tree once fell down in our place, the trunk of which was so wide that *sixteen* waggons were drawn abreast upon it. *Bechoroth*, fol. 57, col. 2.

Note.—Who can estimate the loss the world sustains in its ignorance of the trees of the Talmud? What a sapling in comparison with this giant cedar of Lebanon must the far-famed Mammoth tree have been which was lately cut down in California, and was the largest known to the present generation! And that, report says, was above 400 feet high and fully 100 feet in circumference, a section of which was lately exhibited in San Francisco, hollowed out into a furnished chamber which could with ease accommodate a hundred and forty children!

51. Rabbi Yochanan plaintively records, "I remember the time when a young man and a young woman *sixteen* or *seventeen* years of age could walk together in the streets and no harm came of it." *Bava Bathra*, fol. 91, col. 2.

52. On the deposition of Rabbon Gamliel, Rabbi Eleazar ben Azariah was chosen as his successor to the presidential chair of the academy. On being told of his elevation, he consulted with his wife as to whether or not he should accept the appointment. "What if they should depose thee also?" asked his wife. He replied, "Use the precious bowl while thou hast it, even if it be broken the

next." But she rejoined, "Thou art only *eighteen* years old, and how canst thou at such an age expect folks to venerate thee?" By a miracle eighteen of his locks turned suddenly grey, so that he could say, "I am as one of seventy."

Berachoth, fol. 27, col. 2.

53. The Rabbis have taught that Shimon Happikoli had arranged the *eighteen* benedictions before Rabbon Gamliel at Javneh. Rabbon Gamliel appealed to the sages, "Is there not a man who knows how to compose an imprecation against the Sadducees?" Then Samuel the Little stood up and extemporised it.

Ibid., fol. 28, col. 2.

NOTE.—The ברכת צדוקים (*supra*, and fol. 29, col. 1), "imprecation against the Sadducees," stands twelfth among the collects of the Shemoneh Esreh. It is popularly known as ולמלשינים, "Velamaleshinim," from its opening words, and is given thus in modern Ashkenazi liturgies:—"Oh, let the slanderers have no hope, all the wicked be annihilated speedily, and all the tyrants be cut off, hurled down and reduced speedily; humble Thou them quickly in our days. Blessed art Thou, O Lord, who destroyest enemies and humblest tyrants." There has been much misconception with regard to this collect against heretics. There is every reason to believe it was composed without any reference whatever to the Christians. One point of interest, however, in connection with it is worth relating here. Some have sought to identify the author of it, Samuel the Little, with the Apostle Paul, grounding the conclusion on his original Hebrew name, Saul. They take שאול as an abbreviation of שמואל, and Paulus as equal to *pusillus*, which means "very little" or "the less," and answers to the Hebrew הקטן. *Hakaton*, a term of similar import. Samuel, however, died a good Jew (see Semachoth, chap. 8), and Rabbon Gamliel Hazaken and Rabbi Eleazar ben Azariah pronounced a funeral oration at his burial. "His key and his diary were placed on his coffin, because he had no son to succeed him." (See also Sanhedrin, fol. 11, col. 1.)

54. *Eighteen* denunciations did Isaiah make against the people of Israel, and he recovered not his equanimity

until he was able to add, " The child shall behave himself proudly against the ancient, and the base against the honourable" (Isa. iii. 5).   *Chaggigah*, fol, 14, col. 1.

55. The Rabbis have related that there was once a family in Jerusalem the members of which died off regularly at *eighteen* years of age. Rabbi Yochanan ben Zacchai shrewdly guessed that they were descendants of Eli, regarding whom it is said (1 Sam. ii. 25), " And all the increase of thine house shall die in the flower of their age;" and he accordingly advised them to devote themselves to the study of the law, as the certain and only means of neutralising the curse. They acted upon the advice of the Rabbi; their lives were in consequence prolonged; and they thenceforth went by the name of their spiritual father.   *Rosh Hashanah*, fol. 18, col. 1.

56. At *eighteen* לחופה, to the nuptial canopy.
Avoth, chap. 5.

57. *Eighteen* handbreadths was the height of the golden candlestick.   *Menachoth*, fol. 28, col. 2.

58. If a man remain unmarried after the age of *twenty*, his life is a constant transgression. The Holy One— blessed be He!—waits until that period to see if one enters the matrimonial state, and curses his bones if he remain single.   *Kiddushin*, fol. 29, col. 2.

59. A woman marrying under *twenty* years of age will bear till she is sixty; if she marries at twenty she will bear until she is forty; if she marries at forty she will not have any family.   *Bava Bathra*, fol. 119, col. 2.

60. At twenty pursue the study of the law.
Avoth, chap. 5.

61. Rabbi Yehudah says the early Pietists (חסידים) used to suffer some *twenty* days before death from diarrhœa,

the effect of which was to purge and purify them for the world to come; for it is said, " As the fining pot for silver, and the furnace for gold, so is a man to his praise" (Prov. xxvii. 21). *Semachoth*, chap. 3, mish. 10.

> NOTE.—It may not be out of place to append two or three parallel passages here by way of illustration :—" Bodily suffering purges away sin" (*Berachoth*, fol. 5, col. 1). " He who suffers will not see hell" (*Eiruvin*, fol. 41, col. 2). " To die of diarrhœa is an augury for good, for most of the righteous die of that ailment " (*Kethuboth*, fol. 103, col. 2, and elsewhere).

62. The bathing season at (the hot baths of) Dimsis lasted *twenty-one* days. *Shabbath*, fol. 147, col. 2.

63. A fowl hatches in *twenty-one* days, and the almond tree ripens its fruit in twenty-one days.

Bechoroth, fol. 8, col. 1.

64. Rabbi Levi says the realisation of a good dream may be hopefully expected for *twenty-two* years; for it is written (Gen. xxxvii. 2), "These are the generations of Jacob, Joseph being seventeen years old when he had the dreams." And it is written also (Gen. xli. 46), " And Joseph was thirty years old when he stood before Pharaoh," &c. From seventeen to thirty are thirteen, to which add the seven years of plenty and the two years of famine, which make the sum total of twenty-two.

Berachoth, fol. 55, col. 2.

> NOTE.—In the pages which precede and follow the above quotation there is much that is interesting on the subject of dreams and their interpretation, and one is strongly tempted to append selections, but we refrain in order to make room for a prayer which occurs in the morning service for the various festivals, and is given in the preceding context :—" Sovereign of the Universe ! I am thine, and my dreams are thine. I have dreamed a dream, but know not what it portendeth. May it be acceptable in Thy presence, O Lord my God, and the God of my fathers, that all my dreams concerning myself and concerning all Israel may be for my good. Whether I have

dreamt concerning myself, or whether I have dreamt concerning others, or whether others have dreamt concerning me, if they be good, strengthen and fortify them, that they may be accomplished in me, as were the dreams of the righteous Joseph ; and if they require cure, heal them as Thou didst Hezekiah, king of Judah, from his sickness ; as Miriam the prophetess from her leprosy, and Naaman from his leprosy ; as the bitter waters of Marah by the hands of our legislator Moses, and those of Jericho by the hands of Elisha. And as Thou wast pleased to turn the curse of Balaam, the son of Beor, to a blessing, be pleased to convert all my dreams concerning me and all Israel to a good end. Oh, guard me ; let me be acceptable to Thee, and grant me life. Amen."*

65. Rabbi Levi said, "Come and see how unlike the character of the Holy One—blessed be He !—is to that of those who inherit the flesh and blood of humanity. God blessed Israel with *twenty-two* benedictions and cursed them with eight curses (Lev. xxvi. 3–13, xv. 43). But Moses, our Rabbi, blessed them with eight benedictions and cursed them with twenty-two imprecations " (see Deut. xxviii. 1–4, xv. 68).   *Bava Bathra*, fol. 59, col. 1.

66. Once as they were journeying to Chesib (in Palestine), some of Rabbi Akiva's disciples were overtaken by a band of robbers, who demanded to know where they were going to. "We are going to Acco," was the reply ; but on arriving at Chesib, they went no farther. The robbers then asked them who they were ? "Disciples of Rabbi Akiva," they replied. Upon hearing this the robbers exclaimed, "Blessed surely is Rabbi Akiva and his disciples too, for no man can ever do them any harm." Once as Rabbi Menasi was travelling to Thurtha (in Babylonia), some thieves surprised him on the road and asked him where he was bound for. "For Pumbeditha," was the reply ; but upon reaching Thurtha, he stayed and went no farther. The highwaymen, thus balked, retorted,

* The translation of this prayer is borrowed from the Jewish liturgy.

"Thou art the disciple of Yehuda the deceiver!" "Oh, you know my master, do you?" said the Rabbi. "Then in the name of God be every one of you anathematised." For *twenty-two* years thereafter they carried on their nefarious trade, but all their attempts at violence ended only in disappointment. Then all save one of them came to the Rabbi and craved his pardon, which was immediately granted. The one who did not come to confess his guilt and obtain absolution was a weaver, and he was eventually devoured by a lion. Hence the proverbs, "If a weaver does not humble himself, he shortens his life;" and, "Come and see the difference there is between the thieves of Babylon and the banditti of the land of Israel."

Avodah Zarah, fol. 26, col. 1.

67. Rabbi Eliezer ben Hyrcanus was *twenty-two* years of age when, contrary to the wishes of his father, he went to Rabbon Yochanan ben Zaccai purposing to devote himself to the study of the law. By the time he arrived at Rabbon Yochanan's he had been without food four-and-twenty hours, and yet, though repeatedly asked whether he had had anything to eat, refused to confess he was hungry. His father having come to know where he was, went one day to the place on purpose to disinherit him before the assembled Rabbis. It so happened that Rabbon Yochanan was at that time lecturing before some of the great men of Jerusalem, and when he saw the father enter, he pressed Rabbi Eliezer to deliver an exposition. So racy and cogent were his observations that Rabbon Yochanan rose and styled him his own Rabbi, and thanked him in the name of the rest for the instruction he had afforded them. Then the father of Rabbi Eliezer said, "Rabbis, I came here for the purpose of disinheriting my son, but now I declare him sole heir of all I have, to the exclusion of his brothers." *Avoth d'Rab. Nathan*, chap. 6.

NOTE.—The father of Eliezer acts more magnanimously by his son than does the father of St. Francis. Like the

Rabbi, as Mr. Ruskin relates in his "Mornings in Florence," St. Francis, one of whose three great virtues was obedience, "begins his spiritual life by quarrelling with his father. He 'commercially invests' some of his father's goods in charity. His father objects to that investment, on which St. Francis runs away, taking what he can find about the house along with him. His father follows to claim his property, but finds it is all gone already, and that St. Francis has made friends with the Bishop of Assisi. His father flies into an indecent passion, and declares he will disinherit him; on which St. Francis, then and there, takes all his clothes off, throws them frantically in his father's face, and says he has nothing more to do with clothes or father."

68. Not the same strict scrutiny is required in money matters as in cases of capital punishment; for it is said (Lev. xxiv. 23), "Ye shall have one manner of law." What distinction is there made between them? With regard to money matters three judges are deemed sufficient, while in cases of capital offence *twenty-three* are required, &c. *Sanhedrin*, fol. 32, col. 1.

69. Rabbi Yehoshua ben Levi said, "In *twenty-four* cases doth the tribunal excommunicate for the honour of a Rabbi, and all are explained in our Mishna." Rabbi Elazer interposed and asked, "Where are they?" The reply was, "Go and seek, and thou shalt find." He went accordingly and sought, but found only three—the case of the man who lightly esteems the washing of hands;* of him who whispers evil behind the bier of a disciple of the wise; and of him who behaves haughtily towards the Most High. *Berachoth*, fol. 19, col. 1.

Note.—There are three degrees of excommunication, נדוי חרם שמתא, *i.e.*, separation, exclusion, and execration. That mentioned in the above extract is of the lowest degree, and lasts never less than thirty days. The second degree of excommunication is a prolongation of the first by thirty days more. The third or highest degree lasts

* Cf. Matt. xv. 2; Mark vii. 23.

for an indefinite time. See Moed Katon, fol. 17, col.
1 ; Shevuoth, fol. 36, col. 1 ; and consult Index II.
appended.

70. A certain matron מטרוניתא, once said to Rabbi
Yehuda ben Elaei, "Thy face is like that of one who
breeds pigs and lends money on usury." He replied,
" These offices are forbidden me by the rules of my religion,
but between my residence and the academy there are
twenty-four latrinæ (בית הכסא) ; these I regularly visit as
I need." *Berachoth*, fol. 55, col. 1.

 Note.—The Rabbi meant to say that paying attention
  to the regular action of his excretory organs was the
  secret of his healthy looks, and to imply that a dis-
  ordered stomach is the root of most diseases,—a physio-
  logical opinion well worthy of regard by us moderns.

71. Rav Birim says that the venerable Rav Benaah once
went to all the interpreters of dreams in Jerusalem, *twenty-
four* in number. Every one of them gave a different interpretation, and each was fulfilled ; which substantiates
the saying that it is the interpretation and not the dream
that comes true. *Ibid.*, fol. 55, col. 2.

72. *Twenty-four* fasts were observed by the men of the
Great Synagogue, in order that the writers of books, phylacteries, and Mezuzahs might not grow rich, lest in becoming rich they might be tempted not to write any
more. *P'sachim*, fol. 50, col. 2.

73. When Solomon was desirous of conveying the Ark
into the Temple, the doors shut themselves of their own
accord against him. He recited *twenty-four* psalms, yet
they opened not. In vain he cried, " Lift up your heads,
O ye gates " (Ps. xxiv. 9). But when he prayed, " O Lord
God, turn not Thy face away from Thine anointed ; remember the mercies of David, Thy servant " (2 Chron. vi. 42),
then the gates flew open at once. Then the enemies of

David turned black in the face, for all knew by this that God had pardoned David's transgression with Bathsheba.

Moed Katon, fol. 9, col. 1.

> NOTE.—In the Midrash Rabbah (Devarim, chap. 15) the same story is told, with this additional circumstance among others, that a sacred respect was paid to the gates when the Temple was sacked at the time of the Captivity. When the glorious vessels and furniture of the Temple were being carried away into Babylon, the gates, which were so zealous for the glory of God, were buried on the spot (see Lam. ii. 9), there to await the restoration of Israel. This romantic episode is alluded to in the נעילה, or closing service for the Day of Atonement. (See the Machzor, D. Levi's edition, p. 195.)

74. There are *twenty-four* species of unclean birds, but the clean birds are innumerable. *Chullin*, fol. 63, col. 2.

75. In *twenty-four* places priests are called Levites, and this is one of them (Ezek. xliv. 15), " But the priests, the Levites, the sons of Zadok." *Tamid*, fol. 27, col. 1.

76. There are *twenty-four* extremities of members in the human body which do not suffer defilement in the case of diseased flesh (see Lev. xiii. 10, 24). The tip-ends of the fingers and toes, the edges of the ears, the tip of the nose, &c. *Negaim*, chap. 6, mish. 7.

77. *Twenty-five* children is the highest number there should be in a class for elementary instruction. There should be an assistant appointed, if there be forty in number; and if fifty, there should be two competent teachers. Rava says, " If there be two teachers in a place, one teaching the children more than the other, the one that teaches less is not to be dismissed, because if so, the other is liable to lapse into negligence also." Rav Deimi of Nehardaa, on the other hand, thinks the dismissal of the former will make the latter all the more eager to teach more, both out of fear lest he also be dismissed, and

out of gratitude that he has been preferred to the other. Mar says, "The emulation of the scribes (or teachers) increaseth wisdom." Rava also says, "When there are two teachers, one teaching much but superficially, and one teaching thoroughly but not so much, the former is to be preferred, for the children will, in the long-run, improve most by learning much." Rav Deimi of Nehardaa, however, thinks the latter is to be preferred, for a mistake or an error once learned is difficult to unlearn; as it is written in 1 Kings xi. 16, "For six months did Joab remain there with all Israel, until he cut off every male (זָכָר, zachar) in Edom." When David asked Joab why he killed only the males and not the females, he replied, "Because it is written in Deut. xxv. 19, 'Thou shalt blot out (זָכָר עֲמָלֵק) the male portion of Amalek.'" "But," said David, "we read (זֵכָר, zeichar) 'the *remembrance* of Amalek.'" To this Joab replied, "My teacher taught me to read זָכָר, and not זֵכָר" (zachar and not zeichar), *i.e.*, *male*, and not *remembrance*. The teacher of Joab was sent for; and being found guilty of having taught his pupil in a superficial manner, he was condemned to be beheaded. The poor teacher pleaded in vain for his life, for the king's judgment was based on Scripture (Jer. xlviii. 10), "Cursed be he that doeth the work of the Lord deceitfully, and cursed be he that keepeth back his sword from blood."

Bava Bathra, fol. 21, col. 1.

Note.—Teachers will excuse me if I ask them to bear this lesson in mind when they impart instruction!

78. The Romans faithfully observed their compact with Israel for *twenty-six* years. After that time they began to oppress them.　　　　*Avoda Zarah*, fol. 8, col. 2.

79. The Rabbis have taught that a small salt fish will cause death if partaken of after seven, seventeen, or *twenty-seven* days; some say after twenty-three days. This is said with reference to half-cooked fish, but when properly

cooked there is no harm in it. Neither does any harm result from eating half-cooked fish, if strong drink (שכרא) be taken after it. *Berachoth*, fol. 44, col. 2.

80. On the *twenty-eighth* day of Adar there came good news to the Jews. The Roman Government had passed a decree ordaining that they should neither study the law, nor circumcise their children, nor observe the Sabbath-days. Yehudah ben Shamua and his associates went to consult a certain matron, whom all the magnates of Rome were in the habit of visiting. She advised them to come at night and raise a loud outcry against the decree they complained of. They did so, and cried, " O heavens! are we not your brethren? are we not the children of one mother ?" (Alluding to Rebekah, the mother of Jacob and Esau.) "Wherein are we worse than all other nations and tongues, that you should oppress us with such harsh decrees ?" Thereupon the decrees were revoked; to commemorate which the Jews established a festival. *Rosh Hashanah*, fol. 19, col. 1.

81. The renewal of the moon comes round in not less than *twenty-nine* days and a half and forty minutes.
Ibid., fol. 25, col. 1.

82. Rav Mari reports that Rabbi Yochanan had said, " He who indulges in the practice of eating lentils once in *thirty* days keeps away quinsey, but they are not good to be eaten regularly because by them the breath is corrupted." He used also to say that mustard eaten once in thirty days drives away sickness, but if taken every day the action of the heart is apt to be affected.
Berachoth, fol. 40, col. 1.

83. He who eates unripe dates and does not wash his hands will for *thirty* days be in constant fear, without knowing why, of something untoward happening.
P'sachim, fol. 111, col. 2.

84. The Rabbis have taught that נידוי, the lighter kind of excommunication, is not to last less than *thirty* days, and נזיפה, censure, not less than seven. The latter is inferred from what is said in Num. xii. 14, "If her father had but spit in her face, should she not be ashamed seven days?" (See Note to No. 69, *supra*.)

Moed Katon, fol. 16, col. 1.

85. If we meet a friend during any of the *thirty* days of his mourning for a deceased relative, we must condole with him but not salute him; but after that time he may be saluted but not condoled with. If a man (because he has no family) re-marries within *thirty* days of the death of his wife, he should not be condoled with at home (lest it might hurt the feelings of his new partner); but if met with out of doors, he should be addressed in an undertone of voice, accompanied with a slight inclination of the head.

Ibid., fol. 21, col. 2.

86. During the *thirty* days of mourning for deceased friends or relatives, the bereaved should not trim their hair; but if they have lost their parents, they are not to attend to such matters until their friends force them to do so.

Ibid., fol. 22, col. 2.

87. "And Haman told them of the glory of his riches and the multitude of his children" (Esth. v. 11). And how many children were there? Rav said *thirty;* ten had died, ten were hanged, and ten went about begging from door to door. The Rabbis say, "Those that went about begging from door to door were seventy; for it is written (1 Sam. ii. 5), 'They that were full have hired themselves for bread.'" Read not שְׂבֵעִים, svyim = *that were full*, but שִׁבְעִים, shivim = *seventy*. Rami bar Abba said, "They were *two hundred and eight* in all; for it is said, וְרוֹב בָּנָיו, 'the multitude of his sons.'" רוֹב, by Gematria, equals two hundred and eight, &c.

Meggillah, fol. 15, col. 2.

88. When Rabbi Chanena bar Pappa was about to die, the Angel of Death was told to go and render him some friendly service. He accordingly went and made himself known to him. The Rabbi requested him to leave him for *thirty* days, until he had repeated what he had been learning; for it is said, "Blessed is he who comes here with his studies in his hand." He accordingly left, and at the expiration of thirty days returned to him. The Rabbi then asked to be shown his place in Paradise, and the Angel of Death consented to show him while life was still in him. Then said the Rabbi, "Lend me thy sword, lest thou surprise me on the road and cheat me of my expectation." To this the Angel of Death said, "Dost thou mean to serve me as thy friend Rabbi Yoshua did?" and he declined to intrust the sword to the Rabbi. (See chap. ix. No. 7, note, *supra*.) *Kethuboth*, fol. 77, col. 2.

89. If a man says to a woman, "Thou art betrothed to me after *thirty* days," and in the interim another comes and betroths her, she is the second suitor's.

Kiddushin, fol. 58, col. 2.

Note.—Is this on the principle that a bird in the hand is worth two in the bush?

90. If one finds a scroll, he may peruse it once in *thirty* days, but he must not teach out of it, nor may another join him in reading it; if he does not know how to read, he must unroll it. If a garment be found, it should be shaken and spread out once in *thirty* days, for its own sake (to preserve it), but not for display. Silver and copper articles should be used to take care of them, but not for the sake of ornament. Gold and glass vessels he should not meddle with עד שיבוא אליהו—till the coming of Elijah. *Bava Metzia*, fol. 29, col. 2.

91. Rabbi Zira so inured his body (to endurance) that the fire of Gehenna had no power over it. Every *thirty*

days he experimented on himself, ascending a fiery furnace, and finally sitting down in the midst of it without being affected by the fire. One day, however, as the Rabbis fixed their eyes upon him, his hips became singed, and from that day onward he was noted in Jewry as the little man with the singed hips.	*Bava Metzia*, fol. 85, col. 1.

> NOTE.—This is the anticlimax of the saying ascribed to the people of Verona when they pointed out to a stranger the passing figure of the sorrow-stricken Dante, "See! there goes the man that has been in hell."

92. An Arab once said to Rabbah bar bar Channah, "Come and I will show thee the place where Korah and his accomplices were swallowed up." "There," says the Rabbi, "I observed smoke coming out from two cracks in the ground. Into one of these he inserted some wool tied on to the end of his spear, and when he drew it out again it was scorched. Then he bade me listen. I did so, and as I listened heard them groan out, 'Moses and his law are true, but we are liars.' The Arab then told me that they come round to this place once in every *thirty* days, being stirred about in the hell-surge like meat in a boiling caldron."	*Bava Bathra*, fol. 74, col. 1.

93. Rabbi Yochanan, in expounding Isa. liv. 12, said, "The Holy One—blessed be He!—will bring precious stones and pearls, each measuring *thirty* cubits by *thirty*, and polishing them down to twenty cubits by ten, will place them in the gates of Jerusalem." A certain disciple contemptuously observed, "No one has ever yet seen a precious stone as large as a small bird's egg, and is it likely that such immense ones as these have any existence?" He happened one day after this to go forth on a voyage, and there in the sea he saw the angels quarrying precious stones and pearls like those his Rabbi had told him of, and upon inquiry he learned that they were intended for the gates of Jerusalem. On his return he went straight to Rabbi Yochanan and told him what he had

seen and heard. "Raca!" said the latter, "hadst thou not seen them thou wouldst have kept on deriding the words of the wise!" Then fixing his gaze intently upon him, he with the glance of his eye reduced to a heap of bones the carcase of his body.

Bava Bathra, fol. 75, col. 1.

94. He who lends unconditionally a sum of money to his neighbour is not entitled to demand it back within *thirty* days thereafter. *Maccoth*, fol. 3, col. 2.

95. If a man has lost a relative, he is forbidden to engage in business until *thirty* days after the death. In the case of the decease of a father or a mother, he is not to resume work until his friends rebuke him and urge him to return. *Semachoth*, chap. 9.

96. It is unlawful for one to enter a banqueting-house for *thirty* days after the death of a relative; but he must refrain from so doing for twelve months after the demise of either father or mother, unless on the behest of some higher requirement of piety. *Ibid.*

97. But I know not whether there are *thirty* righteous men here and fifteen in the land of Israel, or *vice versâ*. (See ante, No. 47.) *Chullin*, fol. 92, col. 1.

98. *Thirty* days in a year are equivalent to a whole year. *Niddah*, fol. 44, col. 2.

> Note.—Almost answering to the well-known proverb, "Annus inceptus habetur pro completo,"—a year begun is regarded as completed; but see the context.

99. "Moses, thou didst say unto me, 'What is Thy name?' And now thou dost say, 'Neither hast Thou delivered Thy people at all.' Now shalt thou see what I will do to Pharaoh (Exod. v. 23, vi. 1), but not what I am about to do to the *thirty-one* kings."

Sanhedrin, fol. 111, col. 1.

100. When Rav Deimi arrived at Babylon, he reported

that the Romans had fought *thirty-two* battles with the Greeks without once conquering them, until they allied themselves with Israel, on the stipulation that where Rome appointed the commanding officers the Jews should appoint the governors, and *vice versâ*.

Avodah Zarah, fol. 8, col. 2.

101. Manasseh did penance *thirty-three* years.

Sanhedrin, fol. 103, col. 1.

102. Balaam was *thirty-three* years of age when Phineas, the robber, slew him.   *Ibid.*, fol. 106, col. 2.

103. For *thirty-four* years the kingdom of Persia lasted contemporaneously with the Temple.

Avodah Zarah, fol. 9, col. 1.

104. Abaii has said, "There are never fewer than *thirty-six* righteous men in every generation who receive the presence of the Shechinah; for it is said (Isa. xxx. 18), 'Blessed are all those who wait upon *Him*.'" The numerical value (by Gematria) of *Him*, לו, is *thirty-six*.

Sanhedrin, fol. 97, col. 2.

105. The sons of Esau, of Ishmael, and of Keturah went on purpose to dispute the burial (of Jacob); but when they saw that Joseph had placed his crown upon the coffin, they did the same with theirs. There were *thirty-six* crowns in all, tradition says. "And they mourned with a great and very sore lamentation." Even the very horses and asses joined in it, we are told. On arriving at the Cave of Machpelah, Esau once more protested, and said, "Adam and Eve, Abraham and Sarah, Isaac and Rebekah, are all buried here. Jacob disposed of his share when he buried Leah in it, and the remaining one belongs to me." "But thou didst sell thy share with thy birthright," remonstrated the sons of Jacob. "Nay," rejoined Esau, "that did not include my share in the burial-place." "Indeed it did," they argued, "for our father, just before he died, said (Gen. l. 5), 'In my grave which I have bought

for myself.'" "Where are the title-deeds?" demanded Esau. "In Egypt," was the answer. And immediately the swift-footed Naphthali started for the records. ("So light of foot was he," says the Book of Jasher, "that he could go upon the ears of corn without crushing them.") Hushim, the son of Dan, being deaf, asked what was the cause of the commotion. On being told what it was, he snatched up a club and smote Esau so hard that his eyes dropped out and fell upon the feet of Jacob; at which Jacob opened his eyes and grimly smiled. This is that which is written (Ps. lviii. 10), "The righteous shall rejoice when he sees vengeance; he shall wash his feet in the blood of the wicked." Then Rebekah's prophecy came to pass (Gen. xxvii. 45), "Why shall I be deprived also of you both in one day?" For although they did not both die on the same day, they were both buried on the same day. *Soteh*, fol. 13, col. 1.

Note.—This story, slightly varied, is repeated in the Book of Jasher and in the Targum of Ben Uzziel.

106. The principal works of the hand are *forty* save one:—To sow, to plough, to reap, to bind in sheaves, to thrash, to winnow, to sift corn, to grind, to bolt meal, to knead, to bake, to shear, to wash wool, to comb wool, to dye it, to spin, to warp, to shoot two threads, to weave two threads, to cut and tie two threads, to tie, to untie, to sew two stiches, to tear two threads with intent to sew, to hunt game, to slay, to skin, to salt a hide, to singe, to tan, to cut up a skin, to write two letters, to scratch out two letters with intent to write, to build, to pull down, to put out a fire, to light a fire, to smite with a hammer, to convey from one Reshuth * to another. *Shabbath*, fol. 73, col. 1.

107. King Yanai had a single tree on the royal mound, whence once a month they collected *forty* seahs (about fifteen bushels) of young pigeons of three different breeds. *Berachoth*, fol. 44, col. 1.

* A private property in opposition to a public.

108. *Forty* years before the destruction of the Temple the Sanhedrin were exiled, and they sat in the Halls of Commerce.   *Shabbath*, fol. 15, col. 1.

109. Until one is *forty* eating is more advantageous than drinking.   After that age the rule is reversed.

Ibid., fol. 152, col. 1.

110. The Rabbis have taught that during the *forty* years in which Simeon the Just officiated in the Temple the lot always fell on the right (see Lev. xvi. 8–10).   After that time it sometimes fell on the right and sometimes on the left.   The crimson band also, which in his time had always turned white, after that period sometimes turned white, and at others it did not change colour at all.

Yoma, fol. 39, col. 1.

111. The Rabbis have taught:—*Forty* years before the destruction of the Temple the lot did not fall on the right, and the crimson band did not turn white; the light in the west did not burn, and the gates of the Temple opened of themselves, so that Rabbi Yochanan ben Zacchai rebuked them, and said, "O Temple! Temple! why art thou dismayed?   I know thy end will be that thou shalt be destroyed, for Zachariah the son of Iddo has already predicted respecting thee (Zech. xi. 1), 'Open thy doors, O Lebanon, that the fire may devour thy cedars.'"

Ibid., fol. 39, col. 2.

112. During the *forty* years that Israel were in the wilderness there was not a midnight in which the north wind did not blow.   *Yevamoth*, fol. 71, col. 1.

113. Rabbi Zadok fasted *forty* years that Jerusalem might not be destroyed, and so emaciated was he, that when he ate anything it might be seen going down his throat.   *Gittin*, fol. 56, col. 1.

114. *Forty* days before the formation of a child a Bath Kol proclaims, "The daughter of so-and-so shall marry the son of so-and-so; the premises of so-and-so shall be the property of so-and-so." *Sotah,* fol. 2, col. 1.

115. Rav Hunna and Rav Chasda were so angry with one another that they did not meet for *forty* years. After that Rav Chasda fasted *forty* days for having annoyed Rav Hunna, and Rav Hunna fasted *forty* days for having suspected Rav Chasda. *Bava Metzia,* fol. 33, col. 1.

116. A female who marries at *forty* will never have any children. (See No. 59, *supra.*)

117. He who eats black cummin the weight of a denarius will have his heart torn out; so also will he who eats *forty* eggs or *forty* nuts, or a quarter of honey.
Tract Calah.

118. He that cooks in milk the nerve Nashe (גיד הנשה *i.e.,* "the sinew that shrank") on a yearly festival, and then eats it, receives five times *forty* stripes save one, &c. (See chap. v. 16, *supra.*) *Baitza,* fol. 12, col. 1.

119. He who passes *forty* consecutive days without suffering some affliction has received his good reward in his lifetime (*cf.* Luke xvi. 25). *Erachin,* fol. 16, col. 2.

120. If a bath contain *forty* measures of water and some mud, people may, according to Rabbi Elazar, immerse themselves in the water of it, but not in the mud; while Rabbi Yehoshua says they may do so in both.
Mikvaoth, chap. ii. 10.

121. Rav Yehudah said in the name of Rav:—The Divine name, which consists of *forty-two* letters, is revealed only to him who is prudent and meek, who has reached the meridian of life, is not prone to wrath, not given to drink, and

not revengeful.   He that knows that name, and acts circumspectly in regard to it, and retains it sacredly, is beloved in heaven and esteemed on earth; he inspires men with reverence, and is heir both to the world that now is and that which is to come.

Kiddushin, fol. 71, col. 1.

122. A man should always devote himself to the study of the law and to the practice of good deeds, even if he does not do so for their own sake, as self-satisfied performance may follow in due course. Thus, in recompense for the *forty-two* sacrifices he offered, Balak was accounted worthy to become the ancestor of Ruth. Rav Yossi bar Hunna has said, Ruth was the daughter of Eglon, the grandson of Balak, king of Moab.

Sanhedrin, fol. 105, col. 2.

123. These are the *forty-five* righteous men for whose sake the world is preserved.   (See *ante*, No. 47.)

Chullin, fol. 92, col. 1.

124. Rabbi Meir had a disciple named Sumchus, who in every case assigned *forty-eight* reasons why one thing should be called clean and why another should be called unclean, though Scripture declared the contrary.   (A striking illustration of Rabbinical ingenuity!)

Eiruvin, fol. 13, col. 2.

125. *Forty-eight* prophets and seven prophetesses prophesied unto Israel, and they have neither diminished nor added to that which is written in the law, except the reading of the Book of Esther.   *Megillah*, fol. 14, col. 1.

NOTE.—The Rabbis teach that in future (in the days of the Messiah) all Scripture will be abolished except the Book of Esther, also all festivals except the feast of Purim. (See Menorath Hamaor, fol. 135, col. 1.)

126. By *forty-eight* things the law is acquired. These are study, attention, careful conversation, mental discernment, solicitude, reverential fear, meekness, geniality of

soul, purity, attention to the wise, mutual discussion, debating, sedateness, learning in the Scripture and the Mishna, not dabbling in commerce, self-denial, moderation in sleep, aversion to gossip, &c., &c. *Avoth*, chap. 6.

127. When God gave the law to Moses, He assigned *forty-nine* reasons in every case for pronouncing one thing unclean and as many for pronouncing other things clean.
Sophrim, chap. 16, mish. 6.

128. He that has *fifty* zouzim, and trades therewith, may not glean what is left in the corner of the field (Lev. xix. 9). He that takes it, and has no right to it, will come to want before the day of his departure. And if one who is entitled to it leaves it to others more needy, before he dies he will not only be able to support himself, but be a stay to others. *Peah*, chap. 8, mish. 9.

129. *Fifty* measures of understanding were created in the world, and all except one were given to Moses; as it is said (Ps. viii. 5), "Thou hast made him a little lower than the angels." *Rosh Hashanah*, fol. 21, col. 2.

130. Poverty in a house is harder to bear than *fifty* plagues. *Bava Bathra*, fol. 116, col. 1.

Note.—The above saying is based on Job xix. 21, compared with Exod. viii. 19.

131. For *fifty-two* years no man travelled through the land of Judea. *Yoma*, fol. 54, col. 1.

132. Black cummin is one of the *sixty* deadly drugs.
Berachoth, fol. 40, col. 1.

133. Ulla and Rav Chasda were once travelling together, when they came up to the gate of the house of Rav Chena bar Chenelai. At sight of it Rav Chasda stooped and sighed. "Why sighest thou?" asked Ulla, "seeing, as Rav says, sighing breaks the body in halves; for it is

said (Ezek. xxi. 6), 'Sigh, therefore, O son of man, with the breaking of thy loins;' and Rabbi Yochanan says a sigh breaks up the whole constitution; for it is said (Ezek. xxi. 7), 'And it shall be when they say unto thee, Wherefore sighest thou? that thou shalt answer, For the tidings because it cometh, and the whole heart shall melt,'" &c. To this Rav Chasda replied, "How can I help sighing over this house, where *sixty* bakers used to be employed during the day, and *sixty* during the night, to make bread for the poor and needy; and Rav Chena had his hand always at his purse, for he thought the slightest hesitation might cause a poor but respectable man to blush; and besides he kept four doors open, one to each quarter of the heavens, so that all might enter and be satisfied? Over and above this, in time of famine he scattered wheat and barley abroad, so that they who were ashamed to gather by day might do so by night; but now this house has fallen into ruin, and ought I not to sigh?"

Berachoth, fol. 58, col. 2.

134. Egypt is a *sixtieth* of Ethiopia, Ethiopia a *sixtieth* of the world, the world is a *sixtieth* part of the garden of Eden, the garden itself is but a *sixtieth* of Eden, and Eden a *sixtieth* of Gehenna. Hence the world in proportion to Gehenna is but as the lid to a caldron.

P'sachim, fol. 94, col. 1.

135. They led forth Metatron and struck him *sixty* bastinadoes (Rashi, בישטוינאדי) with a cudgel of fire.

Chaggigah, fol. 15, col. 1.

NOTE.—In the context of the foregoing quotation occurs an anecdote of Rabbi Elisha ben Abuyah which is too racy to let pass, and too characteristic to need note or comment. One day Elisha ben Abuyah was privileged to pry into Paradise, where he saw the recording angel Metatron on a seat registering the merits of the holy of Israel. Struck with astonishment at the sight, he exclaimed, "Is it not laid down that there is no *sitting* in heaven, no shortsightedness or fatigue?" Then Metatron,

thus discovered, was ordered out and flogged with sixty
lashes from a fiery scourge. Smarting with pain, the
angel asked and obtained leave to cancel the merits of
the prying Rabbi.   One day—it chanced to be on Yom
Kippur and Sabbath—as Elisha was riding along by the
wall where the Holy of Holies once stood, he heard a
Bath Kol proclaiming, " Return, ye backsliding children,
but Acher abide thou in thy sin " (Acher was the Rabbi's
nickname).   A faithful disciple of his hearing this, and
bent on reclaiming and reforming him, invited him to
go and hear the lads of a school close by repeat their
lessons.   The Rabbi went, and from that to another
and another, until he had gone the round of a dozen
seminaries, in the last of which he called up a lad to
repeat a verse who had an impediment in his speech.
The verse happened to be Ps. l. 16, " But unto the
wicked, God saith, Why dost thou declare my law?" Acher
fancied the boy said ולאלישע, *and to Elisha* (his own
name), instead of ולרשע, *and to Rasha*, that is, the wicked.
This roused the Rabbi into such fury of passion, that
he sprang to his feet, exclaiming, " If I only had a knife
at hand I would cut this boy into a dozen pieces, and
send a piece to each school I have visited!"

136. A woman of *sixty* runs after music like a girl of
six.   *Moed Katon*, fol. 9, col. 2.

137. Rabba, who only studied the law, lived forty years;
Abaii, who both studied the law and exercised benevolence, lived *sixty*.   *Rosh Hashanah*, fol. 18, col. 1.

138. The manna which came down upon Israel was
sixty ells deep.   *Yoma*, fol. 76, col. 1.

139. It is not right for a man to sleep in the daytime
any longer than a horse sleeps. And how long is the sleep
of a horse ? *Sixty* respirations.   *Succah*, fol. 26, col. 2.

140. Abaii says, " When I left Rabbah, I was not at all
hungry ; but when I arrived at Meree, they served up
before me *sixty* dishes, with as many sorts of viands, and

I ate half of each, but as for צלי קדרה, hotch-potch, which the last dish contained, I ate up all of it, and would fain have eaten up the dish too." Abaii said, "This illustrates the proverb, current among the people, ' The poor man is hungry, and does not know when he has eaten enough; or, there is always room for a tit-bit.' "

Megillah, fol. 7, col. 2.

Note.—צלי קדרה literally means *Pot-roast;* meat hermetically sealed in a pot and then baked in a closed oven.

141. There are *sixty* kinds of wine; the best of all is the red aromatic wine, and bad white wine is the worst.

Gittin, fol. 70, col. 1.

142. Samson's shoulders were *sixty* ells broad.

Soteh, fol. 10, col. 1.

143. Ebal and Gerizim were *sixty* miles from Jordan.

Ibid., fol. 36, col. 1.

144. One who makes a good breakfast can outstrip *sixty* runners in a race (who have not).

Bava Kama, fol. 92, col. 2.

145. A (hungry) person who looks on while another eats, experiences *sixty* unpleasant sensations in his teeth.

Ibid.

146. His wife made him daily *sixty* sorts of dainties, and these restored him again.

Bava Metzia, fol. 84, col. 2.

Note.—Rabbi Elazar, the son of Rabbi Shimon, once vindictively caused a man to be put to death, merely because he had spoken of him as Vinegar the son of Wine, a roundabout way of reproaching him that he was the bad son of a good father, though it turned out afterwards that the condemned man deserved death for a crime (שהוא ובנו בעלו נערה מאורשה ביום הכיפורים) that he was not known to be guilty of at the time of his execution; yet the mind of the Rabbi was ill at ease, and he voluntarily did penance by subjecting himself in a peculiar fashion to great bodily suffering. Sixty woollen cloths were regularly spread under him every night, and these were found soaked in the morning with his profuse perspiration. The result of this was greater and greater bodily prostration, which his wife strove, as related above, day after day to repair, detaining him from College, lest the debates there should prove too much for his weakened frame. When his wife found that he persisted in courting these sufferings, and that her tender care, as well as her own patrimony, were being lavished on him in vain, she tired of her assiduity, and left him to his fate. And now, waited on by some sailors, who believed they owed to him deliverance from a watery grave, he was free to do as he liked. One day, being ministered to by them after a night's perspiration of the kind referred to, he went straight to college, and there decided sixty doubtful cases against the unanimous dissent of the assembly. Providential circumstances, which happened afterwards, both proved that he was right in his judgment and that his wife was wrong in suffering her fondness for him to stand in the way of the performance of his public duties.

147. Elijah frequently attended the Rabbi's seat of instruction (כתיבתא), and once, on the first of a month, he came in later than usual. Rabbi asked what had kept him so late. Elijah answered, "I have to wake up Abraham, Isaac, and Jacob one after the other, to wash the hands of each, and to wait until each has said his prayers and retired to rest again." "But," said Rabbi, "why do they not all get up at the same time?" The answer was, "Because if they prayed all at once, their united prayers would hurry on the coming of the Messiah before the time appointed." Then said Rabbi, "Are there any such praying people among us?" Elijah mentioned Rabbi Cheyah and his sons. Then Rabbi announced a fast, and the Rabbi Cheyah and his sons came to celebrate it. In the course of repeating the Shemoneh Esreh * they were about to say, "Thou restorest life to the dead" when the world was convulsed, and the question was asked in heaven, "Who told *them* the secret?" So Elijah was bastinadoed *sixty* strokes with a cudgel of fire. Then he

* A prayer consisting of eighteen Collects, which is repeated three times each day.

came down like a fiery bear, and dashing in among the people, scattered the congregation. (See No. 135, *supra*.)

Bava Metzia, fol. 85, col. 2.

148. When love was strong, we could lie, as it were, on the edge of a sword; but now, when love is diminished, a bed *sixty* ells wide is not broad enough for us.

Sanhedrin, fol. 7, col. 1.

149. The pig bears in *sixty* days.

Bechoroth, fol. 8, col. 1.

150. *Sixty* iron mines are suspended in the sting of a gnat.   *Chullin*, fol. 58, col. 2.

151. An egg once dropped out of the nest of a bird called Bar-Yuchnei, which deluged *sixty* cities and swept away three hundred cedars.   The question therefore arose, " Does the bird generally throw out its eggs ? "   Rav Ashi replied, " No; that was a rotten one."

Bechoroth, fol. 57, col. 2.

152. Everybody knows why a bride enters the nuptial chamber, but against him who sullies his lips by talking about it, the decree for good, though of *seventy* years' standing, shall be reversed into a decree for evil.   Rav Chasda says, " Whosoever disgraces his mouth (by evil communication), Gehenna shall be deepened for him; for it is said in Prov. xxii. 14, ' A deep pit for the mouth of strange words (immoral talk).' "   Rav Nachman bar Yitzchak says, " The same punishment will be inflicted on him who listens to it and is silent; for it is said (Prov. xxii. 14), ' And he that is abhorred of the Lord shall fall therein.' "

Shabbath, fol. 33, col. 1.

Note.—So then a little perversion of Scripture for a good purpose is no harm, for *the end sanctifies the means!*

153. (Jer. xxiii. 29), " Like a hammer that breaketh the rock in pieces," so is every utterance which proceedeth from the mouth of God, divided though it be into *seventy* languages.   *Ibid.*, fol. 88, col. 2.

154. Rabbi Eliezer asked, "For whose benefit were those *seventy* bullocks intended?" See Num. xxix. 12–36. For the *seventy* nations into which the Gentile world is divided; and Rashi plainly asserts that the *seventy* bullocks were intended to *atone* for them, that rain might descend *all over the world*, for on the Feast of Tabernacles judgment is given respecting rain, &c. Woe to the Gentile nations for their loss, and they know not what they have lost! for as long as the Temple existed, the altar made atonement for them; but *now, who* is to atone for them?

Succah, fol. 55, col. 2.

155. Choni, the Maagol, once saw in his travels an old man planting a carob-tree, and he asked him when he thought the tree would bear fruit. "After *seventy* years," was the reply. "What!" said Choni, "dost thou expect to live *seventy* years and eat the fruit of thy labour?" "I did not find the world desolate when I entered it," said the old man; "and as my fathers planted for me before I was born, so I plant for those that will come after me." *Taanith*, fol. 23, col. 1.

156. Mordecai was one of those who sat in the hall of the Temple, and he knew *seventy* languages.

Megillah, fol. 13, col. 2.

157. The Rabbis have taught:—During a prosperous year in Israel, a place that is sown with a single measure of seed produces five myriad cors of grain. In the tilled districts of Zoan, one measure of seed produces *seventy* cors; for we are told that Rabbi Meir said he himself had witnessed in the vale of Bethshean an instance of one measure of seed producing *seventy* cors. And there is no better land anywhere than the land of Egypt; for it is said, "As the garden of the Lord, like the land of Egypt." And there is no better land in all Egypt than Zoan, where several kings have resided; for it is written (Isa. xxx. 4), "His princes were in Zoan." In all Israel there was no

more unsuitable soil than Hebron, for it was a burying-place, and yet Hebron was seven times more prolific than Zoan; for it is written (Num. xiii. 22), "Now Hebron שבע שנים נבנתה, was built seven years before Zoan in Egypt." What does נבנתה mean? Literally it means *built;* but is it likely that a man would build a house for his youngest son before he built one for his eldest? For it is said (Gen. x. 6), "And the sons of Ham, Cush, Mizraim (that is, Egypt), Phut, and Canaan" (that is, Israel). It must, therefore, mean that it was seven times more prolific (the verb meaning both *to build* and *to produce*) than Zoan. This is only in the unsuitable soil of the land of Israel, Hebron, but in the suitable soil (the increase) is five hundred times. All this applies to a year of average return, but in one of special prosperity, it is written (Gen. xxvi. 12), "Then Isaac sowed in that land, and received in the same year an hundredfold, and the Lord blessed him." (The word שנים = years, is conveniently overlooked in working out the argument.)

Kethuboth, fol. 112, col. 1.

158. The astrologers in Egypt said to Pharaoh, "What! shall a slave whose master bought him for twenty pieces of silver rule over us?" Pharaoh replied, "But I find him endowed with kingly qualities." "If that is the case," they answered, "he must know *seventy* languages." Then came the Angel Gabriel and taught him *seventy* languages.

Sotah, fol. 36, col. 2.

159. When the leviathan makes the deep boil, the sea does not recover its calm for *seventy* years; for it is said (Job xli. 32), "One would think the deep to be hoary," and we cannot take the word "hoary" to imply a term of less than *seventy* years.

Bava Bathra, fol. 75, col. 1.

Note.—See Avoth, chap. 5, where it is said, "at seventy he is *grey*," *i.e.*, *hoary*.

160. Abba Chalepha Keruya once remarked to Rav

Cheyah bar Abba, " The sum total of Jacob's family thou findest reckoned at *seventy*, whereas the numbers added up make only sixty-nine. How is that ?" Rav Cheyah made answer that the particle את, in verse 15, implies that Dinah must have been one of twin-sisters. " But," objected the other, " the same particle occurs also in connection with Benjamin, to say nothing of other instances." " Alas !" said Rav Cheyah, " I am possessed of a secret worth knowing, and thou art trying to worm it out of me." Then interposed Rav Chama bar Chanena, " The number may be made up by reckoning Jochebed in, for of her it is said (Num. xxvi. 59) ' that her mother bare her to Levi in Egypt;' her birth took place in Egypt, though she was conceived on the journey."

Bava Bathra, fol. 123, cols. 1, 2.

161. Rav Yehudah says in the name of Shemuel :—There is yet another festival in Rome, which is observed only once in *seventy* years, and this is the manner of its celebration. They take an able-bodied man, without physical defect, and cause him to ride upon the back of a lame one. They dress up the former in the garments of Adam (such as God made for him in Paradise), and cover his face with the skin of the face of Rabbi Ishmael, the high priest, and adorn his neck with a precious stone. They illuminate the streets, and then lead the two men through the city, a herald proclaiming before them, " The account of our Lord was false; it is the brother of our Lord that is the deceiver! He that sees this festival sees it, and he that does not see it now will never see it. What advantage to the deceiver is his deception, and to the crafty his craftiness ?" The proclamation finishes up thus—" Woe to this one when the other shall rise again !"

Avodah Zarah, fol. 11, col. 2.

NOTE.—The Targum Yarushalmi informs us that the Lord God wrought for Adam and his wife robes of honour from the cast-off skin of the serpent. We learn elsewhere that Nimrod came into possession of Adam's coat through Ham, who stole it from Noah while in the Ark. The glib tongue of tradition also tells how Esau slew Nimrod and appropriated the garment, and wore it for luck when hunting; but that on the day when he went to seek venison at the request of his dying parent, in his hurry he forgot the embroidered robe of Adam, and had bad luck in consequence. Then Jacob borrowed the left-off garment, and kept it for himself.—The mask alluded to is accounted for thus:—The daughter of a Roman emperor took a fancy to have the skin of Rabbi Ishmael's face, and it accordingly, when he was dead, was taken off, and so embalmed as to retain its features, expression, and complexion, and the Jews say that it is still preserved among the relics at Rome. The able-bodied man in this prophetic mystery-play represents Esau, and the limping man is intended for Jacob. Rome (or Esau) is uppermost in that ceremonial, but the time is coming when Jacob will rise and invest himself in the blessings he so craftily obtained the reversion of.

162. Rabbi Yochanan said:—None were elected to sit in the High Council of the Sanhedrin except men of stature, of wisdom, of imposing appearance, and of mature age; men who knew witchcraft and *seventy* languages, in order that the High Council of the Sanhedrin should have no need of an interpreter.　　*Sanhedrin*, fol. 17, col. 1.

163. Yehudah and Chiskiyah, the sons of Rabbi Cheyah, once sat down to a meal before Rabbi (the Holy) without speaking a word. "Give the boys some wine," said Rabbi, "that they may have boldness to speak." When they had partaken of the wine, they said, "The son of David will not come until the two patriarchal houses of Israel are no more," that is, the head of the Captivity in Babylon and the Prince in the land of Israel; for it is written (Isa. viii. 14), "And he shall be for a sanctuary, and for a stone of stumbling and a rock of offence to both the houses of Israel." "Why, children," said Rabbi (who was patriarch of Tiberias), "you are thrusting thorns into my eyes." Rabbi Cheyah said, "Do not be offended at them. *Wine*,

ין, is given with *seventy*, and so is a *secret*, סוד (the numerical value of each of these words is seventy); when wine
enters the secret oozes out."   *Sanhedrin*, fol. 38, col. 1.

164. A certain star appears once in *seventy* years and
deceives the sailors (who guide their vessels by the position of the heavenly bodies; and this star appears sometimes in the north and sometimes in the south.—*Rashi*.)
Horayoth, fol. 10, col. 1.

165. As eating olive berries causes one to forget things
that he has known for *seventy* years, so olive oil brings
back to the memory things which happened *seventy* years
before.   *Ibid.*, fol. 13, col. 2.

166. The outside of the shell of the purple mollusc re-
sembles the sea in colour; its bodily conformation is like
that of a fish; it rises once in *seventy* years; its blood is
used to dye wool purple, and therefore this colour is dear.
Menachoth, fol. 44, col. 1.

167. The bearing-time of the flat-headed otter lasts
seventy years; a parallel may be found in the carob-tree,
from the planting to the ripening of the pods of which is
seventy years.   *Bechoroth*, fol. 8, col. 1.

168. The Sanhedrin consisted of *seventy-one* members.
It is recorded that Rabbi Yossi said, "Seldom was
there contention in Israel, but the judicial court of
seventy-one sat in the Lishkath-hagazith (לשכת הגזית,
i.e., Paved Hall), and two (ordinary) courts of justice
consisting of *twenty-three*, one of which sat at the entrance
of the Temple-Mount, and the other at the entrance of
the ante-court; and also (provincial) courts of justice,
also comprising twenty-three members, which held their
sessions in all the cities of Israel. When an Israelite had
a question to propose, he asked it first of the court in his
own city. If they understood the case, they settled the

receivers of bribes may well look to their souls.　If I feel partial who have not even taken a bribe of what was my own, how perverted must the disposition of those become who receive bribes at the hands of others!" (*Kethuboth*, fol. 105, col. 1.)

(*f.*) The judge who takes a bribe only provokes wrath, instead of allaying it; for is it not said (Prov. xxi. 14), "A reward in the bosom bringeth strong wrath"? (*Bara Bathra*, fol. 9, col. 2.)

(*g.*) Let judges know with whom and before whom they judge, and who it is that will one day exact account of their judgments; for it is said (Ps. lxxxii. 1), "God standeth in the assembly of God, and judgeth *with* the judges." (*Sanhedrin*, fol. 6, col. 2.)

(*h.*) A judge who does not judge justly causeth the Shechinah to depart from Israel; for it is said (Ps. xii. 5), "For the oppression of the poor, the sighing of the needy, now will I depart, saith the Lord." (*Ibid.*, fol. 7, col. 1.)

(*i.*) The judge should ever regard himself as if he had a sword laid upon his thigh, and Gehenna were yawning near him; as it is said (Solomon's Song. iii. 7, 8), "Behold the bed of Solomon (the judgment-seat of God), threescore valiant men are about it, of the valiant of Israel. They all hold swords, being expert in war (with injustice). Every one has his sword upon his thigh, for fear of the night" (the confusion that would follow). (*Yevamoth*, fol. 109, col. 2; *Sanhedrin*, fol. 7, col. 1.)

(*j.*) Seven have, in the popular regard, no portion in the world to come: a notary, a schoolmaster, the best of doctors, a judge in his native place, a conjuror, a congregational reader, and a butcher. (*Avoth d' Rabbi Nathan*, chap. 36.)

WITNESSES.

(*a.*) An ignoramus is ineligible for a witness. (See Chap. vi., No. 7.)

(*b.*) The following are ineligible as witnesses of the appearance of the new moon :—Dice-players, usurers, pigeonfliers, sellers of the produce of the year of release, and slaves. This is the general rule; in any case in which women are inadmissible as witnesses, they also are inadmissible here. (*Rosh Hashanah*, fol. 22, col. 1.)

(*c.*) Two disciples of the wise happened to be shipwrecked with Rabbi Yossi ben Simaii, and the Rabbi allowed

their widows to re-marry on the testimony of women.
Even the testimony of a hundred women is only equal
to the evidence of one man (and that only in a case like
the foregoing; it is inadmissible in any other matter).
(*Yeramoth*, fol. 115, col. 1.)

(*d.*) "Whosoever is not instructed in Scripture, in the
Mishna, and in good manners," says Rabbi Yochanan,
"is not qualified to act as a witness." "He who eats
in the street," say the Rabbis, "is like a dog;" and
some add that such a one is ineligible as a witness, and
Rav Iddi bar Avin says the Halachah is as "some
say." (*Kiddushin*, fol. 40, col. 2.)

(*e.*) Even when a witness is paid, his testimony is not
thereby invalidated. (*Ibid.*, fol. 58, col. 2.)

(*f.*) Testimony that is invalidated in part is invalidated
entirely. (*Bava Kama*, fol. 73, col. 1.)

(*g.*) Let witnesses know with whom and before whom they
bear testimony, and who will one day call them to
account; for it is said (Deut. xix. 17), "Both the men
between whom the controversy is shall stand before
the Lord." (*Sanhedrin*, fol. 6, col. 2.)

(*h.*) Those that eat another thing (*i.e.*, not pork, but those
who receive charity from a Gentile.—*Rashi and Tosefoth*) are disqualified from being witnesses. When is
this the case? When done publicly; but if in secret,
not so. (*Ibid.*, fol. 26, col. 2.)

(*i.*) He who swears falsely in a capital case is unreliable as
a witness in any other suit at law; but if he has per-
jured himself in a civil case only, his evidence may be
relied upon in cases where life and death are concerned.
(*Ibid.*, fol. 27, col. 1.)

(*j.*) He who disavows a loan is fit to be a witness; but he
who disowns a deposit in trust is unfit. (*Shevuoth*,
fol. 40, col. 2.)

(*k.*) Shimon ben Shetach says, "Fully examine the witnesses; be careful with thy words, lest from them they
learn to lie." (*Avoth*, chap. 1.)

CRIMINALS AND CRIMINAL PUNISHMENTS.

Four kinds of capital punishment were decreed by
the court of justice:—Stoning, burning, beheading, and
strangling; or, as Rabbi Shimon arranges them—Burning,
stoning, strangling, and beheading. As soon as the sentence
of death is pronounced, the criminal is led out to be

stoned, the stoning-place being at a distance from the court of justice; for it is said (Lev. xxiv. 14), "*Bring forth* him that hath cursed *without* the camp." Then one official stands at the door of the court of justice with a flag in his hand, and another is stationed on horseback at such a distance as to be able to see the former. If, meanwhile, one comes and declares before the court, " I have something further to urge in defence of the prisoner," the man at the door waves his flag, and the mounted official rides forward and stops the procession. Even if the criminal himself says, " I have yet something to plead in my defence," he is to be brought back, even four or five times over, provided there is something of importance in his deposition. If the evidence is exculpatory, he is discharged; if not, he is led out to be stoned. As he proceeds to the place of execution, a public crier goes before him and proclaims, " So-and-so, the son of So-and-so, goes out to be stoned because he has committed such-and-such a crime, and So-and-so and So-and-so are the witnesses. Let him who knows of anything that pleads in his defence come forward and state it." When about ten yards from the stoning-place, the condemned is called upon to confess his guilt. (All about to be executed were urged to confess, as by making confession every criminal made good a portion in the world to come; for so we find it in the case of Achan, when Joshua said unto him (Josh. vii. 19), " My son, give, I pray thee, glory to the Lord God of Israel, and make confession unto him," &c. " And Achan answered Joshua, and said, Indeed I have sinned." But where are we taught that his confession was his atonement? Where it is said (ibid., v. 25), " And Joshua said, Why hast thou troubled us? The Lord shall trouble thee *this day;*" as if to say, " *This day* thou shalt be troubled, but in the world to come thou shalt not be troubled.") About four yards from the stoning-place they stripped off the criminal's clothes, covering a male in front, but a female both before and behind. These are the words of Rabbi Yehudah; but the sages say a man was stoned naked, but not a female.

The stoning-place was twice the height of a man, and this the criminal ascended. One of the witnesses then pushed him from behind, and he tumbled down upon his chest. He was then turned over upon his back: if he was killed, the execution was complete; but if not quite dead, the second witness took a heavy stone and cast it upon his chest; and if this did not prove effectual, then the stoning was completed by all present joining in the act; as it is said (Deut. xvii. 7), "The hands of the witnesses shall be first upon him to put him to death, and afterwards the hands of all the people."

"Criminals who were stoned dead were afterwards hanged." These are the words of Rabbi Eliezer; but the sages say none were hanged but the blasphemer and the idolator. "They hanged a man with his face towards the people, but a woman with her face towards the gallows." These are the words of Rabbi Eliezer; but the sages say a man is hanged, but no woman is hanged. . . . How then did they hang the man? A post was firmly fixed into the ground, from which an arm of wood projected, and they tied the hands of the corpse together and so suspended it. Rabbi Yossi says, "The beam simply leant against a wall, and so they hung up the body as butchers do an ox or a sheep, and it was soon afterwards taken down again, for if it remained over night a prohibition of the law would have been thereby transgressed." For it is said (Deut. xxi. 23), "His body shall not remain all night upon the tree, but thou shalt in any wise bury him that day; for he that is hanged is accursed of God," &c. That is to say, people would ask why this one was hanged; and as the reply would needs be, "Because he blasphemed God," this would lead to the use of God's name under circumstances in which it would be blasphemed.

The sentence of burning was carried out thus:—They

fixed the criminal up to his knees (בַּבֶּל) in manure, and a hard cloth wrapped in a softer material was passed round his neck. One of the witnesses, taking hold of this, pulled it one way, and another the other, until the criminal was forced to open his mouth; then a wick of lead (שׁל אבר) was lighted and thrust into his mouth, the molten lead running down into his bowels and burning them. Rabbi Yehudah asks, "If the criminal should die in their hands, how would that fulfil the commandment respecting burning?" But they forcibly open his mouth with a pair of tongs and the lighted wire (the molten lead) is thrust into his mouth, so that it goes down into his bowels and burns his inside.

The sentence of beheading was executed thus:—They sometimes cut off the criminal's head with a sword, as is done among the Romans. But Rabbi Yehudah says this was degrading, and in some cases they placed the culprit's head upon the block and struck it off with an axe. Some one remarked to him that such a death is more degrading still.

The sentence of strangling was carried out thus:— They fixed the criminal up to his knees in manure, and having twined a hard cloth within a soft one round his neck, one witness pulled one way and the other pulled in an opposite direction till life was extinct.

Sanhedrin, fol. 42, col. 2 ; fol. 49, col. 2 ; fol. 52, cols. 1, 2.

Note.—(*a.*) The above, which has been translated almost literally from the Talmud, may serve to remove many misconceptions now current as to the modes of capital punishment that obtained in Jewry.

(*b.*) In further illustration of this topic, we will append some of the legal decisions that are recorded in the Talmud, authenticating each by reference to folio and column. Examples might be multiplied by the score, but a sufficient number will be quoted to give a fair idea of Rabbinic jurisprudence.

(*c.*) If one who intends to kill a beast (accidentally) kill a man ; or if, purposing to kill a Gentile, he slay an Israelite ; or if he destroy a *fœtus* in mistake for an *embryo*, he shall be free; (פטור), *i.e.*, not guilty. (*Sanhedrin*, fol. 78, col. 2.)

(*d.*) He who has been flogged and exposes himself again to the same punishment is to be shut up in a narrow cell, in which he can only stand upright, and fed with barley till he burst. (*Ibid.*, fol. 81, col. 2.)

(*e.*) If one commits murder, and there is not sufficient legal evidence (שלא בעדים, literally, *without witnesses*), he is to be shut up in a narrow cell and fed with "the bread of adversity and the water of affliction" (Isa. xxx. 20). They give him this diet till his bowels shrink, and then he is fed with barley till (as it swells in his bowels) his intestines burst. (*Ibid.*)

(*f.*) A woman who is doomed, being *enceinte*, to suffer the extreme penalty of the law, is first beaten, בית כנגד הרין, about the womb, lest a mishap occur at the execution. (*Erachin*, fol. 7, col. 1.)

(*g.*) If a woman who has vowed the vow of a Nazarite drink wine or defile herself by contact with a dead body (see Num. vi. 2–6), she is to undergo the punishment of forty stripes. (*Nazir*, fol. 23, col. 1.)

(*h.*) The Rabbis teach that when the woman has to be flogged, the man has only to bring a sacrifice ; and that if she is not to be flogged, the man is not required to bring a sacrifice. (This is in reference to Lev. xix. 20, 21.) (*Kerithoth*, fol. 11, col. 1.)

(*i.*) Rav Yehudah says, "He that eats a בניתא (an aquatic insect, the swallowing of which while drinking would involve no penalty whatever—*Tosefoth*), receives forty stripes save one (the penalty for transgressing negative precepts), for it belongs to the class of 'creeping things that do creep upon *the earth*' (Lev. xi. 29)." Rav Yehudah once gave a practical exemplification of this ruling of his.

Abaii says, "He that eats a פוטיתא (an animalcule found in stagnant water), receives four times forty stripes save one. For eating an ant this penalty is five times repeated, and for eating a wasp it is inflicted six times." (*Maccoth*, fol. 16, col. 2.)

(*j.*) When one is ordered to construct a booth, or to prepare a palm-branch for the Feast of Tabernacles, or to make fringes, and does not do so, he is to be flogged, עד שתצא נפשו, *i.e.*, till his soul comes out of him. (*Chullin*, fol. 132, col. 2.)

(*k.*) Once on a time, as the Rabbis relate, the wicked

Government sent two officers (סרדיוטות) to the wise men of Israel, saying, "Teach us your law." This being put into their hands, three times over they perused it; and when about to leave they returned it, remarking, "We have carefully studied your law, and find it equitable save in one particular. You say: When the ox of an Israelite gores to death the ox of an alien, its owner is not liable to make compensation; but if the ox of an alien gore to death the ox of an Israelite, its owner must make full amends for the loss of the animal; whether it be the *first or second* time that the ox has so killed another (in which case an Israelite would have to pay to another Israelite only *half* the value of the loss), or the *third* time (when he would be fined to the full extent of his neighbour's loss). Either ' *neighbour* ' (in Exod. xxi. 35, for such the word signifies in the original Hebrew, though the Authorised Version has *another*) is taken strictly as referring to an Israelite only, and then an alien should be exempted as well; or if the word ' *neighbour* ' is to be taken in its widest sense, why should not an Israelite be bound to pay when his ox gores to death the ox of an alien?" "This legal point," was the answer, "we do not tell the Government." As Rashi says in reference to a preceding Halacha, "an alien forfeits the right to his own property in favour of the Jews." (*Bava Kama*, fol. 38, col. 1.)

For more on this subject see Index II.

169. Ptolemy, the king (of Egypt), assembled *seventy-two* elders of Israel and lodged them in *seventy-two* separate chambers, but did not tell them why he did so. Then he visited each one in turn and said, "Write out for me the law of Moses your Rabbi." The Holy One—blessed be He!—went and counselled the minds of every one of them, so that they all agreed, and wrote, "God created in the beginning," &c. *Megillah*, fol. 9, col. 1.

NOTE.—The Talmudic story of the origin of the Septuagint agrees in the main with the account of Aristeas and Josephus, but Philo gives a different version. Many of the Christian fathers believed it to be the work of inspiration.

170. Abraham was as tall as *seventy-four* people; what

he ate and drank was enough to satisfy *seventy-four* ordinary men, and his strength was proportionate.

Sophrim, chap. 21, 9.

171. The venerable Hillel had *eighty* disciples, thirty of whom were worthy that the Shechinah should rest upon them, as it rested upon Moses our Rabbi; and thirty of them were worthy that the sun should stand still (for them), as it did for Joshua the son of Nun; and twenty of them stood midway in worth. The greatest of all of them was Jonathan ben Uzziel, and the least of all was Rabbi Yochanan ben Zacchai. It is said of Rabbi Yochanan ben Zacchai that he did not leave unstudied the Bible, the Mishna, the Gemara, the constitutions, the legends, the minutiæ of the law, the niceties of the scribes, the arguments *à fortiori* and from similar premises, the theory of the change of the moon, the Gematria, the parable of the unripe grapes and the foxes, the language of demons, of palm-trees, and of ministering angels.

Bava Bathra, fol. 134, col. 1.

172. A male criminal is to be hanged with his face towards the people, but a female with her face towards the gibbet. So says Rabbi Eliezer; but the sages say the man only is hanged, not the woman. Rabbi Eliezer retorted, "Did not Simeon the son of Shetach hang women in Askelon?" To this they replied, "He indeed caused *eighty* women to be hanged, though two criminals are not to be condemned in one day."

Sanhedrin, fol. 45, col. 2.

NOTE.—We may here repeat the story of the execution of the eighty women here alluded to, as that is told by Rashi on the preceding page of the Talmud. Once a publican, an Israelite but a sinner, and a great and good man of the same place, having died on the same day, were about to be buried. While the citizens were engaged with the funeral of the latter, the relations of the other crossed their path, bearing the corpse to the sepulchre. Of a sudden a troop of enemies came upon the scene and caused them all to take to flight, one faithful disciple alone remaining by the bier of his Rabbi. After a while the citizens returned to inter the remains they had so unceremoniously left, but by some mistake they took the wrong bier and buried the publican with honour, in spite of the remonstrance of the disciple, while the relatives of the publican buried the Rabbi ignominiously. The poor disciple felt inconsolably distressed, and was anxious to know for what sin the great man had been buried with contempt, and for what merit the wicked man had been buried with such honour. His Rabbi then appeared to him in a dream, and said, "Comfort thou thy heart, and come I will show thee the honour I hold in Paradise, and I will also show thee that man in Gehenna, the hinge of the door of which even now creaks in his ears.* But because once on a time I listened to contemptuous talk about the Rabbis and did not check it, I have suffered an ignoble burial, while the publican enjoyed the honour that was intended for me because he once distributed gratuitously among the poor of the city a banquet he had prepared for the governor, but of which the governor did not come to partake." The disciple having asked the Rabbi how long this publican was to be thus severely treated, he replied, "Until the death of Simeon the son of Shetach, who is to take the publican's place in Gehenna." "Why so?" "Because, though he knows there are several Jewish witches in Askelon, he idly suffers them to ply their infernal trade and does not take any steps to extirpate them." On the morrow the disciple reported this speech to Simeon the son of Shetach, who at once proceeded to take action against the obnoxious witches. He engaged eighty stalwart young men, and choosing a rainy day, supplied each with an extra garment folded up and stowed away in an earthen vessel. Thus provided, they were each at a given signal to snatch up one of the eighty witches and carry her away, a task they would find of easy execution, as, except in contact with the earth, these creatures were powerless. Then Simeon the son of Shetach, leaving his men in ambush, entered the rendezvous of the witches, who, accosting him, asked, "Who art thou?" He replied, "I am a wizard, and am come to experiment in magic." "What trick have you to show?" they said. He answered, "Even though the day

---

* Which were formed into sockets for the gates of hell to turn in.

is wet I can produce eighty young men all in dry clothes."
They smiled incredulously and said, " Let us see !" He
went to the door, and at the signal the young men took
the dry clothes out of the jars and put them on, then
starting from their ambush, they rushed into the witches'
den, and each seizing one, lifted her up and carried
her off as directed. Thus overpowered, they were
brought before the court, convicted of malpractices and
led forth to execution. (*Sanhedrin*, fol. 44, col. 2.)

173. (Exod. xxiii. 35), "And I will take away sickness
from the midst of thee." It is taught that sickness
(מהלה, Machlah) means the bile. But why is it termed
Machlah ? Because *eighty-three* diseases are in it. Machlah by Gematria equals *eighty-three;* and all may be
avoided by an early breakfast of bread and salt and a
bottle of water. *Bava Kama*, fol. 92, col. 2.

174. If in a book of the law the writing is obliterated
all but *eighty-five* letters—as, for instance, in Num. x. 35,
36, "And it came to pass when the ark set forward," &c.,
—it may be rescued on the Sabbath from a fire, but not
otherwise. *Sabbath*, fol. 116, col. 1.

175. Elijah said to Rabbi Judah the brother of Rav
Salla the Pious, "The world will not last less than *eighty-
five* jubilees, and in the last jubilee the son of David will
come." *Sanhedrin*, fol. 97, col. 2.

176. There was not a single individual in Israel who
had not *ninety* Lybian donkeys laden with the gold and
silver of Egypt. (See chap. xii. No. 36, *infra*).
Bechoroth, fol. 5, col. 2.

177. (2 Sam. xix. 35), "Can thy servant taste what I
eat or what I drink ?" From this we learn that in the
aged the sense of taste is destroyed. . . . Rav says, " Bar-
zillai the Gileadite reports falsely, for the cook at the
house of Rabbi (the Holy) was *ninety-two* years old, and
yet could judge by taste of what was cooking in the pot."
Shabbath, fol. 152, col. 1.

178. Rava said, "Life, children, and competency do not depend on one's merit, but on luck; for instance, Rabbah and Rav Chasda were both righteous Rabbis; the one prayed for rain and it came, and the other did so likewise with the like result; yet Rav Chasda lived *ninety-two* years and Rabbah only forty. Rav Chasda, moreover, had sixty weddings in his family during his lifetime, whereas Rabbah had sixty serious illnesses in his during the short period of his life. At the house of the former even the dogs refused to eat bread made of the finest wheat flour, whereas the family of the latter were content to eat rough bread of barley and could not always obtain it." Rava also added, " For these three things I prayed to Heaven, two of which were and one was not granted unto me. I prayed for the wisdom of Rav Hunna and for the riches of Rav Chasda, and both these were granted unto me; but the humility and meekness of Rabbah, the son of Rav Hunna, for which I also prayed, was not granted."

Moed Katon, fol. 28, col. 1.

179. The judges who issued decrees at Jerusalem received for salary *ninety-nine* manahs from the contributions of the chamber. *Kethuboth*, fol. 105, col. 1.

180. *Ninety-nine* die from an evil eye for one who dies in the usual manner. *Bava Metzia*, fol. 107, col. 2.

CHAPTER XII.

TALMUDIC NUMBERS, RANGING FROM 'ONE HUNDRED' TO 'NINE HUNDRED AND NINETY-NINE' INCLUSIVE.

1. THE Rabbis have taught us who they are that are to be accounted rich. "Every one," says Rabbi Meir, "who enjoys his riches." But Rabbi Tarphon says, "Every one who has a *hundred* vineyards and a *hundred* fields, with a *hundred* slaves to labour in them." Rabbi Akiva pronounces him well off who has a wife that is becoming in all her ways; whereas Rabbi Yossi says, "He is rich who has a בית הכסא not far from his table."

Shabbath, fol. 25, col. 2.

2. A light for one is a light for a *hundred*.

Ibid., fol. 122, col. 1.

NOTE.—When a Gentile lights a candle or a lamp on the Sabbath-eve for his own use, an Israelite is permitted to avail himself of its light, as a light for one is a light for a hundred; but it is unlawful for an Israelite to order a Gentile to kindle a light for his use.

3. A *hundred* Rav Papas and not one (like) Ravina! (See chap. iv. No. 28, *supra*.)

4. A *hundred* zouzim employed in commerce will allow the merchant meat and wine at his table daily, but a *hundred* zouzim employed in farming will allow their owner only salt and vegetables.　*Yevamoth*, fol. 63, col. 1.

5. A *hundred* women are equal to only one witness (compare Deut. xvii. 6 and xix. 15).

Ibid., fol. 88, col. 2.

6. If song should cease, a *hundred* geese or a *hundred* measures of wheat might be offered for one zouz, and even then the buyer would refuse paying such a sum for them.

Soteh, fol. 48, col. 1.

Note.—Rav *in loco* says, " The ear that often listens to song shall be rooted out." Music, according to the idea here, raises the price of provisions. Do away with music and provisions will be so abundant that a goose would be considered dear at a penny. Theatres and music-halls are abominations to orthodox Jews, and the Talmud considers the voice of a woman to be immoral. (See "Genesis," p. 124, No. 43.)

7. When Rabbi Zira returned to the land of Israel he fasted a *hundred* times in order that he might forget the Babylonian Talmud (גמרא בבלאה).

Bava Metzia, fol. 85, col. 1.

Note.—This passage, as also that on p. 23, No. 15, will appear not a little surprising to many a reader, as we confess it does to ourselves. We must, however, give the Talmud great credit for recording such passages, and also the custodians of the Talmud for not having expunged them from its pages.

8. " Ye shall hear the small as well as the great" (Deut. i. 17). Resh Lakish said, " A lawsuit about a prutah (the smallest coin there is) should be esteemed of as much account as a suit of a *hundred* manahs."

Sanhedrin, fol. 8, col. 1.

9. Rav Yitzchak asks, " Why was Obadiah accounted worthy to be a prophet?" Because, he answers, he concealed a *hundred* prophets in a cave; as it is said (1 Kings xviii. 4), " When Jezebel cut off the prophets of the Lord, Obadiah took a *hundred* prophets and hid them by fifty in a cave." Why by fifties? Rabbi Eliezer explains, " He copied the plan from Jacob, who said, ' If Esau come to one company and smite it, then the other company which is left may escape.' " Rabbi Abuhu says, " It was because the caves would not hold any more."

Ibid., fol. 39, col. 2.

10. "And it came to pass after these things that God did test Abraham" (Gen. xxii. 1). After what things? Rabbi Yochanan, in the name of Rabbi Yossi ben Zimra, replies, "After the words of Satan, who said, 'Lord of the Universe! Thou didst bestow a son upon that old man when he was a *hundred* years of age, and yet he spared not a single dove from the festival to sacrifice to Thee.' God replied, 'Did he not make this festival for the sake of his son? and yet I know he would not refuse to sacrifice that son at my command.' To prove this, God did put Abraham to the test, saying unto him, 'Take now thy son;' just as an earthly king might say to a veteran warrior who had conquered in many a hard-fought battle, 'Fight, I pray thee, this severest battle of all, lest it should be said that thy previous encounters were mere haphazard skirmishes.' Thus did the Holy One—blessed be He!—address Abraham, 'I have tried thee in various ways, and not in vain either; stand this test also, for fear it should be insinuated that the former trials were trivial and therefore easily overcome. Take thy son.' Abraham replied, 'I have two sons.' 'Take thine only son.' Abraham answered, 'Each is the only son of his mother.' 'Take him whom thou lovest.' 'I love both of them,' said Abraham. 'Take Isaac.' Thus Abraham's mind was gradually prepared for this trial. While on the way to carry out this Divine command Satan met him, and (parodying Job iv. 2–5) said, 'Why ought grievous trials to be inflicted upon thee? Behold thou hast instructed many, and thou hast strengthened the weak hands. Thy words have supported him that was falling, and now this sore burden is laid upon thee.' Abraham answered (anticipating Ps. xxvi. 11), 'I will walk in my integrity.' Then said Satan (see Job iv. 6), 'Is not the fear (of God) thy folly? Remember, I pray thee, who ever perished being innocent?' Then finding that he could not persuade him, he said (perverting Job iv. 12), 'Now a word came to me by stealth. I overheard it behind the veil (in the Holy

of Holies above).   A lamb will be the sacrifice, and not Isaac.' Abraham said, ' It is the just desert of a liar not to be believed even when he speaks the truth.'"

Sanhedrin, fol. 89, col. 2.

11. It is better to have ten inches to stand upon than a *hundred* yards to fall.   *Avoth d'Rab. Nathan, chap. 1.*

12. When Israel went up to Jerusalem to worship their Father who is in heaven, they sat so close together that no one could insert a finger between them, yet when they had to kneel and to prostrate themselves there was room enough for them all to do so.   The greatest wonder of all was that even when a *hundred* prostrated themselves at the same time there was no need for the governor of the synagogue to request one to make room for another. (See p. 148, No. 2, *supra*.)   *Ibid., chap. 35.*

13. A man is bound to repeat a *hundred* blessings every day.   *Menachoth, fol. 43, col. 2.*

Note.—(*a.*) This duty, as Rashi tells us, is based upon Deut. x. 12, altering the word מה (what) into מאה (a hundred), by the addition of the letter א; and from the Tosafoth we learn the curious fact that " the text counts *a hundred letters*, with the addition of an א to the word מה, the verse itself containing ninety and nine. (See the " Aruch," *s. v.* מאה)

(*b.*) This is what the so-called Pagan Goethe, intent on self-culture as the first if not the final duty of man, makes Serlo in his " Meister" lay down as a rule which one should observe daily. " One," he says, " ought every day to hear a little song, read a good poem, see a fine picture, and, if possible, speak a few reasonable words." The contrast between this advice and that of the Talmud here and elsewhere is suggestive of reflections.

14. He who possesses one manah may buy, in addition to his bread, a litra of vegetables ; the owner of ten manahs

may add to his bread a litra of fish; he that has fifty
manahs may add a litra of meat; while the possessor of a
hundred may have pottage every day.

Chullin, fol. 84, col. 1.

15. Ben Hey-Hey said to Hillel, "What does this mean
that is written in Mal. iii. 18, 'Then shall ye return, and
discern between the righteous and the wicked, between
him that serveth God and him that serveth Him not'?
Does the righteous here mean him that serveth God, and
the wicked him that serveth Him not? Why this repetition?" To this Hillel replied, "The expressions, 'he that
serveth God, and he that serveth Him not,' are both to
be understood as denoting 'perfectly righteous,' but he who
repeats his lesson a *hundred* times is not to be compared
with one who repeats it *a hundred and one* times." Then
said Ben Hey-Hey, "What! because he has repeated what
he has learned only one time less than the other, is he to
be considered as 'one who serveth Him not'?" "Yes!"
was the reply; "go and learn a lesson from the published
tariff of the donkey-drivers—ten miles for one zouz, eleven
for two. *Chagqigah*, fol. 9, col. 2.

> Note.—Hillel was great and good and clever, but his exposi-
> tion of Scripture, as we see from the above, is not always
> to be depended upon. If, indeed, he was the teacher of
> Jesus, as some suppose him to have been, then Jesus
> must, even from a Rabbinical stand-point, be regarded as
> greater than Hillel the Great, for He never handled the
> Scriptures with such irreverence.

16. *One hundred and three* chapters (or psalms) were
uttered by David, and he did not pronounce the word
Hallelujah until he came to contemplate the downfall of
the wicked; as it is written (Ps. civ. 35), "Let the sinners
be consumed out of the earth, and let the wicked be no
more. Bless the Lord, O my soul, Hallelujah!" Instead
of *one hundred and three* we ought to say *a hundred and
four*, but we infer from this that "Blessed is the man,"

&c., and "Why do the heathen rage?" &c., are but one
psalm.   *Berachoth*, fol. 9, col. 2.

NOTE.—(*a*.) See chap. i. No. 28, *supra*. The first is an instructive psalm, the second a prophetic, and the reason why the two psalms are merged into one is because the first begins and the second ends with the same word, אשרי, "blessed."

(*b*.) One of the most charming women that we find figuring in the Talmud was the wife of Rabbi Meir, Beruriah by name; and as we meet with her in the immediate context of the above quotation, it may be well to introduce her here to the attention of the reader. The context speaks of a set of ignorant fellows (probably Greeks) who sorely vexed the soul of Rabbi Meir, her husband, and he ardently prayed God to take them away. Then Beruriah reasoned with her husband thus:—"Is it, pray, because it is written (Ps. civ. 35), 'Let the sinners be consumed'? It is not written חוטאים, 'sinners,' but חטאים, 'sins.' Besides, a little farther on in the text it is said, 'And the wicked will be no more;' that is to say, ויתמו חטאים, 'Let sins cease, and the wicked will cease too.' Pray, therefore, on their behalf that they may be led to repentance, and these wicked will be no more." This he therefore did, and they repented and ceased to vex him. Of this excellent and humane woman it may well be said, "She openeth her mouth with wisdom, and in her tongue is the law of kindness" (Prov. xxxi. 26). Her end was tragic. She was entrapped by a disciple of her husband, and out of shame she committed suicide. (See particulars by Rashi in Avodah Zarah, fol. 18, col. 2, and "Genesis," p. 187, notes *b* and *c*.)

17. The Hasmoneans ruled over Israel during the time of the second Temple a *hundred and three* years; and for a *hundred and three* the government was in the hands of the family of Herod.   *Avodah Zarah*, fol. 9, col. 1.

18. Rabbi Yochanan the son of Zacchai lived a *hundred and twenty* years; forty he devoted to commerce, forty to study, and forty to teaching. ¶

                     Rosh Hashanah, fol. 30, col. 2.

19. *One hundred and twenty* elders, and among them

several prophets, bore a part in composing the Eighteen Blessings (the Shemonah Esreh).

Meggillah, fol. 17, col. 2.

> Note.—A similar tradition was current among the early Christians with reference to the composition of the Creed. Its different sentences were ascribed to different apostles. However fitly this tradition may represent the community of faith with which the prophets on the one hand and the apostles on the other were inspired, it is not recommended by the critic as a proceeding calculated to ensure unity in a work of art.

20. Rabbi Shemuel says advantage may be taken of the mistakes of a Gentile. He once bought a gold plate as a copper one of a Gentile for four zouzim, and then cheated him out of one zouz into the bargain. Rav Cahana purchased *a hundred and twenty* vessels of wine from a Gentile for a hundred zouzim, and swindled him in the payment out of one of the hundred, and that while the Gentile assured him that he confidently trusted to his honesty. Rava once went parts with a Gentile and bought a tree, which was cut up into logs. This done, he bade his servant go and pick him out the largest logs, but to be sure to take no more than the proper number, because the Gentile knew how many there were. As Rav Ashi was walking abroad one day he saw some grapes growing in a roadside vineyard, and sent his servant to see whom they belonged to. "If they belong to a Gentile," he said, "bring some here to me; but if they belong to an Israelite, do not meddle with them." The owner, who happened to be in the vineyard, overheard the Rabbi's order and called out, "What! is it lawful to rob a Gentile?" "Oh, no," said the Rabbi evasively; "a Gentile might sell, but an Israelite would not." *Bava Kama*, fol. 113, col. 2.

> Note.—This is given simply as a sample of the teaching of the Talmud on the subject both by precept and example. There is no intention to cast a slight on general Jewish integrity, or suggest distrust in regard to their ethical creed.

21. Rabbon Gamliel, Rabbi Eliezer ben Azaryah, Rabbi Yehoshua, and Rabbi Akiva once went on a journey to Rome, and at Puteoli they already heard the noisy din of the city, though at a distance of a *hundred and twenty* miles. At the sound all shed tears except Akiva, who began to laugh. "Why laughest thou?" they asked. "Why do you cry?" he retorted. They answered, "These Romans, who worship idols of wood and stone and offer incense to stars and planets, abide in peace and quietness, while our Temple, which was the footstool of our God, is consumed by fire; how can we help weeping?" "That is just the very reason," said he, "why I rejoice; for if such be the lot of those who transgress His laws, what shall the lot of those be who observe and do them?"

Maccoth, fol. 24, col. 2.

22. When Adam observed that his sin was the cause of the decree which made death universal he fasted *one hundred and thirty* years, abstained all that space from intercourse with his wife, and wore girdles of fig-leaves round his loins. All these years he lived under divine displeasure, and begat devils, demons, and spectres; as it is said (Gen. v. 3), "And Adam lived a *hundred and thirty* years, and begat in his own likeness, after his image," which implies that, until the close of those years, his offspring were not after his own image.

Eiruvin, fol. 18, col. 2.

23. There is a tradition that there was once a disciple in Yabneh who gave a *hundred and fifty* reasons to prove a reptile to be clean (which the Scripture regards as unclean.—Compare Lev. xi. 29.)　　　*Ibid.*, fol. 13, col. 2.

24. The ablutionary tank made by Solomon was as large as a *hundred and fifty* lavatories.

Ibid., fol. 14, col. 1.

25. A *hundred and eighty* years before the destruction

of the Temple, the empire of idolatry (Rome) began the conquest of Israel. *Shabbath*, fol. 15, col. 1.

> NOTE.—The empire of Rome was, some think, so designated, because it strove with all its might to drag down the worship of God to the worship of man, and resolve the cause of God into the cause of the Emperor.

26. During the time of the second Temple Persia domineered over Israel for thirty-four years and the Greeks held sway a *hundred and eighty*.

Avodah Zarah, fol. 9, col. 1.

27. Foolish saints, crafty villains, sanctimonious women, and self-afflicting Pharisees are the destroyers of the world. What is it to be a foolish saint? To see a woman drowning in the river and refrain from trying to save her because of the look of the thing. Who is to be regarded as a crafty villain? Rabbi Yochanan says, "He who prejudices the magistrates by prepossessing them in favour of his cause before his opponent has had time to make his appearance." Rabbi Abhu says, "He who gives a denarius to a poor man to make up for him the sum total of *two hundred* zouzim; for it is enacted that he who possesses *two hundred* zouzim is not entitled to receive any gleanings, neither what is forgotten in the field, nor what is left in the corner of it (see Lev. xxiii. 22), nor poor relief either. But if he is only one short of the *two hundred* zouzim, and a thousand people give anything to him, he is still entitled to the poor man's perquisites."

Soteh, fol. 21, col. 2.

28. The cup of David in the world to come will contain *two hundred and twenty-one* logs; as it is said (Ps. xxiii. 5), "My cup runneth over," the numerical value of the Hebrew word (רויה), "runneth over," being *two hundred and twenty-one*. *Yoma*, fol. 76, col. 1.

> NOTE.—In the world to come the Holy One will make a grand banquet for the righteous from the flesh of the leviathan. Bava Bathra, fol. 75, col. 1. (See the Morn-

ing Service for the middle days of the Feast of Tabernacles.) God will make a banquet for the righteous on the day when He shows His mercy to the posterity of Isaac. After the meal the cup of blessing will be handed to Abraham, in order that he may pronounce the blessing, but he will plead excuse because he begat Ishmael. Then Isaac will be told to take the cup and speak the benediction of grace, but he also will plead his unworthiness because he begat Esau. Next Jacob also will refuse because he married two sisters. Then Moses, on the ground that he was unworthy to enter the land of promise, or even to be buried in it ; and finally Joshua will plead unworthiness because he had no son. David will then be called upon to take the cup and bless, and he will respond, " Yea, I will bless, for I am worthy to bless ; as it is said (Ps. cxvi. 13), ' I will take the cup of salvation, and call upon the name of the Lord.'" Psachim, fol. 119, col. 2. This cup, as we are told above, will contain *two hundred and twenty-one* logs (the לג, as the Rabbis tell us, is the twenty-fourth part of a seah, therefore this cup will hold rather more than one-third of a hogshead of wine).

29. Beruriah once found a certain disciple who studied in silence. As soon as she saw him she spurned him and said, " Is it not thus written (2 Sam. xxiii. 5), ' Ordered in all and sure ?' If *ordered* with all the *two hundred and forty-eight* members of thy body, it will be *sure ;* if not, it will not be sure." It is recorded that Rabbi Eliezer had a disciple who also studied in silence, but that after three years he forgot all that he had learned.

Eiruvin, fol. 53, col. 2, and fol. 54, col. 1.

Note.—In continuation of the above we read that Shemuel said to Rav Yehudah, " Shrewd fellow, open thy mouth when thou readest, &c., so that thy reading may remain and thy life may be lengthened ; as it is written in Prov. iv. 22, ' For they are life unto those that find them ;' read not למצאיהם, 'that find them,' but read למוציאיהם, ' that bring them forth by the mouth,' *i.e.*, that read them aloud." It was and is still a common custom in the East to study aloud.

30. As an anathema enters all the *two hundred and*

forty-eight members of the body, so does it issue from them all. Of the entering-in of the anathema it is written, (Josh. vi. 17), "And the city shall be הרם, accursed;" הרם, by Gematria amounting to *two hundred and forty-eight.* Of the coming-out of the anathema it is written (Hab. iii. 2), "In wrath remember רהם, mercy;" רהם, a transposition of the letters of the word for *accursed*, also amounting by Gematria to *two hundred and forty-eight.* Rabbi Joseph says, "Hang an anathema on the tail of a dog and he will still go on doing mischief."

Moed Katon, fol. 17, col. 1.

31. The human body has *two hundred and forty-eight* members:—Thirty in the foot—that is, six in each toe—ten in the ankle, two in the thigh, five in the knee, one in the hip, three in the hip-ball, eleven ribs, thirty in the hand—that is, six in each finger—two in the fore-arm, two in the elbow, one in the upper arm, four in the shoulder. Thus we have *one hundred and one* on each side; to this add eighteen vertebræ in the spine, nine in the head, eight in the neck, six in the chest, and five in the loins.

Oholoth, chap. 1, mish. 8.

Note.—See also Eiruvin, fol. 53, col. 2, and the Musaph for the second day of Pentecost. In the Musaph for the New Year there is a prayer that runs thus, "Oh, deign to hear the voice of those who glorify Thee with all their members, according to the number of the *two hundred and forty-eight* affirmative precepts. In this month they blow thirty sounds, according to the thirty members of the soles of their feet; the additional offerings of the day are ten, according to the ten in their ankles; they approach the altar twice, according to their two legs; five are called to the law, according to the five joints in their knees; they observe the appointed time to sound the cornet on the first day of the month, according to the one in their thigh; they sound the horn thrice, according to the three in their hips; lo! with the additional offering of the new moon they are eleven, according to their eleven ribs; they pour out the supplication with nine blessings, according to the muscles in their arms, and which contain thirty verses, according to the thirty

P

in the palms of their hands; they daily repeat the prayer of eighteen blessings, according to the eighteen vertebræ in the spine; at the offering of the continual sacrifice they sound nine times, according to the nine muscles in their head," &c., &c.

32. It is related of Rabbi Ishmael's disciples that they dissected a low woman who had been condemned by the Government to be burned, and upon examination they found that her body contained *two hundred and fifty-two* members.   *Bechoroth*, fol. 45, col. 1.

33. The regular period of gestation is either *two hundred and seventy-one*, two hundred and seventy-two, or two hundred and seventy-three days.

Niddah, fol. 38, col. 1.

34. Revere the memory of Chananiah ben Chiskiyah, for had it not been for him the Book of Ezekiel would have been suppressed, because of the contradictions it offers to the words of the law. By the help of *three hundred* bottles of oil, which were brought up into an upper chamber, he prolonged his lucubrations till he succeeded in reconciling all the discrepancies.

Shabbath, fol. 13, col. 2.

35. It is related of Johanan, the son of Narbai, that he used to eat *three hundred* calves, and to drink *three hundred* bottles of wine, and to consume forty measures of young pigeons by way of dessert. (Rashi says this was because he had to train many priests in his house.)

P'sachim, fol. 57, col. 1.

36. The keys of the treasury of Korah were so many that it required *three hundred* white mules to carry them. These, with the locks, were said to be made of white leather. (See chap. xi. No. 176, *supra*.)

Ibid., fol. 119, col. 1.

Note.—The Midrash repeats the same story, and adds, " His wealth was his ruin." "He is as rich as Korah " is now a Jewish proverb.

37. Rav Chiya, the son of Adda, was tutor to the children of Resh Lakish, and once absented himself from his duties for three days. On his return he was questioned as to the reason of his conduct, and he gave the following reply: "My father bequeathed to me a vine, trained on high trellis-work as a bower, from which I gathered the first day *three hundred* bunches, each of which yielded a gerav of wine (a gerav is a measure containing as much as 288 egg-shells would contain). On the second day I again gathered *three hundred* bunches of smaller size, two only producing one gerav (one bunch yielding the quantity of wine 144 egg-shells would contain). The third day I also gathered *three hundred* bunches, but only three bunches to the gerav, and have yet left more than half of the grapes free for any one to gather them." Thereupon Resh Lakish observed to him, "If thou hadst not been so negligent (losing time in the instruction of my children), it would have yielded still more."

Kethuboth, fol. 111, col. 2.

38. There were *three hundred* species of male demons in Sichin, but what the female demon herself was like is known to no one. *Gittin*, fol. 68, col. 1.

39. "Now, when Job's three friends heard of all this evil that was come upon him, they came each from his own place; Eliphaz the Temanite, Bildah the Shuhite, and Zophar the Naamathite: for they had made an appointment together to come and mourn with him, and to comfort him" (Job ii. 11). What is meant when it is said, "They had made an appointment together?" Rab. Yehudah says in the name of Rav, "This is to teach that they all came in by one gate." But there is a tradition that each lived *three hundred* miles away from the other. How then came they to know of Job's sad condition? Some say they had wreaths, others say trees (each representing an absent friend), and when any friend was in distress the

one representing him straightway began to wither. Rava said, "Hence the proverb, ' Either a friend as the friends of Job, or death.'" *Bava Bathra*, fol. 16, col. 2.

NOTE.—Rashi tenders this explanation, that Job and his friends had each wreaths with their names engraved on them, and if affliction befell any one his name upon the wreath would change colour.

40. Rabbi Yochanan says that Rabbi Meir knew *three hundred* fables about foxes, but we have only three of them, viz., "The fathers have eaten sour grapes, and the children's teeth are set on edge" (Ezek. xviii. 2); "Just balances and just weights" (Lev. xix. 36); "The righteous is delivered out of trouble, and the wicked cometh in his stead" (Prov. xi. 8).

Sanhedrin, fol. 38, col. 2, and fol. 39, col. 1.

NOTE.—Quite *apropos* to this we glean the following from Rashi :—A fox once induced a wolf to enter a Jewish dwelling to help the inmates to get ready the Sabbath meal. No sooner did he enter than the whole household set upon him, and so belaboured him with cudgels that he was obliged to flee for his life. For this trick the wolf was indignant at the fox, and sought to kill him, but he pacified him with the remark, "They would not have beaten thee if thy father had not on a former occasion belied confidence, and eaten up the choicest pieces that were set aside for the meal." "What!" rejoined the wolf, "the fathers have eaten sour grapes, and shall the children's teeth be set on edge?" "Well," interrupted the fox, "come with me now and I will show thee a place where thou mayest eat and be satisfied." He thereupon took him to a well. across the top of which rested a transverse axle with a rope coiled round it, to each extremity of which a bucket was attached. The fox, entering the bucket, which happened to be at the top, soon descended by his own weight to the bottom of the well, and thereby raised the other bucket to the top. On the wolf inquiring at the fox why he had gone down there, he replied, because he knew there was meat and cheese to eat and be satisfied, in proof of which he pointed to a cheese, which happened to be the reflection of the moon on the water. Upon which the wolf inquired, "And how am I to get down beside you?" The fox replied, "By getting into the bucket at the top." He did as directed, and as he descended the bucket with the fox rose to the top. The wolf in this plight again appealed to the fox. "But how am I to get out?" The reply was, "The righteous is delivered out of trouble, and the wicked cometh in his stead;" and is it not written, "Just balances just weights"?

41. When Rabbi Eliezer, on his deathbed, taught Rabbi Akiva *three hundred* particulars to be observed in regard to the white spot covered with hair which was the sign of leprosy, the former lifted up his arms and placed them on his chest and exclaimed, "Woe is me, because of these my two arms, these two scrolls of the law, that are about to depart from this world; for if all the seas were ink, and all the reeds were quills, and all the men were scribes, they could not record all I have learned and all I have taught, and how much I have heard at the lips of sages in the schools. And what is more, I also taught *three hundred* laws based on the text, 'A witch shall not live.'"

Avoth d'Rab. Nathan, chap. 25.

Note.—This truly Oriental exaggeration, which Rabbi Eliezer ben Azariah so complacently applies to himself, was spoken also of Rabbi Yochanan before him (Bereshith Rabba); and an acrostic poem in the Morning Service for Pentecost adopts the same hyperbole almost word for word, and turns it to very pious account. It is interesting to note how contemporary sacred literature abounds in similar hyperbolic expressions. In John xxi. 25 it is said, "There are also many other things which Jesus did, the which, if they should be written every one, I suppose that even the world itself could not contain the books that should be written." Cicero, too, speaks of a glory of such a weight that even heaven itself is scarcely able to contain it; and Livy, on one occasion, describes the power of Rome as with difficulty restrained within the limits of the world.

Here it may not be out of place if we introduce a few of the many passages in the Talmud that treat of enchantment and witchcraft, as well as magic, charms, to a hundred, but we must confine ourselves to a score or so.

(*a.*) The daughters of Israel burn incense for (purposes of) sorcery. (*Berachoth*, fol. 53, col. 1.)

(*b.*) Ben Azai (son of impudence), says, " . . . he who seats himself and then feels . . . . (which must not be explained), the effects of witchcraft, even when practised in Spain, will come upon him. What is the remedy when one forgets and first sits down and then feels? . . . When he rises let him say, לא תחים ולא תחתים, 'Not these and not of these; not the witchcraft of sorcerers and not the sorcery of witches.'" (*Ibid.*, fol. 62, col. 1.)

(*c.*) The daughters of Israel in later generations lapsed into the practice of witchcraft. (*Eiruvin*, fol. 64, col. 2.)

(*d.*) Ameimar says, "The superior of the witches told me that when a person meets any of them he should mutter thus, 'May a potsherd of boiling dung be stuffed into your mouths, you ugly witches! May the hair with which you perform your sorcery be torn from your heads, so that ye become bald. May the wind scatter the crumbs wherewith ye do your divinations. May your spices be scattered, and may the wind blow away the saffron you hold in your hands for the practising of sorcery.'" (*Psachim*, fol. 110, col. 1, 2.)

(*e.*) Yohanna, the daughter of Ratibi, was a widow, who bewitched women in their confinement. (See *Rashi* on *Sotah*, fol. 22, col. 1.)

(*f.*) Rabbi Shimon ben Gamliel, in the name of Rabbi Yehoshua, says, "Since the destruction of the Temple a day has not passed without a curse; the dew does not come down with a blessing, and the fruits have lost their proper taste." Rabbi Yossi adds, " Also the lusciousness of the fruit is gone." Rabbi Shimon ben Elazar says, " With the decay of purity the taste and aroma (of the fruit) has disappeared, and with the tithes the richness of the corn." The sages say, " Lewdness and witchcraft ruin everything." (*Sotah*, fol. 48, col. 1.)

(*g.*) A certain magician used to strip the dead of their shrouds. Once when he came to the tomb of Rav Tovi bar Mathna, he was seized and held fast by the beard, but Abaii having interceded on behalf of his friend, the grip was let go and he was set at liberty. Next year he came again on the same errand, and again he was seized by the beard. This time Abaii's intercession was

of no avail, and he was not liberated until they brought
a pair of scissors and cut off his beard. (*Bava Bathra*,
fol. 58, col. 1.)

(*h.*) None were allowed to sit in the Sanhedrin unless
they had a knowledge of magic. (*Sanhedrin*, fol. 17,
col. 1.)

(*i.*) Rabbi Shimon said, "An enchanter is הכיעביר
על העין שבעה מיני זבור, one who passeth the exudation
(שכבת זרע) of *seven* different sorts of male creatures over
the eye." The sages say he is one who practises and
palms off optical illusions. Rabbi Akiva says, " He is
one who calculates times and hours, and says To-day is
good to start on a journey, To-morrow will be a lucky
day for selling, The year before the Sabbatical year is
generally good for growing wheat, The pulling up* of
pease will preserve them from being spoiled." According
to the Rabbis, " An enchanter is he who augurs ill when
his bread drops from his mouth, or if he drops the stick
that supports him from his hand, or if his son calls after
him, or a crow caws in his hearing, or a deer crosses his
path, or he sees a serpent at his right hand or a fox on
his left, or if he says to the tax-gatherer, ' Do not begin
with me the first in the morning;' or, ' It is the first of
the month ;' or, ' It is the exit of the Sabbath,' *i.e.*, the
commencement of a new week." (*Sanhedrin*, fol. 65,
col. 2.)

(*j.*) " By the term witch," the Rabbis say, " we are
to understand either male or female." " If so," it is
asked, " why the term מכשפה ' witch,' in Exod. xxii. 18,
in the Hebrew verse 17, is in the feminine gender?"
" Because," it is answered, " most *women* are witches."
(*Ibid.*, fol. 67, col. 1.)

(*k.*) If the proud (in Israel) were to cease, the magi-
cians would also cease ; as it is written (Isa. i. 25), " I
will purge away thy dross and take away all thy tin."
(*Ibid.*, fol. 98, col. 1.)

(*l.*) Among those who have no portion in the world
to come is he who reads the books of the strangers,
foreign books (ספרי החיצונים, books of outsiders. See
also *Sanhedrin*, fol. 90, col. 1). Now Rav Yoseph says,
" It is unlawful to read the Book of the Son of Sirach,
. . . because it is written therein (Ecclesiasticus xlii. 9,
&c., as quoted, or rather misquoted, in the Talmud),
' A daughter is a false treasure to her father : because of

* Instead of cutting.

anxiety for her he cannot sleep at night; when she is young, for fear she should be seduced; in her virginity, lest she play the harlot; in her marriageable age, lest she should not get married; and when married, lest she should be childless; and when grown old, lest she practise witchcraft.'" (*Sanhedrin*, fol. 100, col. 2.)

(*m.*) He who multiplieth wives multiplieth witchcraft. (*Avoth*, chap. 2.)

(*n.*) Most donkey-drivers are wicked, but most sailors are pious. The best physicians are destined for hell, the most upright butcher is a partner of Amalek. Bastards are mostly cunning, and servants mostly handsome. Those who are well-descended are bashful, and children mostly resemble their mother's brother. Rabbi Shimon ben Yochai bids us " kill the best of Gentiles " (modern editions qualify this by adding, *in time of war*), "and smash the head of the best of serpents." " The best among women," he says, " is a witch." Blessed is he who does the will of God ! (*Sophrim*, chap. 15, hal. 10.)

(*o.*) On the Sabbath one may carry a grasshopper's egg as a charm against earache, the tooth of a living fox to promote sleep, the tooth of a dead fox to prevent sleep, and the nail of one crucified (as a remedy) for inflammation or swelling. For cutaneous disorders he is to repeat Baz Baziah, Mass Massiah, Cass Cassiah, Sharlaii, and Amarlaii (names of angels), &c. . . . As the mules do not increase and multiply, so may the skin disease not increase and spread upon the body of N., the son of the woman N., &c. (*Shabbath*, fol. 67, col. 1.)

(*p.*) " For night-blindness, let a man take a hair-rope and bind one end of it to his own leg and the other to a dog's, then let children clatter a potsherd after him, and call out, 'Old man ! dog ! fool ! cock !' Let him now collect seven pieces of meat from seven (different) houses; let him set them on the cross-bar of the threshold, then let him eat them on the town middens ; and after that let him undo the hair-rope, then let him say thus : ' Blindness of So-and-so, son of Mrs. So-and-so, leave So-and-so, son of Mrs. So-and-so, and be brushed into the pupil of the eye of the dog.'" (Quoted from " The Fragment," by Rev. W. H. Lowe of Cambridge.) (*Gittin*, fol. 69, col. 1.)

(*q.*) According to the Rabbis, a man should not drink water by night, for thus he exposes himself to the power of Shavriri, the demon of blindness. What then should he do if he is thirsty? If there be another man with him, let him rouse him up and say, "I am thirsty;" but if he be alone, let him tap upon the lid of the jug (to make the demon fancy there's some one with him), and addressing himself by his own name and the name of his mother, let him say, "Thy mother has bid thee beware of *Shavriri, vriri, riri, iri, ri,*" in a white cup. Rashi says by this incantation the demon gradually contracts and vanishes as the sounds of the word Shavriri decrease. (*Avodah Zarah*, fol. 12, col. 2.)

(*r.*) A python is a familiar spirit who speaks from his arm-pits; a wizard is one who speaks with the mouth. As the Rabbis have taught, a familiar spirit is one who speaks from his joints and his wrists; a wizard is one who, putting a certain bone into his mouth, causes it to speak. (*Sanhedrin*, fol. 65, col. 1, 2.)

(*s.*) He who says to a raven, "Croak," and to a hen raven, "Droop thy tail and turn it this way as a lucky sign," is an imitator of the ways of the Amorites (Lev. xviii. 3). (*Shabbath*, fol. 67, col. 2.)

(*t.*) Women going out on the Sabbath-day are allowed, as the Rabbis teach, to carry with them אבן תקומה, a certain stone believed to counteract abortion.

Abaii interrupts his exposition of this Halachah in order to enumerate certain antidotes to chronic fever which, he says, he had learned from his mother. Take a new zouz and then procure its weight in sea-salt; hang this round the neck, suspended by a papyrus fibre, so that it may rest just in the hollow in front. If this does not answer, go where two or more roads meet and watch for the first big ant that is going home loaded; lay hold of it and place it in a brass tube; stop up the end of the tube with lead, putting as many seals upon it as possible; then shake it, saying the while, "My load be upon thee, and thine upon me." To this Rav Acha, the son of Rav Hunna, objected to Rav Ashi, and asked, "Might not the ant have been already laden with another man's fever?" "True," observed the other; "nevertheless let him say, 'My load be upon thee as well as thine own.'" If this be not effective, then take a new earthenware pot, and going to the nearest stream, say, "Stream, stream, lend me a pot full of water for one who is on a visit to me." Wave it seven times round thy head and then throw the water back again, saying, "Stream, stream, take back thy borrowed water, for my guest came and went the same day."

Rav Hunna then adds a prescription for a tertian fever, and Rabbi Yochanan gives the following as effective against a burning fever:—Take an iron knife, and having fastened a papyrus fibre to the nearest bramble, cut off a piece and say, " And the Angel of the Lord appeared to him in a *flame of fire*," &c., as in Exod. iii. 2. On the morrow cut off another piece and say, "The Lord saw that he (the fever) *turned aside;*" then upon the third day say, " Draw not hither," and stooping down, pray, " Bush, bush! the Holy One—blessed be He!—caused His Shechinah to lodge upon thee, not because thou art the loftiest, for thou art the lowest of all trees ; and as when thou didst see the fire of Hananiah, Mishael, and Azariah, thou didst flee therefrom, so see the fire (fever) of this sufferer and flee from it." (*Shabbath*, fol. 66, col. 2, &c.)

(*u.*) Rabba once created a man (out of dust) and sent him to Rabbi Zira, who having addressed the figure and received no answer, said, " Thou art (made) by witchcraft ; return to thy native dust." Rav Chaneanah and Rav Oshayah sat together every Sabbath eve studying ‏כפר יצירה‎, the book Yetzirah (*i.e.*, the book of Creation), until they were able to create for themselves a calf (as large as a) three-year old, and they did eat thereof. (*Sanhedrin*, fol. 65, col. 2.)

(*v.*) Yannai once turned in to a certain inn, and asked for water to drink, when they gave him ‏שתיתא‎ (Shethitha, *i.e.*, water mixed with flour). He noticed that the lips of the woman who brought it moved (and so suspecting that something was wrong), he poured out a little of it and it became scorpions. He then said, " I have drunk of thine, now thou shalt drink of mine." The woman drank and was transformed into an ass, which he mounted and rode to the market-place. One of her companions having come up, broke the spell, and the ass he had ridden was on the spot transformed back again into a woman. In reference to the above, Rashi naïvely remarks that " we are not to suppose that Yannai was a Rabbi, for he was not held in esteem, because he practised witchcraft." But Rashi is mistaken ; see Sophrim, chap. 16, hal. 6. (*Sanhedrin*, fol. 67, col. 2.)

(*w.*) Ten measures of witchcraft came into the world; Egypt received nine measures, and the rest of the world one. (*Kiddushin*, fol. 49, col. 2.)

(*x.*) The Rabbis say that on the Sabbath סם ומשבין בבני מים, serpents and scorpions may be tamed by charming; that a metal ring, such as may be carried on the Sabbath, may be applied as a remedy to a sore eye; but that demons may not be consulted on that day about lost property. Rabbi Yossi has said, "This ought not to be done even on week-days." Rav Hunna says, "The Halachah does not enjoin as Rabbi Yossi says, and even he prohibits it only because of the risk there is in consulting demons. For instance, Rav Yitzchak bar Yoseph was once desperately delivered from the attacks of a vicious demon by a cedar-tree opening of its own accord and enclosing him in its trunk." (*Sanhedrin*, fol. 101, col. 1.)

(*y.*) Rabbi Yochanan ben Zachai acquired a knowledge of the language of angels and demons for purposes of incantation. (*Bava Bathra*, fol. 134, col. 1.)

(*z.*) "Neither shall ye use enchantments" . . . (Lev. xix. 26). Such, for instance, as those practised with cats, fowls, and fishes. (*Sanhedrin*, fol. 66, col. 1.)

(*aa.*) Rav Ketina happened once, in his travels, to hear the noise of an earthquake just as he came opposite to the abode of one who was wont to conjure with human bones. Happening to mutter aloud to himself as he passed, "Does the conjurer really know what that noise is?" a voice answered, "Ketina, Ketina, why shouldn't I know? When the Holy One—blessed be He!—thinks of His children who dwell in sorrowful circumstances among the nations of the earth, He lets fall two tears into the great sea, and His voice is heard from one end of the world to the other, and that is the rumbling noise we hear." Upon which Rav Ketina protested, "The conjurer is a liar, his words are not true; they might have been true, had there been two rumbling noises." The fact was, two such noises were heard, but Rav Ketina would not acknowledge it, lest, by so doing, he should increase the popularity of the conjurer. Rav Ketina is of opinion that the rumbling noise is caused by God clapping His hands together, as it is said (Ezek. xxi. 22; A. V., ver. 17), "I will also smite My hands together, and I will cause My fury to rest." (*Berachoth*, fol. 59, col. 1.)

42. Rabbi Elazar ben Azariah proclaimed this anathema with the blast of *three hundred* trumpets:—"Whoever shall take drink from the hand of a bride, no matter whether she be the daughter of a disciple of the wise or the daughter of an Amhaaretz, it is all one as if he drunk it from the hand of a harlot." Again, it is said, "He who receives a cup from the hands of a bride and drinks it therefrom, has no portion whatever in the world to come."

Tract Calah.

43. There was a place for collecting the ashes in the middle of the altar, and there were at times in it nearly as much as *three hundred* cors (equal to about 2830 bushels) of ashes. On Rava remarking that this must be an exaggeration, Rav Ammi said the law, the prophets, and the sages are wont to use hyperbolical language. Thus the law speaks of "Cities great and walled up to heaven" (Deut. i. 28); the prophets speak of "the earth rent with the sound of them" (1 Kings i. 40); the sages speak as above and also as follows. There was a golden vine at the entrance of the Temple, trailing on crystals, on which devotees who could used to suspend offerings of fruit and grape clusters. "It happened once," said Rabbi Elazer ben Rabbi Zadoc, "that *three hundred* priests were counted off to clear the vine of the offerings."

Chullin, fol. 90, col. 2.

44. *Three hundred* priests were told off to draw the veil (of the Temple) aside; for it is taught that Rabbi Shimon ben Gamliel declared in the name of Rabbi Shimon the Sagan (or high priest's substitute), that the thickness of the veil was a handbreadth. It was woven of seventy-two cords, and each cord consisted of twenty-four strands. It was forty cubits long and twenty wide. Eighty-two myriads of damsels worked at it, and two such veils were made every year. When it became soiled, it took *three hundred* priests to immerse and cleanse it.

Ibid., fol. 90, col. 2.

45. When Moses was about to enter Paradise he turned to Joshua and said, " If any doubtful matters remain, ask me now and I will explain them." To this Joshua replied, " Have I ever left thy side for an hour and gone away to any other? Hast thou not thyself written concerning me (Exod. xxxiii. 11), ' His servant Joshua, the son of Nun, a young man, departed not out of the Tabernacle?'" As a punishment for this pert reply, which must have distressed and confounded his master, Joshua's power of brain was immediately weakened, so that he forgot *three hundred* Halachahs, and seven hundred doubts sprang up to perplex him. All Israel then rose up to murder him, but the Holy One—blessed be He!—said unto him, " To teach thee the Halachahs and their explanation is impossible, but go and trouble them with work; as it is said (Josh. i. 1), ' Now after the death of Moses, the servant of the Lord, it came to pass that the Lord spake unto Joshua,'" &c. *Temurah*, fol. 16, col. 1.

46. In the future God will assign to each righteous man *three hundred and ten* worlds as an inheritance; for it is said (Prov. viii. 21), " That I may cause those that love me to inherit (שׁי) substance, and I will fill their treasures." שׁי by Gematria equals *three hundred and ten*. *Sanhedrin*, fol. 100, col. 1, and *Okitzin*, chap. 3, mish. 12.

47. An old woman once complained before Rav Nachman that the Head of the Captivity and certain Rabbis with him were enjoying themselves in her booth, which they had surreptitiously taken possession of and would not surrender, but Rav Nachman gave no heed to her remonstrance. Then she raised her voice and cried aloud, " A woman whose father had *three hundred and eighteen* slaves is now pleading before you, and you paying no heed to her!" Upon which Rav Nachman turned to his associates and said, " She is a bawling woman, but she has no right to claim the booth, only the value of its timber." *Succah*, fol. 31, col. 1.

48. Elijah the Tishbite once said to Rav Yehudah, the brother of Rav Salla the Holy, " You ask why the Messiah does not come, but though it is just now the Day of Atonement," ואביעיל כמה בתולתא בנהרדעא. "And what," asked the Rabbi, " does the Holy One—blessed be He!— say to that ?" "He says, ' Sin lieth at the door '" (Gen. iv. 7). "And what has Satan to say ?" "He has no permission to accuse any one on the Day of Atonement." "How do we know this ?" Ramma bar Chamma replied, " Satan (השטן) by Gematria equals *three hundred and sixty-four*, therefore on that number of days only has he permission to accuse ; but on the Day of Atonement (*i.e.*, the 365th day) he cannot accuse." *Yoma*, fol. 20, col. 1.

49. Rav Yitzchak said, " What is the meaning of that which is written (Ps. cxl. 8), ' Grant not, O Lord, the desires of the wicked ; further not his wicked device, lest they exalt themselves. Selah ?'" It is the prayer of Jacob to the Lord of the universe that He would not grant to Esau, " the wicked, the desires of his heart." " Further not his wicked device," this refers to Germamia of Edom (*i.e.*, Rome), for if they (the Romans) were suffered to go forward they would destroy the whole world ! Rav Chama bar Chanena said, " There are *three hundred* crowned heads in Germamia of Edom, and there are *three hundred and sixty-five* dukes in Babylon. These encounter each other daily, and one of them commits murder, and they strive to set up a king."   *Megyillah*, fol. 6, col. 2.

50. In the great city (of Rome) there were *three hundred and sixty-five* streets, and in each street there were *three hundred and sixty-five* palaces, and in every one of these there were *three hundred and sixty-five* steps, each of which palaces contained sufficient store to maintain the whole world.   *P'sachim*, fol. 118, col. 2.

51. There are *three hundred and sixty-five* negative precepts. (See No. 84, *infra.*)

52. There were *three hundred and ninety-four* courts of law in Jerusalem, and as many synagogues; also the same number of high schools, colleges, and academies, and as many offices for public notaries.

Kethuboth, fol. 105, col. 1.

53. Rav Hunna had *four hundred* casks of wine which had turned into vinegar. On hearing of his misfortune, Rav Yehudah, the brother of Rav Salla the Holy, or, as some say, Rav Adda bar Ahavah, came and visited him, accompanied by the Rabbis. "Let the master," said they, "examine himself carefully." "What!" said he, "do you suppose me to have been guilty of wrong-doing?" "Shall we then," said they, "suspect the Holy One—blessed be He!—of executing judgment without justice?" "Well," said Rav Hunna, "if you have heard anything against me, don't conceal it." "It has been reported to us," said they, "that the master has withheld the gardener's share of the prunings." "What else, pray, did he leave me?" retorted Rav Hunna; "he has stolen all the produce of my vineyard." They replied, "There is a saying that whoever steals from a thief smells of theft." "Then," said he, "I hereby promise to give him his share." Thereupon, according to some, the vinegar turned to wine again; and, according to others, the price of vinegar rose to the price of wine.

Berachoth, fol. 5, col. 2.

54. Rav Adda bar Ahavah once saw a Gentile woman in the market-place wearing a red head-dress, and supposing that she was a daughter of Israel, he impatiently tore it off her head. For this outrage he was fined a fine of *four hundred* zouzim. He asked the woman what her name was, and she replied, "My name is Mathan." "Methun, Methun," he wittily rejoined, "is worth *four hundred* zouzim." (See No. 69, *infra.*)

Ibid., fol. 20, col. 1.

Note.—(*a.*) מתון sounds like מאתן, Methun or Mathan. The former means *patience* and the latter means *two hundred.* The point lies either in the application of the term *Methun,* which means *patience,* as if to say, had he been so patient as to have first ascertained what the woman was, he would have saved his *four hundred* zouzim ; or in the identity of the sound Mathan, *i.e., two hundred,* which *doubled,* equals *four hundred.* This has long since passed into a proverb, and expresses the value of *patience.*

(*b.*) From the foregoing extract it would seem that it was not the fashion among Jewish females to wear head-dresses of a red colour, as it was presumed to indicate a certain lightness on the part of the wearer ; so Rav Adda in his pious zeal thought he was doing a good work in tearing it off from the head of the supposed Jewess. " Patience, patience is worth *four hundred* zouzim."

(*c.*) *Custom* among the Jews had then, as now, the force of religion. The Talmud says, "A man should never deviate from a settled custom. Moses ascended on high and did not eat bread (for *there* it is not the custom) ; angels came down to earth and did eat bread (for *here* it is the custom so to do)." *Bava Metzia,* fol. 86, col. 2.

(*d.*) In the olden time it was not the fashion for a Jew to wear *black* shoes (Taanith, fol. 22, col. 1). Even now, in Poland, a pious Jew, or a Chasid, would on no account wear *polished* boots or a *short* coat, or neglect to wear a *girdle.* He would at once lose caste and be subjected to persecution, direct or indirect, were he to depart from a custom. מנהג בטיל, *Custom is law,* is an oft-quoted Jewish proverb, one among the most familiar of their household words, as usus est tyrannus, "Custom is a tyrant," is among ours. Another saying we have is, " Custom is the plague of wise men, but is the idol of fools."

55. The following anecdotes are related by way of practically illustrating Ps. ii. 11, " Rejoice with trembling." Mar, the son of Ravina, made a grand marriage-feast for his son, and when the Rabbis were at the height of their merriment on the occasion, he brought in a very costly cup, worth *four hundred* zouzim, and broke it before them, and this occasioned them sorrow and trembling. Rav Ashi made a grand marriage-feast for his son, and when

he noticed the Rabbis in high jubilation, he brought in a costly cup of white glass and broke it before them, and this made them sorrowful. The Rabbis challenged Rav Hamnunah on the wedding of his son Ravina, saying, " Give us a song, sir," and he sung, " Woe be to us, for we must die! Woe be to us, for we must die!" " And what shall we sing?" they asked in chorus by way of response. He replied, " Sing ye, 'Alas! where is the law we have studied? where the good works we have done? that they may protect us from the punishment of hell!'" Rabbi Yochanan, in the name of Rabbi Shimon ben Yochai, says, " It is unlawful for a man to fill his mouth with laughter in this world, for it is said in Ps. cxxvi., 'Then (but not now) will our mouth be filled with laughter,'" &c. It is related of Resh Lakish that he never once laughed again all the rest of his life from the time that he heard this from Rabbi Yochanan, his teacher.

Berachoth, fol. 30, col. 2, and fol. 31, col. 1.

56. A man once laid a wager with another that he would put Hillel out of temper. If he succeeded he was to receive, but if he failed he was to forfeit, *four hundred* zouzim. It was close upon Sabbath-eve, and Hillel was washing himself, when the man passed by his door, shouting, " Where is Hillel? where is Hillel?" Hillel wrapped his mantle round him and sallied forth to see what the man wanted. " I want to ask thee a question," was the reply. " Ask on, my son," said Hillel. Whereupon the man said, " I want to know why the Babylonians have such round heads?" " A very important question, my son," said Hillel; " the reason is because their midwives are not clever." The man went away, but after an hour he returned, calling out as before, " Where is Hillel? where is Hillel?" Hillel again threw on his mantle and went out, meekly asking, " What now, my son?" " I want to know," said he, " why the people of Tadmor are weak-eyed?" Hillel replied, " This is an important question, my

son, and the reason is this, they live in a sandy country." Away went the man, but in another hour's time he returned as before, crying out, "Where is Hillel? where is Hillel?" Out came Hillel again, as gentle as ever, blandly requesting to know what more he wanted. "I have a question to ask," said the man. "Ask on, my son," said Hillel. "Well, why have the Africans such broad feet?" said he. "Because they live in a marshy land," said Hillel. "I have many more questions to ask," said the man, "but I am afraid that I shall only try thy patience and make thee angry." Hillel, drawing his mantle around him, sat down and bade the man ask all the questions he wished. "Art thou Hillel," said he, "whom they call a prince in Israel?" "Yes," was the reply. "Well," said the other, "I pray there may not be many more in Israel like thee!" "Why," said Hillel, "how is that?" "Because," said the man, "I have betted *four hundred* zouzim that I could put thee out of temper, and I have lost them all through thee." "Be warned for the future," said Hillel; "better it is that thou shouldst lose *four hundred* zouzim, and *four hundred* more after them, than it should be said of Hillel he lost his temper!" *Shabbath*, fol. 31, col. 1.

57. Rabbi Perida had a pupil to whom he had to re-hearse a lesson *four hundred* times before the latter comprehended it. One day the Rabbi was hurriedly called away to perform some charitable act, but before he went he repeated the lesson in hand the usual *four hundred* times, but this time his pupil failed to learn it. "What is the reason, my son," said he to his dull pupil, "that this time my repetitions have been thrown away?" "Because, master," naïvely replied the youth, "my mind was so pre-occupied with the summons you received to discharge another duty." "Well, then," said the Rabbi to his pupil, "let us begin again." And he repeated the lesson a second *four hundred* times.

Eiruvin, fol. 54, col. 2.

58. Between Azel and Azel (1 Chron. viii. 38 and ix. 44) there are *four hundred* camel-loads of critical researches due to the presence of manifold contradictions.

P'sachim, fol. 62, col. 2.

59. Egypt has an area of *four hundred* square miles.

Ibid., fol. 94, col. 1.

60. The Targum of the Pentateuch was executed by Onkelos the proselyte at the dictation of Rabbi Eliezer and Rabbi Yehoshua, and the Targum of the prophets was executed by Jonathan ben Uzziel at the dictation of Haggai, Zachariah, and Malachi (!), at which time the land of Israel was convulsed over an area of *four hundred* square miles. *Meggillah*, fol. 3, col. 1.

61. Mar Ukva was in the habit of sending on the Day of Atonement *four hundred* zouzim to a poor neighbour of his. Once he sent the money by his own son, who returned bringing it back with him, remarking, "There is no need to bestow charity upon a man who, as I myself have seen, is able to indulge himself in expensive old wine." " Well," said his father, "since he is so dainty in his taste, he must have seen better days. I will therefore double the amount for the future." And this accordingly he at once remitted to him.

Kethuboth, fol. 67, col. 2.

62. " And Joseph took an oath of the children of Israel, . . . ye shall carry up my bones from hence" (Gen. l. 25). Rabbi Chanena said, " There is a reason for this oath. As Joseph knew that he was perfectly righteous, why then, if the dead are to rise in other countries as well as in the land of Israel, did he trouble his brethren to carry his bones *four hundred* miles ?" The reply is, " He feared lest, if buried in Egypt, he might have to worm his way through subterranean passages from his grave into the land of Israel." *Ibid.*, fol. 111, col. 1.

Note.—To this day among the Polish Jews the dead are

provided for their long subterranean journey with little wooden forks, with which, at the sound of the great trumpet, they are to dig and burrow their way from where they happen to be buried till they arrive in Palestine. To avoid this inconvenience there are some among them who, on the approach of old age, migrate to the Holy Land, that their bones may rest there against the morning of the resurrection. In the context of our quotation more may be found on this quaint conceit in regard to the resurrection of the body.

63. Rav Cahana was once selling ladies' baskets when he was exposed to the trial of a sinful temptation. He pled with his tempter to let him off and he promised to return, but instead of doing so he went up to the roof of the house and threw himself down headlong. Before he reached the ground, however, Elijah came and caught him, and reproached him, as he caught him up, with having brought him a distance of *four hundred* miles to save him from an act of wilful self-destruction. The Rabbi told him that it was his poverty which had given to the temptation the power of seduction. Thereupon Elijah gave him a vessel full of gold denarii and departed.

Kiddushin, fol. 40, col. 1.

64. "Pashur, the son of Immer the priest" (Jer. xx. 1) had *four hundred* servants, and every one of them rose to the rank of the priesthood. One consequence was that an insolent priest hardly ever appeared in Israel but his genealogy could be traced to this base-born, low-bred ancestry. Rabbi Elazar said, "If thou seest an impudent priest, do not think evil of him, for it is said (Hos. iv. 4), ' Thy people are as they that strive with the priest.' "

Ibid., fol. 70, col. 2.

65. David had *four hundred* young men, handsome in appearance and with their hair cut close upon their foreheads, but with long flowing curls behind, who used to ride in chariots of gold at the head of the army. These were men of power (men of the *fist*, in the original), the mighty

men of the house of David, who went about to strike terror into the world (בעלי אגרופים דאזלי לביעותי עלמא).

Kiddushin, fol. 76, col. 2.

66. *Four hundred* boys and as many girls were once kidnapped and torn from their relations. When they learnt the purpose of their capture, they all exclaimed, " Better drown ourselves in the sea ; then shall we have an inheritance in the world to come." The eldest then explained to them the text (Ps. lxviii. 22), " The Lord said, I will bring again from Bashan ; I will bring again from the depths of the sea." " From Bashan," *i.e.*, from the teeth of the lion ; " from the depths of the sea," *i.e.*, those that drown themselves in the sea. When the girls heard this explanation they at once jumped all together into the sea, and the boys with alacrity followed their example. It is with reference to these that Scripture says (Ps. xliv. 22), " For thy sake we are killed all the day long ; we are counted as sheep for the slaughter."

Gittin, fol. 57, col. 2.

67. There were *four hundred* synagogues in the city of Byther, in each there were *four hundred* elementary teachers, and each had *four hundred* pupils. When the enemy entered the city, they pierced him with their pointers ; but when at last the enemy overpowered them, he wrapped them in their books and then set fire to them ; and this is what is written (Lam. iii. 51), " Mine eye affecteth my heart because of all the daughters of my city."

Ibid., fol. 58, col. 1.

Note.—The total population of Byther must have been something enormous, when the children in it amounted to 64,000,000 ! The elementary teachers alone came to 160,000.

68. Once when the Hasmonean kings were engaged in civil war it happened that Hyrcanus was outside Jerusalem and Aristobulus within. Every day the besieged let down a box containing gold denarii, and received in

return lambs for the daily sacrifices. There chanced to be an old man in the city who was familiar with the wisdom of the Greeks, and he hinted to the besiegers in the Greek language that so long as the Temple services were kept up the city could not be taken. The next day accordingly, when the money had been let down, they sent back a pig in return. When about half-way up the animal pushed with its feet against the stones of the wall, and thereupon an earthquake was felt throughout the land of Israel to the extent of *four hundred* miles. At that time it was the saying arose, " Cursed be he that rears swine, and he who shall teach his son the wisdom of the Greeks." (See Matt. viii. 30.) *Sotah*, fol. 49, col. 2.

69. If one strikes his neighbour with his fist, he must pay him one sela; if he slaps his face, he is to pay *two hundred* zouzim; but for a back-handed slap the assailant is to pay *four hundred* zouzim. If he pulls the ear of another, or plucks his hair, or spits upon him, or pulls off his mantle, or tears a woman's head-dress off in the street, in each of these cases he is fined *four hundred* zouzim. (See No. 54, *supra.*) *Bava Kama*, fol. 90, col. 1.

70. There was once a dispute between Rabbi Eliezer and the Mishnic sages as to whether a baking-oven, constructed from certain materials and of a particular shape, was clean or unclean. The former decided that it was clean, but the latter were of a contrary opinion. Having replied to all the objections the sages had brought against his decision, and finding that they still refused to acquiesce, the Rabbi turned to them and said, " If the Halacha (the law) is according to my decision, let this carob-tree attest." Whereupon the carob-tree rooted itself up and transplanted itself to a distance of one hundred, some say *four hundred*, yards from the spot. But the sages demurred and said, " We cannot admit the evidence of a carob-tree." " Well, then," said Rabbi Eliezer, " let this running brook be a

proof;" and the brook at once reversed its natural course and flowed back. The sages refused to admit this proof also. "Then let the walls of the college bear witness that the law is according to my decision;" upon which the walls began to bend, and were about to fall, when Rabbi Joshuah interposed and rebuked them, saying, "If the disciples of the sages wrangle with each other in the Halacha, what is that to you? Be ye quiet!" Therefore, out of respect to Rabbi Joshuah, they did not fall, and out of respect to Rabbi Eliezer they did not resume their former upright position, but remained toppling, which they continue to do to this day. Then said Rabbi Eliezer to the sages, "Let Heaven itself testify that the Halacha is according to my judgment." And a Bath Kol or voice from heaven was heard, saying, "What have ye to do with Rabbi Eliezer? for the Halacha is on every point according to his decision!" Rabbi Joshuah then stood up and proved from Scripture that even a voice from heaven was not to be regarded, "For Thou, O God, didst long ago write down in the law which Thou gavest on Sinai (Exod. xxiii. 2), 'Thou shalt follow the multitude.'" (See context.) We have it on the testimony of Elijah the prophet, given to Rabbi Nathan on an oath, that it was with reference to this dispute about the oven God himself confessed and said, נצחוני בני נצחוני בני, "My children have vanquished me! My children have vanquished me!" *Bava Metzia*, fol. 59, col. 1.

> Note.—In the sequel to the above we are told that all the legal documents of Rabbi Eliezer containing his decisions respecting things "clean" were publicly burned with fire, and he himself excommunicated. In consequence of this the whole world was smitten with blight, a third in the olives, a third in the barley, and a third in the wheat; and the Rabbi himself, though excommunicated, continued to be held in the highest regard in Israel.

71. The Rabbis said to Rabbi Hamnuna, "Rav Ami

has written or copied *four hundred* copies of the law." He replied to them, "Perhaps only (Deut. xxxiii. 4) 'Moses commanded us a law.'" (He meant he did not imagine that any one man could possibly write out *four hundred* complete copies of the Pentateuch.)

Bava Bathra, fol. 14, col. 1.

72. Rabbi Chanena said, "If *four hundred* years after the destruction of the Temple one offers thee a field worth a thousand denarii for one denarius, don't buy it."

Avodah Zarah, fol. 9, col. 2.

73. We know by tradition that the treatise "Avodah Zarah," which our father Abraham possessed, contained *four hundred* chapters, but the treatise as we now have it contains only five.   (See chap. iii. No. 40, notes *c, d*.)

Ibid., fol. 14, col. 2.

74. The camp of Sennacherib was *four hundred* miles in length.   *Sanhedrin*, fol. 95, col. 2.

75. "Curse ye Meroz," &c. (Judges v. 23).   Barak excommunicated Meroz at the blast of *four hundred* trumpets (lit. horns or cornets).   *Shevuoth*, fol. 36, col. 1.

76. What is the meaning where it is written (Ps. x. 27), "The fear of the Lord prolongeth days, but the years of the wicked shall be shortened?"   "The fear of the Lord prolongeth days" alludes to the *four hundred and ten* years the first Temple stood, during which period the succession of high priests numbered only eighteen.   But "the years of the wicked shall be shortened" is illustrated by the fact that during the *four hundred and twenty* years that the second Temple stood the succession of high priests numbered more than three hundred.   If we deduct the forty years during which Shimon the Righteous held office, and the eighty of Rabbi Yochanan, and the ten of Rabbi Ishmael ben Rabbi, it is evident that not one of

the remaining high priests lived to hold office for a whole year.
Yoma, fol. 9, col. 1.

77. "The souls which they had gotten in Haran" (Gen. xii. 5). From this time to the giving of the law was *four hundred and forty-eight* years.
Avodah Zarah, fol. 9, col. 1.

78. A young girl and ten of her maid-servants were once kidnapped, when a certain Gentile bought them and brought them to his house. One day he gave a pitcher to the child and bade her fetch him water, but one of her servants took the pitcher from her, intending to go instead. The master, observing this, asked the maid why she did so. The servant replied, "By the life of thy head, my lord, I am one of no less than *five hundred* servants of this child's mother." The master was so touched that he granted them all their freedom.
Avoth d'Rab. Nathan, chap. 17.

79. Cæsar once said to Rabbi Yoshua ben Chananja, "This God of yours is compared to a lion, as it is written (Amos iii. 8), 'The lion hath roared, who will not fear?' Wherein consists his excellency? A horseman kills a lion." The Rabbi replied, "He is not compared to an ordinary lion, but to a lion of the forest Ilaei." "Show me that lion at once," said the Emperor. "But thou canst not behold him," said the Rabbi. Still the Emperor insisted on seeing the lion; so the Rabbi prayed to God to help him in his perplexity. His prayer was heard; the lion came forth from his lair and roared, upon which, though it was *four hundred* miles away, all the walls of Rome trembled and fell to the ground. Approaching *three hundred* miles nearer, he roared again, and this time the teeth of the people dropped out of their mouths and the Emperor fell from his throne quaking. "Alas! Rabbi, pray to thy God that He order the lion back to his abode in the forest."
Chullin, fol. 59, col. 2.

NOTE.—All this is as nothing compared to the voice of Judah, which made all Egypt quake and tremble, and Pharaoh fall from his throne headlong, &c., &c. See Jasher, chap. 64, verses 46, 47.

80. The distance from the earth to the firmament is *five hundred* years' journey, and so it is from each successive firmament to the next, throughout the series of the seven heavens. (See chap. vii. No. 7.)

Psachim, fol. 94, col. 2.

81. "Now, as I beheld the living creatures, behold, one wheel upon the earth by the living creatures" (Ezek. i. 15). Rabbi Elazar says it was an angel who stood upon the earth, and his head reached to the living creatures. It is recorded in a Mishna that his name is Sandalphon, who towers above his fellow-angels to a height of *five hundred* years' journey; he stands behind the chariot and binds crowns on the head of his Creator.

Chaggigah, fol. 13, col. 2.

NOTE.—In the Liturgy for the Feast of Tabernacles it is said that Sandalphon gathers in his hands the prayers of Israel, and, forming a wreath of them, he adjures it to ascend as an orb for the head of the supreme King of kings.

82. The mount of the Temple was *five hundred* yards square. *Middoth*, chap. 2.

83. One Scripture text (1 Chron. xxi. 25) says, "So David gave to Ornan for the place *six hundred* shekels of gold by weight." And another Scripture (2 Sam. xxiv. 24) says, "So David bought the threshing-floor and the oxen for fifty shekels of silver." How is this? David took from each tribe fifty shekels, and they made together the total *six hundred, i.e.*, he took silver to the value of fifty shekels of gold. *Zevachim*, fol. 116, col. 2.

84. Rabbi Samlai explains that *six hundred and thirteen* commandments were communicated to Moses; *three hundred and sixty-five* negative, according to the number of

days in the year, and *two hundred and forty-eight* positive, according to the number of members in the human body. Rav Hammunah asked what was the Scripture proof for this. The reply was (Deut. xxxiii. iv.), "Moses commanded us a law" (תורה, Torah). תורה, by Gematria answers to six hundred and eleven. "I am," and "Thou shalt have no other," which we heard from the Almighty Himself, together make up *six hundred and thirteen.*

Maccoth, fol. 23, col. 2.

> NOTE.—David, we are told, reduced these commandments, here reckoned at six hundred and thirteen, to eleven, and Isaiah still further to six, and then afterwards to two. "Thus saith the Eternal, Observe justice and act righteously, for my salvation is near." Finally came Habakkuk, and he reduced the number to one all-comprehensive precept (chap. ii. 4), "The just shall live by faith." (See Maccoth, fol. 24, col. 1.)

85. The precept concerning fringes is as weighty as all the other precepts put together; for it is written, says Rashi (Num. xv. 39), "And remember all the commandments of the Lord." Now the numerical value of the word ציצת, "fringes," is *six hundred,* and this with *eight* threads and *five* knots makes *six hundred and thirteen.*

Shevuoth, fol. 29, col. 1.

86. "For behold, the Lord, the Lord of hosts, doth take away from Jerusalem and from Judah the stay and the staff, the whole stay of bread and the whole stay of water, the mighty man and the man of war, the judge and the prophet," &c. (Isa. iii. 1, 2). By "the stay" is meant men mighty in the Scriptures, and by "the staff" men learned in the Mishna; such, for instance, as Rabbi Yehudah ben Tima and his associates. Rav Pappa and the Rabbis differed as to the Mishna; the former said there were *six hundred* orders of the Mishna, and the latter that there were *seven hundred* orders. "The whole stay of bread" means men distinguished in the Talmud; for it is said, "Come, eat of my bread, and drink of the wine which I

have mingled" (Prov. ix. 5).   And "the whole stay of
water" means men skilful in the Haggadoth, who draw
out the heart of man like water by means of a pretty
story or legend, &c.   *Chaggigah*, fol. 14, col. 1.

87. There are *seven hundred* species of fish, *eight hundred* of locusts, twenty-four of birds that are unclean,
while the species of birds that are clean cannot be numbered.   *Chullin*, fol. 63, col. 2.

88. "The same was Adino the Eznite," &c. (2 Sam.
xxiii. 8).   This mighty man when studying the law was
as pliant as a worm; but when engaged in war he was as
firm and unyielding as a tree; and when he discharged an
arrow he killed *eight hundred* men at one shot.
Moed Katon, fol. 16, col. 2.

89. "Ye shall soon utterly perish from off the land"
(Deut. iv. 26).   The term *soon* uttered by the Lord of the
Universe means *eight hundred and fifty-two* years.
Sanhedrin, fol. 38, col. 1.

Note.—This calculation is based on the numerical value of
the word ונושנתם in the previous verse, a word represented in the English version by "And ye shall have
remained long" in the land.

90. There are *nine hundred and three* sorts of deaths in
the world; for the expression occurs (Ps. lxviii. 20), "Issues
of death."   The numerical value of תוצאות, "issues," is *nine
hundred and three*.   The hardest of all deaths is by quinsey, and the easiest is the Divine kiss (of which Moses,
Aaron, and Miriam died).   Quinsey is like the forcible
extraction of prickly thorns from wool, or like a thick
rope drawn through a small aperture; the kiss referred
to is like the extracting of a hair from milk.   (See Note
on p. 102, *supra*.)   *Berachoth*, fol. 8, col. 1.

91. When Moses went up on high, the ministering
angels asked, "What has one born of a woman to do
among us?"   "He has come to receive the law," was the

Divine answer. "What!" they remonstrated again, "that cherished treasure which has lain with Thee for *nine hundred and seventy-four* generations before the world was created, art Thou about to bestow it upon flesh and blood? What is mortal man that Thou art mindful of him, and the son of earth that Thou thus visitest him? O Lord! our Lord! is not Thy name already sufficiently exalted in the earth? Confer Thy glory upon the heavens" (Ps. viii. 4, 6). The Holy One—blessed be He!—then called upon Moses to refute the objection of the envious angels. "I fear," pleaded he, "lest they consume me with the fiery breath of their mouth." Thereupon, by way of protection, he was bid approach and lay hold of the throne of God; as it is said (Job xxvi. 9), "He lays hold of the face of His throne and spreads His cloud over him." Thus encouraged, Moses went over the Decalogue, and demanded of the angels whether they had suffered an Egyptian bondage and dwelt among idolatrous nations, so as to require the first commandment; or were they so hardworked as to need a day of rest, &c., &c. Then the angels at once confessed that they were wrong in seeking to withhold the law from Israel, and they then repeated the words, "O Lord, how excellent is Thy name in all the earth!" (Ps. viii. 9), omitting the words, "Confer Thy glory upon the heavens." And not only so, but they positively befriended Moses, and each of them revealed to him some useful secret; as it is said (Ps. lxviii. 18), "Thou hast ascended on high, thou hast captured spoil, thou hast received gifts; because they have contemptuously called thee man." *Shabbath*, fol. 88, col. 2.

92. *Nine hundred and seventy-four* generations before the world was created the law was written and deposited in the bosom of the Holy One—blessed be He!—and sang praises with the ministering angels.

Avoth d'Rab. Nathan, chap. 31.

Note.—In an Haggadah we are told that the law dates back to *two thousand years before the foundation of the world.*

93. If one is sick and at the point of death, he is expected to confess, for all confess who are about to suffer the last penalty of the law. When a man goes to the market-place, let him consider himself as handed over to the custody of the officers of judgment. If he has a headache, let him deem himself fastened with a chain by the neck. If confined to his bed, let him regard himself as mounting the steps to be judged; for when this happens to him, he is saved from death only if he have competent advocates, and these advocates are repentance and good works. And if *nine hundred and ninety-nine* plead against him, and only *one* for him, he is saved; as it is said (Job xxxiii. 23), "If there be an interceding angel, one among a thousand to declare for man his uprightness, then He is gracious unto him and saith, Deliver him from going down to the pit." *Shabbath*, fol. 32, col. 1.

CHAPTER XIII.

TALMUDIC NUMBERS, RANGING FROM 'ONE THOUSAND'
TO 'MILLIONS.'

1. WHEN Solomon married the daughter of Pharaoh, she introduced to him *a thousand* different kinds of musical instruments, and taught him the chants to the various idols. *Shabbath*, fol. 56, col. 2.

2. When Buneis, the son of Buneis, called on Rabbi (the Holy), the latter exclaimed, "Make way for one worth a hundred manahs!" Presently another visitor came, and Rabbi said, "Make way for one worth two hundred manahs." Upon which Rabbi Ishmael, the son of Rabbi Yossi, remonstrated, saying, "Rabbi, the father of the first-comer, owns *a thousand* ships at sea and *a thousand* towns ashore!" "Well," replied Rabbi, "when thou seest his father, tell him to send his son better clad next time." Rabbi paid great respect to those that were rich, and so did Rabbi Akiva. *Eiruvin*, fol. 86, col. 1.

3. Rabbi Elazer ben Charsom inherited from his father *a thousand* towns and *a thousand* ships, and yet he went about with a leather sack of flour at his back, roaming from town to town and from province to province in order to study the law. This great Rabbi never once set eye on his immense patrimony, for he was engaged in the study of the law all day and all night long. And so strange was he to his own servants, that they, on one occasion, not knowing who he was, pressed him against his will to do a

day's work as a menial; and though he pled with them as a suppliant to be left alone to pursue his studies in the law, they refused, and swore, saying, "By the life of Rabbi Elazer ben Charsom, our master, we will not let thee go till thy task is completed." He then let himself be enforced rather than make himself known to them. (See context in "Genesis According to the Talmud," p. 200, No. 21.)

Yoma, fol. 35, col. 2.

4. The wife of Potiphar coaxed Joseph with loving words, but in vain. She then threatened to immure him in prison, but he replied (anticipating Ps. cxlvi. 7), "The Lord looseth the prisoners." Then she said, "I will bow thee down with distress; I will blind thine eyes." He only answered (*ibid.*, ver. 8), "The Lord openeth the eyes of the blind and raiseth them that are bowed down." She then tried to bribe him with *a thousand* talents of silver if he would comply with her request, but in vain.

Ibid.

Note.—A Midrash tells us that Potiphar's wife not only falsely accused Joseph herself, but that she also suborned several of her female friends to do likewise. The Book of Jasher, which embodies the Talmudic story quoted above, tells us that an infant in the cradle spoke up and testified to Joseph's innocence, and that while Joseph was in prison his *inamorata* daily visited him. More on this topic may be found in the Koran, chap. xii. The amours of Joseph and Zulicka, as told by the glib tongue of tradition, fitly find their consummation in marriage, and certain Moslems affect to see in all this an allegorical type of Divine love, an allegory which some other divines find in the Song of Solomon.

5. The thickness of the earth is *a thousand* paces or ells.

Succah, fol. 53, col. 2.

Note.—The crust of the earth as far as the abyss is a thousand ells, and the abyss under the earth is fifteen thousand. There is an upper and a lower abyss mentioned in Taanith, fol. 25, col. 2. Riddia, the angel who has the command of the waters, and resides between the two

abysses, says to the upper, חישור מימך, "disperse thy
waters," and to the lower, אבע כימך, "let thy waters
flow up."

6. Many may ask after thy peace, but tell thy secret
only to one of *a thousand*.   *Yevamoth*, fol. 63, col. 2.

7. The Rabbis have taught that if the value of stolen
property is *a thousand*, and the thief is only worth, say,
five hundred, he is to be sold into slavery twice. But if
the reverse, he is not to be sold at all.

Kiddushin, fol. 18, col. 2.

8. The Behemoth upon *a thousand* hills (Ps. l. 10), God
created them male and female, but had they been allowed
to propagate they would have destroyed the whole world.
What did He do? He castrated the male and spayed the
female, and then preserved them that they might serve for
the righteous at the Messianic banquet; as it is said (Job
xl. 16), "His strength is in his loins (*i.e.*, the male), and
his force in the navel of his belly" (*i.e.*, the female). (See
"Genesis According to the Talmud," p. 58, ver. 21, ii.)

Bava Bathra, fol. 74, col. 2.

NOTE.—This provision for the coming Messianic banquet is
considered of sufficient importance to be mentioned year
after year in the service for the Day of Atonement and
also at the Feast of Tabernacles. The remark of D.
Levi, that the feast here referred to is to be understood
allegorically, involves rather sweeping consequences, as it
is open to any one to annihilate many other expectations
on the same principle.

9. The Holy One—blessed be He!—will add to Jerusalem gardens extending to *a thousand* times the numerical value of טפף, which equals one hundred and sixty-
nine, &c.   *Ibid.*, fol. 75, col. 2.

NOTE.—The above is a Rabbinical estimate of the extent of
the Messianic Jerusalem.

10. "Moreover Manasseh shed innocent blood very

much " (2 Kings xxi. 16).   Here (in Babylon) it is interpreted to mean that he murdered Isaiah, but in the West
(*i.e.*, in Palestine) they say that he made an image of the
weight of *a thousand* men, which was the number he
massacred every day (as Rashi says, by the heaviness of
its weight).   *Sanhedrin*, fol. 103, col. 2.

<blockquote>

Note.—(*a*.) See Josephus, Antiq., Book X. chap. iii., sec. 1, for
corroborative evidence.   Tradition says that Manasseh
caused Isaiah to be sawn asunder with a wooden saw.
(See also Yevamoth, fol. 49, col. 2 ; Sanhedrin, fol. 103,
col. 2.)

(*b*.) Nowhere in the Talmud do we find the name of
the great image here referred to.   What if we christen it
the "Juggernaut of the Talmud"?   May the tradition
not be a prelusion or a reflex of that man-crushing mon-
ster?   Anyhow, scholars are aware of a community of
no inconsiderable extent between the conceptions and
legends of the Hindoos and the Rabbis.   One notable
contrast, however, between this Juggernaut and that of
the Hindoos is, that whereas in both cases the innocent
suffered for the guilty, in the former the sacrifices were
exacted to propitiate Satan, while in the latter they were
freely offered in supposed propitiation of the gods.

</blockquote>

11. The food consumed by Og, king of Bashan, consisted of *a thousand* oxen and as many of all sorts
of other beasts, and his drink consisted of *a thousand*
measures, &c.   *Sophrim*, chap. 21, mish. 9.

12. Solomon made ten candelabra for the Temple; for
each he set aside *a thousand* talents of gold, which he
refined in a crucible until they were reduced to the weight
of one talent.   *Menachoth*, fol. 29, col. 1.

13. There was an organ in the Temple which produced
a thousand kinds of melody.   *Eirchin*, fol. 11, col. 1.

<blockquote>

Note.—The Magrepha (מגריפה), with its ten pipes and its
ten-times-ten various notes (Eirchin, fol. 10, col. 2, and
fol. 11, col. 1), which was said to have been used in the
Temple service, must have been an instrument far
superior to any organ in use at the time elsewhere.

</blockquote>

14. If from a town numbering *fifteen hundred* footmen, such, for example, as the village of Accho, nine people be borne forth dead in the course of three successive days, it is a sure sign of the presence of the plague; but if this happen in one day or in four, then it is not the plague.

Taanith, fol. 21, col. 1.

15. *Seventeen hundred* of the arguments and minute rules of the Scribes were forgotten during the days of mourning for Moses. Othniel, the son of Kenaz, by his shrewd arguing restored them all as if they had never lapsed from the memory. *Temurah*, fol. 16, col. 1.

16. There was a great court at Jerusalem called Beth Yaazek, where all witnesses (who could testify to the time of the appearance of the new moon) used to assemble, and where they were examined by the authorities. Grand feasts were prepared for them as an inducement to them to come (and give in their testimony). Formerly they did not move from the place they happened to be in when overtaken by the Sabbath, but Rabbon Gamliel the elder ordained that they might in that case move *two thousand* cubits either way. *Rosh Hashanah*, fol. 21, col. 2.

17. He that is abroad (on the Sabbath) and does not know the limit of the Sabbath-day's journey may walk *two thousand* moderate paces, and that is a Sabbath-day's journey. *Eiruvin*, fol. 42, col. 1.

18. Rabbon Gamliel had a hollow tube, through which, when he looked, he could distinguish a distance of *two thousand* cubits, whether by land or sea. By the same tube he could ascertain the depth of a valley or the height of a palm-tree. *Ibid.*, fol. 43, col. 2.

Note.—This is one evidence among several of the scientific and mechanical ingenuity of this Rabbi. The instrument here introduced must have been some rude anticipation of our modern theodolite.

19. He who observes carefully the precepts respecting fringes will, as a reward, have *two thousand eight hundred* slaves to wait upon him; for it is said (Zech. viii. 23), "Thus saith the Lord of hosts; In those days it shall come to pass that ten men shall take hold out of all languages of the nations, even shall take hold of the skirt of him that is a Jew, saying, We will go with you, for we have heard that God is with you."

Shabbath, fol. 32, col. 2.

Note.—(*a.*) Rashi's explanation of this matter is very simple. The merit of the fringes lies in their being duly attached to "the four quarters" or skirts of the garments (Deut. xxii. 12). There are seventy nations in the whole world, and ten of each nation will take hold of each corner of the garment, which gives $70 \times 10 \times 4 = 2800$. Rabbi B'chai, commenting on Num. xv. 39, 40, repeats the same story almost word for word.

(*b.*) This passage (Zech. viii. 23) has lately been construed by some into a prophecy of the recent Berlin Congress, and the *ten* men mentioned are found in the representatives of the contracting parties, *i.e.*, England, France, Germany, Turkey, Russia, Austria, Italy, Greece, Roumania, and Servia.

20. Rav Hammunah said, "What is it that is written (1 Kings iv. 32), 'And he spoke *three thousand* proverbs, and his songs were a *thousand and five?*'" It is intended to teach that Solomon uttered *three thousand* proverbs upon each and every word of the law, and for every word of the Scribes he assigned *a thousand and five* reasons.

Eiruvin, fol. 21, col. 2.

21. When Rabbi Eliezer was sick he was visited by Rabbi Akiva and his party. . . . "Wherefore have ye come?" he asked. "To learn the law," was the reply. "And why did you not come sooner?" "Because we had no leisure," said they. "I shall be much surprised," said he, "if you die a natural death." Then turning to Rabbi Akiva he said, "Thy death shall be the worst of all" (see how his words came to pass on page 2, No.

4, *supra*). Then folding his arms upon his breast, he exclaimed:—" Woe unto my two arms! for they are like two scrolls of the law rolled up, so that their contents are hidden. Had they waited upon me, they might have added much to their knowledge of the law, but now that knowledge will perish with me. I have in my time learned much and taught much, and yet I have no more diminished the knowledge of my Rabbis by what I have derived from them than the waters of the sea are reduced by a dog lapping them. Over and above this I expounded *three hundred*," some allege he said *three thousand*, " Halachahs with reference to the growing of Egyptian cucumbers, and yet no one except Akiva ben Yoseph has ever proposed a single question to me respecting them. He and I were walking along the road one day when he asked me to instruct him regarding the cultivation of Egyptian cucumbers. I made but one remark, when the entire field became full of them. Then at his request I made a remark about cutting them, when lo! they all collected themselves together in one spot." Thus Rabbi Eliezer kept on talking, when all of a sudden he fell back and expired.   *Sanhedrin*, fol. 68, col. 1.

> Note.—The last words of this eminent Rabbi derive a tragic interest from the fact that he died while under sentence of excommunication. (See p. 246. No. 70, *supra*.)

22. *Three thousand* Halachoth were forgotten at the time of mourning for Moses, and among them the Halachah respecting an animal intended for a sin-offering the owner of which died before sacrificing it.

Temurah, fol. 16, col. 1.

23. All the prophets were rich men. This we infer from the account of Moses, Samuel, Amos, and Jonah. Of Moses, as it is written (Num. xvi. 15), " I have not taken one ass from them." Of Samuel, as it is written (1 Sam. xii. 3), " Behold, here I am ; witness against me before the Lord, and before His anointed, whose ox have

I taken? or whose ass have I taken?" Of Amos, as it is written (Amos vii. 14), "I was an herdsman and a gatherer of sycamore fruit," *i.e.*, I am proprietor of my herds and own sycamores in the valley. Of Jonah, as it is written (Jonah i. 3), "So he paid the fare thereof and went down into it." Rabbi Yochanan says he hired the whole ship. Rabbi Rumanus says the hire of the ship amounted to *four thousand* golden denarii.

Nedarim, fol. 38, col. 1.

24. *Four thousand two hundred and thirty-one* years after the creation of the world, if any one offers thee for one single denarius a field worth a thousand denarii, do not buy it. *Avodah Zarah*, fol. 9, col. 2.

> Note.—Rashi gives this as the reason of the prohibition: For then the restoration of the Jews to their own land will take place, so that the denarius paid for a field in a foreign land would be money thrown away.

25. *Four thousand two hundred and ninety-one* years after the creation of the world the wars of the dragons and the wars of Gog and Magog will cease, and the rest of the time will be the days of the Messiah; and the Holy One—blessed be He!—will not renew His world till after seven thousand years. . . . Rabbi Jonathan said, "May the bones of those who compute the latter days (when the Messiah shall appear) be blown; for some say, 'Because the time (of Messiah) has come and Himself has not, therefore He will never come!' But wait thou for Him, as it is said (Hab. ii. 3), 'Though He tarry, wait for Him.' Perhaps you will say, 'We wait, but He does not wait;' learn rather to say (Isa. xxx. 18), 'And therefore will the Lord wait, that He may be gracious unto you; and therefore will He be exalted, that He may have mercy upon you.'" *Sanhedrin*, fol. 97, col. 2.

26. It is related of Rabbi Tarphon (probably the Tryphon of polemic fame) that he was very rich, but gave nothing

to the poor. Once Rabbi Akiva met him and said, " Rabbi, dost thou wish me to purchase for thee a town or two ? " " I do," said he, and at once gave him *four thousand* gold denarii. Rabbi Akiva took this sum and distributed it among the poor. Some time after Rabbi Tarphon met Rabbi Akiva and said, " Where are the towns thou purchasedst for me ? " The latter seized hold of him by the arm and led him to the Beth Hamedrash, where, taking up a psalter, they read together till they came to this verse, " He hath dispersed, he hath given to the poor, his righteousness endureth for ever " (Ps. cxii. 9). Here Rabbi Akiva paused and said, " This is the place I purchased for thee," and Rabbi Tarphon saluted him with a kiss.

Tract. Callah.

27. The Pentateuch contains *five thousand eight hundred and eighty-eight* verses. The Psalms have eight verses more than, and the Chronicles eight verses short of, that number. *Kiddushin,* fol. 30, col. 1.

> NOTE.—The number of verses in the Pentateuch is usually stated at 5845, the *mnemonic* sign of which is the word החמה in Isaiah xxx. 26, the letters of which stand for 5845. The verse reads, " Moreover, the light of the moon shall be as the light of the sun " (החמה). The Masorites tell us that the number of verses in the Psalms is 2527, and in the two Books of Chronicles 1656.

28. The world is to last *six thousand* years. *Two thousand* of these are termed the period of disorder, *two thousand* belong to the dispensation of the law, and *two thousand* are the days of the Messiah ; but because of our iniquities a large fraction of the latter term is already passed and gone without the Messiah giving any sign of His appearing. *Sanhedrin,* fol. 97, col. 1.

29. As the land of Canaan had one year of release in seven, so has the world one millennium of release in *seven thousand* years ; for it is said (Isa. ii. 17), " And the Lord alone will be exalted in that day ; " and again (Ps. xcii. 1),

"A psalm or song for the Sabbath-day," which means a long Sabbatic period; and again (Ps. xc. 4), "For a thousand years in Thy sight are but as (יום אתכול) the day of yesterday."   *Sanhedrin*, fol. 97, col. 1.

30. Tradition records that the ladder (mentioned Gen. xxviii. 12) was *eight thousand* miles wide, for it is written, "And behold the angels of God ascending and descending upon it." Angels ascending, being in the plural, cannot be fewer than two at a time, and so likewise must those descending, so that when they passed they were four abreast at least. In Daniel x. 6 it is said of the angel, "His body was like Tarshish," and there is a story that Tarshish extended *two thousand* miles.

Chullin, fol. 91, col. 2.

31. The tithes from the herds of Elazer ben Azaryah amounted to *twelve thousand* calves annually.

Shabbath, fol. 54, col. 2.

32. It is said that Rabbi Akiva had *twelve thousand* pairs of disciples dispersed about between Gabbath and Antipatris, and all of them died within a short period because they paid no honour to one another. The land was then desolate until Rabbi Akiva came among our Rabbis of the south and taught the law to Rabbis Meir, Yehudah, Yossi, Shimon, and Elazer ben Shamua, who re-established its authority.   *Yevamoth*, fol. 26, col. 2.

33. After a lapse of twelve years, he returned accompanied by *twelve thousand* disciples, &c. (See *ante*, chap. xi. No. 14, note.)

34. Ravah bar Nachmaini was impeached for depriving the revenue of the poll-tax on *twelve thousand* Jews, by detaining them annually at his academy for one month in the spring, and for another month in the autumn; for great multitudes from various parts of the country were

wont, at the two seasons of the Passover and the Feast of
Tabernacles, to come to hear him preach, so that when the
king's officers came to collect the taxes they found none
of them at home.   A royal messenger was accordingly
despatched to apprehend him, but he failed to find him,
for the Rabbi fled to Pumbeditha, and from thence to
Akra, to Agmi, Sichin, Zeripha, Ein d'Maya, and back
again to Pumbeditha.   Arrived at this place, both the royal
messenger and the fugitive Rabbi happened to put up
at the same inn.   Two cups were placed before the former
on a table, when, strange to say, after he had drunk and
the table was removed, his face was forcibly turned round
to his back.   (This was done by evil spirits because he
drank even numbers—זוגות, pairs—against which we are
earnestly warned in P'sachim, fol. 110, col. 1.)   The inn-
keeper, fearing the consequences of such a misfortune
happening to so high an official at his inn, sought advice
of the lurking Rabbi, when the latter suggested that the
table be placed again before him with one cup only
on it, and thus the even number would become odd, and
his face would return to its natural position.   They did
so, and it was as the Rabbi had said.   The official then
remarked to his host, " I know the man I want is here,"
and he hastened and found him.   " If I knew for certain,"
he said to the Rabbi, " that thy escape would cost my life
only, I would let thee go, but I fear bodily torture, and
therefore I must secure thee."   And thereupon he locked
him up.   Upon this the Rabbi prayed, till the prison walls
miraculously giving way; he made his escape to Agma,
where he seated himself at the root of a tree and gave
himself up to meditation.   Whilst thus engaged he all at
once heard a discussion in the academy of heaven on the
subject of the hair mentioned in Lev. xiii. 25.   The
Holy One — blessed be He !—declared the case to be
" clean," but the whole academy were of a different
opinion, and declared the case to be " unclean."   The

question then arose, " Who shall decide ? "   " Ravah bar Nachmaini shall decide," was the unanimous reply, " for he said, ' I am one in matters of leprosy; I am one in questions about tents; and there is none to equal me.' " Then the angel of death was sent for to bring him up, but he was unable to approach him, because the Rabbi's lips never ceased repeating the law of the Lord. The angel of death thereupon assumed the appearance of a troop of cavalry, and the Rabbi, apprehensive of being seized and carried off, exclaimed, " I would rather die through that one (meaning the angel of death) than be delivered into the hands of the Government ! " At that very instant he was asked to decide the question in dispute, and just as the verdict " clean " issued from his lips his soul departed from his body, and a voice was heard from heaven proclaiming, " Blessed art thou, Ravah bar Nachmaini, for thy body is clean. ' Clean ' was the word on thy lips when thy spirit departed." Then a scroll fell down from heaven into Pumbeditha announcing that Ravah bar Nachmaini was admitted into the academy of heaven. Apprised of this, Abaii, in company with many other Rabbis, went in search of the body to inter it, but not knowing the spot where he lay, they went to Agma, where they noticed a great number of birds hovering in the air, and concluded that the shadow of their wings shielded the body of the departed. There, accordingly, they found and buried him ; and after mourning three days and three nights over his grave, they arose to depart, when another scroll descended threatening them with excommunication if they did so. They therefore continued mourning for seven days and seven nights, when, at the end of these, a third scroll descended and bade them go home in peace. On the day of the death of this Rabbi there arose, it is said, such a mighty tempest in the air that an Arab merchant and the camel on which he was riding were blown bodily over from one side of the river Pappa to the other. " What meaneth such a storm as this?" cried the merchant, as he lay on the ground. A voice from heaven answered, "Ravah bar Nachmaini is dead." Then he prayed and pled, "Lord of the universe, the whole world is Thine, and Ravah bar Nachmaini is Thine! Thou art Ravah's and Ravah is Thine; but wherefore wilt thou destroy the world?" On this the storm immediately abated, and there was a perfect calm. *Bava Metzia*, fol. 86, col. 1.

> NOTE.—The above seems to be a Rabbinical satire on the Talmud itself, although the orthodox Jews believe that every word in it is historically true. Well, perhaps it is so; and we outsiders are ignorant, and without the means of judging.

35. Now we know what God does during the day (see chap. xi. No. 16), but how does He occupy Himself in the night-time? We may say He does the same as at day-time; or that during the night He rides on a swift cherub over *eighteen thousand* worlds; as it is said (Ps. lxviii. 17), "The chariots of God are *twenty thousand*," less *two thousand* Shinan; read not Shinan but She-einan (אל תקרי שנאן אלא שאינן), *i.e., two thousand less than twenty thousand*, therefore *eighteen thousand*.

Avodah Zarah, fol. 3, col. 2.

36. Prince Contrukos asked Rabbon Yochanan ben Zacchai how, when the detailed enumeration of the Levites amounted to *twenty-two thousand three hundred* (the Gershonites, 7500; the Kohathites, 8600; the Merarites, 6200, making in all 22,300), the sum total given is only *twenty-two thousand*, omitting the *three hundred.* "Was Moses, your Rabbi," he asked, "a cheat or a bad calculator?" He answered, "They were first-borns, and therefore could not be substitutes for the first-born of Israel."

Bechoroth, fol. 5, col. 1.

37. "And the inhabitants of Jerusalem did him honour at his death" (2 Chron. xxxii. 33). This is Hezekiah,

king of Judah, at whose funeral *thirty-six thousand* people attended bare-shouldered, . . . and upon his bier was laid a roll of the law, and it was said, "This man has fulfilled what is written in this book."

Bava Kama, fol. 17, col. 1.

38. Sennacherib the wicked invaded (Jewry) with *forty-five thousand* princes in golden coronets, and they had with them their wives and odalisques; also *eighty thousand* mighty men clad in mail and *sixty thousand* swordsmen ran before him, and the rest were cavalry. With a similar army they came against Abraham, and a like force is to come up with Gog and Magog. A tradition teaches that the extent of his camp was *four hundred* parsaes or leagues, the extent of the horses' necks was *forty* parsaes. The total muster of his army was *two hundred and sixty myriads of thousands*, less one. Abaii asked, "Less *one myriad*, or *one thousand*, or *one hundred?* or more literally less *one?*"

Sanhedrin, fol. 95, col. 2.

Note.—In the immediate context of the above extract we have the following legend concerning Sennacherib :—As Rabbi Abhu has said, "Were it not for this Scripture text it would be impossible to repeat what is written (Isa. vii. 20), ' In the same day shall the Lord shave with a razor that is hired, by them beyond the river, by the king of Assyria, the head and the hair of the feet; and it shall also consume the beard.'" The story is this :—The Holy One—blessed be He !—once disguised Himself as an elderly man and came to Sennacherib, and said, "When thou comest to the kings of the East and of the West, to force their sons into thine army, what wilt thou say unto them?" He replied, "On that very account I am in fear. What shall I do?" God answered him, "Go and disguise thyself." "How can I disguise myself?" said he. God replied, "Go and fetch me a pair of scissors and I will cut thy hair." Sennacherib asked, "Whence shall I fetch them?" "Go to yonder house and bring them." He went accordingly and observed a pair, but there he met the ministering angels disguised as men, grinding date-stones. He asked them for the scissors, but they said, "Grind thou first a measure of date-stones, and then thou shalt have the scissors." He did as he was told, and so obtained the scissors. It was dark before he returned, and God said unto him, " Go and fetch some fire." This also he did, but whilst blowing the embers his beard was singed. Upon which God came and shaved his head and his beard, and said, " This is it which is written (Isa. vii. 20), ' It shall also consume the beard.' " Rav Pappa says this is the proverb current among the people, " Singe the face of a Syrian, and, if it pleases him, also set his beard in fire, and thou wilt not be able to laugh enough." (*Sanhedrin*, fol. 95, col. 2, and fol. 96, col. 1.)

39. " He hath cut off in His fierce anger all the horn of Israel," &c. (Lam. ii. 3). These are the *eighty thousand* war-horns or battering-rams that entered the city of Byther, in which he massacred so many men, women, and children, that their blood ran like a river and flowed into the Mediterranean Sea, which was a mile away from the place. *Gittin*, fol. 57, col. 1.

40. That mule had a label attached to his neck on which it was stated that its breeding cost *a hundred thousand* zouzim. *Bechoroth*, fol. 8, col. 2.

41. Rabbi Yossi said, " I have seen Sepphoris (Cyprus) in the days of its prosperity, and there were in it *a hundred and eighty thousand* marts for sauces. *Bava Bathra*, fol. 75, col. 2.

42. Rav Assi said *three hundred thousand* swordsmen went up to the Royal Mount and there slaughtered the people for three days and three nights, and yet while on the one side of the mount they were mourning, on the other they were merry ; those on the one side did not know the affairs of those on the other. *Gittin*, fol. 57, col. 1.

CHAPTER XIV.

1. A CERTAIN disciple prayed before Rabbi Chanina, and said, "O God! who art great, mighty, formidable, magnificent, strong, terrible, valiant, powerful, real and honoured!" He waited until he had finished, and then said to him, "Hast thou ended all the praises of thy God? Need we enumerate so many? As for us, even the three terms of praise which we usually repeat, we should not dare to utter, had not Moses, our master, pronounced them in the law (Deut. x. 17), and had not the men of the Great Synagogue ordained them for prayer; and yet thou hast repeated so many and still seemest inclined to go on. It is as if one were to compliment a king because of his silver, who is master of *a thousand thousands* of gold denarii. Wouldst thou think that becoming?"

Berachoth, fol. 33, col. 2.

2. Rabbi Yossi ben Kisma relates, "I once met a man in my travels and we saluted one another. In reply to a question of his I said, 'I am from a great city of sages and scribes.' Upon this he offered me *a thousand thousand* golden denarii, and precious stones and pearls, if I would agree to go and dwell in his native place. But I replied, saying, 'If thou wert to give me all the gold and silver, all the precious stones and pearls in the world, I would not reside anywhere else than in the place where the law is studied.'"

Avoth, chap. 6.

3. *Thousands on thousands* in Israel were named after Aaron; for had it not been for Aaron these *thousands of thousands* would not have been born. Aaron went about making peace between quarrelling couples, and those who were born after the reconciliation were regularly named after him. *Aroth d'Rab. Nathan*, chap. 12.

4. It is related by the Rabbis that Rabbon Yochanan ben Zacchai was once riding out of Jerusalem accompanied by his disciples, when he saw a young woman picking barley out of the dung on the road. On his asking her name, she told him that she was the daughter of Nikodemon ben Gorion (see chap. xi. No. 13). "What has become of thy father's riches?" said he, "and what has become of thy dowry?" "Dost thou not remember," said she, "that charity is the salt of riches?" (Her father had not been noted for this virtue.) "Dost thou not remember signing my marriage contract?" said the woman. "Yes," said the Rabbi, "I well remember it. It stipulated for a *million* gold denarii from thy father, besides the allowance from thy husband," &c. *Kethuboth*, fol. 66, col. 2.

5. Abba Benjamin says, "If our eye were permitted to see the malignant sprites that beset us, we could not rest on account of them." Abaii has said, "They outnumber us, they surround us as the earthed-up soil on our garden-beds." Rav Hunna says, "Every one has a *thousand* at his left side and *ten thousand* at his right" (Ps. xci. 7). Rava adds, "The crowding at the schools is caused by their pushing in; they cause the weariness which the Rabbis experience in their knees, and even tear their clothes by hustling against them. If one would discover traces of their presence, let him sift some ashes upon the floor at his bedside, and next morning he will see, as it were, the footmarks of fowls on the surface. But if one would see the demons themselves, he must

burn to ashes the after-birth of a first-born black kitten, the offspring of a first-born black cat, and then put a little of the ashes into his eyes, and he will not fail to see them," &c., &c. *Berachoth*, fol. 6, col. 1.

6. In each camp there are suspended *three hundred and sixty-five myriads* of stars, &c. (See chap. xi. No. 7.)

7. Agrippa, being anxious to ascertain the number of the male population of Israel, instructed the priest to take accurate note of the Paschal lambs. On taking account of the kidneys, it was found that there were *sixty myriad* couples, (which indicated) double the number of those that came up out of Egypt, not reckoning those that were ceremonially unclean and those that were out travelling. There was not a Paschal lamb in which less than ten had a share, so that the number represented over six hundred myriads of men. *Pesachim*, fol. 64, col. 2.

NOTE.—(*a.*) "It is unlawful to enumerate Israel even with a view to a meritorious deed" (Yoma, fol. 22, col. 2). From Rashi's comment on the former text it seems that the priest merely held up the duplicate kidneys, upon which the king's agent regularly laid aside a pea or a pebble into a small heap, which were afterwards counted up. See also Josephus, Book VI. chap. ix. sec. 3.

(*b.*) It might not be amiss to remind the reader in passing that if one were to reckon *one hundred* per minute for *ten hours* a day, it would take no less than sixteen days six hours forty minutes to count a *million;* and that it would take *twenty* men, reckoning at the same rate, to sum up the total number stated in the text in *one day*, so as to ascertain that there were 1,200,000 sacrifices at the Passover under notice, representing no less than 12,000,000 celebrants.

8. At the time when Israel in their eagerness first said, "We will do," and then, "We will hear" (Exod. xxix. 7), there came *sixty myriads* of ministering angels to crown each Israelite with two crowns, one for "we will do" and one for "we will hear." But when after this Israel sinned,

there came down *a hundred and twenty myriads* of destroying angels and took the crowns away from them, as it is said (Exod. xxxiii. 6), "And the children of Israel stripped themselves of their ornaments by Mount Horeb." ·Resh Lakish says, "The Holy One—blessed be He!—will, in the future, return them to us; for it is said (Isa. xxxv. 10), 'The ransomed of the Lord shall return and come to Zion with songs and everlasting joy upon their heads,' *i.e.*, the joy they had in days of yore, upon their heads."

Shabbath, fol. 88, col. 1.

9. Let no one venture out alone at night-time on Wednesdays and Saturdays, for Agrath, the daughter of Machloth, roams about accompanied by *eighteen myriads* of evil genii, each one of which has power to destroy.

P'sachim, fol. 112, col. 2.

10. It is related of Rabbi Elazar ben Charsom that his mother made him a shirt which cost *two myriads* of manahs, but his fellow-priests would not allow him to wear it, because he appeared in it as though he were naked.

Yoma, fol. 35, col. 2.

11. He who has not seen the double gallery of the Synagogue in Alexandria of Egypt, has not seen the glory of Israel. . . . There were seventy-one seats arranged in it according to the number of the seventy-one members of the greater Sanhedrin, each seat of no less value than *twenty-one myriads* of golden talents. A wooden pulpit was in the centre, upon which stood the reader holding a Sudarium (a kind of flag) in his hand, which he waved when the vast congregation were required to say Amen at the end of any benediction, which, of course, it was impossible for all to hear in so stupendous a synagogue. The congregation did not sit promiscuously, but in guilds; goldsmiths apart, silversmiths apart, blacksmiths, coppersmiths, embroiderers, weavers, &c., all apart from each other. When a poor craftsman came in, he took his seat

among the people of his guild, who maintained him till
he found employment. Abaii says all this immense
population was massacred by Alexander of Macedon.
Why were they thus punished? Because they transgressed the Scripture, which says (Deut. xvii. 16), "Ye
shall henceforth return no more that way."

Succah, fol. 51, col. 2.

12. The Rabbis teach that during a prosperous year in the
land of Israel, a place sown with a measure of seed produces *five myriad* cors (a cor being equal to thirty measures). Kethuboth, fol. 112, col. 1.

13. Rav Ulla was once asked, "To what extent is one
bound to honour his father and mother?" To which he
replied, "See what a Gentile of Askelon once did, Dammah
ben Nethina by name. The sages one day required goods
to the value of *sixty myriads*, for which they were ready
to pay the price, but the key of the store-room happened to
be under the pillow of his father, who was fast asleep, and
Dammah would not disturb him." Rabbi Eliezer was
once asked the same question, and he gave the same
answer, adding an interesting fact to the illustration:—
"The sages were seeking after precious stones for the
high priest's breastplate, to the value of some *sixty* or
eighty myriads of golden denarii, but the key of the jewel-
chest happened to be under the pillow of his father, who
was asleep at the time, and he would not wake him. In
the following year, however, the Holy One—blessed be
He!—rewarded him with the birth of a red heifer among
his herds, for which the sages readily paid him such a
sum as compensated him fully for the loss he sustained
in honouring his parent." Kiddushin, fol. 31, col. 1.

14. "The Lord hath swallowed up all the habitations
of Jacob" (Lam. ii. 2). Ravin came to Babylon and said
in the name of Rabbi Yochanan, "These are the *sixty
myriads* of cities which King Yannai (Jannæus) possessed

on the royal mount. The population of each equalled
the number that went up out of Egypt, except that of
three cities in which that number was doubled. And
these three cities were כפר ביש, Caphar Bish (literally,
the village of evil), so called because there was no hospice
for the reception of strangers therein; כפר שיהליים,
Caphar Shichlaiim (village of water-cresses), so called
because it was chiefly on that herb that the people sub-
sisted; כפר דכריא, Caphar Dichraya (the village of
male children), so called, says Rabbi Yochanan, because
its women first gave birth to boys, and afterwards to
girls, and then left off bearing." Ulla said, "I have seen
that place, and am sure that it could not hold sixty myriads
of sticks." A Sadducee upon this said to Rabbi Chanina,
" Ye do not speak the truth." The response was, "It is
written (Jer. iii. 19), נהלת צבי, 'The inheritance of a
deer,' as the skin of a deer, unoccupied by the body of the
animal, *shrinks*, so also the land of Israel, unoccupied by
its rightful owners, *became contracted*."

Gittin, fol. 57, col. 1.

15. Rabbi Yoshua, the son of Korcha, relates:—"An
aged inhabitant of Jerusalem once told me that in this
valley *two hundred and eleven myriads* were massacred
by Nebuzaradan, captain of the guard, and in Jerusalem itself he slaughtered upon one stone *ninety-four
myriads*, so that the blood flowed till it touched the blood
of Zachariah, that it might be fulfilled which is said (Hos.
ii. 4), ' And blood toucheth blood.' When he saw the
blood of Zachariah, and noticed that it was boiling and
agitated, he asked, ' What is this ?' and he was told that
it was the spilled blood of the sacrifices. Then he ordered
blood from the sacrifices to be brought and compared it with
the blood of the murdered prophet, when, finding the one
unlike the other, he said, ' If ye tell me the truth, well and
good ; if not, I will comb your flesh with iron currycombs ! '
Upon this they confessed, ' He was a prophet, and because

he rebuked us on matters of religion, we arose and killed him, and it is now some years since his blood has been in the restless condition in which thou seest it.' 'Well,' said he, 'I will pacify him.' He then brought the greater and lesser Sanhedrin and slaughtered them, but the blood of the prophet did not rest. He next slaughtered young men and maidens, but the blood continued restless as before. He finally brought school-children and slaughtered them, but the blood being still unpacified, he exclaimed, 'Zachariah! Zachariah! I have for thy sake killed the best among them; will it please thee if I kill them all?' As he said this the blood of the prophet stood still and quiescent. He then reasoned within himself thus, 'If the blood of one individual has brought about so great a punishment, how much greater will my punishment be for the slaughter of so many!' In short, he repented, fled from his house, and became a Jewish proselyte." *Gittin*, fol. 57, col. 2.

Note.—The same story is repeated in Sanhedrin, fol. 96, col. 2, with some variations; notably this, among others, that it was because the prophet prophesied the destruction of Jerusalem that they put him to death.

16. (Gen. xxvii. 2), "The voice is the voice of Jacob, but the hands are the hands of Esau." The first-named "voice" alludes to the voice of lamentation caused by Hadrian, who had at Alexandria in Egypt massacred twice the number of Jews that had come forth under Moses. The "voice of Jacob" refers to a similar lamentation occasioned by Vespasian, who put to death in the city of Byther *four hundred myriads*, or, as some say, *four thousand myriads*. "The hands are the hands of Esau," that is, the empire which destroyed our house, burned our Temple, and banished us from our country. Or the "voice of Jacob" means that there is no effectual prayer that is not offered up by the progeny of Jacob; and "the hands are the hands of Esau," that there is no victorious battle which is not fought by the descendants of Esau. *Ibid.*

17. Tamar and Zimri both committed fornication. The former (actuated by a good motive, see Gen. xxxviii. 26) became the ancestress of kings and prophets. The latter brought about the destruction of *myriads* in Israel. Rav Nachman bar Yitzchak says, " To do evil from a good motive is better than observing the law from a bad one " (*e.g.*, Tamar and Zimri, Lot and his daughters).

Nazir, fol. 23, col. 2.

18. The Rabbis have taught that the text, " And when it rested, he said, Return, O Lord, to the myriads and thousands of Israel " (Num. x. 36), intimates that the Shechinah does not rest upon less than *two myriads and two thousands* (two being the minimum plurality). Suppose one of the *twenty-two thousand* neglect the duty of procreation, is he not the cause of the Shechinah's departure from Israel ?   *Yevamoth*, fol. 64, col. 1.

19. " And place over them to be rulers of thousands, and rulers of hundreds, and rulers of fifties, and rulers of tens " (Exod. xviii. 21). The rulers of thousands were *six hundred* in number, the rulers of hundreds *six thousand*, of fifties *twelve thousand*, and rulers of tens *six myriads*. The total number of rulers in Israel, therefore, was *seven myriad eight thousand six hundred*.

Sanhedrin, fol. 18, col. 1.

20. Once upon a time the people of Egypt appeared before Alexander of Macedon to complain of Israel. " It is said (Exod. xii. 36), they argued, ' The Lord gave the people favour in the sight of the Egyptians, so that they lent unto them,' &c. ; " and they prayed, " Give us now back the gold and the silver that ye took from us." Givia ben Pesisa said to the wise men (of Israel), " Give me permission to plead against them before Alexander. If they overcome me, say, ' You have overcome a plebeian only,' but if I overcome them, say, ' The law of Moses our master has triumphed over you.' " They accordingly gave him

leave, and he went and argued thus, " Whence do ye produce your proof?" " From the law," said they. Then said he, " I will bring no other evidence but from the law. It is said (Exod. xii. 40), ' The sojourning of the children of Israel, who dwelt in Egypt, was *four hundred and thirty* years.' Pay us now the usufruct of the labour of the *sixty myriads* whom ye enslaved in Egypt for *four hundred and thirty* years." Alexander gave the Egyptians three days' grace to prepare a reply, but they never put in an appearance. In fact, they fled away and left both their fields and vineyards.   *Sanhedrin*, fol. 91, col. 1.

21. " And Jethro said, Blessed be the Lord, who hath delivered you" (Exod. xviii. 10). A tradition says, in the name of Rabbi Papyes, " Shame upon Moses and upon the *sixty myriads* (of Israel), because they had not said, ' Blessed be the Lord,' till Jethro came and set the example."   *Ibid.*, fol. 94, col. 1.

22. " And let him dip his foot in oil" (Deut. xxxiii. 24), the Rabbis say, refers to the portion of Asher, which produces oil like a well. Once on a time, they relate, the Laodiceans sent an agent to Jerusalem with instructions to purchase a *hundred myriads'* worth of oil. He proceeded first to Tyre, and thence to Gush-halab, where he met with the oil merchant earthing up his olive-trees, and asked him whether he could supply a *hundred myriads'* worth of oil. " Stop till I have finished my work," was the reply. The other, when he saw the business-like way in which he set to work, could not help incredulously exclaiming, " What! hast thou really a *hundred myriads'* worth of oil to sell? Surely the Jews have meant to make game of me." However, he went to the house with the oil merchant, where a female slave brought hot water for him to wash his hands and feet, and a golden bowl of oil to dip them in afterwards, thus fulfilling Deut. xxxiii. 24 to the very letter. After they had eaten together, the

merchant measured out to him the *hundred myriads'* worth of oil, and then asked whether he would purchase more from him. "Yes," said the agent, "but I have no more money here with me." "Never mind," said the merchant; "buy it and I will go with thee to thy home for the money." Then he measured out *eighteen myriads'* worth more. It is said that he hired every horse, mule, camel, and ass he could find in all Israel to carry the oil, and that on nearing his city the people turned out to meet him and compliment him for the service he had done them. "Don't praise me," said the agent, "but this, my companion, to whom I owe *eighteen myriads.*" This, says the narrator, illustrates what is said (Prov. xiii. 7), "There is that maketh himself (appear to be) rich, yet hath nothing; there is that maketh himself poor, yet hath great riches."

Menachoth, fol. 85, col. 2.

A
CENTURY OF EXTRACTS FROM THE MIDRASHIM.

————

ויקר בעיני ה׳ אנדה כמבואר במדרשים.

"Precious in the sight of the Lord is the Aggadah, as explained in the Midrashim."

INTRODUCTION TO THE MIDRASHIM.

Our "Century of Extracts from the Midrashim" naturally calls for a few words by way of introduction and explanation.

The Midrashim are ancient Rabbinical expositions of Holy Writ. The term Midrash (of which Midrashim is the plural form) occurs twice in the Hebrew Bible (2 Chron. xiii. 22, and xxiv. 27); and in both passages it is oddly represented in the Anglican version by the word "story," while the more correct translation, "commentary," is relegated to the margin. "Legendary exposition" best expresses the full meaning of the word Midrash, which is derived from the Aramaic דרש, Darash, "to lay open, to investigate," and, according to Rabbinical terminology, "to expound, or to preach." Other cognate terms are Darashah, "a sermon or exposition;" Darshan, "a preacher or expositor;" and one which deserves more than a passing notice, viz., Darshanith, "*a female expounder*." In the Talmud (Bava Bathra, fol. 119, col. 2), the daughters of Zelophehad, the five wise virgins of Rabbinic lore, as we may fairly style them, are uniquely honoured with the titles of חכמניות, דרשניות, צדקניות, *i.e.*, sages, expounders, righteous women; and it is on this ground that the second of these, the strangest of the three, is alleged to have been applied to them. In Num. xxvii. 4 these daughters of Zelophehad are represented as pleading and saying, "Why should the name of our father be done away from among his family because he hath no

son? Give unto us, therefore, a possession among the
brethren of our father;" and thus, by their suggestion,
settling once for all a moot-point in the law given to
Israel. It stands to reason that if they had not been
דרשניות, Darshaneeyoth, that is, female expounders,
they could not have known the correct interpretation of
the law, which even Moses, the prime legislator himself, as
we see from the context, was not aware of; while we have
the Divine testimony to justify the conclusion that they
were correct in their exposition, and, in the whole case,
a warrant for the inference, which is inevitable, that education in the law was not forbidden to females by Moses.
Only those who affected to "sit in Moses' seat" have enacted
the harsh dogma, ישרפו דברי תורה ולא ימסרו ד"ת לנשים.,
"Let the words of the law be burned, but let not the
words of the law be imparted to women" (see Tosaphoth
in Sotch, fol. 21, col. 2, and for more on this subject, Index II. appended to this work).

The Midrashim, for the most part, originated in a
praiseworthy desire to familiarise the people with Holy
Writ, which had, in consequence of changes in the ver-
nacular, become to them, in the course of time, almost a
dead letter. These Midrashim have little or nothing to
do with the Halachoth or legal decisions of the Talmud,
except in aim, which is that of illustration and explanation. They are not literal interpretations, but figurative
and paraphrastic; oftentimes they are allegorical, and as
such enigmatic. They are, however, to be received as
utterances of the sages, and some even regard them of as
binding obligation as the law of Moses itself (see Menorath Hammaor, vol. i. p. 96), so that he who treats them
with disrespect may expect to be punished in Gehenna
for the slight בצואה רותחת, by being boiled in excrement.
(See Eiruvin, fol. 21, col. 2.) Even the gossip, we are
told, of the disciples of the wise, is to be regarded with
reverent attention; how much more, then, their deliberately
recorded utterances!

Nehemiah (chap. viii. 48) supplies an illustration of
the circumstances in which many of these extempore
Midrashim originated, more especially the Targumim or
Chaldee paraphrases of the law, the prophets, and other
sacred writings.   Though not a few quotations from
various Midrashim are given in the notes interspersed
throughout this volume, we have kept the Yalkut Eliezer
in reserve to supply the extracts which follow. These
we take to be fairly typical specimens of that homiletic
literature of the Geonastic period of Jewish history.

This grand Miscellany of Haggadoth, better known by
the title of ‏ילקוט אליעזר‎, Yalkut Eliezer, ranges so freely
over the whole field of sacred history, lingering especially
on the salient features of the five books of Moses, that it
is aptly suited to our purpose here, which is that of illustrating the motto taken from its preface, " Precious in
the eyes of the Lord is the Aggadah, as explained in the
Midrashim."

CHAPTER XV.

1. The name of Abraham always precedes those of Isaac and Jacob except in one place (Lev. xxvi. 42), where it is said, "And I will remember my covenant with Jacob, and also my covenant with Isaac, and also my covenant with Abraham will I remember;" and thus we learn that all were of equal importance.

Midrash Rabbah, Gen. chap. 1.

Note.—So that this precedence is on this exegesis merely an instance of *primus inter pares* among the patriarchal three. In the Selichoth * for the Day of Atonement the above reversal of the usual order of the names of Abraham, Isaac, and Jacob is thus referred to: "The first covenant Thou didst exalt, and the order of the contracting parties to it Thou hast reversed."

2. Abraham deserved to have been created before Adam, but the Holy One—blessed be He!—said, "Should he pervert things as I make them, then there will be no one to rectify them; so behold I will create Adam first, and if he should make things crooked, then Abraham following him will make them straight again."

Ibid., chap. 14.

3. Abram was called Abraham, and Isaac was also called Abraham; as it is written (Gen. xxv. 19), "Isaac, Abraham's son, Abraham." *Ibid.*, chap. 63.

Note.—This is a sample of what we may term a Procrustean quotation (a practice not confined to Rabbinic ingenuity), whereby the Scriptures are cut to measure, and made to fit according to fancy.

---

* A certain portion of the Jewish liturgy.

4. "And he lay down in *that* place" (Gen. xxviii. 11).
Rabbi Yuda said, "*There* he lay down, but he did not lie
down during all the fourteen years he was hid in the house
of Eber." Rabbi Nehemiah said, "*There* he lay down, but he
did not lie down all the twenty years in which he stood
in the house of Laban." *Midrash Rabbah*, chap. 68.

5. וַיִּשָּׁקֵהוּ, Vayash Kihu. "And kissed him" (Gen. xxxiii.
4). Rabbi Yanai asks, "Why is this word (in the original
Hebrew) so pointed?" "It is to teach that Esau did not
come to kiss him, but to *bite* him; only the neck of Jacob
our father became as hard as marble, and this blunted the
teeth of the wicked one." "And what is taught by the
expression 'And they wept?'" "The one wept for his
neck and the other for his teeth." *Ibid.*, chap. 78.

Note.—Rabbi Shimon ben Yochai in Sifri deliberately contro-
verts this interpretation, and Aben Ezra says it is an
"exposition fit only for children."

6. Esau said, "I will not kill my brother Jacob with
bow and arrow, but with my mouth I will suck his blood,"
as it is said (Gen. xxxiii. 4), "And Esau ran to meet him,
and embraced him, and kissed him, and they wept,"
(א"ת וישקהו אלא וישכהו). Read not "and he kissed him,"
but read, "and he bit him." The neck of Jacob, however,
became as hard as ivory, and it is respecting him that
Scripture says (Cant. vii. 5), "Thy neck is as a tower of
ivory,"—so that the teeth of Esau became blunted; and
when he saw that his desire could not be gratified, he
began to be angry, and gnashed his teeth, as it is said
(Ps. cxii. 10), "The wicked shall see it and be grieved; he
shall gnash with his teeth."

Pirke d'Rab. Eliezer, chap. 36.

Note.—See also the previous quotation from the Midrash
Rabbah. The Targum of Jonathan and also the Yerushalmi record the same fantastic tradition. In the latter
it is given thus, "And Esau ran to meet him, and hugged

him, and fell upon his neck and kissed him. Esau wept
for the crushing of his teeth, and Jacob wept for the
tenderness of his neck."

7. Abraham made a covenant with the people of the
land, and when the angels presented themselves to him,
he thought they were mere wayfarers, and he ran to meet
them, purposing to make a banquet for them. This
banquet he told Sarah to get prepared, but just as she was
kneading (ראתה דם נדה). For this reason he did not
offer them the cakes which she had made, but "ran to
fetch a calf, tender and good." The calf in trepidation
ran away from him and hid itself in the cave of Machpelah, into which he followed it. Here he found Adam and
Eve fast asleep, with lamps burning over their couches,
and the place pervaded with a sweet-smelling odour.
Hence the fancy he took to the cave of Machpelah for a
"possession of a burying-place."

Pirke d'Rab. Eliezer, chap. 36.

Note.—Compare the words ראתה דם נדה with the matter-of-
fact statement in Gen. xviii. 11, חדל להיות לשרה ארח
כנשים.

8. Shechem, the son of Hamor, assembled girls together
playing on tambourines outside the tent of Dinah, and
when she "went out to see them," he carried her off, . . .
and she bare him Osenath. The sons of Jacob wished to kill
her, lest the people of the land should begin to talk scan-
dal of the house of their father. Jacob, however, engraved
the holy Name on a metal plate, suspended it upon her
neck, and sent her away. All this being observed before
the Holy One—blessed be He !—the angel Michael was
sent down, who led her to Egypt, into the house of Poti-
pherah; for Osenath was worthy to become the wife of
Joseph.   *Ibid.*, chap. 48.

Note.—In Yalkut Yehoshua 9, Osenath is styled a proselyte ;
and indeed it might seem likely enough that Joseph induced her to worship the true God. The Targum of
Jonathan agrees with the version of the Midrash above,

while another tradition makes Joseph marry Zuleika,
the virgin widow of Potiphar, and says that she was the
same woman that is called Osenath (Koran, note to p.
193).

9. When Joseph's brethren recognised him, and were
about to kill him, an angel came down and dispersed them
to the four corners of the house. Then Judah screamed
with such a loud voice that all the walls of Egypt
were levelled with the dust, all the beasts were smitten
to the ground, and Joseph and Pharaoh, their teeth having
fallen out, were cast down from their thrones; while all
the men that stood before Joseph had their heads twisted
round with their faces towards their backs, and so they
remained till the day of their death; as it is said (Job iv.
10), "The roaring of the lion (Judah), and the voice of the
fierce lion," &c. *Vayegash*, chap. 5.

Note.—For more on this subject see Jasher, chap. 54, and
the Targum of Jonathan, sect. "Vayegash," &c.

10. The tradition of a legend in our possession says
that Judah killed Esau. When? When Isaac died, Jacob
and (the chiefs of) the twelve clans went to bury him; as
it is written (Gen. xxxv. 29), "And his sons Esau and Jacob
buried him." In the Midrash it is, "And Esau and Jacob
and his sons buried him," which fits the legend better.
Arrived at the cave, they entered it, and they stood and
wept. The (heads of the) tribes, out of respect to Jacob,
left the cave, that Jacob might not be put to shame in
their presence. Judah re-entered it, and finding Esau
risen up as if about to murder Jacob, he instantly went
behind him and killed him. But why did he not kill
him from the front? Because the physiognomy of Esau
was exactly like that of Jacob, and it was out of respect
to the latter that he slew Esau from behind.

Midrash Shochar Tov, chap. 18.

Note.—Tradition varies respecting the tragic end of Esau.
The Book of Jasher (chap. 56, v. 64) and the Targum

of Jonathan (in Vayechi) both say that Cushim the· son of Dan slew Esau at the burial, not of Isaac, but of Jacob, because he sought to hinder the funeral obsequies, disputing the title to the sepulchre. (See p. 186, No. 105, *ante.*)

11. " Oh, that I had wings like a dove ! for then I would fly away, and be at rest" (Ps. lv. 6). This is spoken of Abraham. But why like a dove ? Rabbi Azariah, in the name of Rabbi Yudan, says, " Because all birds when tired rest on a rock or on a tree, but a dove, when tired of flying, draws in one wing to rest it, and continues her flight with the other."   *Bereshith Rabbah*, chap. 39.

12. The Holy One—blessed be He !—said unto Abraham, " What should I tell thee ? and with what shall I bless thee ? Shall I tell thee to be perfectly righteous, or that thy wife Sarah be righteous before me ? That ye both are already. Or shall I say that thy children shall be righteous ? They are so already. But I will bless thee so that all thy children which shall in future ages come forth from thee shall be just like thee." Whence do we learn this ? From Gen. xv. 5 : " And he said unto him, So (like thee) shall thy seed be."
   Bamidbar Rabbah, chap. 2.

13. " Every man . . . by his own standard " (Num. ii. 2). The several princes of Israel selected the colours for their banners from the colour of the stones that were upon the breastplate of Aaron. From them other princes have learned to adorn their standards with different distinguishing colours. Reuben had his flag *red*, and leaves of mandrakes upon it. Issachar had his flag *blue*, and the sun and moon upon it. Naphtali had on his flag an olive-tree, for this reason that (Gen. xlix. 20) " Out of Asher his bread shall be fat."   *Ibid.*, chap. 7.

14. " And Abraham rose up early and saddled his ass" (Gen. xxii. 3). This is the ass on which Moses also rode

when he came into Egypt; for it is said (Exod. iv. 20),
"And Moses took his wife and his sons, and set them upon
an ass." This is the ass on which the Son of David also
shall ride; as it is said (Zech. ix. 9), "Poor, and riding
upon an ass."   *Pirke d'Rab. Eliezer*, chap. 31.

> NOTE.—In the morning service for Yom Kippur,* there is an
> allusion to the Scripture passage with which our quota-
> tion opens. It is said that Abraham in "his great joy
> perverted the usual order," which a footnote explains
> thus—"In the greatness of his joy, that he had thus an
> opportunity of showing his obedience to God, he set
> aside the usual order of things, which was that the
> servant should saddle the ass, and saddled the ass himself,
> as mentioned Gen. xxii. 3." The animal referred to in
> the above remarks is spoken of in Sanhedrin, fol. 98,
> col. 1, as being of a hundred colours.

15. When Joseph saw the signs of Judah's anger, he
began to tremble, and said (to himself), "Woe is me, for he
may kill me!" And what were these signs? Tears of
blood rolling down from Judah's right eye, and the hair
that grew on his chest rising and penetrating through the
five garments that he wore. Joseph then kicked the
marble seat on which he was sitting, so that it was
instantly shattered into fragments. Upon this Judah
observed, "He is a mighty man, like one of us."
                                              Yalkut Vayegash.

NOTE.—Compare Jasher, chap. 54; Ber. Rabbah, &c.

16. Abraham married three wives—Sarah, a daughter
of Shem; Keturah, a daughter of Japheth; and Hagar, a
daughter of Ham.   *Yalkut, Job,* chap. 8.

> NOTE.—Rashi supposes that Keturah was one and the same
> with Hagar—so the Midrash, the Targum Yerushalmi,
> and that of Jonathan. The latter says, "Keturah, she is
> Hagar, who had been bound to him from the beginning,"
> as if קטורה meant the *bound one*, from קשר, *to bind or
> tie;* but Aben Ezra and most of the commentators con-

---

* Day of Atonement.

tend that Keturah and Hagar are two distinct persons,
and the use of the plural פלגשים, *concubines*, in verse 6,
bears them out in this assertion.

17. The Holy One—blessed be He!—daily proclaims a
new law in the heavenly court, and even all these were
known to Abraham.　　　　　　　*Yalkut, Job*, chap. 37.

18. A Gentile once asked Rabbi Yoshua ben Kapara,
"Is it true that ye say your God sees the future?"
"Yes," was the reply. "Then how is it that it is written
(Gen. vi. 6), 'And it grieved Him at His heart?'" "Hast
thou," replied the Rabbi, "ever had a boy born to thee?"
"Yes," said the Gentile; "and I rejoiced and made others
rejoice with me." "Didst thou not know that he would
eventually die?" asked the Rabbi. "Yes," answered the
other; "but at the time of joy is joy, and at the time of
mourning, mourning." "So it is before the Holy One—
blessed be He!—seven days He mourned before the deluge
destroyed the world."　　　　*Bereshith Rabbah*, chap. 27.

19. All the strength of the soul's mourning is from the
third to the thirtieth day, during which time she sits on
the grave, still thinking her beloved might yet return (to
the body whence she departed). When she notices that
the colour of the face is changed, she leaves and goes
away; and this is what is written (Job xiv. 22), "But his
flesh upon him shall have pain, and his soul shall mourn
over him." Then the mouth and the belly quarrel with
one another, the former saying to the latter, "All I have
robbed and taken by violence I deposited in thee;" and
the latter, having burst three days after its burial, saying
to the former, "There is all thou hast robbed and taken
by violence! as it is written (Eccles. xii. 6), 'The pitcher
is broken at the fountain.'"　　　　*Ibid.*, chap. 100.

20. Job said, "Even the devil shall not dissuade me
from comforting those that mourn; for I would tell him that

I am not better than my Creator, who comforts Israel; as
it is said (Isa. li. 12), 'I, even I, am He that comforteth
you.'"
Psikta Nachmu.

21. Once Rabbi Shimon ben Yehozedek addressed
Rabbi Sh'muel ben Nachman and said, "I hear that thou
art a Baal Aggadah; canst thou therefore tell me whence
the light was created?"   "We learn," he replied in a
whisper, "that God wrapped Himself with light as with
a garment, and He has caused the splendour thereof to
shine from one end of the world to the other."   The other
said, "Why whisperest thou, I wonder, since Scripture
says so plainly (Ps. civ. 2) 'Who covereth Himself with
light as with a garment'?"   The reply was, "I heard it
in a whisper, and in a whisper I have told it to thee."
Bereshith Rabbah, chap. 3.

22. "As the tents of Kedar" (Cant. i. 5).   As the tents
of the Ishmaelites are ugly without and comely within,
so also the disciples of the wise, though apparently want-
ing in beauty, are nevertheless full of Scripture, and of
the Mishnah and of the Talmud, of the Halacha and of
the Aggadoth.
Shemoth Rabbah, chap. 23.

23. "Write thou these words" (Exod. xxxiv. 37).   That
applies to the Law, the Prophets, and the Hagiographa,
which were given in writing, but not to the Halachoth, the
Midrashim, the Aggadoth, and the Talmud, which were
given by the mouth.
Ibid., chap. 47.

24. Rabbi Samlai said to Rabbi Yonathan, "Instruct
me in the Aggada."   The latter replied, "We have a tradition from our forefathers not to instruct either a Babylonian or a Daromean in the Aggada, for though they are
deficient in knowledge they are haughty in spirit."
Tal. Yerushalmi P'sachim, v. fol. 32, col. 1.

25. He who transcribes the Aggada has no portion in

the world to come; he who expounds it is excommunicated; and he who listens to the exposition of it shall receive no reward.

Tal. Yerushalmi P'sachim, Shabbath, xvi. fol. 30, col. 2.

26. "Day unto day uttereth speech" (Ps. xix. 2, 3, 4); this means the Law, the Prophets, and the Hagiographa. "And night unto night showeth knowledge;" this is the Mishnaioth. "There is no speech or language where their voice is not heard;" these are the Halachoth. "Their line is gone out through all the earth;" these are the Aggadoth, by which His great name is sanctified.

T. debei Aliahu, chap. 2

27. Rabbi Yeremiah, the son of Elazar, said, "When the Holy One—blessed be He!—created Adam, He created him an אנדרוגינוס, for it is written (Gen. v. 2), 'Male and female created He them.'" Rabbi Sh'muel bar Nachman said, "When the Holy One—blessed be He!—created Adam, He created him with two faces; then He sawed him asunder, and split him (in two), making one back to the one-half, and another to the other.

Midrash Rabbah, chap. 8.

Note.—The term אנדרוגינוס is a transliteration of the Greek 'Ανδρόγυνος, from ἀνήρ, ἀνδρός, a man, and γυνή, woman. Latin form Androgynus.

28. "And it repented the Lord that He had made man (Adam) on the earth, and it grieved Him at His heart" (Gen. vi. 6). Rabbi Berachiah says that when God was about to create Adam, He foresaw that both righteous people and wicked people would come forth from him. He reasoned therefore with Himself thus:—"If I create him, then will the wicked proceed from him; but if I do not create him, how then shall the righteous come forth?" What then did God do? He separated the ways of the wicked from before Him, and assuming the attribute of mercy, so He created him. This explains what is written (Ps. i. 6), "For the Lord knoweth the way of the

righteous, but the way of the wicked shall be lost." The way of the wicked was lost before Him, but assuming to Himself the attribute of mercy, He created him. Rabbi Chanina says, לא כן, "It was not so! But when God was about to create Adam, He consulted the ministering angels and said unto them (Gen. i. 26), 'Shall we make man in our image after our likeness?' They replied, 'For what good wilt thou create him?' He responded, 'That the righteous may rise out of him.' This explains what is written, 'For the Lord knoweth the way of the righteous, but the way of the wicked shall be lost.' God informed them only about the righteous, but He said nothing about the wicked, otherwise the ministering angels would not have given their consent that man should be created."

Bereshith Rabbah, chap. 8.

29. Rabbi Hoshaiah said, "When God created Adam the ministering angels mistook him for a divine being, and were about to say, 'Holy! holy! holy!' before him. But God caused a deep sleep to fall upon Adam, so that all knew he was only a man. This explains what is written (Isa. ii. 22), 'Cease ye from man, whose breath is in his nostrils; for wherein is he to be accounted of?'" *Ibid.*

30. Rabbi Yochanan saith, "Adam and Eve seemed as if they were about twenty years old when they were created." *Ibid.*, chap. 14.

31. Rav Acha said when God was about to create Adam He consulted the ministering angels, and asked them, saying, "Shall we make man?" They inquired, "Of what good will this man be?" He replied, "His wisdom will be greater than yours." One day, therefore, He brought together the cattle, the beasts, and the birds, and asked them the name of them severally, but they knew not. He then caused them to pass before Adam, and asked him, "What is the name of this and the other?" Then Adam

replied, "This is an ox, this is an ass," and so on. "And
thou, why is thy name Adam?" (*i.e.*, in Hebrew, man).
"I ought to be called Adam," was his reply, "for I was
created from Adamah" (אדמה = the ground). "And what
is My name?" "It is meet Thou shouldst be called Lord,
for thou art Lord over all Thy creatures." Rav Acha
says, "'I am the Lord, that is My name' (Isa. xlii. 8).
'That is My name which Adam called Me.'"

Bereshith Rabbah, chap. 17.

32. Rabba Eliezer says Adam was skilled in all manner
of crafts. What proof is there of this? It is said (Isa.
xliv. 11), "And the artisans, they are of Adam."

Ibid., chap. 24.

33. "And the Lord said, I will destroy man" (Gen. vi.
7). Rabbi Levi, in the name of Rabbi Yochanan, says
that even millstones were destroyed. Rabbi Yuda, in the
name of Rabbi Yochanan, declares even the very dust of
Adam was destroyed. Rabbi Yuda, in the name of Rabbi
Shimon, insists אפילו לוז של שדרה, even the (resurrection)
bone of the spine, from which God will one day cause man
to sprout forth again, was destroyed.   *Ibid.*, chap. 28.

Note.—Concerning the bone, לוז, the *os coccygis*, there is an
interesting story in Midrash Kohelet (fol. 114, 3), which
may be appropriately inserted here. Hadrian (whose
bones may they be ground, and his name blotted out)
once asked Rabbi Joshua ben Chanania, "From what
shall the human frame be reconstructed when it rises
again?" "From Luz in the backbone," was the answer.
"Prove this to me," said Hadrian. Then the Rabbi took
Luz, a small bone of the spine, and immersed it in water,
but it was not softened; he put it into the fire, but
it was not consumed; he put it into a mill, but it
could not be pounded; he placed it upon an anvil and
struck it with a hammer, but the anvil split and the
hammer was broken. (See also Zohar in "Genesis,"
206, &c., &c.)

34. "A window shalt thou make to the ark" (Gen. vi.
16). Rabbi Amma says, "It was a real window." Rabbi

Levi, on the other hand, maintained that it was a precious stone, and that during the twelve months Noah was in the ark he had no need of the light of the sun by day nor of the moon by night because of that stone, which he had kept suspended, and he knew that it was day when it was dim, and night when it sparkled.

Bereshith Rabbah, chap. 31.

> NOTE.—The צהר = transparency, ascribed to the ark, has given rise to various conjectures which we cannot find room for here. The idea of Rabbi Levi, that it was a precious stone, has the sanction of the Targum of Jonathan; which volunteers the additional information that the gem was found in the river Pison.

35. Noah was deficient in faith, for he did not enter the ark till the water was up to his ankles. *Ibid.*, chap. 32.

36. "And he sent forth a raven" (Gen. viii. 7). The raven remonstrated, remarking, "From all the cattle, beasts, and fowls thou sendest none but me." "What need has the world for thee?" retorted Noah; "thou art good neither for food nor for sacrifice." Rabbi Eliezer says God ordered Noah to receive the raven, as the world would one day be in need of him. "When?" asked Noah. "When the waters are dried up from off the earth, there will in a time to come arise a certain righteous man who shall dry up the world, and then I shall want it." This explains what is written (1 Kings xvii. 6), "And the ravens brought him bread and flesh in the morning."

Ibid., chap. 33.

37. At the time God said to the serpent, "Upon thy belly thou shalt go" (Gen. iii. 14), the ministering angels descended and lopped off his hands and his feet. Then his voice was heard from one end of the world to the other. *Bereshith Midrash Rabbah*, chap. 20.

38. When God said to the serpent, "And upon thy belly thou shalt go" (Gen. iii. 14), the serpent replied, "Lord

of the universe! if this be Thy will, then I shall be as a fish of the sea without feet." But when God said to him, "And dust shalt thou eat," he replied, "If fish eat dust, then I also will eat it." Then God seized hold of the serpent and tore his tongue in two, and said, "O thou wicked one! thou hast commenced (to sin) with thy evil tongue; thus I will proclaim it to all that come into the world that it was thy tongue that caused thee all this."

Letters of Rabbi Akiva.

39. "And Noah only remained" (Gen. vii. 23), except Og, king of Bashan, who sat on a beam of the ladders (which projected from the ark), and swore to Noah and his sons that he would be their slave for ever. Noah made a hole in the ark through which he handed to Og his daily food. Thus *he* also remained, as it is said (Deut. iii. 11), "For only Og, king of Bashan, remained."

Pirke d'Rab. Eliezer, chap. 23.

Note.—See more about the antediluvian fable in regard to Og in chap. iii. No. 7, and chap. xiii. No. 11.

40. "Unto Adam and his wife did the Lord God make coats of skins" (Gen. iii. 21), viz., to cover their nakedness; but with what? With fringes and phylacteries, "Coats of skins," viz., the leathern straps of the phylacteries; "and they sewed fig-leaves" (Gen. iii. 7), viz., fringes; "and made themselves aprons," this means קריאת שמע, the proclaiming of the Shema, "Hear, O Israel," &c.

Yalkut Chadash.

Note.—The בתנות עור, which some (as Rashi, for instance) take to denote *furs*, the Targum of Jonathan says were made "from the skin of the serpent." The wardrobe of Adam afterwards came into the possession of Esau and Jacob (see Targ. Yon. in Toledoth, and p. 199, No. 161, *ante*).

41. All the presents which our father Jacob gave to Esau will one day be returned by the nations of the world to the Messiah, and the proof of this is (Ps. lxxii. 10),

"The kings of Tarshish and the isles shall return pre-sents." יבואו אין כתיב כאן אלא ישיבו. It is not written here, "They shall *bring*," but they shall restore or return.

Midrash Rabbah Vayishlach, chap. 78.

42. A philosopher once posed Rabbi Eliezer with the question, "Does not the prophet say (Mal. i. 4), 'They shall build, but I will throw down?' and do not buildings still exist?" To which the Rabbi answered, "The prophet does not speak of buildings, but of the schemes of designers. Ye all think to contrive and build up devices, to destroy and make an end of us, but He bringeth your counsels to nought. He throweth them down, so that your devices against us have no effect. "By thy life," said the philosopher, "it is even so; we meet annually for the purpose of compassing your ruin, but a certain old man comes and upsets all our projects" (namely, Elijah). *Yalkut Malachi.*

43. When Israel came out of Egypt, Samael rose to accuse them, and thus he spoke:—"Lord of the Universe! these have till now worshipped idols, and art Thou going to divide the sea for such as they?" What did the Holy One—blessed be He!—then do? Job, one of Pharaoh's high counsellors, of whom it is written (Job i. 1), "That man was perfect and upright," He took and delivered to Samael, saying, as He did so, "Behold, he is in thy hand; do with him as thou pleasest." God thought to divert his evil designs by keeping him thus occupied with Job, that Israel meanwhile might cross the sea without any hindrance, after which He would return and rescue Job from his tender mercies. God then said to Moses, "Behold I have delivered Job to Satan; make haste. Speak unto the children of Israel that they go forward" (Exod. xiv. 15). *Midrash Rabbah Shemoth*, chap. 21.

44. No man ever received a mite (in charity) from

Job, and needed to receive such a second time (because of the good-luck it brought along with it).

Midrash Rabbah Shemoth, chap. 21.

NOTE.—A superstitious belief prevails to some extent in Poland, among the Christian population as well as the Jews, that coins obtained in certain circumstances bring luck apart altogether from any virtue they may be supposed to convey from the giver. A penny obtained, for instance, the first thing in the morning, by stumbling on it in the street, by the sale of an article in the market, or by gift of charity, is considered to bode luck, and cherished as a pledge of good fortune by being slightly spat upon several times on receipt, and then carefully stowed away, for a longer or shorter period, in some safe sanctum. Job was the luckiest man that ever lived; his very goats even were so lucky as to kill the wolves that came to devour them; and a beggar, as we see, who received a mite from his hands, never needed afterwards to beg an alms from him again. (See "Genesis according to the Talmud," p. 288, No. 16.)

45. "And Saul said unto the Kenites, Go, depart, &c.; for ye showed kindness to all the children of Israel" (1 Sam. xv. 6). And did they show kindness to all the children of Israel? No; but what is written is to teach that he who receives a disciple of the wise as a guest into his house, and gives him to eat and to drink, is as if he had shown kindness to all the children of Israel.

Midrash Sh'muel, chap. 18.

46. Rabbi Levi says, "When Solomon introduced the ark into the Temple, all the woodwork thereof freshened with sap and began to yield fruit, as it is said (Ps. xcii. 13), 'Those that be planted in the house of the Lord shall flourish in the courts of our God.' And thus it continued to bear fruit, which abundantly supplied the juveniles of the priestly caste till the time of Manasseh; but he, by introducing an image into the Temple, caused the Shechinah to depart and the fruit to wither; as it is said (Nah. i. 4), 'And the flower of Lebanon languisheth.'"

Midrash Tillin Terumah.

47. The land of Israel is situated in the centre of the world, and Jerusalem in the centre of the land of Israel, and the Temple in the centre of Jerusalem, and the Holy of holies in the centre of the Temple, and the אבן שתיה, foundation-stone on which the world was grounded, is situated in front of the ark.

Midrash Tillin Terumah, Kedoshim.

NOTE.—In Ezek. v. 5 we read, " I have set Jerusalem in the midst of the nations and countries that are round about her." On the literal interpretation of these words it was asserted that Jerusalem was the very centre of the world, or, as Jerome quaintly called it, "the navel of the earth." In the Talmud we find a beautiful metaphor in illustration of this view. It is in the last six lines of the ninth chapter of Derech Eretz Zuta, which read thus :—" Issi ben Yochanan, in the name of Shemuel Hakaton, says, ' The world is like the eyeball of man ; the white is the ocean which surrounds the world, the black is the world itself, the pupil is Jerusalem, and the image in the pupil is the Temple. May it be built in our own days, and in the days of all Israel ! Amen !'" The memory of this conceit is kept alive to this day among the Greek Christians, who still show the sacred stone in the Church of the Holy Sepulchre at Jerusalem. This notion is not confined to Jewry. Classic readers will at once call to mind the appellation Omphalos or navel applied to the temple at Delphi (Pindar, Pyth., iv. 131, vi. 3 ; Eurip. Ion., 461 ; Æsch. Chœph., 1034 ; Eum. 40, 167 ; Strabo, &c.).

48. Two sparks issued from between the two cherubim and destroyed the serpents and scorpions and burned the thorns in the wilderness. The smoke thereof, rising and spreading, perfumed the world, so that the nations said (Cant. iii. 6), " Who is this that cometh out of the wilderness like pillars of smoke, perfumed," &c.

Ibid., Vayakhel.

49. Better to lodge in the wilderness of the land of Israel than dwell in the palaces outside of it.

Midrash Rabbah, chap. 39.

50. " And give thee a pleasant land " (ארץ חמדה, a

coveted land) (Jer. iii. 19). Why is it called a coveted land ? Because the Temple was in it. Another reason why it was so called is, because the fathers of the world have coveted it. Rabbi Shimon ben Levi says, " Because they (who are buried) there will be the first to be raised in the days of the Messiah." *Shemoth Rabbah*, chap. 32.

51. " When the Lord thy God shall enlarge thy border, as He hath promised thee " (Deut. xii. 20). Rabbi Yitzchak said, " This scroll no man knows how long and how broad it is, but when unrolled it speaks for itself, and shows how large it is. It is so with the land of Israel, which, for the most part, consists of hills and mountains; but when the Holy One—blessed be He !—shall level it, as it is said (Isa. xl. 4), ' Every valley shall be raised and every mountain and hill shall be made low, and the crooked shall be made straight, and the rough places smooth,' then shall that land speak, as it were, for herself, and its extent stand revealed." *Devarim Rabbah*, chap. 4.

52. Blessed are they who dwell in the land of Israel, for they have no sin, no iniquity, either in their lives or in their deaths. *Midrash Shochar Tov on Ps. lxxv.*

53. " Better is a dry morsel and quietness therewith " (Prov. xvii. 1). This, saith Rabbi, means the land of Israel, for even if a man have nothing but bread and salt to eat, yet if he dwells in the land of Israel he is sure that he is a son of the world to come. " Than a house full of sacrifices with strife." This means the חוצה לארץ, outside of the land, which is full of robbery and violence. Rabbi Y—— says, " He who walks but an hour in the land of Israel and then dies within it may feel assured that he is a son of the world to come ; for it is written (Deut. xxxii. 43), וכפר אדמתו עמו, ' And his earth shall atone for his people.' " *Midrash Mishle.*

Note.—See also the Talmud, Kethuboth, fol. 111, col. 1.

Dr. Benisch renders וכפר אדמתו עמו "and make expiation
for His ground and His people." The Targums of Jonathan and the Yerushalmi have, "He will make atonement for His land and for His people;" and Onkelos
puts it thus, "He will show mercy unto His land and
His people." Our rendering, however, is in accordance
with the sense given to it in the Talmud (see "Genesis
according to the Talmud," p. 224, No. 11). There are
Jews who travel about the world with bags of earth
from the Holy Land, which they sell in small quantities
for high prices to such as can afford it, and believe in its
virtue as a protection against the worms of the grave.

54. Jerusalem is the light of the world; as it is said,
"And the Gentiles shall come to Thy light" (Isa. lx. 3).
And the light of Jerusalem is the Holy One—blessed be
He!—as it is written, but "the Lord shall be unto thee an
everlasting light" (Isa. lx. 19).

Bereshith Rabbah, chap. 59.

55. Ten portions of wisdom, ten portions of the law, and
ten portions of hypocrisy are in the world; nine portions
of each are in the land of Israel and one outside of it.

Midrash Rabbah Esther.

56. "And it shall come to pass that from one new moon
to another, and from one Sabbath to another, shall all flesh
come to worship before Me, saith the Lord" (Isa. lxvi. 23).
But how is it possible that all flesh shall come every new
moon and Sabbath to Jerusalem? Rabbi Levi saith, "In
the future Jerusalem will be as the land of Israel, and the
land of Israel will be as the whole world." But how will
they come from the end of the world every new moon and
Sabbath? "The clouds will come and carry them and
bring them to Jerusalem, where they will perform their
morning prayer, and will carry them back to their several
homes; and this is the meaning of the prophet's saying
(Isa. lx. 8), 'Who are these that fly as a cloud (in the
morning), and as the doves to their windows (in the
evening)?'"

Pesikta.

57. "He stood and measured the earth" (Hab. iii. 6). Rabbi Shimon ben Yochai expounded "He stood and measured" thus:—"The Holy One—blessed be He!—measured all the nations, and He found none worthy to receive the law except the generation in the wilderness. He measured all the mountains, and he found none on which to give the law except Mount Sinai. He measured all cities, and found none in which to build the Temple except Jerusalem. He measured all lands, and found none worthy to be given unto Israel except the one now called the land of Israel. This it is that is written, "He stood up and measured the earth."

Vayckra Rabbah, chap. 13.

58. "I went down to the bottoms of the mountains" (Jonah ii. 6). From this we learn that Jerusalem is situated on seven hills. The world's "foundation-stone" sank to "the depths" under the Temple of the Lord, and upon this the sons of Korah stand and pray. (They) pointed this out to Jonah. The fish said unto him, "Jonah, behold thou art standing under the Temple of the Lord; therefore pray, and thou shalt be answered."

Pirke d'Rab. Eliezer, chap. 10.

59. "And there went out fire from the Lord" (Lev. x. 2). Abba Yossi saith, "Two threads of fire came out from the Holy of holies, and these were disparted into four: two entered the nostrils of the one (*i.e.*, Nadab), and two entered the nostrils of the other (*i.e.*, Abihu), and thus consumed them. Their souls were burned, but not their garments; for it is said, 'So they went near, and carried them in their coats'" (ver. 5). *Torath Cohanim*, sec. *Shemini*.

60. Rabbi Jacob teaches that he who has no wife abideth without good, without help, without joy, without blessing or atonement, to which Rabbi Yehoshua ben Levi adds, (yea) also without peace or life. Rabbi Cheya says that he is not a perfect man, for it is said, "And blessed them

and called their name man" (Gen. v. 2), where both are spoken of together as one man.

Midrash Rabbah Bereshith, chap. 17.

NOTE.—See also Yevamoth, fol. 63, col. 1, and compare the saying that "Woman is an unfinished vessel" . . . (Sanhedrin, fol. 22, col. 2, and Rashi.)

61. "My beloved is like a roe" (1 Cant. ii. 9). As a roe leaps and skips from bush to bush, from covert to covert, from hedge to hedge, so likewise does the Holy One—blessed be He!—pass from synagogue to synagogue, and from academy to academy, that He may bless Israel.

Pesikta.

62. (Cant. v. 1), "I came into My garden," the synagogues and academies; "My sister, My spouse," the congregation of Israel; "I have gathered My myrrh with My spice," the Bible (that is); "I have eaten My honeycomb with My honey," (this means) the Halachoth, Midrashoth, and Aggadoth; "I have drank My wine with My milk," this alludes to the good works which are reserved for the sages of Israel. After that, "Eat, O friends! drink, yea, drink freely, O beloved!"   *Yalkut Eliezer,* fol. 41, col. 2.

63. When Solomon brought the ark into the Temple and said, "Lift up your heads, O ye gates! and the King of glory shall come in," the gates were ready to fall upon him and crush his head, and they would have done so if he had not said at once, "The Lord of hosts, He is the King of glory" (Ps. xxiv. 9, 10). The Holy One—blessed be He!—then said to the gates, "Since ye have thus honoured Me, by your lives! when I destroy My Temple, no man shall have dominion over you!" This was to inform us that while all the vessels of the Temple were carried into captivity, the gates of the Temple were stored away on the very spot where they were erected; for it is said (Lam. ii. 9), "Her gates are sunk into the ground."

Midrash Rabbah Devarim, chap. 15.

Note.—We are reminded of this tradition in the נעילה, or conclusion service for Yom Kippur, where we repeat, "Speedily thou shalt open the hidden gates to those who hold fast Thy law." The allusion is to "the gates of the Temple," which "are supposed to be sunk in the ground."

64. Rabbi Akiva once met on a journey a remarkably ugly man toiling along under a great load of wood. Rabbi Akiva said unto him, "I adjure thee to tell me whether thou art a man or a demon." "Rabbi," said he, "I was once a man, and it is now some time since I left the world. Day after day I have to carry a load like this, under which I am obliged to bow down, and submit three times a day to be burned." Then Rabbi Akiva asked him, "What was the reason of this punishment?" and the reply was, "I committed an immorality on the Day of Atonement." The Rabbi asked him if he knew of anything by which he might obtain for him a remission of his punishment. "I do," was the answer. "When a son whom I have left behind me is called up to the (public) reading of the law, and shall say, 'Blessed be the blessed Lord,' I shall be drawn out of hell and taken into Paradise." The Rabbi noted down the name of the man and his dwelling-place, whither he afterwards went and made inquiries about him. The people of the place only replied, "The name of the wicked shall rot" (Prov. x. 7). Notwithstanding this, the Rabbi insisted, and said, "Bring his son to me." When they brought him, he taught the lad to repeat the blessing, which he did on the ensuing Sabbath at the public reading of the law; upon which his father was immediately removed from hell to Paradise. On the self-same night the father repaired direct to Rabbi Akiva, and gratefully expressed his hope that the Rabbi's mind might be as much at rest as his own was. *Midrash Assereth Hadibroht.*

Note.—See *infra*, No. 83.

65. There are three things which a man does not wish

for :—Grass to grow up among his grain-crops; to have a daughter among his children; or that his wine should turn to vinegar. Yet all these three are ordained to be, for the world stands in need of them. Therefore it is said, "O Lord, my God, Thou art very great! . . . He causeth the grass to grow for the cattle" (Ps. civ. 1, 14).

Midrash Tanchuma.

66. There are four cardinal points in the world, &c. The north point God created but left unfinished; for, said He, "Whoever claims to be God, let him come and finish this corner which I have left, and thus all will know that he is God." This unfinished corner is the dwelling-place of the harmful demons, ghosts, devils, and storms.

Pirke d'Rab. Eliezer, chap. 3.

67. A Min once asked Rabbi Akiva, "Who created this world?" "The Holy One—blessed be He!"—was the reply. "Give me positive proof of this," begged the other. "Come to-morrow," answered the Rabbi. On coming the next day, the Rabbi asked, "What are you dressed in?" "In a garment," was the reply. "Who made it?" asked the Rabbi. "A weaver," said the other. "I don't believe thee," said the Rabbi; "give me a positive proof of this." "I need not demonstrate this," said the Min; "it stands to reason that a weaver made it." "And so thou mayest know that God created the world," observed the Rabbi. When the Min had departed, the Rabbi's disciples asked him, "What is proof positive?" He said, "My children, as a house implies a builder, and a garment a weaver, and a door a carpenter, so likewise the existence of the world implies that the Holy One—blessed be He!—created it." *Midrash Terumah.*

68. When the Holy One—blessed be He!—created the world, it was a level expanse free from mountains; but when Cain slew Abel his brother, whose blood was trod-

den down on the earth, He cursed the ground, and immediately hills and mountains sprang into existence.

Midrash Vayosha.

69. "The Lord your God hath multiplied you, and behold ye are this day as the stars of heaven for multitude" (Deut. i. 10). Why did He bless them with stars? As there are degrees above degrees among these stars, so likewise are there degrees above degrees among Israel. Again, as these stars are without limit, without number, and of great power from one end of the world to the other, so likewise is Israel. (Cf. 1 Cor. xv. 41.)

Midrash Rabbah Devarim.

70. "Flee, my beloved" (A. V. "make haste," Cant. viii. 14). When Israel eat and drink, and bless and praise the Holy One—blessed be He!—He hearkeneth to their voice and is reconciled; but when the Gentiles eat and drink, and blaspheme and provoke the Holy One—blessed be He!—He has a mind to destroy His world, until the Law enters and pleads in defence, "Lord of the universe! before Thou regardest those that blaspheme, look and behold Thy people Israel, who bless, and praise, and extol Thy great Name, with the Law, and with songs and with praises!" And the Holy Spirit shouts, "Flee, my beloved! flee from the Gentiles, and hold fast to Israel!"

Midrash Rabbah Shir-Hashirim.

71. Rabbon Gamaliel called on Chilpa, the son of Caroyna, when the latter asked the Rabbi to pray on his behalf; and he prayed, "The Lord grant thee according to thine own heart" (Ps. xx. 4). Rabbi H——, son of Rabbi Isaac, said, "It was not so; he prayed thus, 'The Lord fulfil all thy petitions;'" for a man often thinks in his heart to steal or commit some other transgression, and therefore 'The Lord grant thee according to thine own heart,' is a prayer not to be offered on behalf of every

man." But the answer was, " His heart was perfect before
his Creator, and therefore he did so pray on his behalf."
Midrash Shochar Tov, 20.

72. Thou wilt find that whithersoever the righteous go
a blessing goes with them. Isaac went down to Gerar,
and a blessing followed him. " Then Isaac sowed," &c.
(Gen. xxvi. 12). Jacob went down to Laban (Gen. xxx.
27), and Laban said, " I have learned by experience that
the Lord hath blessed me for thy sake." Joseph went
down to Potiphar, and " the Lord blessed the Egyptian's
house for Joseph's sake " (Gen. xxxix. 5). Thus also thou
wilt find it was with the ark which came down to the
house of Obed-edom, &c. (2 Sam. vi. 11). Our forefathers
came into the land and a blessing followed at their heels,
as it is said (Deut. vi. 11), " And houses full of good
things," &c. Yalkut Ekev.

73. "And the Lord put a word in Balaam's mouth"
(Num. xxiii. 5). An angel took up his seat in Balaam's
throat, so that when he wished to bless, the angel permitted him, but when he desired to curse, the angel tickled
his throat and stopped him. " Word" in this place means
simply an angel; as it is said (Ps. cvii. 20), " He sent His
word and healed them." Rabbi Yochanan says, " There
was an iron nail in his throat which permitted him when
he wished to bless, but it rasped his throat and prevented
him when about to curse." " Word" in this place means
only an iron nail; for it is said (Num. xxxi. 23), כל דבר,
" Every thing (or word, for the original has both meanings) that may abide the fire." Ibid.

74. Rabbi Avin said four kinds of excellency were
created in the world :—(1.) Man's excellency over the
animal kingdom; (2.) the eagle's excellency over the
feathered tribes; (3.) the excellency of the ox over

domestic cattle; and (4.) the lion's excellency over the wild beasts. All were fixed under the chariot of God; as it is said (Ezek. i. 10), "As for the likeness of their faces, they four had the face of a man, the face of a lion, the face of an ox, and the face of an eagle." And why all this? In order that they should not exalt themselves, but know that there is a kingdom of heaven over them; and on this account it is said (Eccles. v. 8), "He that is higher than the highest regardeth, and there be higher than they." This is the meaning of Exod. xv. 1 : "He hath triumphed gloriously."　　　　　*Midrash Shemoth*, chap. 23.

75. No man in Israel despised himself more than David when the precepts of the Lord were concerned, and this is what he said before God (Ps. cxxxi. 1, 2), "' Lord, my heart was not haughty' when Samuel anointed me king. 'Nor were mine eyes lofty' when I slew Goliath. 'Neither did I exercise myself in matters too great and wonderful for me' when I brought up the ark. 'Have I not behaved myself, and hushed my soul, as a babe that is weaned of his mother?' As a child which is not ashamed to uncover himself before his mother, so have I likened myself before Thee, in not being ashamed to depreciate myself before Thee for Thy glory," &c. (See 2 Sam. vi. 20, 21.)

　　　　　Bamidbar, chap. 4.

76. "I sleep, but my heart waketh" (Cant. v. 2). The synagogue of Israel says "I sleep" with regard to the end of days, "but my heart waketh" with regard to the redemption; "I sleep" with regard to redemption, but the heart of the Holy One—blessed be He!—waketh to redeem me.　　　　　*Midrash Shir Hashirim.*

77. Rabbi Ishmael saith all the five fingers of the right hand of the Holy One of Israel—blessed be He!— are severally the efficient causes of redemptions. (1.)

With His little finger he pointed out to Noah how to construct the ark; as it is said (Gen. vi. 15), " And thus thou shalt make it." (2.) With the finger next to the little one He smote the Egyptians; as it is said (Exod. viii. 19), " This is the finger of God." (3.) With the third finger from the little one He wrote the tables; as it is said (Exod. xxxi. 18), " Tables of stone written by the finger of God." (4.) With the fourth finger, that which is next the thumb, the Holy One—blessed be He!—pointed out to Moses how much the Israelites should give as a ransom for their souls; as it is said (Exod. xxx. 13), " This shall they give." (5.) With the thumb and the whole hand the Holy One—blessed be He!—will in the future destroy the children of Esau, for they oppress the children of Israel, as also the children of Ishmael, for they are their enemies; as it is said (Micah v. 9), " Thine hand shall be uplifted upon thy adversaries, and all thy enemies shall be cut off."　　　　　*Pirke d'Rab. Eliezer*, chap. 48.

78. " For Mine own sake, for Mine own sake, will I do it " (Isa. xlviii. 11). Why this repetition ? The Holy One—blessed be He!—said, " As I redeemed you when you were in Egypt for My name's sake "—(Ps. cvi. 8), " He saved them for His name's sake,"—" so in like manner will I do it from Edom for My own name's sake. Again, as I redeemed you in this world, so likewise will I redeem you in the world to come;" for thus He saith (Eccles. i. 9), " The thing that hath been is that which shall be " (Isa. li. 11); " The redeemed of the Lord shall return;" not the redeemed of Elijah, nor the redeemed of the Messiah, but " the redeemed of the Lord."

　　　　　Midrash Shochar Tov Tehillim, 107.

79. " Her children are gone into captivity before the enemy " (Lam. i. 5). Rabbi Isaac saith, " Come and see how greatly beloved are the children !" The Sanhedrin

were exiled, but the Shechinah was not exiled with them. The Temple guards were exiled, but the Shechinah was not exiled with them. But with the children the *Shechinah* also was exiled. This is that which is written (Lam. i. 5, 6), " Her children are gone, . . . and from the daughter of Zion all her beauty (*i.e.*, the Shechinah) is departed."   *Midrash Rabbah Eicha.*

80. " How doth the city sit solitary ! " (Lam. i. 1). Three have, in prophesying, made use of this word " How "— Moses, Isaiah, and Jeremiah. Moses said (Deut. i. 12), " How can I myself bear your cumbrance ! " Isaiah said (Isa. i. 21), " How is the faithful city become an harlot ! " Jeremiah said (Lam. i. 1), " How doth the city sit solitary ! " Rabbi Levi saith, " The thing is like to a matron (מטרונה, matrona) who has three friends; one saw her in her prosperity, another saw her in her dissipation, and the third saw her in her pollution. So Moses saw Israel in their glory and prosperity, and he said, " How can I myself bear your cumbrance ! " Isaiah saw them in their dissipation, and he said, " How is the faithful city," &c. ; and Jeremiah saw them in their pollution, and he said, " How doth the city sit solitary ! "   *Midrash Rabbah Eicha.*

81. Hezekiah saith the judgment in Gehenna is six months' heat and six months' cold.   *Midrash Reheh.*

82. Gehenna has sixteen mouths, four towards each cardinal point. The Gentiles say, " Hell is for Israel, but Paradise is for us." The Israelites say, " Ours is Paradise."   *Midrash Aggadath Bereshith.*

83. Rabbi Yochanan ben Zachai says, that coming once upon a man who was gathering wood, he addressed him, but at first he made no reply. Afterwards, however, he came up and said, " Rabbi, I'm not a living man, but

a dead one." "If thou art a dead man," said I, "what is this wood for?" He replied, "When I was alive upon earth, I and an associate of mine committed a certain sin in my shop, and when we were taken thence, we were sentenced to the punishment of mutual burning; so I gather wood to burn him, and he does the same to burn me." I then asked him, "How long are you to be punished thus?" He replied, "When I came here my wife was *enceinte*, and I know she gave birth to a boy. May I beg thee, therefore, to see that the child is instructed by a teacher, for as soon as he is able to repeat, 'Bless ye the blessed Lord!' I shall be brought up hence and be free from this punishment in hell." (See No. 64, *supra*.)

Tanu d'by Eliyahu.

84. Rabbi Berachia saith, "In order that the Minim, apostates, and wicked Israelites might not escape hell on account of their circumcision, the Holy One—blessed be He!—sends an angel to undo the effects of it, and they straightway descend to their doom. When Gehenna sees this, she opens her mouth and licks them. This is the purport of (Isa. v. 14), "And she opened her mouth, לִבְלִי חֹק, to those without law" (*i.e.*, to those without the sign of the covenant).

Midrash Rabbath Shemoth, chap. 19.

85. "God hath also set the one over against the other" (Eccles. vii. 14), *i.e.*, the righteous and the wicked, in order that the one should atone for the other. God created the poor and the rich, in order that the one should be maintained by the other. He created Paradise and Gehenna, in order that those in the one should deliver those in the other. And what is the distance between them? Rabbi Chanina saith the width of the wall (between Paradise and Gehenna) is a handbreadth. *Yalkut Koheleth.*

86. "Those passing through the valley of (בכא) weeping make it a well (נם ברכות יעטה מורה); also blessings shall

cover the teacher" (Ps. lxxxiv. 6, A. V.). "The valley of weeping" is Gehenna. "Make it a well," for their tears are like a well or spring. "Also blessings shall cover the teacher." Rabbi Yochanan saith, "The praises of God that ascend from Gehenna are more than those that ascend from Paradise, for each one that is a step higher than his neighbour praises God, and says, 'Happy am I that I am a step higher than the one below me.' 'Also blessings shall cover the teacher,' for they will acknowledge and say, 'Ye have taught well, and ye have instructed well, but we have not obeyed.'" *Yalkut Tehillim,* 84.

87. Those of the house of Eliyahu have taught that Gehenna is above the sky, but some say it is behind the mountains of darkness. *Tanu d'by Eliyahu.*

88. Gehenna was created before Paradise; the former on the second day and the latter on the third. *Yalkut.*

> NOTE.—In T. B. P'sachim, fol. 54, col. 1, it is said that the reason of the omission of the words, "And God saw that it was good," in respect to the second day of the creative week, was *because hell-fire was then created;* but see the context.

89. When Adam saw (through the Spirit) that his posterity would be condemned to Gehenna, he disobeyed the precept פרו ורבו. But when he perceived that after twenty-six generations the Israelites would accept the law, he bestirred himself in compliance; as it said (Gen. iv. 1), "Adam vero cognovit uxorem suam Hevam."
> *Ibid.*

90. "And the souls they had gotten in Haran" (Gen. xii. 5). These are they who had been made proselytes. Whoever attracts a Gentile and proselytises him is as much as if he had created him. Abraham did so to men and Sarah to women. *Bereshith Midrash Rabbah.*

> NOTE.—See also Rashi to the same effect.

91. "Sing and rejoice" (Zech. ii. 10). The Holy One—blessed be He!—will in the future bring all the proselytes that were proselytised in this world, and judge all the nations of the world in their presence. He will say to them, "Why have ye left Me and served idols, which are nothing?" They will reply and say, "Had we applied at Thy door, Thou wouldst not have received us." Then will He say to them, "Let the proselytes that were made from among you come forward and testify against you."

P'sikta.

92. These are the pious female proselytes—Hagar, Osenath, Zipporah, Shiphrah, Puah, the daughter of Pharaoh (Bathia), Rahab, Ruth, and Jael.

Yalkut Yehoshua, 9.

93. "The Lord keepeth the proselytes" (Ps. cxlvi. 9). "I esteem it a great compliment on the part of the proselyte to leave his family and his father's house and come to Me. Therefore I on my part will command respecting him (Deut. x. 19), 'Love ye therefore the proselyte.'"

Midrash Shochar Tov, 146.

94. "I am a God near at hand" (Jer. xxiii. 23). "I am He who drew Jethro near, and did not keep him at a distance;" therefore thou also when a man comes to be proselytised in the name of Heaven, draw him near, do not repulse him or keep him at a distance. From this thou art to learn that whilst one repulses with the left hand he is to draw with the right, and not as Elisha did. (He repulsed Gehazi with both hands.)

Yalkut Jeremiah.

95. Showers of rain are greater than the giving of the Law, for the giving of the Law was a gladsome event to Israel only, but rain is a cause of joy to the wide world, including cattle, beasts, and fowls.

Midrash Shochar Tov, 117.

96. David was the shepherd of Israel, and the Shepherd of David was the Holy One—blessed be He !—as it is said (Ps. xxiii. 1), "The Lord is my Shepherd."

Midrash Rabbah, chap. 59.

97. Rav Pinchas says, "David in the Psalms calls five times upon the Holy One—blessed be He !—to arise. (1.) 'Arise, O Lord; save me, O my God !' (Ps. iii. 7). (2.) 'Arise, O Lord, in Thine anger !' (Ps. vii. 6). (3.) 'Arise, O Lord, let not man prevail !' (Ps. ix. 19). (4.) 'Arise, O Lord; O God, lift up Thine hand: forget not the humble !' (Ps. x. 12). (5.) 'Arise, O Lord; disappoint him !' But the Holy One—blessed be He !—said unto David, 'My son, though thou call upon Me many a time to arise, I will not arise. But when do I arise ? When thou seest the poor oppressed and the needy sighing, then will I arise.'" This explains what is written (Ps. xii. 5), "For the oppression of the poor, for the sighing of the needy, *now will I arise,* saith the Lord."

Bamidbar Rabbah, chap. 75.

98. "And Solomon's wisdom excelled" (1 Kings iv. 30). Thou findest that when Solomon desired to build the Temple he sent to Pharaoh Necho a request to send him artisans on hire. Pharaoh assembled his astrologers, who pointed out to him such artisans as were destined to die in the course of that year, and these he despatched to Solomon; but he, through the Holy Ghost, seeing the fate that impended, provided each of them with a shroud and sent them back to Pharaoh with the message, " Hast thou no shrouds in which to bury thine own dead ? Behold here I have provided them with them !" " For he was wiser than all men" (1 Kings iv. 31); "than *all* men," even than the first man, *Adam.*

Yalkut Eliezer, fol. 65, col. 2, n. 36.

99. "Ye are My witnesses, saith the Lord, that I am God" (Isa. xliii. 12). Rabbi Shimon ben Yochai expounds

these words thus, "If ye are My witnesses, then I am God; but if ye are not My witnesses, then I am not God."

Yalkut Jethro, n. 271.

100. "Let us hear the conclusion of the whole matter" (Eccles. xii. 13).   Thou shalt ever hear the Law, even when thou dost not understand it.   "Fear God," and give thy heart to Him.   "And keep His commandments," for on account of the Law the whole world was created, that the world should study it.

Koheleth, as given in Tse-enah Ure-enah.

דִּבְרֵי חֲכָמִים וְחִידֹתָם

"The words of the wise and their dark sayings" (Prov. i. 6).

SELECTIONS FROM THE KABBALAH.

לשם יחוד קב״ה ושכינתיה ע״י ההוא טמיר ונעלם ברוך ה׳ לעולם!

" In the name of the Union of the Holy and Blessed One and His Shechinah,
the Hidden and the Concealed One, blessed be the Lord for ever !"

PRELIMINARY REMARKS.

————

THE Hebrew word קבל, Kabbal, means "to receive," and its derivative, קבלה, Kabbalah, signifies "a thing received," viz., "Tradition," which, together with the written law, Moses received on Mount Sinai, and we are distinctly told in the Talmud, Rosh Hashanah, fol. 19, col. 1, דברי קבלה כדברי תורה דמו, *i.e.*, "The words of the Kabbalah are just *the same* as the words of the law." In another part of this work we find that the Rabbis declare the Kabbalah to be *above* the law.

The Kabbalah is divided into two parts, viz., the symbolical and the real.

I. THE SYMBOLICAL KABBALAH.

This teaches the secret or mystic sense of Scripture, and the *thirteen* rules by which the observance of the law is, not logically, but Kabbalistically expounded; viz., the rules of "Gematria," of "Notricon," of "Temurah," &c. To give some idea of this kind of exposition, we will explain each of these three rules in a manner which, though in the style of the Rabbis, will easily be understood by the Gentile reader.

1. נכמטריא, "Gematria." This rule depends on the numerical value of each letter in the alphabet. The application of this rule in the solution of a disputed point is often such as to show quite as much absurdity as ingenuity. A sample of the process may be seen in this work, page 51, No. 40, note 1. To make the subject still

more clear, let us assume for the nonce that a standard numerical value is attached to each letter in the *English* alphabet. *A* has the value of 1, *B* 2, *C* 3, *D* 4, *E* 5, *F* 6, *G* 7, *H* 8, *I* 9, *J* 10, *K* 20, *L* 30, *M* 40, *N* 50, *O* 60, *P* 70, *Q* 80, *R* 90, *S* 100, *T* 200, *U* 300, *V* 400, *W* 500, *X* 1000, *Y* 10,000, *Z* 100,000. And let us now assume a point in dispute in order to illustrate how it is solved by Gematria. Suppose that the subject of discussion is the comparative superiority of the Hebrew and English languages, and Hugo and Baruch are the disputants. The former, being a Hebrew, holds that the Hebrew is superior to the English, "because," says he, "the numerical value of the letters that form the word *H e b r e w* is 610; whereas the numerical value of *E n g l i s h* is only 209." The latter, being an Englishman, holds, of course, exactly the contrary opinion, and argues as follows :—" All the learned world must admit that *the English is a living language,* but *not* so the Hebrew; and as it is written (Eccles. ix. 4) that 'A living dog is better than a dead lion,' I therefore maintain that the English is superior to the Hebrew." The dispute was referred to an Oxford authority for decision, and a certain learned doctor decided it by—

2. נוטריקון, "Notricon." This consists in forming a decisive sentence composed of words whose initial letters are in a given word; for instance, *Hebrew :* — " *Hugo's excels Baruch's reasoning every way."* *English :* — " *English no good language, is scarcely harmonious ;"* but *Hebrew :* — " *Holy, elegant, brilliant, resonant, eliciting wonder !"* This is a fair specimen of how to get at the secret sense of a word by the rule of " Notricon," and now we will proceed to explain—

3. תמורה, "Temurah." This means permutation, or a change of the letters of the alphabet after a regularly adopted system. We know only five such permuted alphabets, but there may be more. The technical names of these five alphabets are :—את"בש אט"בח. אל"בם. איק"בכר. ת"שרק, "Atbash," "Atbach," "Albam," "Aiak-

bechar," and "Tashrak."   We will try to explain the first permuted alphabet only, as a mere specimen, for the general reader is not quite prepared to comprehend the rest, and a hint for the scholar is sufficient.

Here let the reader observe that as the letters of the English alphabet are more numerous and differently designated and arranged than those of the Hebrew, the "Atbash" of the Hebrew must necessarily become "Azby" in English.   If now we write on one line and in regular order the first half of the alphabet, and the other half on the second line, but in reversed order, thus:—

$$a \; b \; c \; d \; e \; f \; g \; h \; i \; j \; k \; l \; m$$
$$z \; y \; x \; w \; v \; u \; t \; s \; r \; q \; p \; o \; n$$

we get thirteen couples of letters which exchange one with the other, viz., a and z, b and y, c and x, &c.   These letters, when exchanged, give rise to a permuted alphabet, and this permuted alphabet takes its technical name from the first two couples of letters, a and z, b and y, or "Azby."   Now if we wish to write, "Meddle not with them that are given to change," * you have to change the letters of the couples and the following will be the result: —"Nvwwov mlg drgs gsvn gszg ziv trem gl xszmtv." This is a specimen of the mysterious Temurah, and the "Azby" is the key to it.   The other four permuted alphabets are of a similar nature and character, and are so highly esteemed among the sages and bards of Israel, that they often use them in their literary and poetical compositions. The Machzorim, or the Jewish Liturgies for the festivals, are full of compositions where the first letters of the sentences follow the order of either the "Atbash" or "Tashrak." The latter is simply a reversed order of the alphabet.

II. The Real Kabbalah.

The "Real Kabbalah" consists of theoretical and practical mysteries.

* Prov. xxiv. 21.

1. The theoretical mysteries treat about the ten spheres, the four worlds, the essence and various names of God and of angels, also of the celestial hierarchy and its influences and effects on this lower world, of the mysteries of creation, of מעשה מרכבה, the mystical chariot described by the Prophet Ezekiel, of the different orders and offices of angels and demons, also of a great many other deep subjects, too deep for comprehension and too numerous to be introduced here, some specimens of which, however, will be met with here and there in this work, and especially in this last part of it.

2. The practical Kabbalah is a branch of the theoretical, and treats of the practical use of the mysterious names of God and of angels. By uttering properly the שם המפורש, Shem-hammephorash, *i.e.*, the ineffable name of Jehovah, or the names of certain angels, or by the mere repetition of certain Scripture texts, miracles and wonders were and still are performed in the Jewish world. Specimens of this will be found in the following pages, and also in other parts of this work.

CHAPTER XVI.

EXTRACTS FROM THE KABBALAH.

1. Know thou that the 613 Precepts of the Law form a
compact with the Holy One—blessed be He!—and with
Israel, as it is often explained in the Zohar. It is written (Exod. iii. 15), זה שמי וזה זכרי, "This is My name,
and this is My memorial." שמי׳ עם י״ה, " My name," together with " Yeho," amounts numerically to 365 ; ו"ה עם
זכר"י, "Vah," together with " My memorial," amounts to
248. Here we have the number 613 in the Holy One—
blessed be He ! The soul is a portion of God from above,
and this is mystically intimated by the degrees of נפש רוח
נשמה, "breath, spirit, soul," the initial and final letters
of which amount to 613, while the middle letters of these
amount to the number of יהוה שדי אלהים, " Lord, Almighty, God." The soul of Moses our Rabbi—peace be on
him !—embraced all the souls of Israel ; as it is said, Moses
was שקול כנגד כל ישראל, equivalent to all Israel. מש"ה
רבינ׳ו, " Moses our Rabbi," amounts to 613 ; and אלה"י יהו"ה
ישרא׳ל, " Lord God of Israel," also amounts to 613.

Kitzur Sh'lu, p. 2, col. 2.

Note.—The full title of the work just quoted from is קיצור
שני לוחות הברית, that is, " An Epitome of the Two Tables
of the Covenant," a Kabbalistic work of high repute
with those who hold the theosophy of the Rabbis in
estimation, and are privileged to enter the *sanctum
sanctorum* of Jewish thought.

2. Now let us illustrate the subject of יראה ואהבה,
"fear and love." Fear proceedeth from love and love proceedeth from fear. And this you may demonstrate by

writing their letters one over the other, and then dividing them by horizontal and perpendicular lines, thus, אהבה / יראה Love perfecteth fear, and fear perfecteth love. This is to teach thee that both are united together.

Kitzur Sh'lu, p. 4, col. 2.

3. The Holy One—blessed be He!—often brings affliction on the righteous though they have not sinned, in order that they may learn to keep aloof from the allurements of the world and eschew temptation to sin. From this it is plain that afflictions are good for man, and therefore our Rabbis, of blessed memory, have said, " As men bless with joy and a sincere heart for a benefit received, so likewise ought they joyfully to bless God when He afflicts them, as, though the special blessing be hidden from the children of men, such affliction is surely intended for good. . . . Or most souls being at present in a state of transmigration, God requites a man now for what his soul merited in a bypast time in another body, by having broken some of the 613 precepts."

Ibid., p. 6, col. 1.

4. Thus we have the rule :—No one is perfect unless he has thoroughly observed all the 613 precepts. If this be so, who is he and where is he that has observed all the 613 precepts ? For even the lord of the prophets, Moses our Rabbi—peace be on him!—had not observed them all; for there are four obstacles which hinder one from observing all :—(1.) There is the case of complete prevention, such as the law of the priesthood, the precepts of which only priests can observe, and yet these precepts are included in the 613. Besides, there are among the number precepts appertaining to the Levites which concern neither priests nor Israelites, and also others which are binding on Israelites with which priests and Levites have nothing whatever to do. (2.) Then there are impossible cases, as, for instance, when one cannot observe the

precept which enforces circumcision, because he has not a
son to circumcise. (3 and 4.) There are also conditional
and exceptional cases, as in the case of precepts having
reference to the Temple and to the land of Israel.

Kitzur Sh'lu, p. 6, col. 2.

5. Therefore every Israelite is bound to observe only
such of the 613 precepts as are possible to him; and such
as he has not observed in consequence of hindrances arising from unpreventable causes will be reckoned to him as
if actually performed. Ibid.

> Note.—The Yalkut Shimeoni, in true Rabbinical style,
> amplifies still farther the licence conceded in the above
> quotations. Rabbi Eliezer says that the Israelites be-
> wailed thus before God, exclaiming, " We would fain be
> occupied night and day in the law, but we have not the
> necessary leisure." Then the Holy One—blessed be He!
> —said, " Perform the commandment of the Tephillin,*
> and I will account it as if you were occupied night and
> day in the study of the law."

6. Anyhow, all the precepts are being observed by all
Israel taken together, viz., the priests observe their part,
the Levites theirs, and the Israelites theirs; thus the whole
keep all. For the Holy One—blessed be He !—has written
a law for His faithful servants, the nation of Israel, and
as a nation they keep the whole law. It is as once
when a king wrote to his subjects thus, " Behold, I command you to prepare for war against the enemy; raise the
walls higher, collect arms, and store up victuals;" and
those that were builders looked after the walls, the
armourers after the weapons, the farmers after the stores
of food, &c., &c. Each, according to his ability, did all
that was required of him, and all unitedly fulfilled the
king's command. Ibid.

7. He who neglects to observe any of the 613 precepts, such as were possible for him to observe, is doomed

* Phylacteries.

to undergo transmigration (once or more than once) till he has actually observed all he had neglected to do in a former state of being.   *Kitzur Sh'lu*, p. 6, col. 2.

8. The sages of truth (the Kabbalists) remark that אדם, Adam, contains the initial letters of Adam, David, and Messiah; for after Adam sinned his soul passed into David, and the latter having also sinned, it passed into the Messiah. The full text is, "They shall serve the Lord their God, and David their king, whom I will raise up to them" (Jer. xxx. 9); and it is written, "My servant David shall be their king for ever" (Ezek. xxxvii. 25); and thus "They shall seek the Lord their God, and David their king" (Hosea iii. 5).

Nishmath Chaim, fol. 152, col. 2.

9. Know thou that Cain's essential soul passed into Jethro, but his spirit into Korah, and his animal soul into the Egyptian. This is what Scripture saith. "Cain (יקם) shall be avenged sevenfold" (Gen. iv. 24), ר"ת יק"ם יתרו קרה מצרי, *i.e.*, the initial letters of the Hebrew word rendered "shall be avenged," form the initials of Jethro, Korah, and Egyptian. . . . Samson the hero was possessed by the soul of Japhet, and Job by that of Terah.   *Yalkut Reubeni*, Nos. 9, 18, 24.

10. Cain had robbed the twin sister of Abel, and therefore his soul passed into Jethro. Moses was possessed by the soul of Abel, and therefore Jethro gave his daughter to Moses.   *Yalkut Chadash*, fol. 127, col. 3.

11. If a man be niggardly either in a financial or a spiritual regard, giving nothing of his money to the poor or not imparting of his knowledge to the ignorant, he shall be punished by transmigration into a woman. . . . Know thou that Sarah, Hannah, the Shunammite (2 Kings iv. 8), and the widow of Zarepta were each in turn possessed by the soul of Eve. . . . The soul of Rahab transmigrated

into Heber the Kenite, and afterwards into Hannah; and
this is the mystery of her words, "I am a woman of a
sorrowful spirit" (1 Sam. i. 15), for there still lingered
in her soul a sorrowful sense of inherited defilement. . . .
Eli possessed the soul of Jael, the wife of Heber the
Kenite. . . . Sometimes the souls of pious Jews pass by
metempsychosis into Gentiles, in order that they may
plead on behalf of Israel and treat them kindly. For this
reason have our Rabbis of blessed memory said, "The
pious of the nations of the world have a portion in the
world to come."   *Yalkut Reubeni*, Nos. 1, 8, 61, 63.

12. We have it by tradition that when Moses our
Rabbi—peace be unto him!—said in the law, "O God, the
God of the spirits of all flesh" (Num. xvi. 22), he meant
mystically to intimate that metempsychosis takes place
in all flesh, in beasts, reptiles, and fowls. "Of all flesh "
is, as it were, "in all flesh."

                    Avodath Hakodesh, fol. 49, col. 3.

13. It is also needful that thou shouldst know that
the Kabbalists believe in metempsychosis from the body
of one species into the body of another species. Thou
hast already been informed of the mystery of clean and
unclean animals; and some of the later sages of the Kabbalah say that the soul of an unclean person will trans-
migrate into an unclean animal, or into abominable
creeping things or reptiles. . . . For one form of uncleanness the soul will be invested with the body of a Gentile,
who will (eventually) become a proselyte; for another,
the soul will pass into the body of a mule; for others, it
transmigrates into an ass, a woman of Ashdod, a bat, a
rabbit or a hare, a she-mule or a camel. Ishmael transmigrated first into the she-ass of Balaam, and subsequently
into the ass of Rabbi Pinchas ben Yair.

                    Nishmath Chaim, chap. 13, No. 14.

Note.—The last paragraph may be illustrated by the well-known story of the ass of R. Pinchas, which persistently objected to feed on untithed provender. This is also said of the ass of Rabbi Chanina ben Dossa. See Avoth d'Rab Nathan, chap. 8.

14. Sometimes the soul of a righteous man may be found in the body of a clean animal or fowl.

Caphtor U'pherach, fol. 51, col. 2.

15. It sometimes happens that one sacrifices an animal with a human soul in it. And this is the mystic meaning of (Ps. xxxvi. 6), " O Lord, thou preservest man and beast." It is for this reason that we are commanded to have our slaughtering-knife without defect, for who knows if there be not a transmigrated soul in the animal ? . . . Therefore the slaughter must needs be delicately done and the mode critically examined, on account of that which is written (Lev. xix. 18), "Thou shalt love thy neighbour as thyself."

Nishmath Chaim, chap. 13, No. 4.

16. At each of the three meals of the Sabbath one should eat fish, for into them the souls of the righteous are transmigrated. And in relation to them it is written (Num. xi. 22), " All the fish of the sea shall be gathered together for them." *Yalkut Chadash*, fol. 20, col. 4, No. 9.

17. The soul of a slanderer is transmigrated into a silent stone. *Emeh Hamelech*, fol. 153, col. 2.

18. Rabbi Isaac Luria was once passing the great academy of Rabbi Yochanan in Tiberias, where he showed his disciples a stone in the wall, remarking, " In this stone there is a transmigrated soul, and it cries that I should pray on its behalf. And this is the mystic meaning of (Hab. ii. 11), ' The stone shall cry out of the wall.' "

Ibid., fol. 11, col. 2.

19. The murderer is transmigrated into water. The mystical sign of this is indicated in (Deut. xii. 16), " Ye shall pour it upon the earth as water ; " and the meaning

is, he is continually rolling on and on without any rest. Therefore let no man drink (direct) from a running tap or spout, but from the hollow of his hands, lest a soul pass into him, and that the soul of a wicked sinner.

Emek Hamelech, fol. 153, cols. 1, 2.

20. One who sins with a married woman is, after undergoing the penalty of wandering about as a fugitive and vagabond, transmigrated, together with his accomplice, into the millstone of a water-mill, according to the mystery of (Job xxxi. 10), "Let my wife grind unto another."　　　　　　　　　　　　　　　　　　　*Ibid.*

21. A butcher who kills an animal with a defective knife will die of the plague, and his soul will pass into a dog, whom he thus deprives of what belongs to him; for it is said (Exod. xxii. 31), "Ye shall cast it to the dogs."

Kitzur Sh'lh, fol. 17, col. 2.

NOTE.—An animal slaughtered with an improper knife is considered as if it had been "torn of beasts in the field," and the flesh of it, according to the law, belongs to the dogs. A careless butcher, selling the meat as food for man, deprives the dog of his due.

22. The sages of truth have written, "He who does not wash his hands before eating, as the Rabbis of blessed memory have ordained, will be transmigrated into a cataract, where he will have no rest, even as a murderer, who is also transmigrated into water." *Ibid.*, fol. 21, col. 2.

23. After washing his hands before a meal, he is to stretch out his fingers and turn the palms of his hands upwards, as if in the act of receiving something from a friend, and then repeat (Ps. cxxxiv. 2), "Lift ye up your holy hands, and bless ye the Lord!" *Ibid.*, fol. 21, col. 2.

NOTE.—The following are the usual blessings, "Blessed art Thou, O Lord, our God! King of the universe! who has sanctified us with His commandments, and has commanded us to wash the hands!" "Blessed art Thou, O Lord, our God! King of the universe! who bringeth forth bread from the earth!"

CHAPTER XVII.

1. By means of combining the letters of the ineffable names, as recorded in ספר יצירה, " Book of Creation,"* Rava once created a man and sent him to Rav Zera. The man being unable to reply when spoken to, the Rabbi said to him, " Thou art a creation of the company (initiated in the mysteries of necromancy) ; return to thy dust."

Sanhedrin, fol. 65, col. 2.

> Note.—In the Jerusalem Talmud, Sanhedrin, chap. 7, we read that, by the means above mentioned, a Rabbi created pumpkins, melons, and real deer and roes.

2. There is a living creature in heaven which by day has " Truth " upon its forehead, by which the angels know it is day ; but in the evening it has " Faith " on its forehead, whereby the angels know that night is near. Each time the living creature says, " Bless ye the blessed Lord," all the hosts above respond, " Blessed be the blessed Lord for ever."

Kitzur Sh'lh, fol. 42, col. 2.

3. Truth and faith are the essentials of religion, which are thirteen in number :—

> 1. God exists, and there is no period to His existence. The philosophers call it absolute existence, but the majority of Kabbalists term it אין סוף, "endless," which, by Gematria, is אור, " light ;" and again, by Gematria, is אדון עולם, " Lord of the Universe." He is the cause of causes and the causing of causings, and from or by His existence all beings, spiritual and material, derive their existence.
> 2. He is one, and there is no unity like His, &c.
> 3. He has no bodily likeness, and is not corporeal

---

* A book still much studied among a certain class of Jews.

4. He is first of everything, absolute beginning ; as it is said, "I am the First and I am the Last" (Isa. xliv. 6), and there is no beginning to His beginning.

5. None but Himself is to be worshipped and prayed to.

6. The gift of prophecy He has given to men esteemed and glorified by Him.

7. None arose like unto Moses, &c.

8. A law of truth He gave : this is the law from heaven, "In the beginning" unto "in the sight of all Israel."   Also its comment received orally is likewise הלכה למשה מסיני, "a law (given) unto Moses from Sinai."

9. God will not change or alter His law for ever.   He will never change the law of Moses our Rabbi—peace be unto him !   The law will suffer no addition or diminution, (but it will abide even) as the prophet Malachi sealed it with the seal of the prophets in ending his words (Mal. iv. 4), "Remember ye the law of Moses My servant, which I commanded unto him in Horeb for all Israel." Formerly the law was in a garment of light, but in consequence of sin, נתגשמה התורה, the law became materialised in a garment of skin, in the same proportion as man became materialised in a body of flesh.   In the future, after the redemption, however, the law will have the garment of light restored, and the Messiah will preach the law in terrible mysteries, such as no ear has ever heard, and it will appear to us as a new law.   But the law will not be altered or made new, as the nations of the world say = Jer. xxxi. 30–33.

10. He observeth and knoweth all our secrets, &c.

11. There are rewards and punishments in the future, &c.

12. He will send at the end of days our Messiah from the seed of David to redeem His people Israel from among the nations, and restore to them the kingdom.

13. There will be a revival of the dead, &c.

Kitzur Sh'lh, fol. 7, col. 2.

4. Let a man believe that whatever occurs to him is from the Blessed One ! For instance, when a wicked man meets him and abuses him, and puts him to shame, let him receive it with love, and say, "The Lord told him to curse, and he is the messenger of God on account of my sin."

Ibid., fol. 8, col. 1.

5. In every deed or transaction a man performs by his

own free will, be it a matter of precept or of option, let
the name of God be ready in his mouth. If, for instance,
he erects a building, or buys a vessel, or makes a new garment, let him say with his mouth and utter with his lips,
" This thing I do, לייחד השכינה עם הקב"ה, for (the honour
of) the union of the Shechinah with the Holy One—
blessed be He !"   *Kitzur Sh'lh*, fol. 8, col. 1.

NOTE.—Bismillahi Arrahmani Arraheemi, " In the name of
God, most merciful and compassionate," is the motto of
every work undertaken by a Mohammedan.

6. A man should always desire that his neighbour may
profit by him, and let him not strive to profit by his neighbour. Let his words be pleasant with the children of
men if they shame him, and let him not shame them in
return. If they deceive him, let him not deceive them in
return, and let him take the yoke of the public upon his
shoulders, and not impose it heavily on them in return.
Ibid.

7. If—which God forbid !—thy neighbour has done thee
an evil, pardon him at once ; for thou shouldst love him as
thyself. If one hand is accidentally hurt by the other,
should the wounded hand revenge its injury on the other?
And, as urged before (see No. 4), thou shouldst rather say
in thine heart, " It is from the Lord that it came to thee ;
it came as a messenger from the Holy One—blessed be
He !—as a punishment for some sin."
Ibid., fol. 9, col. 2.

8. A sage who was very sorrowful was once comforted
thus :—" If thy sorrow relates to this world, may God
decrease it ; but if it relates to the world to come, may God
increase it and add sorrow to sorrow." (See 2 Cor. vii. 10.)
Ibid., fol. 10, col. 1.

9. A man should not wade through water or traverse
any dangerous place in company with an apostate, or even

a wicked Jew, lest he be overtaken (in the same ruin) with
him.   (Comp. Eph. v. 7, 8 ; Rev. xviii. 4.)

Kitzur Sh'lh, fol. 10, col. 2.

10. The influence of the son is relatively greater and
more blessed than that of the father, for the merits of the
father do not profit the son except in matters relating
to this world (as by bequeathing him worldly inheritance);
whereas the merits of the son do more than benefit the
father in this world; they benefit him also in the world to
come (by saying " Kadish "), which is enough to deliver
his soul from purgatory.   *Ibid.*, fol. 11, col. 2.

11. A common proverb says, " One father willingly maintains ten sons, but ten sons are not willing to support one
father."   *Ibid.*, fol. 12, col. 2.

12. The proper use of money is that thou learn the art
of dealing honestly, so that thy No be no and thy Yes,
yes;* and as far as possible be benevolent with the
money. " And the liberal by liberal things shall stand "
(Isa. xxxii. 8).   *Ibid.*

13. The sage says, " The eye of a needle is not narrow
enough for two friends, but the world is not wide enough
for two enemies."   *Ibid.*, fol. 14, col. 1.

14. " Create in me a clean heart, O God, and renew
a right spirit within me " (Ps. li. 10). Know thou that
the heart is the source of life, and is placed in the centre
of the body as the Holy of holies, as stated in the Book
Zohar, is the central part of the world. Therefore one
must have his heart cleansed from evil and all evil
thoughts, otherwise he introduces an idol into the inner-
most part of the Temple, which ought to be a dwelling-
place for the Shechinah. (See 1 Cor. iii. 16, 17, and vi.
19.)   *Ibid.*, fol. 14, col. 2.

* Comp. p. 130, Note (o), ante.

15. He who gazes even on the little finger of a woman is as if he looked on her to lust after her. He should not give ear to a woman's voice, for the voice of a woman is lewdness. This sin is much discussed in the Zohar; it causes the husband to come to poverty, and deprives him and her sons of all respect. *Kitzur Sh'lh*, fol. 17, col. 1.

> NOTE.—The sages of the Kabbalah were not singular in this view. The Talmud Yerush. Callah, fol. 58, col. 3, says, "He that looks upon a woman's heel is guilty of an act of lewdness."

16. Eating meat after cheese or cheese after meat is a very serious sin; and it is stated in the Zohar, section Mishpatim, that upon him who is without scruple in this regard, an evil spirit will rest for forty days, his soul will be כסטרא אחרא from the spirit which has no holiness.
Ibid., fol. 18, col. 2.

17. The sages of the Kabbalah have written that it becomes him who has in him the fear of Heaven to have a vessel of water near his bed, in order that (on waking in the morning) he may not need to walk four ells without washing his hands, for he who walks four ells without washing his hands has forfeited his life as a divine punishment. *Ibid.*, fol. 43, col. 2.

18. When a man is dressing, he should first put on the right shoe and leave it unfastened till he has put on and fastened the left; then he should fasten the right, as it is explained in the Shulchan Aruch. *Ibid.*, fol. 44, col. 2.

19. The following are some of the many laws relating to the Shemonah-esreh, or the eighteen blessings which form the most devotional part of daily worship, and which are repeated three times on (ordinary) week-days, and four times on Sabbaths, new moons, and on appointed feasts :—

(*a*.) Before commencing the Shemonah-esreh one should

step back three paces, in order to be able to advance three
steps. The reason of this is that Moses our Rabbi—
peace be on him!—advanced before his prayer into the
three divisions, חשך ענן וערפל, "darkness, clouds, and
thick darkness" (Deut. iv. 11). And this is also the
reason why after finishing the Shemonah-esreh three steps
backward are to be made, returning through these three
parts or divisions.

(*b.*) This prayer is to be performed standing, and the
feet so joined together that they should seem as it were
one foot only, in order to be like the angels, of whom it is
written (Ezek. i. 7), "And their feet were (so in the original) a straight foot," that is to say, their feet appeared as
one foot.

(*c.*) This attitude is a sign that the power of locomo-
tion is gone; he cannot pursue and attain any other object
than God. The Gentiles place their hands together, intending to signify thereby that their hands are as it were
bound; but we, by placing our feet together, intend to
signify that they are as it were entirely bound, which is
indicative of greater humility; for with the hands bound
one could still run away in search of his own pleasure,
which he cannot do when the feet are bound.

Kitzur Sh'lh, fol. 48, col. 2, and fol. 49, col. 1.

(*d.*) It is lawful for him who rides upon an animal to
pray the eighteen benedictions, and when he comes to
the point when he should retrace three steps, he is to
back the animal he is mounted on three steps. And so
also it is lawful to pray the eighteen blessings when sitting
and travelling in a waggon. *Ibid.*, fol. 49, col. 1.

(*e.*) It is necessary to pay attention to the feet when
the worshipper repeats "Holy! holy! holy!" and he is
to lift up his eyes towards heaven. At the instant the
Kiddushah is repeated he needs only lift up his heels, and
thereby his body from the earth towards heaven. . . .

According to Tanchuma it is necessary to lift up the feet from the earth altogether, after the example of the angels, of whom it is written (Isa. vi. 2), "And with two he did fly." It is from this text that the sages have ordained that a man should fly up (as it were) when he repeats "Holy! holy! holy!" והבוחר יבחר. And let the chooser choose, *i.e.*, it is optional either to lift up the heels only or to jump. *Kitzur Sh'lh*, fol. 49, col. 1.

> NOTE.—Any one who visits a synagogue may notice the observance of this practice. In the synagogues of the Chassidim, jumping is preferred to lifting up the heels.

(*f.*) It is written (Ps. cii. 17), "He will *regard* the prayer of the destitute," and it is not written, "He will *hear.*" What else can the term "regard" mean than that there is a distinction between the prayer of an individual and the prayer of a community? For when a community prays, their prayer enters before the Holy One—blessed be He!—and He is not particular to regard and criticise their works and their intentions and thoughts, but receives their prayers immediately. But when an individual prays, the Holy One—blessed be He!—regards and scrutinises his heart, whether it be devout and whether he be a righteous man. Therefore, one should always pray with the community, and this is why the text (Ps. cvii. 17) ends with the words, "And not despise *their* prayer." Although there are some of the community whose prayers, on account of their evil deeds, deserve to be despised, He, nevertheless, does not despise their prayer. *Ibid.*, fol. 51, col. 1.

20. A man should study less on Friday, that he may occupy himself with the preparation for the Sabbath. And accordingly we find in the Gemara that some of the great and esteemed sages occupied themselves on that day in preparing what was needed for the Sabbath. Therefore, though one may have many servants to wait upon him,

it is a great merit personally to prepare for the wants of
the Sabbath in order thus to honour it; and let him not
think it derogatory to his own honour to honour the
Sabbath thus, for it is his honour to honour the Sabbath.
It is written of H'A'ree of blessed memory, that he was
in the habit of sweeping away the cobwebs in his house
(in honour of the Sabbath), and it is well known to the
initiated what a wonderful mystery it is to abolish the unclean spirits from the house, ‏ודל"‏, *i.e.*, "And this is enough
for him that understands" (*verb. sup.*).

Kitzur Sh'lh, fol. 61, col. 1.

21. One should trim his finger-nails every Friday,
never on Thursday, otherwise the nails will commence
growing on the following Sabbath. He should pare the
nails of the left hand first, beginning at the fourth finger
and ending with the thumb; and then he should pare the
nails of the right hand, beginning with the thumb and
ending with the fourth finger; he should not vary the
following order :—4th, 2d, 5th, 3d, 1st of the left hand;
then the 1st, 3d, 5th, 2d, 4th of the right hand. Never
pare two (contiguous) fingers one after the other, for it is
dangerous, and it also impairs the memory. The reason
and mystery about the order for paring the nails are well
known to the expert.   *Ibid.*

22. (*a.*) In the Zohar it is explained that the benefit of
immersion on Friday amounts to the restoration of the
soul to her proper place, for he who is bodily unclean has
no soul.   *Ibid.*, fol. 61, col. 2.

(*b.*) Before entering the ‏מקוה‏, plunging-bath, he is to
repeat (Gen. i. 10), "And God called the dry land earth,
and the (‏מקוה‏) gathering together of the waters called He
seas." When he stands in the water he is to repeat seven
times (Ps. li. 10), "Create in me a clean heart, O God, and
renew a right spirit within me," for the initials of ‏לב"‏
‏"ברא "טהור‏, "Create in me a clean heart," form the word

טבל, "to dip," *i.e.*, to immerse. For it is through immersion that the unclean spirits and the סטרא אהרא, "other side," are separated from him, and he becomes a new creature by examining and confessing his (evil) deeds, and forsaking them, and by engaging himself in repentance, and immersing himself, and meditating on elevating subjects, and especially so if he has immersed himself fourteen times.   *Kitzur Sh'lh*, fol. 61, col. 1.

(c.) When standing in the water he is to stoop four times, so that the water may reach his neck, answering to the four modes of legal execution. After that he is to repeat the form of confession, and while the water reaches up to his throat he is to repeat these three texts—Micah vii. 18–20, Jer. x. 24, and Ps. cxviii. 5, and then say, "As I cleanse my body here below, which is formed of clay, so may the ministering angels cleanse my soul, spirit, and ghost above in the river Dinor; and as I sanctify my body here below, so may the angels of the Most High, the ministering angels, sanctify my spirit, soul, and ghost in the river Dinor above! In the name of Jehovah, He is the God and in the name of Adonai, the Rock of all Ages. Blessed be the name of the glory of His kingdom for ever more!"   *Ibid.*, fol. 62, col. 1.

Note.—According to the Kabbalah, the thoroughgoing orthodox Jew has his hands full on Erev Shabbath, *i.e.*, Friday. We cannot here go over the entire proceeding prescribed, but we will briefly touch upon its salient features in the order as we find them.

After having prepared himself for immersion, as above described, he is to turn his face and bow first towards the west and then towards the east, repeating a certain formula, and then dip himself under the water. This over, he is to turn again east and west and repeat a different formula, and while meditating on certain given letters of certain mystical divine names and other known words, and their respective numerical values, he is to dip a second time under the water. Then turning and bowing again west and east, repeating the while a different formula, he proceeds to meditate on different letters of the divine names, and dips for the third and last time. As dipping fourteen times is the exception and not the rule, no farther directions are given about the matter, except a few additional formulæ and meditations.

When he comes out of the water he is to step backward in the same respectful manner as when he leaves the synagogue, and is to repeat Isa. iv. 3, 4, and Rabbi Akiva's commentary on the text Ezek. xxxvi. 25.

When he begins dressing he is to repeat Isa. liv. 17, and when he subsequently washes his face and hands and feet in warm water, to which is attached a great mystery, he is to say, "Behold, here I am, washing myself in honour of Sabbath the queen;' and add also Isa. iv. 4, and also, "I have washed my feet; how shall I defile them?" (Cant. v. 3.)

Happy is he who is able to provide himself with a complete suit of apparel down to the girdle, the shoes and the hat for wearing on the Sabbath, different from those worn on week-days. Then he is to repeat the Book of Solomon's Song, and if unable to repeat the whole, he is, at all events, to repeat these four verses, the initials of the first word in each of which taken together form the word Jacob, Cant. i. 2, ii. 10, ii. 8, v. 1. After this he is to repeat certain portions of the Mishnah, and something of the Zohar or some other Kabbalistic work.

This over, the devout Israelite goes to the synagogue to meet his God as the bridegroom, and to receive the Sabbath as the bride. The service is well worthy of rehearsal, but we must refer for details to the Liturgy.

The Israelite returns home from the synagogue accompanied by two angels, one good and the other evil; and according to the condition of the domestic arrangements when he re-enters, he is blessed by the good angel or cursed by the evil one. (See more in chap. ii. No. 7, *supra.*)

The Israelite is solemnly warned not to quarrel with his wife on Sabbath-eve, for the devils are very busy then to stir up more strife, as is illustrated by the story of Rabbi Meir.

Having repeated the usual hymn appointed for the Sabbath-eve, and pronounced the form of blessing over the cup of wine, he and his family commence their supper, which is carefully prepared of the very choicest viands, flesh and fish included. Hymns and a certain form of blessing after the meal complete the family duties of the day, and all retire to rest. The head of the family, if he be a pious Israelite, and especially a disciple of the wise, has a particular duty to perform— a duty which is based on Scripture and on the following text (Exod. xxxi. 16), " Wherefore the children of Israel shall keep the Sabbath." The initial letters of "בני "ישראל "את "השבת make up the word ביאה, but what this word means must remain a mystery to all those who are not initiated into the hidden things of the Kabbalah. (The ordinary Hebrew scholar, however, will know what ביאה means.) (*Kitzur Sh'lh*, fol. 64, col. 1.)

23. Of the laws relating to the Sabbath we can here only enumerate a few; and we must deal with these as briefly as possible, consistently with justice to the subject; we shall, however, take them in order as detailed in the book before us, and carefully rendered by us.

Jewish women, maid-servants and girls are warned not to order a Gentile woman on the Sabbath to do this or that, but they may instruct her on a work-day what she is to do on the Sabbath.

Geese, fowl, cats, dogs, &c., are not to be handled on the Sabbath. Neither are pocket-handkerchiefs, spectacles, &c., to be carried on the Sabbath in an unwalled town or village. Radishes are not to be salted in quantities, but each piece is to be dipped separately in salt and eaten. After dinner the Israelite is to take a siesta, for each letter of "ש"ב"ת forms the initial of a word, and the words thus formed are "שינה "בשבת תענוג, " Sleep on the Sabbath is a delight." (See Isa. lviii. 13.) Before he dozes off he is to repeat the last verse of the 90th and the whole of the 91st Psalm. The salutation should not be, as on working-days, "Good morning," but "Good Sabbath;" for respecting this it is said (Exod. xx. 8), " Remember the Sabbath-day to keep it holy." He is not to rise on the Sabbath as early as on the other days of the week, and this is based on Scripture. He is to be very careful with the fur garments that he may be wearing, lest he should pluck a hair therefrom, and for the same reason he is not to scratch his head or touch his beard on the Sabbath. He is not to wash his hands with salt or soap on the Sabbath, nor may he play at ball; he is not to knock with the rapper on a door, or ring the house-bell; nor, if he has married a widow, is he to cohabit with her on that day. *Kitzur Sh'lh*, fols. 65–67.

24. At the close of the Sabbath he is to pronounce over a cup of wine what is technically termed הבדלה, or the "Separation," for the departure of the Sabbath, as given in the prayer-book. He is then to fold up his Tallith or veil and sing "Hamavdil," the first verse of which runs thus:—

"May He who maketh a distinction between the holy (Sabbath) and the profane (days of the week) pardon our sins and multiply our children and our money as the sand and as the stars in the night!"

Should he forget to fold his veil (Tallith), he is to shake it thoroughly the next morning, in order to get rid of the evil spirits that have harboured there during the night, והבטיגם ידוע לכיארי קבלה, and the reason is known to the lords of the Kabbalah. *Ibid.*, fol. 71, col. 1.

25. It is customary then to repeat a number of hymns and songs and legends wherein Elijah the Prophet is mentioned, because he it is that is to come and bring the tidings of redemption, for it is thus stated in Tosephta, that on the exit of the Sabbath Elijah of blessed memory sits under the "Tree of Life" and records in writing the merits of those that keep the Sabbath. Those that are particular repeat, and the very pious write, "Elijah the Prophet, Elijah the Prophet, Elijah the Prophet," a hundred and thirty times, for אליהו הנביא, "Elijah the Pro-

phet," by Gematria equals 120, to which add 10, the number of the letters, and the total is 130.

Kitzur Sh'lh, fol. 71, col. 1.

אליהו אהליו לאיהו להאיו יאלהו יהאלו האליו היאלו ואליה ויאלה
אליוה אהלוי לאיוה להאוי יאלוה יהאול האלוי היאול ואלהי ויאהל
אלהיו אהילו לאהיו להיאו יאהלו יהלאו האילו הילאו ואילה וילאה
אלהוי אהיול לאהוי להיוא יאהול יהלוא האיול הילוא ואיהל וילהא
אלויה אהולי לאויה להואי יאולה יהואל האויל היואל ואהלי ויהאל
אלוהי אהויל לאוהי להויא יאוהל יהולא האולי היולא ואהיל ויהלא
אילהו אוליה ליאהו לואיה ילאהו יואלה הלאיו הואלי ולאיה והאלי
אילוה אולהי ליאוה לואהי ילאוה יואהל הלאוי הואיל ילאהי והאיל
איהלו אוילה ליהאו לויאה ילהאו יולאה הליאו הולאי וליאה והליא
איהול אויהל ליהוא לויהא ילהוא יולהא הליוא הוליא וליהא והלאי
איולה אוהלי ליוהא לוהאי ילואה יוהאל הלוא הוילא ולהאי והיאל
איוהל אוהיל ליואה לוהיא ילוהא יוהלא הלויא הויאל ולהיא והילא
אליהו אליהו אליהו אליהו אליהו אליהו אליהו אליהו אליהו אליהו

המדקדקין יאמרו ק״ל פעמים אליהו במ״ש.

NOTE.—The Hebrew words in the above may look exactly the same, but they are not, as the careful reader will remark. In fact, out of the first hundred and twenty, not two are spelt precisely alike, though they all consist of the same letters. The reader will understand the nature of this precious Kabbalistic curiosity if he will take the trouble of transposing the letters of the English equivalent thus:—

Elijah	Ehlija	Ejahli	Eijahl	Elhija
Elahij	Eljahi	Elhaji	Eljiah	Ealijh
Eahlij	Eajhli	Eaijhl	Eallhij	Ehalij
Ehlaij	Ehijla	Ehjial	Ehialj	Ehjail

&c., &c.*

26. The last day of the month is called יום כפור קטן, "The little Day of Atonement," and it is fit and proper to do penance on that day. On the first day of the month

* *N.B.*—Elijah in Hebrew has five letters and in English *six*, and therefore the English can be transposed more than one hundred and twenty times. Perhaps some reader of a Kabbalistical turn of mind may have the patience to draw out all on paper for the benefit of the curious.

it is a pious act to prepare an extra dish for dinner in
honour of the day. God has given the first of the month
(as a festival) more for women than for men, because the
three annual festivals are according to the three patriarchs,
Abraham. Isaac, and Jacob, and because the twelve months
are according to the twelve tribes ; and as the tribes sinned
in the matter of the golden calf, and the women were
unwilling to give up their golden earrings for that idolatrous purpose, therefore they deserved that God should
give them as their reward the first days of the twelve
months, according to the number of the tribes.

Kitzur Sh'lh, fol. 72, col. 1.

27. It is a very pious act to bless the moon at the close
of the Sabbath, when one is dressed in his best attire and
perfumed. If the blessing is to be performed on the evening of an ordinary week-day the best dress is to be worn.
According to the Kabbalists the blessings upon the moon
are not to be said till seven full days after her birth, but,
according to later authorities, this may be done after three
days. The reason for not performing this monthly service
under a roof, but in the open air, is because it is considered
as the reception of the presence of the Shechinah, and it
would not be respectful so to do anywhere but in the open
air. It depends very much upon circumstances when and
where the new moon is to be consecrated, and also upon
one's own predisposition, for authorities differ. We will
close these remarks with the conclusion of the Kitzur
Sh'lu on the subject, which, at p. 72, col. 2, runs thus :—

"When about to sanctify the new moon, one should
straighten his feet (as at the Shemonah-esreh) and give
one glance at the moon before he begins to repeat the
ritual blessing, and having commenced it he should not
look at her at all. Thus should he begin—' In the united
name of the Holy and Blessed One and His Shechinah,
through that Hidden and Concealed One ! and in the name
of all Israel !' Then he is to proceed with the ' Form of

'Prayer for the New Moon,' word for word, without haste,
but with solemn deliberation, and when he repeats—

ברוך ״יוצרך ברוך ״עושך ברוך ״עושך ברוך ״קונך ברוך ״בוראך

' Blessed is thy Former, blessed is thy Maker, blessed is thy Possessor,
blessed is thy Creator.'

He is to meditate on the initials of the four divine epithets
which form יעק״ב, 'Jacob,' for the moon, which is called
'the lesser light,' is his emblem or symbol, and he is also
called 'little' (see Amos vii. 2). This he is to repeat
three times. He is to skip three times while repeating
thrice the following sentence, and after repeating three
times forwards and backwards : thus (*forwards*)—'Fear and
dread shall fall upon them by the greatness of Thine arm ;
they shall be as still as a stone ;' thus (*backwards*)—'Still
as a stone may they be; by the greatness of Thine arm may
fear and dread fall on them ;' he then is to say to his
neighbour three times, ' Peace be unto you,' and the neighbour is to respond three times, ' Unto you be peace.'
Then he is to say three times (very loudly), ' David, the
king of Israel, liveth and existeth !' and finally, he is to
say three times—

סימן טוב ומזל טוב יהא לנו ולכל ישראל אמן׀

' May a good omen and good luck be upon us and upon all Israel ! Amen.' '

תושלב״ע.

i.e.,

Perfect and finished praise to God the Creator of the world!

[*The two following extracts belong to chaps. vi. and xii. respectively, but were by inadvertence omitted. They are of such interest, however, that the reader will, it is hoped, not object to their insertion here.*]

(*a.*) *Six* blasts of the horn were blown on Sabbath-eve. The first was to set free the labourers in the fields from their work; those that worked near the city waited for those that worked at a distance, and all entered the place together. The second blast was to warn the citizens to suspend their employments and to shut up their shops. At the third blast the women were to have ready the various dishes they had prepared for the Sabbath and to light the lamps in honour of the day. Then *three* more blasts were blown in succession, and the Sabbath commenced.
Shabbath, fol. 35, col. 2.

(*b.*) Rav Hunna says, " A quarrel is like a breach in the bank of a river; when it is once made it grows wider and wider." . . . A certain man used to go about and say, " Blessed is he who submits to a reproach and is silent, for a *hundred* evils depart from him." Shemuel said to Rav Yehuda, " It is written in Scripture (Prov. xvii. 14), 'The beginning of strife is as when one letteth out water.'" Strife (in Hebrew is מדון, the numerical value of which is 100) is the beginning of a hundred lawsuits.
Sanhedrin, fol. 7, col. 1.

INDEX I.

INDEX II.

*The references in this Index are to the page and to the paragraph
in the page.*

Amos, 262. 23
Amram, 34. 47 (a)
Anathemas, 224. 30
Angel of death, the, 127. note ; 183.
  88 ; 266. 34
Angels, 18. 7
Angels, the ministering, 63. 58 ;
  252-3. 91, 92 ; 294. 28, 29, 31
Anger in God, 128. 2, note
Ant, the, 87. 29
Antoninus, 6. 22 ; 7. note ; 153.
  11 (c)
Apologue, 45. 15 (c) ; 48. 25
Apostates, 312. 84
Apostates to be shunned, 8. 26 ;
  331. 9
Apparel, Sabbath, 338. 22, note
Appearances, 255. 2
Arab, the, and his camel, 266. 34
Arising, the, of God, 315. 97
Ark, Noah's, its window, 295. 34
Ark, the, 162. 24 ; 178. 73 ; 299. 46 ;
  308. 72
Artisans, 111. 23 ; 273. 11 ; 295. 32
Asher, 236. 43
Ashmedai, 93. 8, note
Ass of R. Pinchas, 326. 13, note
Ass, the sacred, 289. 14
Atonement, day of, 169. 43 ; 238. 48
Atonement, eve of the day of, 105.
  8, 9
Atonement, the little day of, 341. 26
Avaricious, the, 76. 39
Avodah Zarah, 248. 73
Azai, Ben, 75. 33

Babylon, 23. 15 ; 238. 49
Babylon, the returned from, 139. 22
Babylonians, the, 241. 56
Badger, the, 3. 5
Bakol, 53. 40 (i)
Balaam, 5. 18 ; 186. 102 ; 308. 73
Balaam, disciples of, 61. 48
Balaam's ass, 326. 13
Balak, 190. 122
Banquet, the Messianic, 223. 28,
  note ; 257. 8
Bastards, 232. 41 (n)
Bath, a mud, 189. 120
Bathing, 336. 22 (a), (b), (c)
Bathing at Dimsis, 174. 62
Bath-Kol, 2. 4, note
Battering-rams, 269. 39
Bavaria, Countess of, 136, note
Beard, the, 56. 40 (v)
Beard of Sennacherib, 269. 38, note

Beauty, 138. 21
Beds, 15. 2 ; 146. 47
Beheading, 208. 168
Behemoth, the, 257. 8
Benaiah, 94. 8, note
Benediction, 8. 30 ; 16. 3
Benevolence, 13. 49, note ; 50. 34,
  193. 137
Ben Haniddah, a, 44. 15 (c)
Benjamin, 34. 47 (a)
Benjamin, the righteous, 111. 19
Beruriah, 220. 16 (b) ; 224. 29
Beth Yaazek, 259. 16
Betrothal, 183. 89
Betrothal to five, 82. 8
Betrothal with a Gentile, 134. 14
Bezaleel, 42. 9
Bile, the, 213. 173
Birds, 179. 74.
Birth, proclamation before, 189. 114
Blessing and cursing, 175. 65
Blessings, 218. 13
Blessings of the righteous, 308. 72
Blind, the, 5. 18 ; 6. 22 ; 14. 53
Body, the human, its members,
  225. 31, 32
Bone, the, of the spine, 295. 33
Boneless animals, 159. 21
Books, foreign, 231. 41 (l)
Boraithaoth, the, xiii.
Bowings, 162. 24
Boys, 162. 27 ; 166. 35 ; 169. 46
Bravery, 138. 21
Breakfast, 163. 31 ; 194. 144
Breastplate, the high priest's, 274.
  13
Breath, the, 73. 23
Bribes, 203. 204.
Brides, 109. 13
Brides, their sacredness, 236. 42
Broth, Babylonian, 47. 21
Buneis, 255. 2
Burning, 207, 208.
Butcher, a prosperous, 170. 48
Butcher, knives of the, 62. 57
Buying and selling, 7. 24
Byther, 245. 67 ; 269. 39

Cæsar and the lion, 249. 79
Cahana Rav, 244. 63
Cain, 325. 9, 10
Calamity, national, 27, 29
Calf, a magic, 234. 41 (u)
Calves, the golden, 26. 26
Canaan, his paideutic, 82. 5
Candelabra, the Temple, 258. 12

THE END.

PRINTED BY BALLANTYNE, HANSON AND CO
EDINBURGH AND LONDON.

www.ingramcontent.com/pod-product-compliance
Lightning Source LLC
Chambersburg PA
CBHW032139110726
47902CB00003B/631